Sword and Blood

Book One of
The Vampire Musketeers

Sarah Marques

PRIME BOOKS

SWORD AND BLOOD

Copyright © 2012 by Sarah Hoyt.

Cover art by Timothy Lantz.
Cover design by Telegraphy Harness.

Prime Books
www.prime-books.com

For more information, contact Prime Books:
prime@prime-books.com

ISBN: 978-1-60701-331-0

Thank you to Kate Paulk
for making me write this,
and to Amanda and Marilynn Green
who let me camp in their living room
in the final push to get this novel done.

Historical Note

Contrary to French usage, I chose to capitalize the "D" in names such as D'Artagnan, D'Herblay, etc., because the lowercase "d" looks out of place to many American eyes, and I feared it might distract readers from the story.

Also, I took liberties with the location of the rue Férou, placing it on the Île de la Cité. This was necessary for my plot and, perhaps, in this parallel world with vampires, the street was located there. (I hope, at least, you can forgive me for the fictional geography.)

There are other historical anachronisms, but those are borrowed from Alexandre Dumas, who, in terms of furnishings and various other things, wrote as though the musketeers lived in his own time. I made the judgment of being authentic to Dumas over being authentic to history.

An additional note on the names of the musketeers: Contrary to popular belief, Dumas only gave one of the musketeers a first name—René Chevalier D'Herblay, known as Aramis. I know there is a tradition—and a tourism industry built around it—that D'Artagnan was Charles de Batz (partly because he was Comte D'Artagnan) and the *The Three Musketeers* was based on his diaries. I don't doubt Dumas made use of the de Batz diaries for some of the exploits and perhaps some incidents. However, de Batz' exploits involved three other musketeers who were all Gascons and all his cousins. (This means they knew each other before they met in Paris, the other gentlemen were not using assumed names, and D'Artagnan was not the sole Gascon and noted as such.)

The gentleman widely believed to be Athos did not have a wife, much less one who fit Milady's profile.

Also, the D'Artagnan of Dumas is not a count.

So, while Dumas might have drawn inspiration from Charles de Batz' diaries, the musketeers owe no more than a passing resemblance to the men in de Batz' stories. The fact Dumas himself chose not to name the diary from which he'd taken inspiration implies, to my mind, he didn't mean the two identified as the same story. The fact Dumas himself chose not to name the diary from which he'd taken inspiration to my mind implies he didn't mean the two identified as the same story.

As such, I took the liberty of naming the musketeers anew.

—*The Author*

His Duty Formed Him; Like God the World
—Fernando Pessoa

Prologue

Paris, Wednesday, April 9, 1625

His captors dragged and pulled him past the ruined marble archway, the ropes on his wrists too tight, the ropes on his ankles loosened only enough to allow him the small steps he must take to avoid falling. They had stolen his sword. His blond hair was matted with blood, but he didn't know whose.

Three of them held him on either side, their supernatural strength making it impossible for him to escape.

Still he struggled, his fevered mind knowing only that he must break free from the hands gripping his arms like vises. He must defeat the bone-crushing grasp of fingers on his waist.

Pulled into the shadows of the defiled church—with its broken cross, its holy statues scribbled with obscenities and painted with leers and fangs—he twisted, suddenly. The frantic hands tightened on him. He managed to sink his teeth into one of the implacable fingers holding his arm.

The metallic taste of blood filled his mouth. The one he was biting—a coarse-haired man, who in life must have been a peasant—pulled his hand free and grinned widely, displaying long fangs that sparkled in the guttering light of the candles surrounding the bloodstained altar.

"Oh, good effort!" the bitten man said, speaking as though Athos were a puppy or a kitten. Then, looking up, he said in quite a different voice, "We've brought him, milady."

Athos turned—and his mind stopped.

She stood by the altar, as she had stood by quite a different altar, fifteen years ago, when she had given him her hand in marriage. You could say she was tall and beautiful and slim and blond—but that omitted much of everything she truly was. The first time he had seen her, in the humble cottage that the priest of Athos' parish was given as a prerogative of his office, he'd thought her an angel descended from heaven.

Whatever had happened to her in fifteen years since he had last seen her had changed neither her countenance nor her figure. She retained the perfect oval face with large, expressive violet-blue eyes. Her hair was still that shade of blond on the edge of silver, still a straight, glimmering cascade down to her waist.

She wore simple clothing, albeit much more expensive than it had been when he met her—a white overdress made of velvet with a collar outlined in ermine shining like ice around her neck. A silver belt delineated a waist that could still fit the span of his two hands.

She stepped down from the altar platform, down the marble steps, between the candles, her steps so graceful and lovely that Athos, unable to breathe, could only think he was seeing her ghost—that she had descended from heaven to redeem him. To forgive him for his horrible crime against her.

The last time he had seen her, he'd left her for dead after hanging her by the neck from the branch of a young tree. He looked anxiously at her neck for signs of the ordeal, but by the light of the candles it looked white and perfect, and he wondered if all *this* were a dream.

Or had the other been the dream? An evil nightmare, conjured by a demon? Perhaps the whole world they lived in was a nightmare. Perhaps none of it was true. Perhaps vampires didn't fill half the world and more, maybe France wasn't at war in all but name. Perhaps he and this exquisite beauty were still married and their lives were whole back in Athos' domain of La Fère.

He felt his dry lips move, and heard himself rasp out, "Charlotte!"

She spoke in the voice he remembered, the musical tones that fell on the ears like the caress of soft fingers upon the skin. "Did you miss me, Raphael?"

Looking like she was dancing in air, she drew near, until she was standing close by him, her scent enveloping him. So near that were he not still held immobile, he could have leaned down and kissed her. "Yes," he told her, struggling to embrace her. "Oh, yes."

And then the fact that she was here, and that he had been brought to her by Richelieu's guards penetrated his mind, and he knitted his brow. "Did they . . ." He was about to ask if they'd captured her too, then he remembered one of those holding him had talked as if she'd ordered it. They had called her *milady*. An English term, but proof they held her in respect. He looked at her in horror. "Charlotte!"

She grinned, displaying sharp fangs he had never seen. They glimmered brightly on either side of her mouth. "What else, Raphael?" she said. "How else do you think I could have survived that noose?" She stared up at him, her eyes gleaming. Then, looking away, she told the men holding him, "Strip him!"

Athos twisted, pivoted, trying to avoid them, but a hand reached out and ripped his doublet, then his shirt, and finally his breeches and undergarment, leaving him shivering in the spring night in his stockings and boots. Those too were torn from him.

She said, "The altar."

Two of the vampires lifted him and laid him down on cold marble. They tied him down, arms and legs twisted and bent, to the columnar supports.

Athos and his friends had found corpses tied like this. Blood masses they called these rituals, though Aramis had said no masses were celebrated. There was no ritual, just a group of vampires all feeding on the human victim until he was dead. A communion, perhaps, but not holy.

The cold, hard altar leeched the heat from his skin and thought from his mind. He was immobilized, hand and foot, atop, he was sure, old bloodstains. They tightened a rough rope across his torso, biting into his flesh. This was his last hour. He would die here, bound so he could not move. He would die here, and his friends would find him, dead and pale and defiled.

He licked his lips and managed to summon voice to his dry mouth, "Listen, Charlotte, I don't . . . I don't blame you for wanting your revenge."

She checked the knots at his hands, her light fingers just touching his skin as she adjusted the rope. "Oh, good," she said. "I would hate to think you withheld your forgiveness from me."

13

One of the watching male vampires laughed, but stopped abruptly as Charlotte glanced down at him.

Athos shook his head. Before he died, he must make her understand. "It isn't that," he said. "I just . . . I realized afterwards I judged you too quickly. Just because you . . . just because you were branded with the fleur-de-lis, it didn't mean you were a Judas goat or that you served the vampires. I should never . . . I should have asked you first. Before . . . executing you. Trying to execute you."

She smiled at him and did not say anything. Her fingers moved idly from his wrists, as if of their own accord tracing the contour of muscles on his arm, sculpted and strengthened by his sword fighting day after day for fifteen years. "I think you've grown more muscular, Raphael," she said, smiling a little. "You were too thin when we were married." Her fingers, at his chest now, moved slowly down, cool and velvety soft, tracing his flat stomach.

"And I see I can still make you react," she said as her hand traced the edges of his burning erection.

He shivered. She was a vampire. Other vampires watched them. Yet it took all his will to clamp his lips together to keep from begging her to touch him, to forget it all, to be his wife again.

But no matter how much he still needed her—through the horror and fear and remorse, and the mind-snapping craving of his body— the Comte de la Fère would not beg.

And yet . . . and yet, his bound back lifted fractionally off the marble, attempting to arch his body upward toward her touch.

She looked up at his face, and smiled slowly, knowingly, as though she guessed his thoughts and knew the extent of his need. Then she pulled her hand away and leaned in so close to his face that he could smell the familiar lilac scent she wore. "You are right, you know?" she said, confidentially. "I wasn't a Judas goat."

"No?" he said, relieved and crushed at once, because that meant he had tried to hang an innocent woman, a woman he'd adored with his whole heart, a woman who had survived only to become this. If only he hadn't been so quick to judge. If he hadn't been so proud. If he—

"No," she said, smiling widely, her soft, moist lips glistening, sensuous and inviting. "I was already a vampire."

With that she withdrew and struck, her fangs biting deep into his neck and forcing a scream out of him. Pain burned into his muscles and propagated like fire along his nerves, descending, tortuously, down his spine. He screamed until he could scream no more. Tired and wrung out, he lay still in a puddle of his own sweat and looked up at Charlotte's eyes dancing with amusement.

He tried to speak, but could not find the strength.

Then the feeling changed and instead of pain, bliss radiated from her mouth on his neck, sucking his life away. A tingle of pleasure like nothing he'd ever felt—an overall caress, skin-enveloping, nerve shattering—took him completely and soothed him. Transported on its wings, he felt his body react again, excitement gathering, coursing along his veins—pounding, demanding release.

She bit deeper and his mind fogged. He plunged into the darkness of death.

Ruins and Fallen Angels

Grief carried D'Artagnan to Paris. Like a tidal wave swelling from shock to anger, it propelled him across the devastated country, riding on lonely roads amid denuded fields.

As the anguishing surge receded, it left him sitting on an ornate chair in the private office of Monsieur de Tréville, Captain of the Musketeers.

"I don't know what you heard in the provinces," the captain said. He was a small man, a Gascon, like D'Artagnan. Even though silver threads mingled with the dark in his long straight hair, he didn't look old. No wrinkles marred his mobile olive-skinned face and his eyes remained bright. He stood behind a great armchair facing D'Artagnan. His long thin fingers clasped the frame tightly, flesh dark against the white-painted wood and the threadbare blue-gray velvet of the cushions. "But France is not England. We are not at war with the vampires. Our king and the cardinal have signed a truce between them. His Eminence might have been turned, but he still wants what's best for France. Neither the king, nor the cardinal—nor I, myself—want to experience here the slaughter and mayhem that engulfs the other side of the channel."

All the energy drained from D'Artagnan's body, leaving his arms nerveless and his legs feeling as though they lacked the strength to support his body. He had run to Paris to fight the vampires, and to stand for king and queen. To support the forces of the light. To avenge his parents who'd been turned and had chosen to die as humans rather than live as vampires.

"My father said," he heard his own voice echo back to him, aged and flat, "that I should come and offer my sword to you. That no

17

matter who else had made peace with evil, you never would. That you knew darkness when you saw it."

"Your father." For just a moment, there was a flash of something in Monsieur de Tréville's eyes. What it was, D'Artagnan could not tell. It flickered and vanished. In a changed voice, the captain said, "Your father and I fought side by side thirty-five years ago, when the first vampires came to France from Germany." He sighed deeply. "Other times, my boy, other times. Now there's a treaty in place. Daylighters are not to hunt vampires and vampires are not to turn the unwilling. Those turned must register promptly and become subjects of the cardinal, restrained by his laws. Only undeclared vampires, the ones in hiding, could be a danger, and we don't have those." He opened his hands. "Different times demand—"

Behind D'Artagnan, the door opened. A voice said, "I'm sorry to interrupt you, Captain, but you said you wanted to know when the inseparables came in."

Turning, D'Artagnan saw a thin man in threadbare livery that seemed too big for him, looking in through the half-opened door. Just like all other Parisians, he looked starved, ill-dressed, and not so much worried as anxious. Ready to run at a sound like a hare amid wolves.

D'Artagnan knew no intelligent Parisian could take the truce or the treaty seriously. Monsieur de Tréville did not look that stupid.

In fact, he did not look stupid at all, as his fingers released their death grip on the back of the chair, and his eyes filled with an eager curiosity, leavened by hope and fear. His voice trembling with what appeared to be near-maniacal relief, he said, "All three? Athos, Porthos, Aramis?"

The servant shook his head and looked away as he spoke, as if afraid of seeing the reaction to his words. "Porthos and Aramis, only, sir. Should I send them away?"

Monsieur de Tréville's face froze, the skin taut on the frame of his skull—as though he'd aged a hundred years in that moment and only iron will kept him alive. He licked his lips. "The two?" His expression became impenetrable. He drew his mouth into a straight line and crossed his arms at his chest. "Send them in, Gervase."

The gentlemen had apparently been waiting just outside the door, because as Gervase opened it, they immediately entered.

They were splendid. There was no other word for them. D'Artagnan, who had waited in the captain's antechamber, had seen the rest of the musketeers as something very close to immortal gods. He had listened to them jest about how many vampires they had killed, and taunt each other with the latest court gossip. How—fearless and unabashed— they called evil by its true name—*vampire*. Yet, admirable though they were, they admired others. They too had idols they looked up to.

All through the other musketeer's chatter—like a touchstone, a prayer—he'd heard the names of the inseparables: *Athos, Porthos, Aramis.*

They were, according to their own comrades, the best and the bravest. It was said that in one night, the three of them alone had killed a hundred vampires. It was whispered that if France still had a human king, if the throne still belonged to the living, it was to the credit of none but the three noblemen who hid under the appellations of Porthos, Athos, and Aramis.

D'Artagnan, a Gascon and therefore inclined by nature to discount half of what he heard as exaggeration, and the other half as mere talk, now felt his mouth drop open in wonder at the sight of Porthos and Aramis. He thought that, if anything, the rumors had been an understatement.

Though their clothes looked as worn and their bodies as thin as those of other Parisians, the two inseparables were so muscular and broad-shouldered, and stood with such pride, that they lent their humble threadbare tunics, their frayed doublets, their mended lace and worn cloaks an air of distinction. Pride was an attribute one would have thought departed from mortals since the vampires had taken control.

The smaller of the two—just taller than D'Artagnan—had dark-golden hair and the flexible body of a dancer—or an expert sword fighter. His features were so exactingly drawn that they might have graced a well-favored woman. However old his clothes might be, they looked well matched and even better fitted. Made of dark blue velvet, no mended patches were visible. The ringlets of his hair fell over his shoulders, disposed in the most graceful of ways, with a longer love-lock caught up on the side of his head by a small but perfect diamond pin. Other than that pin, he wore no jewelry save for a plain, flat silver cross on a silver chain around his neck, and an antique signet ring on his left hand.

The other musketeer stood at least a head taller than any man D'Artagnan had ever seen. His chestnut brown hair was shoulder-long, his beard and moustache luxuriant; the bare patches on his tunic had been sewn by an expert hand and embroidered in what looked like gold thread. D'Artagnan only noticed they were skillfully covered rents because there was no other explanation for the haphazard nature of the embroidery, which meandered over his broad torso with the abandon of a gypsy caravan on an endless jaunt. He wore a ring on the finger of each massive hand—most of them ornamented with stones too large to be anything but paste or glass—and on his chest lay a thick gold chain, with a cross composed of rubies and garnets—or their counterfeits—dazzling in its splendor.

This would be Porthos, D'Artagnan surmised. He had heard the man was a giant. Indeed, he had arms like tree trunks, legs like logs, and the most terrified brown eyes that D'Artagnan had ever seen.

His gaze darted around the room in skittish anxiety and, alighting on D'Artagnan, it made the Gascon wish to make his excuses and leave. But the musketeers blocked the path to the door. Porthos' gaze moved on, immediately, to stare in abject fear at his captain, whom Porthos outweighed by at least half again as much.

Looking at Monsieur de Tréville, D'Artagnan could understand at least part of the fear. The captain's face had hardened, and his gaze threatened to bore holes in the two musketeers, if it could. Settling on Porthos, the hard gaze then dismissed him, focusing instead on Aramis, who bowed correctly. D'Artagnan had heard how valiant Porthos was and could only imagine his fear in this instance was that common malady known as timidity or shyness in social situations.

Here stood a man who could destroy vampires with a smile but who would be forever in fear of offending another human or committing a faux pas.

"Aramis," Monsieur de Tréville rasped. "Where is Athos?"

Aramis smiled, as if he had expected this question all along. "He's indisposed, sir. It's nothing serious."

"Nothing serious," the captain said. He turned his back on them and stared out of his window. Through it one could just glimpse the broken cross atop the cathedral, the marble stark white against the lowing sky. "Nothing serious," he said again, his voice heavy, like the closing of a tomb. "The cardinal bragged at his card game with the king last night. He said that Athos had been turned. That Athos was now one of them. The rumor is all over Paris."

"It is . . . not so serious," Aramis said.

"Not so serious," the captain turned around. "So is he only half turned? You men and your careless ways. How many times have I told you not to wander the streets at night after your guard shift? Never to go into dark alleys willingly? And if you must go into them, to guard yourselves carefully? Do you have any idea what Athos will become as a vampire? Do you not know your own friend well enough to know what a disaster this is?" His voice boomed and echoed. Doubtless, the musketeers massed in the antechamber were eagerly drinking in every word he said.

Porthos and Aramis shifted their feet, looked down, and let their hands stray to their sword pommels. It was obvious that had anyone but their captain given them such a sermon, he would have paid dearly for it.

Porthos, who had been squirming like a child in need of the privy, blurted out, "It's just . . . that . . . sir! He has the smallpox!"

"The smallpox?" the Captain asked, with withering sarcasm, even as Aramis gave his friend a baneful, reproachful glance and a minimal headshake. "The smallpox, has Athos, who is over thirty years of age? Do you take me for a fool, Porthos?" His voice made even D'Artagnan—over whom he had, as yet, no power—back away and attempt to disappear against a wall-hung tapestry that illustrated the coronation of Henri IV. "I've given the three of you too much freedom because I thought you'd at least defend each other. How can you have allowed Athos to be taken? From now on, I am making sure that none of my musketeers go anywhere, save as a group. Not after dark. And if I hear of any of you starting a fight with a vamp—"

He stopped mid-word, as steps were heard rushing outside, followed by a man's voice calling out, "I'm here."

A blond man burst through the door. He was taller than Aramis, almost as tall as Porthos, though of a different build. It was not so much that he appeared lithe and lean, though he was both, but on that leanness was superimposed a layer of muscle. D'Artagnan had seen similar bodies in a book of drawings by someone who had visited Greece. The ancients had excelled in the creation of sculptures of ideal men, which they placed as parts of their temples, supporting whole buildings on their backs. The buildings and the men were both a harmony of perfect proportion. Though D'Artagnan imagined this man must be Athos, and that he must, therefore, be over thirty, he looked like a young man in the early prime of his days. It was as though he had halted at the peak of golden youth and from its summit looked through the ages unafraid, carrying the best of his civilization upon his powerful shoulders.

Like most of the other musketeers, he did not exactly wear a uniform. Instead, he wore the fashion of at least ten years before—a black doublet laced tightly in the Spanish fashion and with ballooning sleeves; black knee breeches, beneath which a sliver of carefully mended stockings showed, disappearing into the top of his old but polished riding boots.

But it was his face that attracted and arrested one's gaze as he threw back his head, parting the golden curtain of his hair as he did so. He said, "I heard you were asking for me, Captain, and, as you see, I came in answer to your call."

He looked like the angel guarding the entrance to a ruined cathedral; beautiful, noble, and hopeless. The mass of hair tumbling down his back might have been spun out of gold, his flesh resembling the marble out of which such a statue's features might be chiseled. The noble brow, the heavy-lidded eyes, the high straight nose, the pronounced cheekbones, and square chin, and the lips—full and sensuous, as if hinting at forbidden earthly desires. All of it was too exquisite, too exact; perfection that no human born of woman should be entitled to.

He also looked cold, unreachable, lost, and—except for still standing on his feet and moving—as if he'd died waiting for a miracle that had never come.

Monsieur de Tréville's mouth had remained open. He now closed it with an audible snap, and advanced on the musketeer, hands extended. "Athos! You should not have come. You look pale. Are you wounded?"

Athos shook his head, then shrugged. "A scratch only, Captain," he said. "And you'll be proud to know we laid ten of them down forever, D'Alene among them."

"D'Alene? The Terror of Pont Neuf?" Monsieur de Tréville asked, suddenly gratified.

Athos bowed slightly, and in bowing, flinched a little. His eyes, which had looked black at first sight, caught the light from the window—as he turned his head—and revealed themselves as a deep, dark jade green.

The captain squeezed the musketeer's hands hard. Athos bit his lips, looking as if the touch pained him, though not a sound of complaint escaped him. "As you see," he said, "we do what we can to defend the people of Paris."

"Indeed. Indeed. I was just telling your friends how much I prize men like you, and how brave you are to risk your lives every night, in defense of the people, and how . . ."

Athos, who looked pale and wan as if he were indeed wounded, and, in fact, as if he only remained standing through sheer will, didn't seem able to withstand the barrage of words, or perhaps the additional pain of what must be the captain's iron grip on his hands—so tight that Monsieur de Tréville's knuckles shone white. He made a sound like a sigh, his legs gave out under him, and he began to sink to the floor.

His friends managed to catch his apparently lifeless body and ease him onto the carpet.

Bewildered, D'Artagnan suddenly perceived that the captain must be playing some deep game. The man who'd told him musketeers didn't fight guards clearly was pleased that musketeers did. Which must mean D'Artagnan's father was right and that Monsieur de Tréville fought against the vampires still—only carefully enough to not be caught at fault under the treaty.

D'Artagnan took a step forward to help with the fallen Athos, but the musketeer's two comrades moved, obstructing his path.

The young man stopped, staring. It seemed to him that, as Athos fell—awkwardly caught by Aramis around the chest and Porthos by the shoulders to ease what would otherwise have been a floor-shaking collapse—his hair moved away from his neck revealing two deep, dark puncture marks on his neck.

Athos would not be the first to be bitten by a vampire and live to tell the tale. There was a time, D'Artagnan's father had told him, that this was the basic requirement to become a musketeer—to have felt the bite of the vampire—and his allure—and to have survived it. But the bite mark combined with Athos' pallor seemed to indicate a vampire might have gone too far. Far enough, in fact, that the human thus bitten turned into a vampire within twenty-four hours, and would be prowling the streets for living blood by the next evening.

D'Artagnan moved closer. He was barely breathing as he strove to see the musketeer's neck. Surely, if he had been turned, his friends would not hide it. They were musketeers. Surely—

The two musketeers knelt, one on either side of their comrade, while the captain stood nervously at his feet. Aramis was unlacing Athos' doublet, a sensible action indeed if he was wounded and needed air. With his movements, Aramis had also artlessly pulled Athos' hair to hide what might be punctures on his neck. Perhaps it had indeed been by chance, but D'Artagnan found it hard to trust anyone.

"*Sangre Dieu*," Porthos thundered, looking up and noticing that a crowd had come from the antechamber and gathered at the still-open door, to watch the excitement. "Back, all of you. Can't you see the man needs to breathe?"

At that moment, Aramis lifted a reddened hand that he had just dipped beneath his friend's doublet. "He's all over blood," the musketeer said. "He was badly cut in the fight last night." As he spoke, he undid Athos' doublet altogether, and showed the red-soaked shirt beneath. There was a sound of relief from bystanders as they released long-held breaths in a collective sigh.

Clearly if the musketeer could bleed still and in such quantity, when he could not have fed as a vampire yet, the rumor of him turning would be just that. Yet D'Artagnan was not so sure. Such things could be falsified.

Aramis pulled back the gory shirt to reveal a cut on the pale, burly chest beneath—a cut smeared in blood, some of it dried.

"My surgeon," Monsieur de Tréville said.

"No, please, sir," Aramis said. "Athos wouldn't even let us bandage him last night. You know how private he is and how proud. He wouldn't like it if it was known he suffered such a wound." He looked toward the crowd with worried eyes. "I hope no one speaks of this."

The mass of musketeers backed a step, then two, under his steely gaze.

Porthos stood, then bent down to pick up his unconscious friend. "I'll take him to his lodgings, sir. His servant will bandage him up, been with his family since Athos was a baby. Athos cannot resent him. Yes, Grimaud will look after him."

"Yes," Monsieur de Tréville said, his gaze heavy on the bloodied shirt. "Yes. Do. Take care of my brave Athos."

"We will, sir," Aramis said, bowing a little.

But D'Artagnan had discerned two things. First, the appearance of Athos' chest and the blood on it was wrong. If he had bled so copiously, most of the blood would have crusted around the wound. Instead, it was smeared around the pale skin in irregular streaks looking like it had gone from the shirt to the wound, and not the other way around.

Second, Athos wore no cross. While there was no requirement that musketeers—or indeed anyone—wear a cross, almost everyone did. A cross or some other chosen symbol of their faith that not only stood between them and the vampires, but which showed to the world that they were, indeed, still free men.

Had a vampire managed to get into the ranks of the musketeers? And were his friends hiding him?

When the three inseparables left the room, D'Artagnan slipped out and followed them.

The Destiny of Fools

Athos woke up held in living arms. For a moment, he did not know whose arms, only that they were strong and too warm and alive. That last truth communicated itself to him through smell and temperature, through feeling and his own quickened heartbeat and a desperate lust to feed, which made it hard for him to think.

He was being held like a child—which even his sluggish brain knew meant that the arms belonged to Porthos. But more important, more urgent, was that his head rested on Porthos' shoulder, close enough to hear his friend's heartbeat, close enough to feel the song of living blood through Porthos' neck veins. Close enough to thirst.

Athos tightened his hands into fists and bit his lips together to keep his fangs from extruding. They had already appeared once today, while he was smearing the shirt. Even though he had used sheep's blood, the smell had been enough for the fangs to descend from his gums, alien and demanding, in front of his teeth.

With his lips sealed together, Athos found that he could not speak; he opened them, but kept his teeth clenched. The voice that emerged sounded like something from beyond the grave even to him. "Put me down, Porthos. For the love of—" He remembered in time not to stain the holy name with his cursed tongue. "Put me down."

Porthos looked down at Athos, startled. "Are you sure?" he asked. "You don't look—"

"Down. Now."

Porthos started to lower him, and Athos threw himself at the ground and away. He half tumbled, half ran out of Porthos' embrace, to press his back flat against a wall. The support of stone behind him helped. Its coldness seeped through his clothes to steady his mind with icy sanity. They were in an alley just like the ones he had used to get to Monsieur de Tréville's office. Narrow ancient alleys surrounded by buildings so tall that the bottom floor never saw the light of day. Daylight was only a mild bother here. Not a danger. He could hardly feel its faint sting on his skin. On the way to Monsieur de Tréville's he had ensured that his hair and the lace of his sleeves covered every exposed inch of his skin as well. It was only in the captain's office that he had felt sunlight on his face. Even the attenuated light, coming through the window with its half-drawn curtains, had been enough to fill him with panic and make him want to writhe in pain. That and the temptation to feed when the captain touched him had overwhelmed his senses and caused his faint.

"Athos!" Aramis said. "You are wounded. You bled. Perhaps they didn't take enough to turn you, perhaps—"

Athos heard something between a gasp and a cackle tear through his lips, behind which, and despite all his will power, the fangs were now displaying fully. "It was from mutton," he said. "I cut myself and squeezed the meat Grimaud had in the kitchen. I folded it in my shirt and pounded. I assumed the rumors would have started and you two fools . . . " He shook his head, unable to go on. "Grimaud will never forgive me." He pressed his palms back, flat against the stone, trying to will its coldness into him, trying to find his fast-evaporating control.

Heat rose through him like a fever, and he could smell his friends as he had never smelled anyone before. Blood rushing through their veins spoke of health and strength, filling Athos with an almost uncontrollable yearning.

It wasn't hunger, though the mouth-watering need for bread after a long afternoon of work was contained within it; it wasn't thirst, though the pounding of the blood sounded like the singing of a stream on a hot afternoon when he had been hunting all day. It wasn't desire, but his entire body strained with the need to bite, to suck blood, just as his whole body had once lusted to join with the woman he loved.

He kept from striking only by desperate strength of will, by near-insane force of rationality. He would never bite Porthos and Aramis. They were his friends. He could not wish this hell on them.

And he couldn't bite anyone—anyone—without surrendering his immortal soul, or his remaining honor. He had abandoned his name, his lands, his home—all for the sake of fighting vampires—but he was still the Comte de la Fère. He would not stain that ancient dignity by becoming a bloodthirsty monster, stalking innocents and condemning them to death or damnation.

He controlled his breathing, as it hissed, ragged, between his teeth. He shook his head. "You do me no kindness," he said in a voice tinged with the pain of holding back from feeding, "to refuse to grant me the true death. I beg of you . . ."

"We don't know that you'll become a vampire," Aramis said. "We cannot kill you simply because you've been bitten. Half the musketeers . . ."

Athos' laughter barked out, startling him. "Aramis," he said. "My friend. Don't delude yourself. You wouldn't have chosen these alleys as the way to take me home, if you did not know how it stood with me." He looked up at the distant sky, lost in the shadow between buildings, and decided there was enough light here. Just enough. "I wasn't bitten. After . . . after I parted from you in that fight, they surrounded me. Fifteen of them. They tied me up before I even knew they were there. I was taken to a lair and there . . ." He couldn't bring himself to tell them what he'd found there. The wife he'd thought dead for fifteen years, still alive, or at least in that form of death in life that was vampirism. It wasn't that he didn't wish to. He couldn't. He lacked the strength to pronounce Charlotte's name. "And there I was drained," he said. "Very thoroughly and carefully, to be at that point of almost full depletion at which one becomes a vampire, before the complete emptiness at which one dies." He shook his head, as the sound of her laughter echoed in his memory, her musical voice telling him, as he woke from human death to vampire life, that his only way out, now, was to kill himself. "I was turned, Aramis," he said, lifting his upper lip to reveal the glint of fangs.

Aramis took a step back and crossed himself, paling as he did so.

"Yes, do cross yourself," Athos said. "Pray for me, Aramis. But give me mercy."

"Mercy?" Aramis asked, stunned, his usually agile tongue stumbling over itself.

"Death, Aramis, death. While my soul is still unstained. I'm controlling myself by an effort of will. A . . . great effort of will. I came to that office to avoid you or Porthos being suspected of abetting a rogue vampire and being branded as Judas goats because it might be heard you . . . helped me to my lodgings last night and I have neither registered nor submitted to the cardinal's authority—I'd see him in hell first. People would think you knew. You should have known. Now kill me, and go back. Tell them that you found out I was turned after all, and tell them that you killed me cleanly."

Aramis took a breath, the noise of it so loud it seemed to echo inside Athos' brain. He crossed himself again, but shook his head.

"Aramis," Porthos said. "We are doing him no kindness. He asked for death when we found him yesterday. We should have given it to him. It's the last duty of every musketeer to his comrade to keep him from becoming . . ."

Athos looked up at Porthos, who was now far enough away that Athos did not have to concentrate so hard to avoid to tearing into his veins to satiate his unnatural need. From within his darkening heart and soul, Athos fished a word he wasn't used to uttering, and turning his eyes to his friend, said, "Please."

"Aramis," Porthos said, looking sideways, a panicked expression in his dark brown eyes. "We must grant him final mercy."

But Aramis shook his head again and, looking up, spoke with the sting of his usually sarcastic pronouncements. "Why tell *me* that, Porthos? You have a sword. You want to give him mercy, do so."

Porthos' eyes changed, softening into a sad mix of horror and fear. "I can't," he said. "I . . . I did it when I had to, Aramis. To those I loved. Until I came to Paris, I thought my heart dead to all friendship and love. Without your friendship—the friendship both of you offered me—I'd have become worse than the vam— the things we kill. You two have kept me alive and human. I could not . . . I cannot kill him. No more than I could kill you. Unless . . . unless I had to. To defend myself."

"Well, then," Aramis said, tartly. "Why do you think I could?"

Athos calculated the distance to his friends. He could charge them. He could grip one of them, maybe both. He could feed. Then they would kill him, and then—

29

His heart, straining in his chest, scarcely sustained by insufficient blood, made a noise that sounded like a drum in his ears. His body, his mind, his need, all told him to attack. But once he let himself go, he would no longer be able to control himself. Once he allowed himself strike, he would be a beast, intent only on getting what he needed. He knew how to fight, and he had his sword by his side.

Closing his eyes, to blot out the two of them—standing there, like fools, side by side—he could picture it all like a series of paintings behind his closed eyelids. He saw himself jumping out at them, stabbing Aramis through the heart and seizing Porthos . . . Once he closed his fangs on Porthos' neck, he doubted his friend would fight. Or kill him. Beneath the brazen and admittedly larger than life exterior, Porthos was a shy, gentle creature. Not deficient in courage, but not able to withstand his friend's will. It would end with Porthos dead, or turned.

Once Athos let go of himself, this outcome would follow, as easily and surely as a river flowed downhill. There would be no recall. Oh, they could fight other vampires and win against great odds. But he'd fought by their side for years. He knew their weaknesses. He could get in under their defenses.

"Traitors!" A loud voice called out, to Athos' right side. "Traitors all! You'd allow a vampire to live and call himself a musketeer?"

Athos pivoted to face the voice, and saw a very young man running toward them. Small and slight, he had the olive skin of Gascony, an expression of rage on his face, and his sword drawn. By instinct, Athos drew his own sword, so that as the man came close enough to strike, he found Athos' sword already raised in defense.

The vampire's reflexes were faster, of course, but the boy seemed to have been made of the skin of the devil himself. He countered every one of Athos' attacks, and attacked again, like fury incarnate. Something in the back of Athos' mind whispered, *you should let him give you quietus. It would end this and not stain your friends with your death.*

But his mind raced ahead of the wishful voice. If this boy killed him, he would denounce his friends as Judas goats. They would be branded as such and banned from all lawful contact with humans. Marriage contracts would no longer apply to them. Even simple commerce with humans would be interdict. Their only choice would be to deal with vampires and to serve them. And, if they lied to hide their disgrace from their fellow men, and were found out, they would be killed. Aramis and Porthos would be at the very least dishonored and barred from free society. At the worst, dead.

"Athos," Aramis said, his voice full of anguish. "He's just a boy. What are you doing?"

"Isn't it obvious?" Athos asked. "I'm fighting for all our lives. I would allow him to kill me, but I cannot allow him to condemn you as Judas goats. Do you see what you've done?"

As he spoke, he saw the expression of alarm and realization in the boy's eyes. He also saw the boy's chin jut out in determination. He was, what, a mere youth? From the incipient moustache on his upper lip and the still-childish roundness of his cheeks, he could not be more than nineteen, and Athos would guess closer to sixteen. Full of righteousness and fury. Doubtless, he came to the capital full of innocent eagerness, to fight the evil of vampires. Now he must futilely end his life here, at the hands of Athos, who would truly be much better off dead.

"Halt, in the name of the cardinal," a voice called out behind Athos.

Athos, his sword raised, in the act of parrying the boy's sword, glanced quickly over his shoulder. He could feel and smell and sense Porthos and Aramis, already moving into position behind him, between him and the boy and the guards of the cardinal. He could smell the guards too—the heavy musk that spoke of vampire. The smell he could now detect on his own clothes, though he knew the living could not.

The man who had spoken was Jussac, one of the most feared guards of the cardinal. He had his sword drawn and his fangs bared, his speech almost slurping, as if he were trying not to drool. "What have we here? A rogue vampire and a nice juicy pack of conniving abettors. Best surrender, gentlemen. You've more chance at living with our side." Jussac was accompanied by other vampires whom Athos had met in combat and had been good enough fighters to escape with their heads still attached to their shoulders: Bisarac and Cahusac, and two other nameless adversaries.

"Surrender?" Aramis said. "Never."

"Not while we live," Porthos said.

"And you?" Jussac said, looking directly at Athos. "You at least must see it's in your interest to come with us."

Athos spun around. The boy wasn't trying to fight him—he had gone utterly still, probably dazed by the presence of so many vampires, which had that effect on the living that hadn't become immunized by long habit—nor was he the kind to strike by stealth. Glaring, Athos shook his head at Jussac. "I am not one of yours," he said. "I was not willingly turned." Something very much like a giggle escaped him. "I don't hate vampires less for being one."

Jussac leered at him, displaying his fangs. "Is that so? And you'd fight us? When you're a fledgling of less than a night, and you have not fed yet?"

Athos, thinking the greatest mercy possible would be for him to die here and not at his friends' hands, though he felt as though he were teetering on his legs and staying upright by sheer resolve, sneered back, "I would fight you with my last ounce of strength."

"Oh very well then," Jussac said, "if that is so. But the stranger, the boy, there ... The cardinal needs to at least appear to observe the pact, and I don't think that boy is of legal age to consent. I don't think he's of a legal age to be away from his mother's apron. You, boy—scamper. You're free to go back where you belong. And stay away from dark alleys in Paris, even during the day. That's our territory."

Athos heard the boy draw breath, sharply, as if wounded, and wondered what had brought it about—was it the mention of his mother? Or the idea that he could not walk where he pleased?

And then, breath was drawn again; Athos heard the boy's heart speed up, and the faint rustle as he lowered his sword arm. Was he going to run? Athos thought at the boy's age, he would have. As good as the boy was, how could he face these odds? He had survived one vampire, but only a single vampire who was very weak and who, in truth, did not want to kill him. The guards of the cardinal would not have such compunctions.

A hand dropped on his shoulder, hot even through doublet and shirt. "Sir?" the boy's voice said, hesitantly.

Athos turned around, shaking his shoulder, to flip the hand away. "Yes," he said. He wished the boy would not touch him, but preferred to endure the temptation of living contact than to show his weakness in front of the monsters.

The boy looked curiously shy, and all the younger because of it.

He was gazing down, his slick black hair half-hiding his face. He looked up at Athos, at his word. "Sir, I heard what you said, and if you hate vampires . . . That is . . . It would do me great honor if you would allow me to fight by your side."

"No," Athos said. "Save yourself. Do you see how many of them there are? They have been vampires for years, faster and more cunning than any human being I know of. Even were I a true vampire, I wouldn't be a match for them, I don't have my strength. My friends and I will likely meet our death here. It's only two musketeers and a lamed man against five."

The boy shook his head, his face grave. "No. Two musketeers, a lamed man, and a boy against five," he said, and allowed a little smile to appear.

"You don't have to. You're not a musketeer. Go, go and fight another day."

The boy threw his head back, and looked up. His face seemed to age years in a moment. "When my parents were turned and chose to stand in the sun and die, rather than feed," he said gravely, his voice cracking, "I decided I would be a musketeer and fight vampires. I might not be a real musketeer yet, but in my heart, I am. I must fight by your side."

Athos read the pride and the pain in the boy's face. He thought of the moment when he himself had made the same decision. He had been twenty. The boy looked much younger. But grief was the same at any age. As was courage. "Very well," he said. He turned to his other friends and, though it cost him in self-control, clasped their hands, drawing them together in his strong hand. "Athos, Porthos, Aramis, and . . . what is your name, my friend?"

"D'Artagnan."

"Very well, Athos, Porthos, Aramis, D'Artagnan, All for one—"

His friends answered, "—and one for all." D'Artagnan smiled, clapping his hand atop theirs.

"How touching," Jussac said mockingly. "Have you made a decision then? Any chance of a surrender?"

"Oh, we've made a decision," Athos said and grinned, knowing it displayed his fangs. "We're going to have the pleasure of charging you."

Clean Cutting

D'Artagnan felt as if his heart would burst out of his chest. The beat deafened him. His muscles clenched with the urgency to move, the need to strike.

Some part of him—some ignored part of him—murmured that he'd come to Paris to fight vampires. Now he was fighting beside a vampire and the men helping him. That he was a traitor. That he should kill the musketeer, Athos, and his friends. But the other part— the other part *knew*, with absolute, unflinching certainty that he was doing what he should do. He was fighting against Richelieu and his minions, the bloodsuckers that held Paris and all France hostage.

His sword rose like a living thing, pulling his arm up with it, propelling his feet forward. He charged at the dark vampire who had called him a child. The one who had told him he should go back to his mother's apron. His mother, mon Dieu! The indefatigable, busy wife of a Gascon lord, always bustling about her household and her garden. His mother who would have protected D'Artagnan with her last breath. Dead because of creatures like this one.

The vampire looked startled, but reacted fast. Indeed, D'Artagnan had heard they were faster than any human—striking like the coiled serpent that unwinds when least expected. As D'Artagnan charged— an inchoate scream tearing through his throat—the vampire unsheathed his sword, parried, and grinned at D'Artagnan, flashing his shining fangs.

D'Artagnan was vaguely aware the musketeers had engaged in the fight as well. Porthos, the tall man who looked like a farmer— except that no farmer had ever worn such gold-spangled clothes, such brilliant, if false, jewels—took on the tall vampire, whom he called Bisarac. They fought while exchanging insults, their voices booming over the group.

Aramis fought like a dancer: striking and parrying, flashing and charging everywhere at once. He fought two vampires at one time and made it look easy. His hair—shining dark gold in the dark alley, like the wheat crops France no longer had—flowed behind him as if it had been taught the choreography of this particular dance and knew how to obey it.

Athos—Athos called "Cahusac!" to a dark vampire and charged forward like a wounded tiger. He fought, teeth clamped on his lower lip, as if every step hurt, as if every thrust and parry were pulled, hard won, out of a great, unending desert of exhaustion. Each of his spare and forceful movements bore the feeling of a suppressed groan and a spasm of pain.

And D'Artagnan . . . D'Artagnan was managing to parry—just barely. The Gascon had almost no practice in dueling. His father, a staid gentleman, lord of a small manor, had neither the time nor the habit of picking private quarrels. He had served in the war, and he had taught his son what he knew and guessed about fighting. Specifically about fighting vampires; his father's war was the first great war against vampires as they came like a tide from Germany.

D'Artagnan knew—and bore in mind at all times with startling clarity—that he fought at great disadvantage here. The vampires could hit him anywhere at all, and there was a good chance he would die, if not right then and if not from the bleeding, then from the infection that would follow. But he had to either strike them through the heart or cut their heads off. Any other injury would heal.

He trembled at the thought, but even as he trembled, he parried and charged, aiming for the heart of the vampire, who laughed at him and danced lightly back. "Ah, the boy fights by the book," he said, in a tone of great amusement. "What is it, boy? Salvator Fabris' *Art of Dueling*?" The vampire the others called Jussac stepped away from one of D'Artagnan's thrusts, and swept his sword back with such force that had D'Artagnan not ducked in time, he would have been beheaded himself.

"My father had a copy of that," the vampire said. "With hand-colored illustrations."

"And did you suck your father's blood?" D'Artagnan answered in fury, refusing to see the vampire as someone who could have had a father. Someone who had once been a human infant and a human child.

The vampire's eyes sparkled, "No, nursling. He sucked mine and made me a vampire. For which I thank him."

The vampire expected, D'Artagnan thought, for him to be stunned by this intelligence that a father might turn his own son. And for a moment, ridiculously, he was. The moment almost cost him a thrust through his shoulder before he brought his own sword up, lightning-fast, and parried.

"Ah, the reflexes of youth," the vampire said, grinning, showing feral teeth and sharp fangs. "Think how much faster you'd be as a vampire."

"Think how much *better* you'd be as a human," D'Artagnan said, pressing forward. Jussac had made a mistake in mentioning Salvator Fabris. D'Artagnan had in fact been following Signor Fabris' positions, set by set, place by place. The first guard and the second guard, and the extended fourth guard. He had been playing it by rote, as he had learned it from childhood.

But now he was alert. He was incensed. And he had remembered Fabris' one immutable rule: if you were in a defensive position, you were already at a disadvantage. The better chance belonged to he who attacked.

His ears ringing with fury at his own stupidity and with rage at the vampire who spoke to him as if he were a child freshly weaned, D'Artagnan attacked fast, madly.

What mattered if he died? He pressed forward, his sword diving under the guarding sword of the vampire, and incidentally, almost disdainfully, pushing it aside so that he missed D'Artagnan altogether.

Vampires might be fast, but their brains were still human. Or somewhat human. The vampire was surprised by D'Artagnan's sudden shift in tactics. His sword went wide, pushed out of its path, and seemed to pull his arm with it. It drew him out of balance. He stepped rearward, arm swinging back to regain equilibrium

D'Artagnan's sword found its target in his heart, piercing it through. The vampire screamed an ear splitting death-shriek.

D'Artagnan jumped back, letting go of his sword. He had never before stabbed anyone through. The weight of the body and the death scream undid him, but it lasted only a moment. In the next moment, he forced himself forward and tugged his sword from the vampire's chest, even as dark blood flowed like a tide, soaking the creature's clothing, pouring onto the cobblestones of the street.

The dark blood smelled of corruption—like a corpse, long putrefied. The stench filled D'Artagnan's mouth and nose, stung the back of his throat, and made his bile rise, but D'Artagnan would not show it. Instead, he reached for the vampire's dark cloak and wiped away his fouled sword, as he looked around at his comrades and their opponents. According to the laws of duel, taught to him from a very early age, he knew he could lend assistance to whichever of the others needed it.

He looked first at Aramis, last seen fighting two opponents. But one of Aramis' opponents lay beheaded, pouring out the same miasma of corruption into the air as Jussac. Porthos and Bisarac seemed to be evenly matched, with Porthos perhaps slightly the superior, despite the vampire-reflexes of his opponent.

Then there was Athos. D'Artagnan was not sure how he felt about Athos. His father had told him, over and over, until the belief was as real to him as the creed recited every night before sleep: trust no vampire. They might seem rational or even kind, but their minds are a collective mind tainted by the evil that fathered them. They think like insects, like locusts. Their hunger dominates all.

Yet Athos had said that he didn't hate vampires any the less for being one. And, Athos *was* fighting vampires—madly fighting to keep the bloodsuckers at bay—fighting even though he looked distinctly unwell.

D'Artagnan looked over at the older musketeer. Athos parried Cahusac's thrust, and faltered, his step failing. Cahusac took advantage of it, thrusting at Athos. Athos recovered in time and leapt away, just enough that Cahusac's blade went through his arm, not his heart.

Athos pulled his arm back—free of the blade—and gritted his teeth. There was no blood on the blade, and if any followed out of the wound, it didn't go past sleeve and doublet. It dawned on D'Artagnan—thinking of that strangely smeared wound—that Athos would be nearly dry. He couldn't have fed since being turned. Whatever he was, whatever had been done to him, he was no more guilty than D'Artagnan's parents were. He too had refused to drink living blood.

"To me, Monsieur Cahusac," D'Artagnan said, calling the vampire's attention, and addressing the vampire's curled lip. "What is it, Monsieur Bloodsucker? Are you afraid you cannot withstand a boy?"

Athos collapsed onto one knee, his head lowered, breathing hard.

His strength had failed him. No, not strength. He could have none if he'd not fed. Will. Athos must have been standing and fighting through dauntless discipline alone, and that was the only thing keeping him on his feet.

Turning his full attention to the combat, D'Artagnan parried Cahusac's thrust, and pressed close. He remembered the lesson he'd learned while fighting Jussac and attacked, putting the vampire off his balance. Cahusac, on the defensive, seemed unable to fully employ the vampiric speed of reaction against D'Artagnan. As the death scream of Aramis' opponent echoed, closely followed by a similar cry from Porthos', D'Artagnan could see the sting of fear in the vampire's eyes. All his comrades lay dead. He alone stood.

It was almost worthy of admiration that he did not run—even when he was the last of his kind against all of them.

But his form fell apart. His parrying became increasingly irregular until D'Artagnan had him backed against a wall. He would have finished him then, only Athos called from behind in a voice more breath than words, "Don't. Please. Let me finish what I started."

A look over his shoulder showed D'Artagnan that Athos was back on his feet, and the younger man stepped out of the way as Athos charged Cahusac. The vampire attempted to return the attack. They met halfway, swords clashing. Athos fought like a man possessed. His sword swept in a broad arc, detaching Cahusac's head from his shoulders even as Athos collapsed on both knees and drew in air like a drowning man who crests a wave and does not know when he will again taste air. The sound of his knees hitting the alley's cobblestones resonated against the walls, reinforcing the impression the man was more sinew than muscles, more bone than either.

D'Artagnan found himself running to help him up at the same time that Porthos dashed from the other side. The tall musketeer set a massive hand beneath Athos' elbow. Athos shook his arm free. "Don't," he said. "Don't." He looked at D'Artagnan, his gaze half-forbidding, half-pleading. "Don't touch me. I'm having enough trouble controlling . . . don't."

Porthos opened his mouth, as if to ask what Athos had trouble controlling, but Aramis was on Porthos' other side, pulling at his sleeve, whispering urgently to him. D'Artagnan had no need of such explanations. He knew very well what Athos feared. Losing control over the hunger that must be twisting and biting within him, like a worm eating him from the inside out.

He stepped back, looking at this man who was almost like a golden statue, and yet—and yet unbearably frail within his strength, defenseless from the beast that had invaded his very being and turned all his power to weakness.

Athos took a breath and shook with it, as if the air—tainted as it was with the miasma of dying vampires—carried some needed, vital component that would keep him alive.

"We must go," Aramis whispered urgently. "Athos, others will have sensed their comrades dying. Soon, every vampire who can get here without going out in the sun will be on us." He looked around, his eyes haunted. "There could be hundreds of them in these alleys."

Athos nodded, acknowledging Aramis' words but not showing any response to the emotion beneath them, as though he understood the danger but not the panic. He put a hand on his own knee and braced himself, slowly rising. Porthos retrieved the sword that Athos had let fall, and cleaned it on a dead vampire's tunic before handing it to Athos, who received it and sheathed it solemnly.

"The question is," Porthos said gravely, "what do we do now?"

Athos looked at the giant. "You mean, surely, what do *I* do now? Or what *you* do about me?"

Porthos shrugged. "I mean—" he said, his voice resonant, even though he was speaking in an ordinary tone "—what do we do now? All of us?"

"We leave," Aramis said, managing to hem Athos between his hands—not touching him, but using his hands as brackets within which to herd Athos—whose colder vampire body felt the warmth of Aramis' hands—forward and away from the alley. "We leave very fast." The musketeer saw a bewildered expression on D'Artagnan's young face. "We have fought enough of the creatures to know that at this very moment the feeling and knowledge of these vampires' deaths is flowing through their comrades' brains. That the cardinal himself, in his coffin, will know some of his favorites have been killed. He was not a forgiving man when he was human, and he's even less tolerant now. We must move, quickly, away from here."

Without touching Athos, without shouting at Porthos, whose face had wrinkled in a frown of concern, without saying anything more to D'Artagnan, Aramis managed to force them to walk down the alley, then turned twice into alleys where there was more daylight. Even if not enough to burn Athos, it was enough to make vampires uncomfortable. Enough that other vampires would not think Athos had gone that way. "Go, go," Aramis urged. "Athos, I believe from this maze of alleys we can reach the rue Férou very close to your house, without requiring you to walk in the sunlight until then."

"But . . . my house . . ." Athos said. "The cardinal will know—"

"Doesn't matter. His guards can't dash from alley to door. They won't risk having to stand in the full sun and knock. They, no more than you, cannot stand still in full sunlight."

Athos turned. He'd been stumbling ahead, his expression half-dazed, as if he were sleepy or drunk. Now he faced Aramis with a calm gaze, his arms held down, his hands open, palms toward Aramis, "Wouldn't that perhaps be the best?"

"To get you home without burning you to ashes?" Aramis asked, his voice darkly humorous. "I believe so. It will be very hard indeed to explain to Grimaud that we let you be burnt to nothing."

"Grimaud! Do you think he'll like serving a vampire?"

"No, but I think he will like continuing to serve you. He's spent most of his life serving you. I don't think he now wishes for your death, even if you sorely abused his mutton."

The humor perplexed Athos, who shook his head. "But you must agree," he said, "you know that I cannot possibly be . . . That I am dead already. I am no longer one of you. I am one of them, one of those creatures out there, in the alley, and they—"

"You aren't." The voice, tinged with a Gascon accent, was so decisive D'Artagnan thought in puzzlement that he hadn't known either Athos or Porthos could speak with a Gascon accent. As the voice continued, he realized it was himself speaking. "You are not one of them. You said back there that you did not hate vampires any the less for being turned. And you don't."

Athos looked at him, as surprised as D'Artagnan himself felt at his own words. "But—" he started.

"There are no 'buts' in this," D'Artagnan said. "I would not have fought by a true vampire's side. Not ever. I know what I owe my father's memory."

For just a moment, it seemed as though Athos would dispute this, but then his eyelids lifted, and he shook his head minimally. "But what do I do?" he asked in anguish.

All the time—in front of them, as they advanced—he retreated, step by step, his back turned in the direction he was walking as he stared at his companions. It was, D'Artagnan thought, as though they were pushing him forward against his will, pushing him, as a hunter will push his prey off a cliff.

"What do I do?" he asked again. "Very easy for you to say I'm not a vampire, that I am not dead." He looked accusingly at D'Artagnan. "But my body is one of theirs. I can no longer eat what you eat. I tried. Even water tastes stagnant and poisonous to me. And food . . ." He shrugged and shook his head. "My body won't retain it, much less derive nourishment from it. What can I do? I can't live without eating. Or rather, I can, because being a vampire, this life I have is already not life. But I can't go on with my hunger increasing every second. No. I would rather die, and die now, than become . . . than attack one of you, or Grimaud, or some other innocent."

"You won't," Aramis said. He seemed very assured. "You will not. There are things you can take in. Yes, water will taste foul. As will other liquids not blood, but you will retain most clear liquids and you will derive some nourishment from them."

Athos narrowed his eyes. "Will it be enough?"

"To live? Probably. Though people eventually succumb to the desire for blood, usually."

"Usually?" Athos asked, sounding lost and baffled.

"Other people. People who are not Athos," Aramis said. "That is to say the majority of them." Only a slight smile indicated that he was being facetious, not as confused as Athos sounded. "Stop, my friend."

This last because Athos had been about to walk, backwards, into the full noonday sun of the rue Férou, where buildings were far enough apart for the sun to shine all the way down to the cobblestones. Athos cast a look at it, over his shoulder, and jumped back as if he'd come too close to an open flame.

"I can't—" he said.

Aramis took his finger to his lips, asking for silence, as he walked past Athos.

"But . . . it is midday. It was dimmer light when I departed, and now—"

Aramis came back, "It is but a few doors," he said, "to your own. What did you do before?" He reached for Athos' arms, to pull his sleeves down.

Athos shook his head. "No. I'll do it." He pulled the lace cuffs down forcefully, so the heavy ruffle hid his hands, and, quickly lifting his hat, lowered his head—his mass of hair surged forward, obscuring his face.

Aramis nodded. "You, Porthos," he said. "Go knock at the door. Make sure Grimaud is in and opens it. If he is there, tell him to hold the door open in readiness and make sure the shutters are up or the curtains closed in the rooms we'll enter."

Porthos was gone what seemed like an eternity. Yet D'Artagnan knew that on the street beyond the alley only a couple of people had passed. It could not have been more than a few minutes before the huge musketeer came back to the entrance to the alley and nodded.

Aramis herded Athos forward, while D'Artagnan followed. The house they entered was characteristic of lodgings noble single gentlemen in Paris occupied. It took up the second floor over an establishment that appeared to house a draper. D'Artagnan did not linger to ascertain the nature of the business, but there were bolts of cloth in front of a shop. The door beside it led to a steep and darkened staircase that climbed upwards into deeper dark.

Aramis closed the door and bolted it, while the rest of them started up the polished wooden stairs, which ended in a large landing. The place smelled of both decay and cleanliness, as if great age and scrupulous care mingled here. From this landing—where three candles burned in candlesticks set upon a low table—three doors opened and a smaller stairway led upwards.

Athos paused to pull back his hair, revealing a face that, in the light of the candles, resembled white marble more than ever. He ignored the single closed door and another that opened into a hallway leading to the back of the house.

A man, who looked somewhere between middle and old age, stood at the third door. He was built as solidly as Porthos, but in proportion to a considerably shorter frame. He had russet hair flecked with white, and a face that would usually be grave but was marked now by lines of concern. "Milord," he said to Athos, and then, as though recalling himself and that his master was incognito—at least if the stories D'Artagnan had heard were true—he said, "Monsieur."

Athos inclined his head, and then turned slightly so he could see both D'Artagnan and his servant. "Dear Grimaud," he said, his voice sounding better bred and softer than before. "I wish to make known to you Monsieur D'Artagnan, newly arrived from Gascony. I owe him my life today, so if you prize it, you will from now on consider Monsieur D'Artagnan as an intimate of this house and perform any services you might for him."

"No, pray," D'Artagnan heard himself saying, "you did not . . . That is, I did not save your life at all. It was only—"

"He braved the terrible Cahusac for me," Athos said, "and so tired him out that I had an easy time dispatching him."

The servant raised his eyebrows, then bowed to D'Artagnan and, turning to Athos, said, "Yes, monsieur." His eyes lingered with concern on his master's pale face. He seemed to want to ask something but said nothing. Athos gestured and—seemingly for D'Artagnan's benefit, as if he expected him, indeed, to frequent the house often in the future—said, "Upstairs are Grimaud's quarters. That hallway leads to the back where we have the pantry, a kitchen, and the use of a small garden on the bottom floor. If you should arrive at almost any hour of the day, it is best to come through the garden, and knock on the kitchen door, as Grimaud spends an untold amount of his time there." Athos turned toward the doorway where his servant stood. Grimaud stepped aside to allow him through. "And these are my quarters proper," he said, as he led them through the doorway into a small parlor outfitted with several chairs, a couple of small tables piled with books, several of them with papers and ribbons inserted between the pages.

Against the window, across which heavy curtains had been drawn, stood a small writing desk, on which one might compose a quick letter while standing up. On this desk sat a candlestick with a candle. Other candles sat on the broad mantel of the fireplace opposite, their light reflected from a gilded mirror, whose frame looked too splendid for the room.

As if by long habit, Athos walked to the back wall of the room, against which sat a chair more solid than the others. It looked old and prized. As he sat down, it was hard not to notice the portrait hanging on the wall just above and to the left of his chair, which represented a gentleman who, though wearing the attire of the time of Francis I, looked almost exactly like Athos himself. To the other side hung a magnificent sword of about the same period. Lighter and thinner than today's blades, it looked graceful and frail, like a toy. It would be a thrusting and stabbing sword, not a slicing implement. One would be able to use it to stab a vampire through the heart—at least if the vampire wore no shielding—but there would be no hope of beheading the undead.

In the fifty years since the vamps had been in France, in the hundred years since they'd been awake in the world, armorers had learned to make metal stronger and swords just a little broader, with sharp edges, so they could pierce and slice even through shielding.

Athos' graceful ancestral sword looked as beautiful and as unreal as stories of a world without vampires.

Seated between them, D'Artagnan thought, Athos looked not so much like the scion of an old and respected line as like the statue of such a scion, sculpted in pale stone, and as incapable of life or animation. An immense tiredness had settled on the musketeer's features. He removed his hat, almost reverently, and set it atop a small table to his right. He lowered his face to his hands and covered it.

"*Sangre Dieu*," he moaned. "What am I to do? How can I endure this?"

The Blood and the Flesh

He became aware of pronouncing the divine name with his decidedly unholy lips, but only after he had done so. It added a sense of despair to the tiredness that so weighed upon him. It took all his will and every ounce of fortitude to keep himself from shaking like a leaf. But he would keep himself from trembling, at least while anyone was present.

His arm hurt where Cahusac's sword had penetrated, as did his chest where he had given himself that broad gash. But worst of all was pain from the bite marks on his neck—because it was not all pain. It throbbed and beat with an agonizing torture that—were it anywhere else—he would have judged to be the beginning of an infection. Only the pain was tinged with something else—an edge of pleasure that had flowed through his body as she—as Charlotte had sunk her fangs into him and drained him of life. That pain felt like an odd ravishment, a caress navigating along his nerves raising near-pain as much as near-delight.

Distantly, he heard Aramis say, "Grimaud, if you could make your master some clear broth?"

This brought a drawn breath from Grimaud and, hesitantly, "Will it do any good? Only Monsieur le Comte tried to . . . that is . . . "

Athos did not like his title bandied about. Grimaud had learned long ago not to give any clue to his identity, since Athos' killing of a suspected Judas goat in hiding, without trial, was a crime under the laws of the kingdom. Only the protection of the king and Monsieur de Tréville—and his assumption of a false identity—had kept him from being tried and beheaded for it. But they'd gone well beyond that fear now. He was a vampire. An illegal one.

Grimaud had served the de la Fère family since before Athos' birth and—this Athos knew—loved the musketeer as the son he had never sired. Athos could be as demanding and as severe as he wished at other times, but today he would be lenient. He forced himself to remove his hands from his face, setting them down and clasping his knees tight, to prevent any tremor from being visible. He spoke in a voice that seemed little more than a whisper to his own ears and hurt coming out through his parched throat. "Monsieur Aramis tells me broth will work, Grimaud. It will not taste good, but it will work. If you'd be so kind . . . ?"

Grimaud frowned. "Only, m'sieur, the mutton! It will not be fit. I don't know what you did to it, but it wasn't decent."

"He put it in his shirt and pounded it," Porthos said, sitting on the chair to the left of Athos. "To pretend he'd still had blood in him and had suffered a dueling injury."

"Oh," Grimaud said.

For a moment, meeting his servant's gaze, Athos understood as clearly as if the servant had announced it, that Grimaud had believed Athos had sucked the blood out of the meat. Despite the dryness in his mouth and the fact that all his companions smelled like appetizing meals, he felt a chuckle bubble between his lips. "I did not suck the mutton, Grimaud," he said softly. "It should still do well for broth."

Grimaud bowed and left, and Aramis said, in a pensive voice, "Animal blood will work as well. Dead animal blood. I'm not proposing you should go feed from live animals. But there are plenty of abattoirs in this city and I should be able to procure . . . It won't stop you wanting . . . that is . . . you'll always . . ."

"I'll always crave human blood," Athos said, the realization of his fate settling over him like night falling over the landscape, and just as inevitable.

"But not as you crave it now," Aramis said, in a rallying tone. "Not as you do while you're starving. You won't crave it for your sustenance only . . . but the sustenance part we can supply."

Athos nodded and said nothing. If Aramis was the only one who knew what else vampires craved blood for—the exquisite pleasure that came with having your life sucked or—Athos presumed—

sucking someone else's blood, he was not about to explain it. Besides, he was almost sure Porthos knew already, and D'Artagnan surely wouldn't need to. Not yet. Let the boy preserve what innocence he still had while he could. In this damned world it wouldn't be much or for very long.

He closed his eyes and tried intently to avoid thinking of attacking his friends, or of the pain-pleasure from the bite site, or of Charlotte. The last was the hardest of all. He was engaged in the struggle of not recalling her scent as she bent over him to kill him, nor the exquisite silky texture of her skin as her hands rested on him, when Grimaud returned carrying a tray with a small pot and a porcelain cup.

"I'm afraid the mutton was not usable," he said. "I have made some beef broth."

Athos believed it was beef broth, because Grimaud told him so. To his altered senses, it smelled and tasted like foul ditch water. But he forced himself to take a mouthful of it, and then another. Medicine, he told himself, medicine that would prevent his tearing open the living veins of some innocent and doing to them what had been done to him.

"Thank you, Grimaud," he said, as soon as his mouth felt slightly less parched.

"You might feel quite nauseated. You might need to . . . retch," Aramis said, as soon as Grimaud retreated.

Athos did feel quite nauseated, but he'd be damned if he was going to allow himself to vomit and provide such a show of weakness before his friends. Besides, he could feel the liquid doing him good, and he presumed he needed all that he could keep down.

All the same, the broth, though warm, hit his stomach like cold lead, and made him gag more than once, as he forced himself to swallow. He drank three cups, and then had to pause. He noticed Aramis' gaze was transfixed on Athos' right arm and the sleeve of his doublet. Following his stare, Athos saw that drops of blood showed against the dark fabric. "Ah," he said. Of course, even this little moisture circulating through his veins would seep out. Particularly there and at the cut in his chest.

The Gascon, who had remained standing, took a step forward and then one back, and fished in his sleeve like a child who had lost his handkerchief. What he pulled out was a small cured leather pouch, which he extended to Athos, on a shaking hand. "It is an ointment, Monsieur," he said, "that my mother gave me the secret of. If no vital organ was hit, it will heal the wound utterly in three days and leave no scar."

Athos didn't know whether to laugh or cry. Most such ointments were blessed. He looked up at the boy. "And usable on vampires?"

The boy blushed, as if the very mention of Athos' condition embarrassed him. "It should be, monsieur. It's nothing but herbs boiled together."

"And at that," Aramis said, tartly, "I've noticed you don't look away from our crosses, Athos, so a blessed ointment might not hurt you."

The thought hit Athos like a punch. It wasn't just that it was common knowledge vampires saw crosses as a foci of light so bright they hurt—particularly blessed crosses. Athos had heard the same was true of other sacred symbols. But Athos saw them as crosses—Aramis' polished; D'Artagnan's dark, perhaps made of forged iron; and Porthos'... well, Porthos' did glitter, but not in that way. His mouth fell open in surprise, and he could not find words for a good while. When he did, it was no more than a whisper. "But . . . I'm a vampire."

"Clearly not . . . a vampire as we know them," Aramis said. "I mean, you are not . . ." He paused, considering. "Can you hear them?" he asked. "In your mind?"

"Them?" Athos asked. He had known before—perhaps he'd always known but without giving it any thought—that Aramis of all of the musketeers knew the most about vampires and their constitution. It made a certain sense to Aramis, as they were spiritual enemies and not merely physical ones. When at court Aramis did, perforce, mingle with both sides, and he was more of a court creature than the others. But they'd never before discussed it. Not aloud. Not explicitly.

"The vampires," Aramis said, "it is like . . . There is a reason they know everything, that they are not like us. They do not have the privacy of the mind. Do *you* have the privacy of your mind?"

"I . . ." Athos cleared his throat, and reached into his mind, trying to feel even the distant echoes of a presence. Charlotte's presence? But there was nothing. The only thing she'd left him, was that pleasure-pain on the site of the fang marks. "Yes. They are not in my mind. My mind is as it was." He allowed himself a wry smile. "Save for the craving for blood."

There was a silence, broken by the Gascon stepping forward, waving the little leather sack, "Sir?" he said.

If he should deny the ointment, he would be upsetting the boy. He inclined his head. Given his new state, it appeared he should try to tread as carefully as possible and not upset anyone, if it could be managed.

Sighing, he started to unfasten his doublet. As both Grimaud and Aramis darted forward to help, he said, "No, please. No . . . living touch."

Grimaud froze in bewilderment, but Aramis stepped back, letting Athos know he understood all too well. Athos didn't know which reaction stung more.

He pulled off his doublet and his ruined shirt and flung both from him, as though they'd offended him. A thought passed through his mind, fleeting as a lightening bolt on a darkened sky: only a day ago he would have been embarrassed to be seen half-naked. Only a day ago, he would have held onto the remnants of his frayed dignity as though they meant something. Now, there seemed to be scarcely any point. He was no longer human; no longer a creature that deserved dignity.

From the youth's extended hand, he took the bag of ointment. Dipping out as little as he dared he rubbed it on his wounds, while looking at them dispassionately. He'd been in such a state this morning—half dreaming, as it were, though the dream was a nightmare—that he'd cut himself rather deeper than he meant to over his lowest pair of ribs. Nothing had seemed to hurt then.

Like the sword thrust through his arm, given in the heat of duel, he'd hardly felt the cut. He'd thought at the time he would soon be beyond all mortal cares. Now, with his wounds paining him, he wondered about the healing rate of vampires. He thought it was very rapid, but he'd never had any other involvement with vampires but to kill them, and quickly too.

As he looked up from his task, he found Grimaud standing by his side holding out a bundle of linen strips. As the servant of a musketeer, he always had these handy and prepared. "I thought," he said. "If you should bleed, you'd need bandages to bind your wounds."

Athos looked up and into his servant's clear eyes. He read concern and worry there, but no fear. What were they all made of? His friends, his servant, the young Gascon boy he'd just met? Why would they all trust him? And Grimaud most of all, who was proposing to live alone with a vampire. What sort of man was he?

Athos took the bandages and started wrapping them about his torso. Suddenly Aramis was there, helping, careful not to touch him. As if Athos couldn't feel the heat of the living body and smell the coursing blood in the veins. As though a little distance would put him off. But Athos thought if Aramis hadn't known how things were, he would not be the one to show it to him.

Clamping his teeth on the inside of his lip, telling himself he would not allow his fangs to extrude, he accepted Aramis' help, gravely.

"I wonder," he said, more to distract himself than because he wished to know, "why they can't penetrate my mind. And what that has to do with my not seeing sacred symbols as light, or not feeling them as a burn."

Aramis shrugged. "Do you want me to tell you the theology of it, truly, Athos? There was a Portuguese monk, Matos da Silva, who wrote a treatise about vampires and consent. That was, of course, before . . ."

Athos inclined his head. That was before the king of Portugal himself had become a vampire during an ill-fated expedition to the north of Africa. Now no treatises came out of Portugal—or at least no holy ones. "But, my friend, there are so many vampires who are made without consenting."

Aramis nodded intently, without looking up, his features pinched. Knowing his friend, Athos thought Aramis must be considering how much Athos needed to know, and how much he didn't. Aramis— perhaps because of his profession and its dangers—never gave away more than he needed to. "Most vampires are made without their consent, true," he said. "But then they consent . . . afterwards. It is much, in that, like the sin of . . . of rape compared to seduction." He had the grace to blush. "If a man should take advantage of a maiden in a lone place, and should she call for help in vain, the sin is only his, and in God's eyes she retains that virginal virtue with which she was born. But if the maiden is assailed with praise and compliments, and she yields to the seduction without protest, then she's guilty of the sin the same as the man. Does that make sense?"

"No one assailed me with compliments," Athos said baffled and guilty, remembering the pleasure of Charlotte's taking his life. Was that not consent, that transport of pleasure?

"No," Aramis said. Having tied the bandage neatly around Athos' middle, he started winding another piece about Athos' arm. "But . . . with vampirism, the consent, I think, happens in stages. At least Matos da Silva thought so. If, having been made a vampire one kills oneself, one clearly negates the consent."

"But I tried and—"

"One denies the consent," Aramis said. "But there is some doubt whether one loses one's soul, nonetheless."

D'Artagnan gasped and Athos looked at him quickly. "But that question is not settled," he said, guessing a whole tale in the young man's face, and speaking rapidly to Aramis, trying to soothe the Gascon. "Not settled for sure that one loses one's soul, is it? Because if one is dead, then how can the sin of taking one's life count?"

"There is debate," Aramis said, and pressed his lips together. "Though it is generally held it is better to take one's life than to live on as a vampire if one cannot resist the urge to feed on humans and will, therefore, inevitably, commit the sin of taking human life."

"So it is like that famous philosophical debate on if one were fated to be a murderer, would it not be best to die at one's own hand?" Athos asked, dredging the theological quandary from his school days. He remembered it explained—in Latin—in his aged tutor's calm voice.

This was not a good thought, bringing with it memories of his parents' graves in the little cemetery by the family chapel outside the manor. He didn't want to think of them sleeping there, on hallowed ground, not knowing their only son was worse than dead.

He blinked up at Aramis, who was tying a bandage around his arm.

"Something like that," Aramis said. "But barring death—and that not a sure escape for your soul—your . . . it's more a matter of . . ." He shrugged. "You have been introduced to the sin, but not through your fault. In fact, if there are degrees of repulsion, I'd say yours was very high indeed, because you seem to be all but untainted. Some effects remain—the craving of blood, the fear of the sun . . . but . . . not the rest."

Athos took a deep breath. "And feeding on living blood would destroy it all," he said, more thinking than asking.

"Feeding on living blood would be your assent to being a vampire, Athos, but there are other . . . other ways to allow them into your . . . into your mind. As a collective entity."

He darted a startled look one way and then the other, as though afraid to speak in front of the others. But he didn't need to explain what was on his mind to Athos. Oh, he didn't know for sure. He had never experienced vampirism before and, unlike Aramis, he had not made it his life's study. But he knew what could bring him into intimate contact with the vampires; what could break his resistance; what could make his mind theirs; his soul . . . his soul lost.

He knew what else came with vampirism, besides the craving for blood. He knew it in that deep pleasure that frayed his nerves at the memory of Charlotte's teeth in his neck; in the whole-body joy at the memory of her smell, of her soft skin, of her touch. To give himself to a vampire, to make love to her would be consent.

He knew to do so would make him lose his mind and his soul. It was the same desire that had made him lose his domain: the craving for Charlotte's body and her touch that had led him to marry her, to make her his countess, without so much as investigating her; without caring where she'd come from.

But now, unlike his young and inexperienced self, he was weak, pulled by a craving deep within that seemed to be tied to his very being. He didn't know if he could avoid that hunger as well as his thirst for living blood.

He groaned, deeply.

Aramis, straightening, after finishing Athos' bandage, gave him a sharp look. "The carnal pleasures," he said, "that bind two as one is such a moment—it is almost impossible to hold your mind whole and inviolate against the thrust of the vampire." He spoke so softly the others might not have heard at all. "That craving, too, can cause you to consent. The two are deeply linked."

Revenge and Fear

They'd left Athos' home—D'Artagnan and Porthos and Aramis, the older musketeers escorting the newcomer. "D'Artagnan, we must," Aramis had said, "find you a place to lodge. A *safe* place to lodge."

That had started a walk through the streets of Paris. When D'Artagnan first arrived, the night before, he'd seen very little of the city and all of it seemed to him shabby and almost as abandoned as the villages he'd passed on the way here. But now in the full light of day it looked almost like the city that D'Artagnan's father had described living in thirty years ago.

The narrow alleys were lined with merchandise and the sound of heavy bargaining echoed off the tall buildings. Families and housewives, servants and chaises made the streets impassible at some points. If you squinted a little and didn't look at the threadbare clothes and the haunted look on people's faces, you might think the vampires had never come to France.

But then a dark carriage, heavily curtained against the light, would rush down the street, pulled by black horses whose impetuous careen didn't take mortals into account. The daylight crowd would scurry out of the way of the vampire's carriage, and then—in its awake—a silence fell deep with memory, as though they were remembering a day when humans were their own masters.

They went from the Île de la Cité—where Athos lived—along the nearest bridge, and to other neighborhoods where lodging would be less expensive. The fact the only money D'Artagnan had came from the sale of his old horse should have deterred the musketeers but it hadn't. "In these days," Aramis had said, "knowing there is a man in the house who can use a sword and is not afraid of vampires might be enticement enough."

But it hadn't been. The neighborhoods that Aramis and Porthos deemed safe—those with few windows shuttered against the full light of day, and given over mostly to the housing of the living—were not affordable. Those that were affordable were not safe.

As night approached, they'd come by degrees to the rue des Fossoyeurs, a bourgeois neighborhood that looked well enough until they noticed the blackened ruins of a chapel at the very end of it. "It's been taken by vampires," Aramis said. "Like almost all churches in Paris. It would be good if you do not go near it."

But the owner of the bakery located two blocks down the street had upstairs lodgings to rent and the musketeers managed to convince him to rent it to D'Artagnan for a price the young man could afford.

They'd inspected the three spacious rooms and found them more than sufficient for D'Artagnan's non-existent possessions.

Aramis wrinkled his nose with distaste at the dusty floors, the unfashionable furniture, but Porthos seemed bent on praising the qualities of the abode. It came with a bed, he noted, but it seemed to D'Artagnan that Aramis just stopped himself from noting that it might be infested with vermin.

The width of the street, Porthos had said, would prevent his having any problems with vampires during the day. There was no access from the alley. And during the night . . . ah, during the night, the windows had thick shutters that could be closed from within. It had, too, an earth closet accessible from the inside, and quite private. Something that had only entered the architecture of Paris abodes since the arrival of vampires, it was nevertheless indispensable. A necessity, if one wished to avoid chamber pots—and the dangers of opening a window in the night to empty them—and didn't want to expose himself to an attack on the way to an outdoor privy.

Only as the two of them were leaving, did D'Artagnan speak. "But," he said, "Monsieur Athos cannot visit, if he can't come through the street entrance—the street is too wide. Too much sun. And at night . . ."

Porthos frowned. "We presume," he said. "That if he comes in the night, you'll open the door for him."

"Or not," Aramis said, and frowned slightly.

D'Artagnan's throat constricted at those last words, and he looked questioningly at Aramis, just as Porthos said, "Aramis, Athos is not— "

Aramis turned his clear eyes in D'Artagnan's direction, quite ignoring his friend. He'd removed his gloves, while they inspected D'Artagnan's new lodgings, and now he put them on with exaggerated care, "Athos is not dangerous is what Porthos would say, if I allowed him, and to an extent he's right." He pulled the glove tight to his hand and looked up. "Athos, our friend, whom we've known for so many years, is both far above and far below the common run of men. In matters of nobility and mind, he is the highest of men, his mind schooled far beyond most of his kind, his principles disciplined with rigid but enlightened exactness. He was the only son of a most noble couple, born late in their married life. As such, he was the repository of all their hopes and desires. They formed him as their ideal of perfection." His eyes were intent, giving D'Artagnan a stern look, as though warning him of something. "But he is now a vampire and vampires are more animal than we are. There is, however, more to it than that." He sighed. "If you want the explanation of their nature from a theological perspective, I can offer it. I was destined for the Church and close to ordination when the cardinal disbanded the seminaries and forbade anyone from becoming a priest. What they told us in seminary, as the plague of vampires blotted out the Church, is that vampires are like animals as far as having extra senses, but like angels in that they share their minds with others. Athos does not do that, but I don't know for how long this will be so." He shook his head. "You wonder why, then, I allowed him to live?"

"It does . . . beg the question," D'Artagnan said, and found his hands were clenched one on the other, forcefully. He'd trusted the vampire, even though his father had told him not to. He'd fought by his side, and now his oldest friends cast doubts on his character.

"It's not so easy. If anyone can beat this—if anyone can resist the mind-blighting, the craving for pleasure that are part of vampirism, it will be Athos. It's just—" He sighed deeply. "It's just that to my knowledge no vampire ever has. Not for long. Whichever vampire turned him . . . they . . . as I understand it, they take the measure of the man when they taste his blood. And whoever that vampire is, he or she knows where to push—where the weak point in the defense is and how to break through. Lock your door, my friend, and do not open it at night, even if the voices of those asking you to do so are well known and trusted. In the streets of Paris, in the dark of night, friends become strangers, and acquaintances hideous enemies."

And thus they had left D'Artagnan alone, in his commodious lodging, behind two locked doors—one at the bottom of the steps that led up to the first floor, and one at the top, where his lodgings proper started. Both doors were marked with large embossed crosses. The shine from those crosses alone should blind any vampire attempting to approach the door, much less to break it down. If they persisted, it would burn out their eyes. For younger vampires, D'Artagnan had heard and didn't know how much of it was legend, it blotted out their thoughts as well as their vision.

Behind his two closed doors, with his windows well shuttered against the waxing moon outside, he was safe. As safe as he could be in this time of ruin and evil.

He paced, by the light of two candles—provided by his new landlord—placed on cracked plates, one on the table in the front room—a large table with more chairs than D'Artagnan ever could hope to entertain guests—one on the clothes press in his bedroom, at the foot of the bed. The bed must once have belonged to a much grander household with its posts and headboard carved in curlicues and turns, the gilding on them worn thin in spots.

From outside came a sound that might be dogs, but which reminded D'Artagnan of the wolves that haunted the night of his native Gascony. He'd heard that in Paris no one could leave their dogs outside, lest they fall prey to vampires. But the howling continued, fraying the nerves. Perhaps the wolves—their fear of vampires that roamed the countryside less than their fear of the humans in Paris—had been driven into the city, looking for the scraps that humanity discarded even in these lean times when most of the kingdom lay fallow.

It wouldn't be the first time wolves came into Paris and preyed on the weak there. And even had they come—D'Artagnan paced his floor, measuring forty steps from bedstead, out the door of the bedroom, and across the front room to the door at the top of the stairs—they wouldn't be the most dangerous creatures in Paris at night. Nor the most vile. Compared to a vampire, a wolf was almost a brother of men, an open and honest natural creature.

He paced again, from doorway to bedstead. From outside, through the shutters, came a scream, and the sound of running feet and coarse male laughter.

In his mind, thoughts assembled themselves then drew his attention—one by one—as if they were the beads of a rosary, slowly told through clenching fingers. He'd come to Paris to cleanse it of vampires. His anger so fierce it seemed as though it could, by itself, scour every building of the city, right every upended cross, and rebuild every desecrated cathedral.

He'd come to Paris to serve Monsieur de Tréville's musketeers, but he'd been turned down—put off with pretty words—and Aramis had said that the numbers of the musketeers could not be augmented. That too, was part of the treaty between the cardinal and the king. And the king was not, despite his crown and his anointing, the more powerful of the two.

Until a musketeer died—or enough musketeers died, since there was a waiting list—D'Artagnan would not receive the tunic of a musketeer. And until then, he had no sanction, no help in killing vampires. Even after that, if he understood it properly, he would have to do it stealthily, in the dark, and silence, as though it were a shameful thing. Monsieur de Tréville—or the king himself—might approve of it in secret but would disown him if he were discovered killing registered vampires, the proper subjects of the cardinal.

So why was he here, locked behind safe doors? Safe shutters? Porthos and Aramis had said to stay there in the dark of night, in the dangerous hours, and not to open his door to anyone.

But if that was what he wished to do, then surely he could have stayed in Gascony, barricaded himself, in his parents' house, and kept away from vampires—thus wasting his life as solidly as he was wasting it here in Paris.

Oh, there was a good chance—and he suspected that was Porthos' and Aramis' and even Athos' fear—that if he went out in the dark of night, he would find himself facing a vampire he could not conquer.

He clasped his hands and unclasped them, the tightening of his fists so close that his nails drew blood from his palm. Yes, he was but seventeen. What they called a child and little more. Seventeen or not, what good was life to him? And what did it matter?

On that day when he'd come home to find his parents turned, he'd faced his own death—or at least the death of everything dear to him. Until then, they'd been living peacefully, telling themselves the horrors that ravaged the rest of France could never reach their little domain where they knew everyone and everything. His father had personally made sure the village church's bells continued tolling over the sleepy countryside and that every peasant had plenty of holy water as a defense. He'd sheltered the parish priest, so he could go on blessing holy water.

But no part of the world could be safe when monsters strode abroad spreading their corruption. D'Artagnan knew that now. And his father had known it before he died. As he died, he had blessed his child and told him to kill vampires. To go to Paris and kill vampires.

D'Artagnan took a deep breath, sudden and shattering, as though it had been forced on him from the outside, so violent he felt his ribs would crack.

To kill vampires.

With sudden decision he reached for the sword in its scabbard, which he'd flung on the table. He strapped it on and nodded, as if to a challenge, though he wasn't sure from whom—perhaps from within himself.

He paced to the bedroom and blew out the candle atop the clothes press. Then he blew out the candle on the table.

In the dark, the sounds from the street seemed magnified. Screams and shouts and, now and then—he would swear to it—the clash of metal on metal.

He threw his cloak over his arm—more as a defensive device than as a garment. At the top of his stairs, he opened his cross-marked door and rushed outside into the musty darkness of the stairway. Down, down, down, by feel and not by sight, to the front door.

He checked he had his key in his sleeve, then opened the door and rushed out, slamming the door behind.

Outside the air was clear and cool and the moon in the sky so brilliant it rivaled the sun.

In its luminescent glow every aspect of the buildings stood revealed—the stones visible through the worn-out whitewashing. At the corner stood the desecrated chapel, its cross broken. In its half-ruined tower, a bell shone, silver-bright.

And in the middle of the street—like ghostly figures, outlined in the silver-blue moonlight, there fought Porthos and Aramis, crossing swords with six men—no, six vampires—in the uniform of the cardinal's guards.

Angels and Demons

His parents had given him the name of an angel. The man who for the last fifteen years had called himself Athos, had been baptized in holy water with the proper rites as Raphael de la Fère in peacetime, or at least in a peaceful region, in the bosom of his noble and ancient family, in its secluded and fruitful domain.

Born when his mother was approaching fifty years of age, he'd been viewed by both his parents as a miracle, as amazing—a portent as absolute as the Biblical Isaac born to the aged Sarah when all hope was past. And like Isaac's, his mother held him to be the gift of angels, or of one angel in particular: Raphael, archangel of the presence, whose power and righteousness had cleansed the Earth after the deluge.

By the vacillating light of the only candle remaining lit, Athos looked at himself in the mirror trying to see any sign of that holy promise, that divine gift.

There was none.

It was not true that vampires couldn't see themselves in mirrors. Or, at least, Athos saw himself clearly enough—his pale hair, his square chin, his eyes looking slightly red-rimmed as though he'd slept too little or cried too long. He had done neither—sleeping nor crying.

During the day he'd remained in his lodgings, refusing to give in to the urge—the overwhelming desire—to sleep. He would not be like them—not in what he could control, not in what he could force to obey him. He would force himself to stay awake by day and sleep by night.

But now that it was night, he wondered if that made any sense after all. He could not go out during the day nor keep the duties that would usually be allotted to him—and how he could explain that to Monsieur de Tréville remained to be seen, at least once the period had passed when the captain would be expecting him to recover from his injuries—and he dared not go out by night. Oh, he wanted to—his body trembled with the eagerness to go out. It was like a call . . . and that call he feared.

What he most dreaded was that once outside he might very well—he probably would—follow the urge to seek Charlotte wherever she was and surrender to her entirely. He could feel heat radiating from her bite, and could hear in his mind Charlotte's brilliant laugh.

But he would not give in. He was not just a man. He was Raphael, Comte de la Fère. However pitiful he might be compared to his parents' great dreams, this much he owed them, and this much he would do. He would not succumb to evil. He would not become one of them; a monster in mind and body, whose very essence served evil.

Clenching his teeth so hard his jaw hurt, he reached for the candlestick on the table and clasped it firmly. In his mind, arising from that safe childhood in which he'd been little more than a promise and his parents' dreams, came a litany taught him by his preceptor—an aged Jesuit—"The enemies of the soul are three: the flesh, the world, and the devil."

He'd repeated those words as a child, not knowing what any of it meant, and now he refused to dwell upon them as he trod out of his little sitting room into the main room. Grimaud had bid him good night an hour since and gone up to his room, calmly, to sleep. How the man could sleep like that in a house with a vampire, Athos didn't know. Why his old servant trusted him more than Athos trusted himself, Athos couldn't fathom.

He knew only that at this moment he'd not given in yet. He was certain of the solidity of the candlestick in his hand, and the light cast by its single candle made the shadows recede.

He hoped, without being able to say it, that Grimaud had set a chair against his door. He didn't want to attack Grimaud. He wouldn't go after Grimaud's blood and soul. Not while he was himself. But how long would he be himself?

It seemed to him as if the shadows themselves called to him and beyond that, those other shadows—the greater night outside and the not-quite-full moon shining over Paris. Outside . . . outside his kind would be rampaging: the Lords of the Night whose every whim could be indulged, every desire gratified. Outside, Charlotte would be awake, silk skin and moonlight hair, her high, firm breasts, her narrow waist . . .

He clenched his teeth so hard he thought they'd crack, and held the candlestick tighter. *The enemies of the soul are three. The flesh . . .*

Down the hallway, in the cool darkness, his heightened sense of smell detected a trace of everyone who had occupied this dwelling before him. Earlier, after his friends had left, he had forced another four cups of broth down, though quite a lot of it had come back up. Still he was not hungry. Or not exactly. His body did not thirst for liquid or nourishment. His body *was* craving. A craving spun and woven, and made flesh. A craving for comfort, for union, for pleasure, for . . . Charlotte.

In his room, he set the candle on a table beside the bed, the same table that held his copy of Virgil, thumbed through and marked with a thin ribbon ending in a silver medallion showing the arms de la Fère given to him by his father. He'd started reading it while he was still a living man.

He slid off his boots, a feat that usually required Grimaud's help, but which he managed by dint of struggle and force. Barefoot, he unfastened his old-fashioned breeches and pulled them off with his stockings and his undergarment, and carefully hung them up.

His nursemaid, who, in the way of an old and affectionate servant, had looked after him long after he'd reached adulthood—in fact, until his marriage—had drummed into him that a nobleman simply did not leave his clothing and possessions lying about. Having met and known many other noblemen in the last fifteen years, Athos begged to differ. But at the time, his pattern of perfection had been his father, an exact gentleman and never untidy.

His shirt, no longer tucked into his breeches, came to his upper thighs. For many years it had been his habit to sleep in his shirt. Tonight he wondered if he should remove it, lest blood, seeping through his bandages, would stain it.

But in the end, he decided tonight, of all nights, if he was going to attempt to sleep—when he didn't even know if vampires slept and knew for a certainty they didn't sleep at night—everything must be as familiar as possible.

From his bedside table, he got the leather strap that he used to tie his hair overnight, so it wouldn't become tangled about him, and then he slid into bed.

The linen sheets were cool and strangely rough against his exposed legs and hands, coarser than they'd ever felt before, and they smelled of his own sweat from the previous night.

He didn't think what he'd done was sleep. His friends had found him, crawling in the street, weak, half-dead, undeniably turned. Undeniably turned, that is, unless it were to the embracing arms of friendship, which refused to believe it, which held out hope against hope that he would still live, that he would still be human.

His friends had dragged him home and to bed. He retained a blurry recollection of being shoved—naked, bloodied, and filthy as he'd been—between his sheets. And then there had been the darkness of death until he'd wakened, dewed in sweat and trembling, in the morning, images of blood and need in his mind.

There was a faint, lingering smell of death in the bed. Not as though someone had died in it, or at least not recently. It was more like the odor from a tomb many centuries old.

In the churchyard of La Fère there were three raised sarcophaguses, each of them surmounted by the statue of a crusader, his arms crossed, his blank eyes looking beyond the sky at eternity. Athos' father had told him they were his ancestors, good and revered men.

A solitary, quiet boy Athos might have been, but he would have been more than blood and flesh if, in the daring years of his adolescence, he hadn't opened the tombs, just a crack, to peer inside.

Perhaps others had done so, in the untold centuries since interment. Or perhaps grave robbers had at some point despoiled the tombs. They were empty, nothing within but a little dust.

And the smell from them was age and incense. Something very old and vaguely musky. This smell, Athos now detected on his sheets—not unpleasant, but strange, as though he were dead and buried at the bottom of a tomb.

He closed his eyes and told himself he had to sleep, but the candlelight, shining through his eyelids, made him open them again, and glare at the brightness. The light kept the shadows at bay. But he'd not slept with the candle lit since he was two.

Rising on his elbow, he blew the flame out and the shadows closed in. Cool shadows, scented of powdery death.

His hand went up, by accustomed rote, to trace the sign of the cross on his forehead, but he could not let himself do it. He could not profane with his unnatural hands a sacred gesture. He turned in bed, and then again, his arm paining him, his middle sticking to the bandages by seeping blood.

Through a crack in his shutters—so small he'd never seen it before—moonlight poured in, blinding. By that moonlight, outside, Charlotte . . .

No.

He bit his lip and thought of Latin declensions, which he'd learned by rote as a child. He didn't dare mutter prayers, but this he could mutter, until the sheer repetition of words, like hypnotism, drove every thought from his mind and ushered in sleep or its surfeit. "*Pater, patris, honor honoris, terror terroris, uxor uxoris, salus salutis . . .*"

Not aware of having lulled himself into sleep, he was brought awake by a soft whisper at his ear, "Raphael!"

His eyes opened. The sliver of moonlight coming through the window seemed to have swelled, filling the entire room, making every object resplendent with silver-blue light. His clothes, hanging neatly in their peg. His candle, blown out. His bed, brought from his estate fifteen years ago—not his wedding bed, *quod avertat Deus*—its posts carved and fretted, and shining with polish.

He could see his body, under the covers: large, powerful, and lean as it had been since it had crested adolescence and not ever got quite enough—from the land that had to subsist on its own produce since its neighbors had succumbed to vampires that neither sowed nor reaped—to put on even a little fat. Not from his hunts, even, which always went to feed the needy among his tenants and serfs. The children, the aged, the helpless woman whose vampire husband had left for more friendly lands, the lost young men made vampire-orphans, like the young Gascon now: all those had depended on his charity to survive.

So there were his sturdy long legs, with their nimble knees, his powerful trunk, the chest muscled from incessant dueling. From vampire killing. All of this delineated by the linen sheet and the thin blanket over it. In the light of the moon it looked like a whole landscape. Valleys and peaks, all of it unknown territory, as different and separated from his former self as though it had been the face of the moon.

As much as he did not wish to turn and look to his right—the direction from which the voice had whispered his name—he knew he would have to. Yet he held rigid in stubborn immobility.

She could not have gotten in. She could not be in his room. The site where her teeth had penetrated his flesh burnt like a fire.

"Raphael," Charlotte's voice called again, and this time, he could feel her breath, warm upon his ear, and smell her perfume—like lilac, sweet and intoxicating.

No.

Her laughter rang like music in the room, so loud, so real, that he was sure that even now, upstairs, Grimaud would be slipping his feet into his shoes and coming down to see what was happening.

But there was no sound from above of Grimaud's feet hitting the floor boards. No sound of feet on the stairs. No rescue.

Her laughter came again, like music, like cool water, like a dream. And now her lips touched his ear, the barest caress, so gentle that it might be no more than the wind, or the sliding of a rose petal. So gentle, that it might not be more than a dream.

"Very well," she said, each of her exhalations a soft breeze against his earlobe. "Very well, Monsieur le Comte. We'll dance to your tune."

A trail of kisses, each of them petal-soft, made its way down the underside of his chin, where his well-trimmed beard left the skin bare, and to his Adam's apple, where her tongue came out to flick at his skin, and the teeth touched—just barely. Not enough to be called a bite, or even a nibble. Just a slightly rougher touch.

He'd closed his eyes and it was all he could do not to throw his head back, not to bare his neck, not beg her to take what remained of his life, to finish him—if finishing him brought her pleasure.

The covers were lifted from his chest and thrown back. "What, a shirt? You were never modest," she said.

In his mind, despite himself, their wedding night replayed itself. She'd been virginal, or so she played it. Now thinking on it, he thought there was no way she could have been virginal. Not if she was a vampire and shared the group mind. He'd been virginal but unwilling to admit it, and he'd intruded on her with his caresses, and pushed what he thought were the bounds of her female modesty.

Now it was she who denuded him, pulling his shirt up, to reveal his body, protected by nothing but bandages. It was he who closed his eyes, and hoped against hope that his pleasure in the assault wouldn't show, and she who lowered her mouth to his chest, who kissed sinewy muscles and ran her silken hands over them, to his flat belly and then down twin paths to his thighs. "Oh, Raphael," she said, her voice soft and sweet, as it had been when she married him. "I have missed you."

He opened his eyes then, to see her, straddling his waist. She was naked and her body was as white and perfect as he remembered, each of the flawless breasts crowned by a nipple the delicate coral pink he'd only before seen inside a seashell. Evil she might be but her features, perfect and tender, could have been sculpted for some Madonna before which mortals prayed.

Her gaze rested on him and she smiled, and either her fangs hadn't descended or she hid them. The place where she had drunk his life felt as though it were glowing—a haze of pleasure diffusing from the wound onto his whole body, making his skin more sensitive.

It was as though a layer of his skin had been peeled away, leaving what was beneath, newly exposed and raw, alive to every touch, every caress.

She was stroking him, her hands everywhere, her lips coming down to cover his as she leaned forward.

Her tongue pushed into his mouth, cool and purposeful, tasting like honey and fresh apples. He could not resist her. His tongue followed hers into her mouth, feeling the even, smooth pearls of her teeth. Her thighs, wrapped around his waist felt warm and as soft as silk, compared to the roughness of the linen still enveloping his calves and feet.

"How . . . how?" he asked, as she pulled up, wishing to ask her how she had gotten in, how she could be in his room, and why. But he could not form coherent words and his body, for once in control, did not care to question. She was here, she was his. She could do as she wished with him. He was hers.

She smiled at him and her finger came down to seal his lips in the gesture of silence. Then her mouth returned to his broad chest, tracing the sprinkling of golden hair, down along his belly and ...

She stopped just short of his erection, wringing from him a moan of deep frustration, which brought a soft laugh from her.

And then her lips were at his thighs, now kissing, now nipping, just enough to allow him to feel the touch of her teeth. Her hands roamed upward, touching everything except what he most wanted her to touch.

For fifteen years, every thought of fleshly desire had brought a thought of Charlotte. And every thought of Charlotte brought the memory of her death, the certainty he had killed her, and the doubt of her guilt.

For fifteen years he'd been like a man encased in granite, afraid of all touch, even of his own hand, if that touch brought pleasure and if pleasure brought a memory of Charlotte.

But now Charlotte was here. Charlotte was now straddling his still-covered calves, and caressing him, her touch like fire upon his sensitive skin, her lips by turns soft and teasing on his hips, his thighs, then up again.

A tentative finger touched his testicles. He arched and moaned, and would have begged had any words remained in his overwrought mind.

But she seemed to understand what he could not say, and she sat back and looked at him with vaguely amused eyes. "Was that a plea, Monsieur le Comte?"

His throat and lips worked in vain, and only one word came out, raspy and all breath, "Charlotte!"

"All you have to do is let me in."

He did not understand her. His mind filled with odd images. His grandfather had owned a collection of leather-bound woodcuts depicting, of all things, Roman orgies. Athos suspected his father didn't even know the book existed, high up on a shelf in the library. Athos had stumbled upon it one summer, while looking for reading material. Though none of the pictures interested him particularly, in the inchoate desire of adolescence—desire for everything, so long as it was touch—he'd spent many an afternoon studying them.

Now those images came to mind and, could he have summoned speech, he would have told Charlotte that was impossible.

She must have read his mind or seen something in his eyes, because he saw her eyes widen and, for the first time, a hint of surprise in her gaze. "Raphael!" she said, and her voice sounded both shocked and amused.

Then she leaned forward and kissed him, hard—teeth catching at his tongue and almost, but not quite biting. Lifting her mouth a little, she spoke against his lips, "Into your mind, my dear. Let me in."

With that, he could feel a scraping, a scratching, on the edges of his mind, around it, pushing, tugging, seeking entrance.

"No," he said, but it was almost a sob.

She said nothing. Her hands and mouth returned to their work, caressing, feeling, gentling. Her hands like silk, like rose petals. Her hands on him, heated, warm. And the pain from the bite, radiating, mingling with pleasure, blotting out his thoughts.

His spine arched. His legs locked. He sobbed, close to begging. But let her in, he would not.

His body felt so hot that at any minute it might burst in flames, and the air around him was filled with the scent of her. She leaned forward and her firm breasts pressed against his chest.

"Raphael," she said. It was the tone an adult might use to a disobedient child. And he knew, he knew as certainly as he knew that one day he would be nothing but dust, that if she went on, if this continued—he would give in. He would not be able to resist.

The enemy of the soul is the flesh. The flesh. The—

His body had a mind of its own and glimpsed a way out his mind could not see. Moving swiftly, he lowered his own hand. Her hand tried to intercept his, just too late.

Her nails raked his wrist, and her voice said, "No!"

But his hand, warm, strong, had already closed on his member.

It took only a touch. His whole body spasmed.

It lasted a second or an eternity.

When he became aware again, he was alone, in his rumpled bed, his body cold and soaked with sweat, his breath coming in small, labored gasps.

And Charlotte was quite gone.

The Bells

D'Artagnan plunged into the fray on the street, his sword out, a scream caught in his throat. Both Aramis and Porthos were battling three vampires apiece.

As he took his place next to Porthos, two of the vampires turned to him. They looked gaunt and famished, aged and goat-like, their skin thin and yellowed like parchment stretched over their skulls, the eyes dark and sunken and unreadable. And they moved fast, fast, fast, but with peculiar darting movements. Like snakes or insects, not humans.

On his toes, his heels barely touching the ground as he shifted, D'Artagnan charged when he could, parried when he had to. He wanted to kill vampires. He wanted to sate his rage. But they were fast; unpredictable. They dove under his guard again and again. He couldn't help but parry and retreat, step by step by step.

His coming to relieve them had allowed Porthos and Aramis a respite. They danced forward in unison, shoulder to shoulder, swords flashing, metal clashes ringing in the still night air. They caught up with D'Artagnan and D'Artagnan kept up with them, his shoulder pressed against Porthos' side.

He glided forward, parrying his adversary blindly. His sword moved by instinct, smooth and alive, seeking its vengeance. Porthos' and Aramis' swords flashed beside him.

A smell of corruption told him one of the musketeers—D'Artagnan did not dare look to see which—had killed an adversary. A scream soon told him another vampire had died. Porthos boomed from his right, "*A moi, Monsieur Bloodsucker,*" and one of D'Artagnan's adversaries answered the call, giving D'Artagnan a free hand to press his enemy closer.

But the vampire's sword still flashed too fast, and the cloak he had wrapped around one stick-thin arm parried all of D'Artagnan's thrusts, while the vampire's blade sought out D'Artagnan's heart again and again. It took all of D'Artagnan's concentration to avert those thrusts.

D'Artagnan's blood coursed through his ears with a hissing sound. His heart pounded an unavoidable meter of despair. He could smell with more intensity than ever before, each of the night smells of the city—mud and cooking, smoke and humanity—all in sharp relief beneath the pall of rank vampire blood. The buildings around them, glimpsed at the edge of his vision, were like unreal sketches made in blue and darkness in shining moonlight and crisp night air.

He heard Aramis' adversary scream his death knell. He smelled the corruption of Porthos' dying opponent. He thought nothing of it.

He thought of nothing but movement—his feet on the cobblestones, his fingers, cold and locked around the pommel of the sword. The vampire's sword seeking his death—his sword countering and striking.

Porthos said, "*A moi.*" The vampire turned. As D'Artagnan glanced in the Porthos' direction, it registered that the two friends had been watching him for some time. Their expressions were somewhere between amused and approving.

D'Artagnan's rage flared. They'd come here, in the night, to guard his door. They'd come to protect him. They were cosseting him as if he were a child. Dismissing him. Belittling him. Just like those vampires earlier, telling him to go back to his mother.

He charged haphazardly. Grabbing at the vampire's cloak, he pulled it away from the vampire's arm. He felt resistance and thought he heard a *snap*, a sound like a dry branch breaking, but it did not matter.

He flung the cloak over the vampire's sword, as he plunged his own sword into the vampire's heart. Panting, sweating, he pulled his blade free before the falling corpse could drag it down.

He wiped his forehead with the back of his hand and rounded on the two musketeers with cold fury. "You didn't need to come," he said. "As you see, messieurs, I am quite able to defend myself."

Aramis frowned slightly at him, his eyes blank with seeming incomprehension, and Porthos said, dully, "Yourself."

"Well, yes, myself, as you see, I killed my vampire."

"Yes, but why—" Porthos said.

Aramis tossed back his head, throwing his golden hair into place, every lock falling perfectly as though he'd spent hours arranging it before his mirror. He wore fawn-colored suede gloves, which perfectly matched a suit of velvet highlighted by dove-colored silk.

D'Artagnan was sure that if it were daylight, he would see that both velvet and silk were quite worn and mended. But here, by the silvery light of the moon, Aramis looked all of one piece, perfectly knit, impeccably attired, and the sort of creature—a chevalier of legend, a man who always did what he should—that would intimidate D'Artagnan, the provincial boy with his raw manners.

It did no more than make his gorge rise. He felt he was being put in his place. He did not like his place.

Aramis' mocking dark eyes scrutinized him from head to toe, with an almost pitying gaze. He did not speak to D'Artagnan.

Instead, he turned to Porthos and his gaze sharpened to intentness. "Porthos," he said, urgently. "This is not the time. They will feel these deaths, they will be here. They will be on us."

"They were not the ones they should have been," Porthos said slowly, his forehead wrinkling in thought. "Not the sort I'd expect."

Aramis shrugged, a nervous gesture. "No, not the ones I'd expect for this sort of ambush." He poked one of the fallen corpses with his foot. "Eastern European, I'd say. The older ones. The wraiths. The sort that—"

D'Artagnan heard himself hiss his impatience. "I don't understand why anyone should ambush me? Or what you mean, or—"

"Will you be quiet?" Porthos asked. "This does not concern you."

"Porthos, that was rude." Aramis looked pained. He gave a little dismissive flick with his gloved hand. "D' Artagnan, we are very grateful indeed that you helped us with our adversaries, but now you should go back to your lodging and barricade the door. We must concentrate on how to defend from the next attack which might very well mean our deaths."

D'Artagnan took a deep breath and exhaled. Oh, he knew very well that he had a hot temper. The rest of France assumed all Gascons did, through the infusion of Spanish blood, so near the

border. D'Artagnan thought it was more that Gascony had been at
war so long. Only those quick with a blade survived.

But now he knew nothing could mark him more as a young man
and one who, therefore, deserved to be treated as a child by his more
experienced comrades, than a sudden outburst of fury.

He shook his head and swallowed hard, to control the fury that
would otherwise choke his voice. "I understand that you might feel
worried about me, since I just arrived. I also understand that I am,
compared to you, a novice at killing vampires. And perhaps I should
not—as you said—have left my lodgings. But I came to Paris to kill
vampires and I—"

"Oh, good," Porthos said, softly, his voice almost a whisper. "You
are then about to get your wish, my friend."

Aramis looked over D'Artagnan's shoulder and his eyes narrowed.
The sword he'd never sheathed rose as he stood straighter and called,
loudly, "To me, musketeers," a call echoed by Porthos, in stentorian
tones. "To me, to me, of the king."

Their shouts peeled echoes from the surrounding buildings,
reverberating in the night with an edge of despair.

Half-fearing that a gross joke was being played on him; ignored
by the musketeers; frightened of the bleakness in their gazes,
D'Artagnan turned around.

A wall of vampires advanced toward them. So dark that they
seemed to meld with the surrounding night, three rows of vampires, at
least, walked toward them—shoulder to shoulder, rank on rank, all of
them strange, thin, almost insectile creatures, their faces frozen masks
showing no emotion at all. They weren't even dressed but looked,
rather, as though the clothes they'd worn while living had fallen to
pieces on their bodies, and remained attached only by dirt or rot.

Pieces of them, ragged and encrusted with dirt, flapped with their
movements. But the blades they held shone bright and sharp.

Porthos leaned forward, spread his feet further apart bracing for
better balance, and spared one brief look at Aramis. "To me, of the
king," he shouted. Then, in a lower tone, "No one else is coming."

"No musketeers in this part of town," Aramis said. He sounded
very calm. "We made sure of it. If we could toll the bells . . . If the
churches were still ours. If anyone still knew what the bells meant,

and if that chapel weren't sure to be crawling with vampires." He shrugged gallantly, his expression frozen and lost. "As it is we die here, my friend. We die here. It has been an honor, Monsieur du Vallon, my dear Porthos, to fight evil by your side."

"Likewise, Chevalier D'Herblay, my dear Aramis," Porthos said, his voice light and airy. His features settled in lines like granite.

Aramis made a sign of the cross mid-air, as though blessing Porthos.

"You said the bells . . ." D'Artagnan said. They thought they were going to die. They were going to die here. *But I'm seventeen. I'm only seventeen.*

The man who'd come to Paris to fight vampires and thought he had nothing else to live for heard his own inner wail and wanted to say it didn't matter. He might in many ways still be a boy, but what did that have to say to his time of death? What in this time when death was victorious everywhere?

I've never been on a boat, I've never broken a horse. I've never kissed a woman. His throat closed, dry as dust. It was dry in the tomb. He'd not see another sunrise. *But . . . I'm seventeen!*

"What of the bells? What would the bells do?" The musketeers spoke in riddles. And it was not about him. It had never been about him. They'd kept other musketeers away from here—they'd not do that if they wanted to defend him. They'd said the vampires were not the right type. As if they'd been expecting—waiting for—another type of vampire.

D'Artagnan remembered his father's stories, about calling musketeers—and those who fought vampires—with the sound of bells. About how bells—holy bells, blessed in the service of the church—made vampires uncomfortable. His father had ordered the bells tolled in the village church almost constantly. He said it kept his domain safe.

D'Artagnan raised his sword and looked over his shoulder, behind him, at the little ruined chapel. He was sure he could see a bell gleaming there atop the broken tower, the metal shining in the moonlight. "Will musketeers come to the bells?" he asked, his voice cracking and sounding terribly young. "Would they come to bells if we rang them?"

"There would be a chance, at least," Aramis said. He looked over his shoulder, too, in the direction of D'Artagnan's glance. "Oh, the bells still seem to be there—perhaps they are too well embedded to be pulled off and broken—but we cannot ring them. No one can get to the bells. The chapel itself will be overflowing with vampires."

"I have my sword. But would musketeers come?" D'Artagnan asked.

"Five years ago all would have," Aramis said. "And there may still be musketeers who remember. We used to ring the bells of the church to ask for help when we couldn't call—before the treaty turned all the churches over to the vampires and desecrated them."

"The ones who remember would come," Porthos said. "And others would follow. The patrols are not in this area—"

"But—" Aramis said.

"I will ring the bells," D'Artagnan said.

"Don't be a fool," Porthos said. He put a hand out to stay D'Artagnan. The vampires—advancing unhurriedly, inexorably—were now so close that their smell of must and dirt enveloped the three men. "The vampires have occupied every chapel, every church. There will be a dozen of the foreign ones in there, the ones who don't have a position or a post in French society yet. They will boil out of there and make short work of you."

D'Artagnan looked on the ranks of advancing corruption and rot, their figures moving stiffly, as no human ever had. "As well die there as here, then," D'Artagnan said. "I shall go."

Aramis looked sideways, favoring him with a grin that shaded from feral to amused. "Well," he said. "*En avant*, then, my friend. Go to the tower, Porthos and I will cover you as long as we can. It can't be very long."

As he spoke, the musketeers started slowly retreating in the direction of the tower, swords ready.

Aramis shook his head, as if answering something, then clicked his tongue perhaps in answer to some internal struggle. With a sigh, he reached in his sleeve and handed D'Artagnan a small cloth pouch exquisitely stitched together and monogrammed with an embroidered R and H. "Take this. It's filled with blessed salt. It will confuse the vampires and daze them and give you, for a little while, the advantage of them. Just fling it ahead of you. It is by no means a magical shield, and you'll still have the odds grossly against you, but it might make it possible for you to survive long enough to ring the bells."

"But . . . " D'Artagnan began, wanting to ask why—if Aramis possessed a weapon with such amazing powers—he had not used it before.

Aramis answered with a smile of mingled exasperation and sweetness, one of the most unusual expressions that D'Artagnan had ever seen, and said only, "If we survive I will explain all. Now go. You must make sure you kill every vampire before they understand why they're so confused. You have my word: if we live, you will receive your explanation."

"If," Porthos said, disdainfully.

D'Artagnan understood nothing. Was this all a mad dream? One of those in which common objects acquire momentous significance? One where ordinary events seemed distorted and changed?

But dream or not, he would ring the bells. Dream or not, D'Artagnan wouldn't die without fighting for his life, without trying to give himself and the musketeers a chance at survival.

I've never kissed a woman, he thought, as he loped toward the tower. *I've never touched a woman.*

He poured some of the salt into his hand. He could hear blade striking against blade at his back. He remembered Aramis saying, *It cannot be for very long.*

The chapel had been very small indeed and, judging by the tile embedded on the wall next to the door, it had been dedicated to the archangel Gabriel. A meek, square building with a narrow tower next to it that could hardly hold more than two people at a time—it now smelled evil and filthy. The interior that had once, doubtless, been lit by blessed candles and filled with the sound of holy words, was now a dank hole stinking of blood and rotting flesh.

Past the arched doorway, all was darkness and shadows. Yet something moved in the gloom. Vampires. Only vampires lived in desecrated churches.

D'Artagnan threw the salt ahead of him, so hard he felt his shoulder wrench. In the absolute darkness within the chapel, it seemed to him as though the scattering grains formed bright trails midair, shining with a light of their own.

They fell with sizzling sounds.

There were cries, screams, and little flares of yellow-blue-red light, like fireworks.

D'Artagnan counted five voices, imagined there were others and, wrapping his cloak tight around his left arm, plunged into the darkness swinging his sword left and right.

Nocturnal Pollution

Athos stood naked in a corner of the kitchen—where a hole in the washing sink allowed wastewater to drain outside—pouring water over himself. He'd retied his hair to keep it out of the way. Taking water from one of the three enormous pails Grimaud bought from water carriers every other day, he'd filled a clay jar with cold water then tipped it over his head, letting it run down his naked body.

Shivering, he grabbed the small bar of soap Grimaud kept by the sink and, soaping his hands, rubbed the foam all over his body. He'd removed his bandages, to find his wounds almost healed. And yet the soap stung his skin, as if it were abraded. He'd removed his shirt and thrown it in a corner of the room. He'd rinse it too, later. Better that than to have Grimaud know . . .

A clean shirt, which had been hard enough to find in the clothes press—since Grimaud laid out Athos' clothing every morning—was draped across one of the kitchen stools.

He shivered as he threw another jar of water over his naked body and watched the soapy water flow down the drain. The shiver was half for the cold, and half for the scratch across his arm—blood red and fresh. The scratch made by Charlotte's fingernails in trying to stop his hand.

Were it not for that, he would think that it had all been a dream—that the mad events of the last twenty-four hours and his being changed into a vampire had lessened his ability to control his animal side. That, in fact, what he'd indulged in had been no more than nocturnal pollution.

But the fresh scratch gave it all the lie, and conspired with what he knew in his heart and soul to be true. He'd denied her victory by blunting his craving, by closing his mental ears to her call with his sudden pleasure. By barring the door and locking it, he had taken away the sword with which she would have pried into his soul.

And yet . . . his wife had been there, in his room. Charlotte had been there in body as well as in spirit. She had come bearing pleasure and pain, or pain hiding beneath pleasure, or perhaps—a pleasurable attack, a sweetened death.

He had defeated her this one time, but it might easily have gone the other way. He knew it as well as he knew his own name, or knew he still loved his treacherous wife.

"Monsieur le Comte!"

The voice made him look up from the water circling down the drain hole to the entranceway of the kitchen where Grimaud stood, a single candle in a clay candlestick in one hand and in the other—

Athos felt his lips twitch and didn't know if he was going to laugh and cry. All he could manage was, in a thickened voice: "I don't believe the stake will be needed quite yet, Grimaud. As you see, I am still myself."

Grimaud let the short, sharpened stick fall from his hand to clatter onto the floor with a hollow sound.

"Good thought, though," Athos said as his mind resolved the dilemma on the side of laughter. "Good thought, and it might have saved your life." It was, on the whole, a relief that his old servant, his friend who had almost raised him, should be wary enough to fear the vampire he'd become; smart enough to carry a stake when searching the house in the middle of the night. It was what he should do. If Athos wasn't sure how long he could trust himself—how long he could hold against the onslaught of Charlotte's efforts to take over his mind—why should Grimaud trust him?

Better to know that should he fail, someone he could count on stood ready to stop him before he could kill.

"Monsieur," Grimaud said, a third time, running his broad calloused hand through his grizzled hair. "I didn't mean to . . . That is . . . I heard the clatter in your room, as if you . . . as if you had lost your way." He was looking wide-eyed at Athos, as well he should.

What will he think has come over me, to stand here, naked, over the kitchen drain, washing myself from the scarce water in the kitchen.

78

"If you'd told me you wished a bath," Grimaud said, his voice somewhat dry, "I could have drawn water from the well in the yard. It is not good enough to drink, but it is quite good enough to wash with. I could have warmed you a pot of it and brought out the hip bath."

Athos shook his head. "It doesn't matter," He said, making his face like stone against the embarrassment clouding his mind. "Well, as you see, I am done," he said, and set down the jar, and then reached for the towel he'd laid beside the shirt. "This way I do not have to wet my hair. Besides, I did not wish to wake you in the middle of the night."

He dried himself briskly, the towel, like his sheet, feeling oddly rough against his skin. Then he draped it across the kitchen stool, and slipped his shirt on, tying the neck and the sleeves with meticulous care, as if he were not about to use this as a nightshirt. As if he were preparing himself, in fact, to go out and keep a formal appointment.

Grimaud dove in to rescue the towel, which was in danger of sliding from the stool to the dirty floor, and, clutching it to himself as if he'd just saved something precious, looked up at Athos, "Monsieur! I've known you since you were a child. If there's anything . . . if you find yourself . . . " He seemed to be himself as ill-at-ease as Athos, and couldn't quite bring himself to speak frankly. Instead, he forcefully expelled air through his nose, and said, in a peevish tone—as if Athos had still been a small child roaming through the fields of his father's domain, climbing trees, and coming in with his clothes muddy and torn: "There is no call for you to do foolish things. You could have rung for me and I would more than gladly have arranged a bath for you. You needn't be stumbling around in the middle of the night trying to look after yourself." His gaze reproached Athos, and he spoke in a low, protesting voice. "It is not fit, m'sieur. Not for someone of your quality."

Athos said only, lightly, "It is no matter." He was half amused and half touched at Grimaud's concern for his dignity. He thought he could not now go in search of sheets to change his bed, so he spoke in a voice as abstracted and casual as he could make it. "There is . . . the matter of my sheets."

79

Grimaud, who'd been ready to leave the kitchen, turned back and looked at Athos. For just a moment it looked as if he would ask what sheets, but then he nodded. "Yes, m'sieur. I'll see to them. I'll get some from the linen press right away."

Athos—who'd never paid much close attention to such matters— thought the linen press might be the big armoire just outside the kitchen. And if, as he supposed, Grimaud was as zealous about the linen as everything else, this would involve a careful evaluation of mended sheets versus merely worn ones, and of the various qualities of cloth that might be allowed on a count's bed even in these reduced times. What Athos could do till the servant had settled on the proper sheets was beyond him. He was fairly sure if he should strip his own bed, he would be rewarded with a look more of reproach than anger from Grimaud.

Partly as self-punishment, he decided he would have more broth. He had no more than turned to look for it, when he heard Grimaud's voice from the stairway. "It is in the pot, m'sieur, at the back of the banked fire in the hearth. To keep warm. I'll make sure there is always some broth for you there. Should I come and—"

"No," Athos said, firmly, refraining—but just barely—from clicking his tongue in annoyance. "I do still remember how to fill cups."

Though it turned out he didn't, at least not when it involved reaching into the hearth and past the uncomfortable warmth of the banked cinders and helping himself from a pot he could not hope to lift, not with his bare hands, at least, since it was still hot. He supposed there was a ladle somewhere. In fact, he remembered such instruments—one of finely carved wood and another of brass—but he could not hope to guess where Grimaud had put them. They were not hanging from the walls nor—as Athos thought in amusement at his own exasperation—dancing in the air before his eyes.

In the end he settled for dipping a crockery mug into the warm liquid, and filling it. Some broth dripped across the flagstones as he crossed the kitchen to sit on the stool to sip, but he thought that Grimaud would never notice it before it had dried. Athos felt like a naughty child slipping a treat from under his guardian's eye.

Only the broth was no treat. It still tasted like foul ditch water. He had just finished the cup and was contemplating a second—not sure even his sins deserved that much punishment—when he heard the bells toll.

At first he thought it was a dream, a hallucination—something his overwrought mind had conjured up out of the trials and toils of the last day and night. And the night before, for that matter.

They sounded, then faded, then sounded again, a will-o'-the-wisp sound, something that was there, yet wasn't—something that hadn't been heard in Paris for . . . oh, at least four years. Not since His Majesty—frightened of his powerful and unholy minister his royal powers surrendered to him in all but word—had given the cardinal a treaty that closed every church, so that even the last vestiges of holiness might be destroyed in this poor kingdom.

Yet the bells sounded, silvery bright through the darkness. They sounded as though tolled by an inexperienced hand, since the rhythm was neither funereal nor joyful, but oscillated between the two sounding, repetitive and urgent, like nothing so much as . . . A shout for help.

Athos was on his feet, before he knew what he was doing. His bare feet hit the flagstones of the kitchen in an increasingly faster rhythm. Walking, jogging, running. He passed the armoire in the hall and Grimaud was not there. Athos called out as he ran up the staircase, "Grimaud!"

And then again, in alarm, as—had the wind shifted direction or was Athos being tormented by a ghost of holiness?—the bells became audible again, louder, perfectly clear, "Grimaud!"

Grimaud appeared at the top of the stairs, coming from Athos' room. He had the dirty sheets clutched in his hands, and for just a moment, Athos thought he was going to ask Athos why he was shouting. But then he noted Grimaud was pale and his eyes were wide, his whole expression that of someone hearing something impossible.

Athos leaned against the banister that ran up the wall on the left of the stairway. "Do you hear them?" he asked; it was no more than a whisper.

Grimaud nodded, his mouth opening then closing. In what was for him an almost unspeakable sacrilege, he flung the sheets down, against the wall, not in whatever sacrosanct hideaway he put clothes to be sent to the laundresses. "It's musketeers, m'sieur," he said. "Someone is in trouble."

And though it made no sense, though it was far more likely it was the vampires who now occupied the churches and chapels, the truth was that the bloodsuckers seemed to have almost as much dread of the bells as of the cross, and even when they destroyed them, they sent Judas goats climbing up the towers to break them. It was as though the metal of the bells were imbued with holiness and, thus, the sound dreadful to damned ears.

Athos experienced none of this, but then crosses did not disturb him. He swallowed and nodded. Panicked and filled with energy, he ran up the stairs. "My breeches, Grimaud," he said, as he ran into his room. "My doublet. My sword."

His servant handed him hose, then the articles he asked for, and helped him strap on the sword, then held him by the sleeve. "M'sieur, your boots."

Those took a little longer—and Grimaud's help—to pull on. Athos, sitting on his bed, listening, said, "I think it comes from the rue des Fossoyeurs."

"Is that where Monsieur Porthos and Monsieur Aramis . . ."

"Usually patrol?" Athos finished his question for him and nodded.

The idea that his friends were in danger put yet more urgency into his movements as he stood up.

"Monsieur," Grimaud said, behind him.

He turned.

"I will be coming along also, after I dress," the servant said. As Athos opened his mouth to protest, Grimaud added, "You know Bazin and Mousqueton—the servants of Messieurs Aramis and Porthos—and I have killed vampires in the past. I think this might be a time we need to do so again."

Ringing In

Athos ran all the way to the rue des Fossoyeurs, which required him to run headlong across Pont Neuf. The great span of bridge, with no houses on either side, looked more like an otherworldly construction than something solid.

What made it odder was the bright moonlight—very clear and cold—pouring down on the confusion of other musketeers crossing the bridge, running, one after the other, in scrambling haste. Some of them wore the uniform of musketeers—the blue tunic with the cross on the chest—some wore ordinary clothes, some their nightshirts, but in these days of relaxed regulations and scarce fabric, mostly they knew each other by sight with no need for uniforms. All wore looks of grim determination.

Athos counted at least three men with whom he'd fought shoulder to shoulder many times, D'Embocage, Maritain, Vercin. They ran within steps of him, and didn't spare him a look. Not a glance. To them, if they noticed him at all, he was just Athos, running to the call as they all were.

And then he wondered if any of these vampires they would meet would reveal his nature. It didn't matter. If they did he would simply say it was all lies and nothing more. He knew that Aramis and Porthos, for good and sufficient reason, had made the rue des Fossoyeurs their private policing district.

In fact, the musketeers had no assigned patrol sections and nowhere they were supposed to be after the sun went down—except for the half dozen assigned to guard the royal palace or the royal quarters. By the bounds of the treaty with the vampires, musketeers—daylighters—were not supposed to walk the shadows of the night.

But they did, of course they did, for the same reason and in the same way that they engaged the vampires in duels all around town. To protect the innocent. To hold back the darkness, just a little.

Porthos and Aramis had a particular interest in the rue des Fossoyeurs, where the queen's maid of honor lived. Madame Constance Bonacieux, all of twenty-two, married to a grocer twice her age, was one of the very few and very brave people who used her special status—and not inconsiderable strength of mind and body— to keep the queen of France safe. Safe from murder, of course, but most of all, safe from being made a vampire.

Since the first vampire had been found, during the excavation of a tomb in the frozen steppes of Eastern Europe, kingdom after kingdom, land after land had fallen under the sway of the ancient evil. Kings and queens had been turned, queens impregnated with vampire children.

Most principalities in Germany had fallen to vampires, as had Greece. Portugal and Spain had been taken via the north of Africa where the vampires had gone from the east and where, reports had it, vampires ran rampant. And Italy . . . Italy was *terra incognita*, having fallen under the internal disputes of its many princes. Rome hadn't been heard from in years and no one knew if the world still had a pope.

In the turmoil, the confusion, the half-lies propagated by the vampires, all that was certain was that England ran with rivers of blood, riven by a civil war. And that France still held. For now. For a given value of holding.

If it was capitulating, it was doing so slowly and step by step, succumbing under the machinations of Richelieu, the weakness of the king. Slowly. Man by man, woman by woman, one by one they were being taken by the vampires. Athos would slow that spread yet further if he could.

Without realizing it, he'd crossed Pont Neuf ahead of all the others. It was that extra strength of the vampire and the extra energy. He reached the rue des Fossoyeurs—a quiet street, inhabited by respectable people—to find Aramis and Porthos, their backs to the tower of a little chapel, where the bells rang madly.

Around them was a sea of vampires. Vampire wraiths, so old. Athos wouldn't allow them in his mind, but he could feel them—he could almost taste them. So old they could not have been changed since that tomb in Eastern Europe had been opened fifty years ago, unleashing vampires upon the unsuspecting world. These were those of whom people spoke in hushed tones, when they told of the first vampire awakened going on to wake the ancient ones. He'd moved stones that had stood in front of cave openings from time immemorial. He'd opened crypts. He'd torn burial mounds asunder.

And out of them the ancient dead had poured—so long parted from humanity and feeling, so long kept underground and sharing nothing but their communal mind—so old that their thoughts, their movements, even their appearance, bore little resemblance to humans. They'd swarmed out starving, ravening. Now these wraiths were used as shock troops in any land the vampires were trying to take. Just as now they were pouring into France.

Sensing them made Athos hate them more and feel a revulsion that was more than bone deep. He lay about with his sword, cutting a path through the abominable crowd toward his friends.

They tried to push him, to take him down. They bared their fangs and hissed at him, like things that had forgotten they were once human and had once had voice.

He reacted slower than they, but he could think. He could think for himself and without consulting the communal mind. This made him faster. Perhaps it made him more ruthless too, as his sword cut and sliced and sent pieces of the ancient evil to clatter onto the street. He wasn't even trying to kill them. Just get them out of the way till he could come close to Aramis and Porthos.

He felt a hand on his shoulder, and turned to see a skeletal head with bared fangs descend toward his neck. He didn't have time to react, before a sword, rather close, cut the head neatly at the neck. As it fell, the hand on Athos' shoulder lost force, and the jovial face of D'Embocage, above D'Embocage's lowering sword, grinned at him. "Go on, I'll guard your back."

Athos turned just in time to avert an attack from his other side. Back to back, he and D'Embocage made it to Aramis' and Porthos' side.

There was no time for more than a smile between them, but his comrades' expressions betrayed all the relief in the world, as Athos turned to stand beside them, and more and more musketeers poured in, till there was a line of them, facing the onslaught of vampires.

For a while it was heavy fighting, hand to hand, sword to sword, human facing vampire. There was nothing they could do but slice and cut and cut and slice, while the bells played madly over it all, and more and more musketeers and vampires poured onto the rue des Fossoyeurs.

Under the moonlight, judging from the tightly closed shutters, the silence from the human habitations, they might as well have been alone. No human would come out of the buildings—not unless it was a musketeer. But if Athos read things properly, behind every one of those doors, those windows, behind every shutter, peering through every knothole in every door, there was a human, watching this.

And it was important they should see it, that they should know humans weren't defeated yet, that they should be made aware vampires had not won France. Not yet.

"Athos."

It was almost a whisper, and the hand on his shoulder, this time well known—Aramis' long-fingered hand—the touch of a friend.

Athos had just dispatched the vampire facing him, and now he turned to see Aramis gesturing with a finger to his lips for him to keep silence, and then for him to follow.

Athos followed, and Porthos did also, leaving behind the long line of fighting musketeers, under the sound of the bells, in the moonlit street.

Rounding the corner, Aramis said, "Should we get D'Artagnan from the tower?"

"It was D'Artagnan who rang the bells?" Athos asked. "What? All this time?" Athos said. "The boy must be tired."

Aramis looked confused. "It is just . . ." he said. "If we do take him with us to do what we must do, we'll have to explain . . ."

"Hardly," Porthos said. "What need is there? Only tell him we're performing one of our duties."

"But—" Aramis said.

"I think Porthos has the right of it," Athos said. He looked toward the tower and frowned. The question was *how* to go get the boy. Bells disturbed vampires, but what if the vampires were just out of reach of the sound? What if they were waiting to jump the boy? To send Porthos or Aramis in there, would surely risk their being attacked. While for Athos to go in ... The sound of church bells was known to adversely affect or even kill vampires, but Athos seemed unaffected. Even if the sound began to hinder him, the worst outcome would be death. And if he died ... if he died it meant his struggle would be over and he wouldn't have to fear becoming a monster.

"I will retrieve him," he said, as he went into the tower.

Two vampires were dead, collapsed across the threshold, their hearts pierced, the dark blood that poured from them filled the air with what Athos, logically, knew should be a repulsive smell. But to his own vampire senses, it smelled enticing. It called out to him, like sweets to a hungry child.

He felt his mouth water, and gagged at the thought of what was making him salivate. Mind and body locked in dispute, he turned left past the chapel door, and headed for the spiral stairs that led to the tower.

On the stairs two more vampires lay dead. One of them beheaded, the other merely run through.

Up again to the tower, from which the roof had been removed, but not the bell, perhaps because it was very heavy or perhaps so heavily blessed none of the vampires could find their way this close to the bell and even the Judas goats felt uncomfortable.

Athos felt the bell—it was like a silvery presence, its song insistent in his mind. But if it neither hurt him nor impaired him, as it must have done to the two vampires at the top of the stairs: their heads had literally exploded, brain and blood coating everything, including D'Artagnan, as the boy now hung from the bell rope, making it toll with his weight, and now jumping, only to pull down fully again.

"Enough, my friend," Athos said, softly, smelling the dead vampires, and trying not to think of their blood as food. He'd never heard of a vampire feeding on other vampires. He didn't know if it were even possible. And if it were, he wanted no part of it. "Enough. There are enough musketeers."

The boy let go of the bell rope, and turned to Athos, his face aglow, covered in perspiration. "Did we ... are we winning?"

It was so sudden, so full of the hopefulness of youth, that Athos heard the cackle before he felt it leave his throat. "I believe so. And Porthos and Aramis and I have a . . . duty we must fulfill. Will you come with us?"

D'Artagnan nodded. Athos thought that—human or vampire—if he had spent what must be an hour tolling the bell, he'd be falling with tiredness. But the boy seemed indefatigable as he rushed after Athos down the stairs. "Did you hear the bells?" he asked. "Did you come to the bell tolling?"

"Yes," Athos said, looking over his shoulder, more to avoid thinking of the vampire he was stepping over than because he felt a need to see D'Artagnan's face.

"You don't . . ." D'Artagnan hesitated. "I mean . . . the vampires, when they got close enough and I was ringing the bell . . . You saw how it happened there on the tower."

Athos nodded. He stepped carefully over the last vampire. "It doesn't seem to have that effect on me. At least my head feels remarkably unaffected," he said. "No. I don't know why. It feels . . . odd, that close," he said. "Like . . . a silver light, a silver sound. But it's not . . . lethal or even unpleasant."

D'Artagnan gave him a searching look, as if to determine if he'd offended him, and Athos thought it best to calm the youth's fears. "You fought well. Even if you fought with bells. But now you must help us in a most secret endeavor . . . It's a duty we perform for Her Majesty, the Queen." As he spoke, he was escorting D'Artagnan behind the line of fighting musketeers and around the corner to where Porthos and Aramis waited.

"The queen!" D'Artagnan said.

Athos nodded.

"You told him?" Aramis asked, who was near enough to have heard that ecstatic exclamation.

"No," Athos said. "No more than . . . I don't think it's necessary that he know all." Seeing the look of betrayal in D'Artagnan's face, he added, "It's not that we don't trust you, D'Artagnan, but knowing this secret could cost you your very life."

"Like knowing what you are and not having denounced you?" D'Artagnan asked.

There was just a hint of defiance in the Gascon's face, and in the upward tilt of his eyebrow. Athos wondered—not for the first time—if he were a Judas goat. A Judas goat would act convincingly like that, and he would be, of course, utterly corrupt.

But D'Artagnan had a certain naïve impetuosity that Athos thought could not be feigned, or not this well. He sighed. "We are here to escort one of the guardians of the queen. It is one of the duties the three of us have taken onto ourselves."

"Athos!" Aramis said, dismayed.

"Hush, my friend," Athos said. "D'Artagnan has fought by our sides and he already knows a secret that could get us all killed. Himself, too. There is no reason that he shouldn't know another."

"It is not just our lives we're putting in danger," Aramis said.

"No, but if we are captured, then everything else will come out and you know it, Aramis. You know it better than I."

"But—"

"There are special guardians to Her Majesty," Athos said. "People who have . . . who by their mode of life have the ability to keep Her Majesty safe. And we escort them and keep them safe too, when they need it. Your landlord's wife is one of these. Her name is Madame Bonacieux and she lives on the floor beneath the one you rent. Customarily we meet her at the front door, but I believe tonight, we'd best go to the back entrance."

"Oh," D'Artagnan said. His forehead furrowed. "Women? A woman is a guard for Her Majesty?"

"One of the best," Aramis said—and from the tone of his saying it, it cost him something.

D'Artagnan looked daunted, but merely nodded. "If she guards Her Majesty and keeps her safe from vampires, then it will be an honor to help you escort her."

"Good," Aramis said, drily. "She should have been on her way to the palace an hour ago. She will be impatient and she has a temper. Come."

And he led them, quietly, to the back gate to the house where D'Artagnan lived.

There, in the shadows, a blond woman stood. Blond she was, like Charlotte, but there the resemblance stopped. Where Charlotte was tall and pale blond and looked like a heartbreakingly beautiful statue, Constance Bonacieux, probably many years younger—even if Charlotte's age had frozen at the time of her mortal death—was dark blond, plump, with a heart-shaped face and laughing blue eyes.

"Madame Bonacieux," Aramis said, advancing and bowing. Athos drew himself into the shadows, hoping she didn't see him or that if she saw him, she wouldn't discern what he'd become.

He noted with interest that the rose she wore at the closing of her cloak, the sacred symbol of her particular beliefs, didn't look any more shining or confusing to him than did the cross.

And then she looked through the darkness, straight at him, and asked, in an altered voice, "What is *that* doing here?"

The Rose in the Thorn

"Madame," Athos said, the word coming out through suddenly rigid lips. He bowed politely, removing his hat as he did. "*That* has escorted your guardians to you. And if it's not needed anymore, it will now take itself off."

Even as he heard in his voice the forbidding chill of offense, Athos felt baffled at the sting of the one word. His pride rose within him, reproving this woman, a commoner, lowborn, for speaking of him as though he were less than human.

Yet at the same time, he understood. He *was* less than human. How many times had the inseparables referred to vampires as *it*? Vampires were not, after all, truly human. Theologically, mentally, emotionally.

The bewildered gaze of Madame Bonacieux' blue eyes expressed all that. "But—" she said and then, as though confused by his stare on her, "But surely . . ."

"Surely I was turned and surely I am less than human," Athos said, his umbrage and his understanding, his confusion, his shame and anger catching in his throat and making his voice strangled. "But while I can, I'll do what good I can, which I did, by bringing your rescuers to you. And now I shall take my leave."

"Oh, Athos, stay," Porthos said. With the sudden, explosive frankness of the very shy, Porthos could voice things other people would not. Athos knew him well enough to understand how uncomfortable Porthos felt in company, and how his blurted pronouncements often originated in his discomfort, not stupidity as many assumed. Now his words expressed the annoyance that shone in eyes.

Before he could say more, Athos spoke. "No, Porthos, she is right. I've been telling you the same myself, since that first night when you found me crawling home, after being unwillingly turned. You should have killed me then. I *am* dangerous." Finding he agreed with the words as they left his mouth didn't placate his fury, at himself, at her, or at the world in general for playing this joke on him.

"Oh, God's Teeth, man, will you let it rest?" Porthos said. "You are not—"

Athos would never know what he was not, because they were interrupted by the sound of running feet. Since the running feet belonged to Grimaud—who was past the age where he should be madly running alone at night through the vampire-infested streets of Paris—his exertions tired him. He stopped, hands on knees, breathing heavily. Athos forgot all else.

Grimaud spoke through sudden gulps of panting breath, "Monsieur. Monsieur. You must come, or both shall die."

Athos felt his hand falling to his hip, grabbing at the hilt of his sword. "Both?" he said.

"Bazin and Mousqueton."

"Bazin!" Aramis said. His body became taut.

"Mousqueton!" Porthos said and stepped toward Grimaud.

"How will they die?"

"There is a church full of vampires, m'sieur, and they are . . . they're holding a blood mass."

In Athos' mind he was lying on an altar and Charlotte . . . He swallowed hard. "What are they doing? Bazin and Mousqueton?"

"Trying to rescue a family. There's a mother and father and a young man. Little more than a boy." Grimaud looked up at him, the lines on his face seemingly more marked than they'd been just this morning. "Monsieur . . ."

"I'll come," Athos said, at once.

"And I also," Porthos said.

"Porthos, you must stay and guard—" Aramis said.

Porthos shook his head. "Take D'Artagnan. He fights like the Devil himself."

Aramis opened his mouth, looked at the Gascon.

D'Artagnan's face was a study in confusion. He looked to Porthos, then to Aramis, and at last he bowed as if to say that he was willing to do what he must.

Aramis quickly contemplated the young man, then looking back at Athos and Porthos saw the calculations behind Aramis' shrewd eyes. Aramis inclined his head slightly. "You're more likely to need experience in fighting vampires than I, and in fighting vampires under such circumstances that— Go!"

Athos nodded to Grimaud. "Show us where they are."

They ran with Grimaud, along darkened streets, and into an alley. Moving shadows along the side of the alley were either vampire or human. Athos did not stop to investigate.

As he ran, Athos wondered if Aramis believed Porthos was choosing to go with Athos out of pique. But Porthos wasn't. Porthos, loyal Porthos, could not bear the thought of Athos going alone to face the vampires. It would never occur to Porthos that Athos might be at greater risk of joining with the vampires than of being killed.

It occurred to Athos. Judging from what the smell of blood— vampire blood—did to his mind in the ruined chapel, he imagined how much harder it would be to face a feeding frenzy while remaining human.

But he could not refuse to go to the rescue. Not when his own servant, his friends' servants, were risking their lives for strangers. By staying behind, he would be killing the victims as much as if he joined in. And the Comte de la Fère could not do this.

They turned from the alley into another again, and suddenly they were in a relatively open plaza. In the center of it stood . . . Les Penitents. What remained of the church of Les Penitents.

Athos' knees buckled, mid-run, and he stopped. He recognized the stone spires, the shattered stained glass windows, the oak doors hanging askew from their hinges atop the stained marble stairs.

Les Penitents. Once a fine, large building, maybe three hundred years old, with two towers and a soaring nave, now utterly in ruins. The church of the repentant sinner. For just a moment, Athos wondered if Charlotte had a sense of humor, and must have smiled, because Grimaud looked worried.

Athos met his servant's gaze. "I am well, Grimaud. Where are Mousqueton and Bazin?"

"I convinced them to not charge in immediately," Grimaud said. "It was not easy. They await around the corner, monsieur." He pointed left, into another narrow street, where a ruined portico had once been a place for stabling beasts, judging from the abandoned piles of rotting hay and the remains of a trough.

As they approached, Bazin's short, rotund figure—made lighter by the years of scarce food, but still rounder than anyone else he knew—and Mousqueton's imposing one came out of the shadows. "Monsieur," Bazin said, and bowed slightly to Athos. "You came." Was there perhaps a hint of surprise in those words?

Mousqueton smiled at Porthos and said, "I knew you'd come."

Athos nodded. "How came you to find what was happening inside?" he asked.

"Mousqueton found it. He was looking for reinforcements. For places where musketeers might be."

"And he looked in a church?" Athos asked, puzzled. Ten years ago, even, when the churches were still holy, still subordinate to the authority of Rome, to have found a musketeer in a church one needed to have very good luck. Taverns and bawdy houses were by far more likely. Now, with the churches in the power of the cardinal . . . Well, the only musketeers found in churches had been captured and had become vampires.

Mousqueton—a darker and rougher version of his master, a peasant who had reason to fight against vampires and had chosen to be a musketeer's servant when he could no longer be a monk—shook his head. "No, Monsieur Athos. I didn't look there, till I heard from the nave, through the open window, very faintly, the call of '*A moi*, musketeers.' And then I looked." He shook his head. "There was a corpse, and there was a woman, being tied to the altar. It was plain they'd removed the last victim from the same place. There was a young boy tied up against the wall. And there were half a half dozen vampires."

"And you thought you'd take them on alone?" Athos asked.

A shadow crossed Mousqueton's gaze and he nodded once. "If Grimaud couldn't have brought you, messieurs, we would have. Because it's more than flesh and blood can stand, to be here and know they are in there, doing that to . . . one of us. A . . . person."

More than flesh and blood could stand. Athos didn't question either that or the shadow in Mousqueton's eyes. There was no use

SWORD & BLOOD

asking the stories of those who chose to fight vampires. The details varied, but they were all the same. Evil worked from a limited text.

"Very well," he said.

"Come with us," Grimaud said. "There is a place from which you can see what is happening inside, if you wish to plan an attack."

"I think," Porthos said, "we should attack as quickly as possible—"

"Oh, undoubtedly," Athos said, keeping his voice firm by an effort of will, because there was something tugging at him—something he could neither identify nor name—a feeling, a wish, a push. Something like a tether being pulled taut in the direction of the church, and he didn't know why or how. His stomach had turned into a cold knot of fear, and he'd rather do anything at all than enter the church, but he'd be damned if he let his comrades see his terror. "But a plan, dear Porthos, will be quicker in the long run."

"This way, then, monsieur," Grimaud said.

"And be silent as the grave," Bazin added.

Athos followed, and Porthos behind him, their servants bringing up the rear. Anyone who saw Porthos would think he was a clumsy oaf, a brute who would topple buildings, or perhaps wreck everything he touched. But of them all he was the stealthiest, and the most graceful of swordsmen. He'd once told Athos that in his youth, before he'd married and returned to his native land, he'd been a fencing master in Paris—his technique proved it still, his light footwork, his dazzling swordplay. They were all good fencers, but only Porthos made it look easy.

He noted that the servants were carrying, in addition to long knives, sharpened stakes. He also noted two huddled corpses they passed exuded the smell of dead vampire. Which meant the men must have killed guardian vampires and did not think it worth mentioning.

The smell of vampire blood called to Athos' thirst, mingling burning need with nausea at knowing what it was that he craved.

Further on, where a statue of a saint leaned, headless, against the stone wall of the church, there was what had been, at one time, a fine stained glass window. Now a few bits of glass hung from a lead frame, but mostly it was open space through which shone a line of candles and the escaped sounds of . . .

95

Athos couldn't identify the sounds. It was a low humming, as would come from many throats, but tuneless and barren of melody as the song of insects. It sounded more like scraping than singing.

He didn't remember hearing anything like it, when he'd been turned, but then he remembered very little but the feel of Charlotte's teeth on his neck. He bit his tongue, to keep himself calm.

In the church, it was as their servants had described, but now there were corpses beside the altar: middle-aged, respectable burghers, in dark clothing. A man and a woman. It was not possible to tell whether the stripling tied to the pale marble altar was their son. From this distance any facial resemblance could not be discerned.

All he could tell for sure was that the boy was restrained in the same position Athos had been, his head was bent back in that painful-ecstatic stretch Athos remembered too well, while a burly male vampire drank at his neck. Athos felt a sudden overwhelming desire for blood in his mouth, for the flavor of life running down his throat. His whole body tensed with desire, aching with need. Never had he felt this desperate longing for food.

"They've been taking turns," Mousqueton said, in an almost inaudible whisper, surely lost in the humming that came from four other vampires around the altar. "We should move fast."

Athos nodded. Four vampires. Something about the humming made his nerves jangle, as though a fingernail were being run across glass, and that glass were embedded in his skull. He suspected that whatever they were doing affected him. He suspected his turned body, his changed nervous system, was linked to blood masses. He was, after all, a vampire and therefore their kin. But his mind was yet his own, and his mind he wouldn't give them. He shook his head.

Looking around, he made quick calculations. There were only two fighters, himself and Porthos. Bazin had been a lay brother in some disbanded order. Aramis had probably taken him on as a servant to keep the man from being caught and turned within a week. He was pious and well-meaning, but that was the best that could be said for him. Mousqueton had learned whatever he'd learned from Porthos. Athos had met Porthos when he was already attended by Mousqueton and had never asked where the young man had come from. Grimaud had served Athos' father. All of that seemed irrelevant now. He knew Grimaud was handy with a knife, good with a club, and deadly with a stake. They were all good with a stake—the slain guardian vampires proved that. But how good against vampires energized by a blood mass?

Athos backed a few steps away from the window, breathing deeply, telling himself the miasma of the blood mass didn't feel like a delicious beckoning to his mind and body.

He motioned for the others to gather around. "The two transept doors are gone, and the way unblocked," he said. "That's the closest path to the altar. I suggest Porthos and I each take one, and fall upon the vampires before they have time to know we're there. You two," he pointed at Grimaud and Mousqueton, "follow us, and prevent our being attacked from behind. Are there any other sentinels?" He motioned with his head to the two dead vampires.

"We disposed of those," Mousqueton said. "Bazin and I, while we were waiting. We saw no others."

Athos nodded grimly, and became aware that Bazin was trying to catch his gaze. He looked at the man's doughy, placid face as the dark, perfectly arched eyebrows descended over his dark, pebble-like eyes. Bazin said, in an almost sullen tone, "I have some blessed salt, from . . . My master gave me some. I used it on the guards and I would use it, only . . . we don't know how you . . . "

Athos swallowed to repress a chuckle that he couldn't explain. "I understand," he said. "I don't know Bazin. The crosses do not affect me, and the bells did not cause my head to explode. But come in behind us, and keep the salt in reserve unless it's absolutely needed." He hoped, hoped with all his might, that it would not be needed.

They nodded at each other. Porthos was biting the corner of his moustache, which he did only when he was nervous. Athos took a deep breath. The humming continued, pulling his nerves taut and rubbing them raw. It increased the attraction of the blood. It tore into his defenses. He would have to strike very, very fast. Fast enough that it couldn't penetrate his mind and confuse him, while he was trying to kill the vampires and free the boy.

He walked as swiftly as he dared to the side entrance to the church, hearing Grimaud behind him, his footsteps against the boom of Athos' own heartbeat, the words he repeated to himself to keep his mind clear: kill the vampires, free the boy. He had not told Porthos how to signal he was in position. He had not—

Looking across the church, gritting his teeth till his jaws ached, he saw, through the other door, a glimmer of movement. Porthos had managed to catch the light of candles on one of his many false jewels and was sending a signal.

How to respond? Nothing on him would reflect the candlelight. His sword. He'd have to use his sword. He grasped it beneath the pommel, just above the sharpened part of the blade, caught the light, and sent it reflecting in Porthos' direction.

Fortunately, he thought—as he slid into the doorway, to see Porthos slide the opposite way into the church—the only vampire in a position to see the reflection was fangs-deep in the boy's neck and unlikely to notice anything but his own pleasure. The pleasure of drinking someone's life. That was a very bad thought, one that caused him to almost keen with desire.

He loped into the church and toward the altar, matching Porthos' movement.

The humming was like a scream in his head, a scream so loud that it deafened all thinking and stopped all reason: kill the vampires, free the boy. He could feel the pressure in his ears, in his skull.

Blindly, unable to see his surroundings as more than blurry shapes, he pushed his sword toward the darkened spot that his memory of the scene told him was the nearest vampire.

Through blind sweat and what felt like the burn of fire climbing up his sword arm to his heart, he felt the sword penetrate something. The scream of the dying vampire sounded and echoed close by. He hoped the echo came from Porthos' killing the other acolyte in the blood mass.

The humming stopped.

It felt like a sudden cold, refreshing wind in the pit of hell itself. Athos' vision cleared and he could see . . .

He could see the vampire who remained alive had his sword out and was dueling Porthos and showing quite a bit of science with it. And the one who had been feeding upon the boy . . .

Athos blinked. He was standing in front of Athos, grinning, displaying bloodstained fangs, his sword in his hand. "Hello, halfling," he said, in the tone of a vampire who knew his own strength—in the tone of a vampire who had just fed—and who would, therefore, be far more powerful than Athos.

The vampire swung his sword at Athos. To Athos, time and motion slowed. His heart thumped hard, his knees felt weak, and he wanted to move, but he didn't remember how. He couldn't remember how.

The vampire's blade, swung in a lazy half-arc, aimed at Athos' neck, clashed with something Athos couldn't see, and suddenly the spell was broken. Turning, he saw it had clashed with Grimaud's blade, and he gritted his teeth and leapt forward.

Grimaud couldn't take a full vampire, not with that pitiful knife against a sword.

"To me," he said. "To me, and leave my servant alone."

But the vampire laughed and where he had stood now stood Charlotte, wearing a white dress and smiling a tempting half-smile. "Raphael. Have you come to seek me?"

Hearts and Shields

D'Artagnan could feel the tension between Aramis and the beautiful woman they were guarding. He fell into step behind the pair, his ears alert to any sound or menace in the night. It was clear the two had known each other for quite a while and were . . . not enemies exactly, but rather in the habit of disagreeing with each other.

They eyed each other with challenge, if not with antagonism, Aramis directly, frowning down at the comely Madame Bonacieux, and she, from beneath lowered lashes, glancing at him sideways and up now and then.

"I can't believe," she said at last with the sound of something long held back, "that you would lend yourself to that sort of thing, monsieur."

"To what sort of thing?" he asked, his voice revealing all too clearly he knew what she was trying to refer to, but he wasn't willing to gratify her by responding.

"Well!" she said.

He looked at her and frowned slightly, but D'Artagnan would swear that the corners of his mouth twitched, if not quite in a smile, at least in amusement. They set off toward Pont Neuf, though they described a wide circle around the rue des Fossoyeurs, where D'Artagnan would guess the fight might very well still be going on.

She walked rapidly, her dainty hand clasping the fold of her cloak at the center showing small, plump fingers, like the hand of a child. D'Artagnan found himself glancing at it and feeling a wave of tenderness for the woman. The fingers clenched tight on the wool and she said, her tone again hinting she had long held the words back and couldn't be expected to do it any longer, "Well!" And then, after expelling his breath in a long, hissing sound, "I'd never have thought a man like you could compromise his principles so, Father."

Aramis still frowned but D'Artagnan could now easily tell that his eyes were alight with amusement. "It is sad debased times we live in, is it not, madame? In better, more morally certain times, the Holy Mother Church would happily have burned the likes of you, and I'd never have entertained any qualms as to the rightness of it." He sighed with a theatrical feeling. "So might we have done with all of our colleagues. The war against the Huguenots and heretics. Oh, how I miss it." His eyes sparkled with something quite like a challenge. "But in these doomed and dark times, we've learned to band together all the forces that work against the vampires. And as sure as I am that your faith is demented, or as convinced you may be mine is oppressive—both of them work against the darkness. Therefore we must continue working together."

She was looking at him, her mouth partly open, as though words had fled her and, in fleeing, left her unable to close her lips.

He grinned at her, a grin as false as his sigh had been. "But take heart, my dear Madame Bonacieux. As soon as the last vampire is conquered, we'll definitely be able to resume hostilities."

She closed her mouth with a snap and pearly white teeth came out to bite at her lower lip. For just a moment, D'Artagnan had the impression that she was suppressing laughter, but when she spoke her voice was not only dry, but didactic, the sort of voice a grown woman might use for a small child, "You speak a great deal of nonsense, D'Herblay."

"Do I?" he asked, in the supercilious way D'Artagnan thought Aramis used when he was trying to goad someone. "Do you wish to make a small wager that as soon as the last vampire dies, the hostilities will resume?" He now lowered his eyelashes coyly in what was clearly a challenge and a prod to her.

"I thought men of your persuasion did not make such wagers?"

"Oh, my dear, let us then make the proceeds be to charity," he said.

"And would the last vampire to die be your friend Athos?"

The last word fell into the night with an unnatural resounding clap. The silence following resembled that following a deafening boom of thunder. The two looked at each other and D'Artagnan, behind them, had the impression their countenances had changed from amusement to dead seriousness. But he only gave them part of his attention.

Something, not quite a sound—as if of wings, or perhaps sheets being shaken vigorously in a high wind—and not quite a feeling, was pricking at his conscience. They were approaching Pont Neuf, that vast unencumbered stretch over the Seine, and the hair at the back of D'Artagnan's neck rose. He felt as though a cold hand were running upward along his spine. And he couldn't say why—he couldn't even think.

It was just that, as some horses will shy away from an unsafe area, all of D'Artagnan's instincts told him to grab his friend and the woman they were protecting, and to pull them away and run away from the bridge, toward one of the areas with narrow streets and tall houses.

It made absolutely no sense, because, as he had learned today, the alleys were, even during the day, the province of vampires, while the bridge . . . Well, surely they'd see any enemy before he came near, would they not?

And yet, his hair prickled at the back of his neck, and his throat felt so dry it ached, and his breath tore through in little, panicked puffs.

"Listen," he said, only his voice came out constricted, and small.

"Athos, madame," Aramis said, his voice terrible enough and cold enough to feel like a sharp blade, "is not part of this discussion."

"Is he not, D'Herblay? Would you care to tell me why not? Would you let him that near me? Do you not know that they all know the same? That they all hear the same? That now all of them will know that I—"

"Madame. Athos is not part of the collective mind. Do not presume to judge a world that you—"

"Judge! How do you know? Because he told you? You believe a—"

"Listen," D'Artagnan said, managing to speak louder. "There is something wrong. I can't explain it. I can't tell you how I know, but there is something very wrong, something—"

They both looked at him. The woman frowned. "A sensitive?" she asked Aramis.

"Not . . . that I know of." He seemed at a disadvantage, having had his thought wrenched from its track. "What do you sense?"

She paused, looked ahead, frowned, then shrugged. "Nothing. Oh, I mean, trouble enough, in the city, but nothing directly in our path, nothing lying in wait for us. However, I believe I must tell you that things are not . . . That is, my husband could not help in certain necessary rites."

With that, the look of amusement returned to Aramis' eyes, even though the worry remained, creasing his features. "Madame, my most sincere regrets."

"Regrets will do nothing for me."

"Nor will I. Dispensation I might have, but not so far as helping in the rites of another religion!"

She pressed her lips together. "Never mind. For this my energy is enough. Have I not seen us safe along this route a hundred times, and detected ambush when there was one? There is nothing bad ahead."

Aramis frowned, at the bridge, at the river, then looked back at D'Artagnan. "How sure of it are you, my friend?" he asked, with a tone of great kindness.

D'Artagnan shook his head, trying to clear it, but it didn't help. His panic had eased once they'd stopped physically advancing toward the bridge, but it was not gone. "I don't know," he said. "My reason tells me that this makes no sense, and yet, all my feelings, my . . . instinct, warns me away from the bridge."

"Where does it tell you you'd be safe?"

"Anywhere," D'Artagnan said. "In a street, with houses on either side. Anywhere else."

Aramis looked at him a long while, so intently that D'Artagnan felt as though the musketeer were trying to peer into his soul, then sighed. "It could be vampire influence. They control some minds. We don't know how exactly, but it's related to the way in which they speak to each other. Some minds are more open to their influence. In fact, all of us gain defenses to their arts over time. And . . ." He shook his head. "I'm sure they are trying to influence you, to . . . attract you. Perhaps not you specifically, but all who will react to it."

He looked out at the moonlight shining on the open space of Pont Neuf, just a few feet away. It did not appear menacing, but open, incapable of hiding anything. It had been the first bridge in Paris built with no accommodation for houses on either side, but only a low parapet with sidewalks, and, in the middle, space enough for two carriages to pass comfortably. Before the vampires, it had been a famous promenade where everyone in town went to see and be seen.

It still retained its open quality and looking at it, D'Artagnan couldn't understand why it should scare him so. It was plain that Aramis didn't either. They were so close they could hear the whispers of the river, and see the moonlight shining on the water below.

"Come," Aramis said. "We're expected at the Palais Royale and must, perforce, cross the bridge. There was once a vampire called The Terror of Pont Neuf; Athos killed him. Besides, he only terrorized the neighborhood hereabouts, not the bridge itself." He gestured with his hand. "As you see, it is almost impossible for anyone to attack you unawares on the bridge."

D'Artagnan didn't like the idea that the creeping fear he felt was being put in his mind by vampires. He didn't like to think his thoughts—his most private self—might be open to manipulation of the creatures. But if it were, as Aramis said, a matter of growing inured to them and of improving your defenses to their wiles, perhaps he could not hope otherwise.

He inclined his head. "It is probably as you say," he said. "I am probably being called toward one of the alleys by one of the creatures."

He noted the woman was looking at him with a faint, sweet smile. "It takes a real man," she said, "to admit he might be flawed."

He felt hot blood suffuse his cheeks, but he smiled. And as the two resumed walking toward the bridge, he walked behind them, though it caused sweat to break out all over his body and every hair to stand on end.

It was all he could do, it took all his strength to step onto the bridge and to keep walking. Below, the Seine gurgled, and ahead of him, Aramis' and Madame Bonacieux' steps echoed side by side. He followed, by an effort of will, straining every nerve against the impulse to run away.

In the middle of the bridge, he stopped, unable to force himself to go any further. Like a horse that had been pulled so far, his body refused to go another step. It seemed to him he heard a sound, just barely, under the babble of the Seine. A rustle.

His companions stopped, noticing he wasn't following, and turned around to look at him, Madame Bonacieux with puzzled intensity; Aramis with intent enquiry.

"Dry leaves," D'Artagnan said, as his mouth found the answer before his brain could stop it. He saw a crease forming between Aramis' eyebrows and said, "That's the sound. Listen. There's a rustle of dry leaves."

Aramis' brows rose with a look of surprise, and he opened his lips. D'Artagnan didn't doubt Aramis was about to say that he heard it too, but he had no time to speak.

Swarming over the parapets of the bridge, uncountable in number, like ants out of a disturbed anthill, came vampire-wraiths. They were of the long-dead type, like those they had fought in the rue des Fossoyeurs.

D'Artagnan heard the clack of Aramis' heel hitting the pavement as the musketeer stepped backward, even as D'Artagnan took a step back himself, so that his back was to Aramis. As more vampires approached, shambling toward them in that walk that was not quite human, D'Artagnan did not doubt they would die here. This was death as sure as if they'd laid down their heads upon the executioner's block and seen the ax descend.

When facing odds of double or triple the number of one's comrades, it was possible to hope. When there was hope of getting succor from other musketeers, it might be possible to hold out a thought of prevailing. But here, in this bleak night, under the shining light of the moon, there was no hope of help, unless it came from heaven—a heaven that, for decades now, had left humans to their own wiles. And the prospect of death was almost freeing. If there were nothing else to be done, then he would die well.

He heard Aramis' sword hiss out of its sheath, like boiling water about to be poured on infection, and he pulled his own sword out. For a moment, battle-mad, watching his executioners approach, he forgot there were only three of them, and one an unarmed woman.

And then, as the vampires closed in, making an odd clicking sound as though they'd long been deprived of speech and must now click to communicate, Aramis leaned back and turned minimally, "I am lost, my friend, but if you would do me a last favor . . . I will help you as much as I can, only for the love of heaven take Madame Bonacieux out of this. If you can contrive to get her out of this unscathed, my blessing and my gratitude go with you."

"What, and run away?" D'Artagnan asked, shocked, as he cast a look at the lady who was standing with her back to D'Artagnan's left side and who held in her hand something, which looked—and smelled— like a handful of dried rose petals. "I am not so dishonorable."

Aramis laughed, a laughter that came out dry and almost sound- less, like the rattle of breath that preceded death. "For heaven's sake, D'Artagnan, do not believe it will be easy, nor that I ask you to do what I would not. If there is a chance, indeed, I'll join in the flight. But you must for the sake of your honor, your chivalry, and our faith, keep Madame Bonacieux safe. It is more important than my life or yours."

Madame Bonacieux cleared her throat, "Gentlemen, I am not a frail—"

But at that moment, their talk ceased because the vampires were upon them. Unholy hands, caked in what had to be grave dirt, reached for them, grabbing at shoulder and arm with vise force.

D'Artagnan heard Aramis' sword meet age-hardened flesh and old bone, and plied his sword in turn, careful only not to hit Aramis or the lady. It was hopeless, of course. The more he killed, the more of them were there, surging rank on rank: unstoppable, darkened flesh, rotted cloth and that smell of corruption that escaped when a vampire died.

Vampire heads rolled and bodies fell, twitching, and yet more vampires came.

There was a smell of roses, and D'Artagnan saw the lady was dipping into a sack at her waist and spreading what seemed to be no more than crumbled dried rose petals. The smell, though, was much stronger than dried petals would warrant. Its effect on the vampires was the same as that of the salt Aramis had given him. It didn't kill them, but it fell on them like sparks of fire, and made them stop and stumble around.

Aramis expected D'Artagnan to get the woman out of here. Suddenly, D'Artagnan's quick brain saw it. There was no possible way they could attain either end of the bridge, but they could reach the nearest parapet no more than twenty steps away. They could, that was, if the woman would only strew her rose petals before them.

He dared not ask if she could swim, because that would tell the vampires what they were about to do. He didn't know how much will or intelligence remained in these desiccated creatures, but neither did he wish to find out.

He reached for the woman with his left hand, even as the sword in his right made short work of vampires in front and to the right of him, "Lady, strew your petals as we go," he said.

"Go where?" she asked, and for a moment, the tenseness of the supple muscles on her arm under his hand, gave him the impression that she meant to shake his grasp off.

"Out of here," he said.

"If you think—" she said.

"I think that you were introduced to me as a brave and capable woman," he said, casting his voice just loud enough for her to hear. "A brave and capable woman would not wish to die in vain."

She said nothing, though D'Artagnan could swear that Aramis' back, pressed to his own, shook once, convulsively, in what might be laughter or a cough. He did not know which, nor did he stop to discover. Instead, he started cutting his way forward, toward the parapet, while holding to her arm. He breathed a sigh of relief, as she seemed to know what was wanted, and began to strew the petals forward, as well as to the side, addling those vampires directly in his path.

Just as well, too, that Aramis seemed to have perceived the gist of D'Artagnan's plan, because he kept right behind them, his back to D'Artagnan's. There was a good chance, D'Artagnan thought, that they could all three get out of here and alive. Or not a good chance, perhaps, but a chance, which in this moment was all he could care about. He fought his way forward, stepping on vampire bones and skulls, which felt as brittle as spun-sugar confections under his boots, but whose crushing poured forth the stench of a thousand open graves.

Suddenly vampires ceased to be in front of him, and the parapet appeared. A vampire stepped up onto the parapet, only to be cut down. The way was clear. Possibly only for a moment. D'Artagnan grabbed at Madame Bonacieux' arm, made a final sweep with his sword, sheathed it. He could not swim while holding onto a woman with one hand and a sword with the other. He shouted, "Jump!"

Vampires reached for his legs, held onto his ankles. He suspected the like were holding onto hers. He flung himself and her forward with force. They cleared the parapet and fell into the open space with water beneath.

D'Artagnan didn't know the Seine, nor its depth, and though he knew that ships sailed on it, he also knew some places were shallower than the others. He had heard there were league masters devoted wholly to the navigation of the river, and he could only breathe a prayer under his breath that they would fall into deep enough water not to break their necks.

He hit the river with his feet, and went down, down, down as water closed over him, dark and cold. In the panic of falling—instinct against decision—he'd somehow let go of Madame Bonacieux. What if she could not swim?

He rose to the surface, and broke the water with a cry, half-ready to fight any vampires that might surround him. He was almost shocked to see none in the water, then relieved to see Madame Bonacieux' head break the water only a few hand spans away, and to hear her gasp for breath, as she tread water very capably.

"Aramis?" he asked her.

She had lost her cap and her blond hair had come loose, obscuring most of her face in a honey-brown mess, but she flinched at his question, and looked toward the bridge.

He looked too, and comprehended exactly the problem they faced. They had never had a prayer. There were vampires all over the underside of the bridge, and the pillars leading to it, holding on to the underside and the vertical surfaces with the gravity-defying, repulsive stubbornness of insects. The bridge itself boiled with them—hundreds, perhaps thousands.

Aramis was not visible at all.

Honeyed Death

Perhaps it was the sound of his baptismal name that made Athos stop and drop the sword from nerveless hands. Perhaps it was Charlotte's voice.

What remained of his reason, beating madly against the inside of his mind like a captive bird, told him this was folly, and the worst kind of folly at that. That the person standing before him was not Charlotte, but a burly, male vampire who had just been sating his unnatural lusts in the blood of the young man tied to the altar—who might be dead or alive. And if alive, needed help.

But the evidence of his eyes told him Charlotte was there—his Charlotte—the only woman to whom he had ever given his heart and, if marriage to a vampire were possible, who remained his wife. He opened his mouth to ask her how she had come here, but she smiled before he could speak.

"No," she said, sadly. "You did not come to seek me, did you? You came to rescue this foolish boy. It is so like you, Raphael."

Her hand, almost ethereally soft, touched his face, which felt, suddenly, as though it had turned to granite. He seemed incapable of moving it, and it felt as cold as stone. "It is so like you to behave in this impracticably chivalrous way and to come to free a boy you don't even know." She smiled at him. "I knew you would come."

Her fingers caressed his neck, flitted butterfly-like down his throat, over his Adam's apple, and lingered, in heated caress on the bite mark she had given him. There it held, and she said, "But you're not one of them, Raphael. Not anymore. You're one of mine. You're of my kind. Don't you see? Now we can be together and be joined once more."

109

He could barely breathe with the touch of her fingers on him. It raised a pleasure in him out of all proportion with that simple gesture. His breath labored in desperate gasps, as if each one had to be earned and as if at any moment his ability to breathe might cease. He wanted to hold her in his arms. He wanted to kiss her. Her lips called to him like the source of all delight.

Touching her was the price of continuing to draw breath. He stumbled forward, blindly, his hands extended.

She stepped back, smiling. "Ah, no, Raphael. Not like that. What kind of woman would I be if I let you have your way with me when you neither love me nor respect me?"

"Love . . . ?" Athos said, not sure he understood the word, not sure what it could mean in these circumstances. Did he love her? Did he respect her? He did not know. He craved her and he hated his subjugation to her and the utter lack of control he felt when she was near. And he wanted, he wanted more than anything—more than he'd ever wanted honor, or power, or even love—to hold her in his arms.

"Let me into your mind," she said, her voice dripping sweetness and yet as sharp as a blade glimmering in the light of the moon. "And we'll be one again. We'll be one forever."

It seemed easy. Athos could feel, within himself, the lock—the restraints—which held his individual thoughts inviolate, and which held the core of himself free of her. Free of vampires. Which kept him from being a vampire like the others—a creature that shared all thought and sensation with the vast multitude of the damned.

He could feel how easy it would be—to open that door, to unlock it. His will pushed on it and it gave . . . It was like a hand reaching to open a gate.

And then he stopped. The thought of his friends rose from his baffled mind. His friends who had fought to keep him from being a vampire like the others. Who trusted him not to be a vampire like the others. The image of Grimaud, with a stake in his hand, creeping along the corridors of his house in the rue Férou in the dark of night wounded him with a sharp stab.

Let them never be deceived in him, and let Grimaud never need that stake. Athos stopped. His body felt cold and rigid all over, granite never to be animated by human touch. Through lips like ice, and about as mobile, he said, "No. Pray God, I never—"

On those words, Charlotte vanished like a soap bubble in the warm air, and something similar to stinging rain bit at Athos' hands and face. Athos was left on the steps of the altar, trembling. The burly vampire lay dead across the steps, his black blood pouring onto the marble. His blood smelled to Athos like the finest brandy, yet Athos had the presence of mind to do no more than lick his lips, and look around dazed.

He didn't know how long his dream of Charlotte lasted. That Porthos had just killed the male vampire was obvious, as Athos' friend was wiping his blade on the vampire's silken doublet and looked up. Bazin was glaring and there were white grains all over Athos' clothes and hands. Blessed salt.

"Who was she?" he asked Athos.

"She?" Athos said. He was covered in sweat, which made his clothes cling damply to him. He ran the back of his hand over his brow, to prevent the sweat from falling into his eyes.

"She, man, the blond angel-like vampire, who appeared, yet was not wholly here. I'd heard they could do that, provided they were within five hundred yards or so, and there was a Judas goat of their making or a vampire they turned, on the premises. But I confess I'd never seen it."

"She . . . she was . . ." Athos' mind and body were moving so slowly he could not find words at all and, for once, Porthos was the nimble-tongued one.

"It's no use telling me you don't know her," Porthos said, as he moved to the side of the altar and felt the boy's neck for a pulse, then nodded and, taking out his sword, started cutting at the ropes holding him. The servants had surrounded them, even Bazin, who crossed himself looking at the boy, but—on a frown from Porthos—stepped forward to help free him.

Porthos looked at Athos, even as he worked. "I've never seen a woman have that effect on you, and I doubt that an unknown vampire could. There are few female ones, I grant you, but you've killed them with as little thought as you killed the males."

Athos drew in breath in three stages, three slow aspirations, each of them seeming to be all he could get. He had to fight for the next.

Win it. He expelled the hard-gained air in one long sigh and shook himself, feeling as if he'd just woken.

He shook his head at Porthos. It was a characteristic of Monsieur Porthos—loyal to a fault; huge, graceful fencer and shy to the point of rarely speaking or at least rarely making sense save in the company of those he knew very well—that when he once fastened to a puzzle, he would continue asking about it until he got an answer.

And what secrets did Athos have left? Wasn't it better if Porthos knew what had caused his friend to act so oddly? The vampires had more of a hold over Athos than he would have thought. Athos had never imagined that Charlotte—or her presence—could appear to him in public, or so paralyze him. Much less had he thought that others would be capable of seeing her.

"My wife," Athos said, speaking with apparent disinterest, but knowing he would not fool anyone who'd seen his meeting with her.

He wondered why she'd married him—raw, innocent provincial that he'd been. Likely he'd never know. He wondered also, how she'd contrived to be in sunlight during their life together. And she'd eaten, he was sure of it, not just pretended. She had eaten very little, but she had eaten.

Had she lied to him about being a vampire then? Had she not truly been such then? But she'd survived hanging! And he remembered how often he'd caught her retching after eating. He'd thought . . .

His head spinning, he retrieved his sword and sheathed it, and stepped forward to help them with the boy, who was just waking. To Athos' relief—a relief so profound that he didn't even mind risking the temptation of touching mortal flesh, warm and alluring though it was—the boy felt warm to the touch and not at all as one who had been turned. They must have stopped the vampires before they could drain him.

"Your wife!" Porthos said. "I didn't know you were married."

"It was a long time ago," he said. "Before . . . before you met me."

He could barely stand the look of mingled curiosity and pity that Porthos directed at him, and for a moment he was afraid that Porthos would assume that, like his own family, in his own distant domain, Athos' wife had been turned against her will and after their marriage. It didn't bear thinking, and it was no part of his intention to fool his friend. But neither did he wish to gratify his curiosity and that of the servants, as well as that of this anonymous boy.

But Porthos asked no more, because at that moment the boy's eyes fluttered open, and he looked uncomprehending around himself before saying, in the voice of one who recollects long-ago events, "Musketeers. Oh."

"Yes, musketeers," Porthos said, speaking in that paternal tone that Athos had heard him use when dealing with the very young, with women who did not excite his interest, and with the sick. "Do not worry, young man, the king's musketeers are here, now."

"But . . ." The boy blinked, first at Porthos and then at Athos. "Mother. And Father."

Athos looked to the side, where the corpses lay, but said nothing, and Porthos clucked his tongue on the roof of his mouth. "It can't be helped," he said, bracingly. "It can't be helped, and who of us these sad days haven't suffered like losses. Who are you, boy?"

"Renard Planchet," he said quickly, turning brown, trusting eyes toward Porthos and determinedly avoiding looking at the corpses. "My father . . ." Now he looked, but then away again, quickly. "My family owned a pastry shop in the rue des Mystères," he said. "They . . . they broke down the door and took us. Father said they'd used Judas goats to get past the cross." He crossed himself, fervently. "No one . . . no one is safe now."

Porthos inclined his head. "Perhaps not. Or perhaps they had a vendetta against you and your family. At any rate, we must leave here, and quickly, because more are bound to come. What with the deaths of their kind and your charming visitor, Athos."

Athos nodded. He did not doubt that even at this moment vampires were swarming toward them. On the contrary. If anything, he expected them to already be surrounding the church, making the musketeers' escape impossible.

He didn't say anything. No reason to increase the anxiety of his companions. No good could come of that, anyway. Instead, he asked the boy, "Can you walk?" as he reached for his arm and supported him.

The boy swallowed and nodded. The swallow had the feel of an attempt to overcome nausea, which might be brought on by his being nearly drained, or it might be brought on by the smell of vampire blood, which Athos must remind himself, did not smell as enticing to humans as to himself.

Porthos and Athos, each at one elbow, brought Planchet to his feet, only to find their servants at their elbows, moving as if of common accord, or as though they'd made a plan.

"Monsieur," Grimaud said, as Mousqueton echoed, "Monsieur Porthos?"

"What?" Porthos asked, impatiently, helping the young man forward, along the rubble-strewn nave.

"Bazin?" Porthos asked.

"He went ahead, monsieur," Mousqueton replied.

"It is as well, perhaps," Grimaud said, "if Messieurs Athos and Porthos allow Mousqueton and I to help this young man, so that the two people who can use a sword and use it well might defend us from any coming ambush."

Athos would have sworn there was a tone of amusement in Grimaud's voice, except that he knew his servant too well to suppose he could be amused in these dire circumstances.

He stepped out of the way, hastily, letting Grimaud take the boy's elbow, while Mousqueton took the other. Athos, beside Porthos, stepped through one of the doors on the transept, and outside.

He expected to meet with a group of vampires—perhaps guards of the cardinal—all armed to the teeth and ready to fight. But instead, he met with blue night, and the distant sounds of the city—a night city, infested by vampires that crawled like unclean insects along its deserted lanes, its ruined churches.

"Where can they be?" he asked, feeling almost more alarmed by the lack of vampires than he would have been by finding himself amid an ambush.

"Never mind," Porthos said. "Let's be glad they're not here."

The two of them leading, they set off upon a relatively safe route, away from the ruined church. There were places vampires did not tend to go, and those areas heavily patrolled by musketeers were some of them. They passed several patrols in fact, and were hailed, and hailed back, all without anyone asking them what they were doing. That was patent to all. They were rescuing a young man, as musketeers did.

It wasn't till they were in front of Monsieur de Tréville's home that they stopped and there, amid musketeers, in as safe a place as could be found in all of Paris, Porthos asked the boy. "Where do you live?"

"I can't!" The boy said.

"Oh, come, rue des Mystères, you said?"

But the boy shook his head. "I can't go back to my parents' home. I can't go back to the shop." He trembled all over. "I can't."

"Let's take him," Grimaud said, wearily, "to Monsieur Athos' lodging, until we decide where he might go."

Athos was about to protest that bringing a young man to his house was the most foolish of decisions. He wasn't sure he was even safe to Grimaud, who had served him for so many years, and who was as wily a vampire fighter as anyone outside the musketeers. But the rue Férou was the closest of all their lodgings and there they could seek safety for a few moments at least. He nodded grimly and led the way.

It was uneventful. Too uneventful, Athos thought, as hair prickled at the back of his neck. His mind was trying to assemble the pieces of the evening, and not at all liking the picture that formed. Charlotte had said she was waiting for him, that she was sure he'd come to the rescue of the boy. Charlotte had known he was coming. He was sure of it. He didn't understand her ability to appear there. He'd half wanted to believe that her presence in his bed was but a dream. But Porthos had also seen her in the church. What new power was this? Vampires needed no more powers. They'd been winning the battle over humans too easily.

Recalling the touch of Charlotte's hand he shivered. He would swear she had been there, present in body as well as in spirit, and if so, what did this mean? Would she come again?

Was his house safe? He wondered as Grimaud swung the door open and stepped cautiously within. What if they were ambushing him in his own house?

He had a feeling he was being played with, as a cat with a mouse, and if he were, then their recent victory was for nothing. It was all for nothing.

"It is safe," Grimaud said, coming back.

Into the house they went, up the steps. Someone—Athos thought Bazin—locked the door tightly behind them. And then across the house, to the kitchen at the back, where Grimaud and Mousqueton helped Planchet onto a stool. Grimaud then examined the bite mark on the boy's neck.

"It will need to be treated," he said, reporting to Athos as he had so many times, when they'd rescued some unfortunate victim of vampires. "At least cleaned and bandaged," he said. "But I don't think they came close to turning him, m'sieur. Not even close. His temperature is good, his heart is beating strong, and as you know, they both drop and the heart stops for hours, upon turning, before starting again."

Athos nodded. He could be presumed to know, but in fact, he knew nothing at all. He remembered nothing of his own turning, save falling into bed and in what felt like a death-sleep. And he'd never before been around anyone through their turning.

He wondered if Grimaud had monitored him through the night after his turning, expecting, awaiting—what? What kind of fool sat by and waited for a vampire to wake, starving as they always did after death?

A devoted fool. A fool who expected, as Aramis had put it, that Athos was not like the majority of people—all the people who were not Athos. A fool who had been as much Athos' father as Monsieur le Comte Henri de la Fère—in nurture if not in nature.

To hide his confusion and his emotion—his unworthiness, considering how he let Charlotte affect him, and how vulnerable he was to her—he stepped to the fireplace and filled a cup of broth by dipping it into the warm pot.

He was conscious of Grimaud's glance on his back, and he turned around braced for Grimaud's stern glare and his slight shake of the head at Athos neglecting to use a ladle.

At that moment, someone knocked at the door. Not civilly, as friends did, or even as acquaintances did when visiting, but in a desperate pounding beat.

Just as the guards of the cardinal might do, if they'd surrounded the house and were ready to take one on charges they thought would stand before the king. Such as the charge of being a secret—undeclared—vampire, or indictments of being of Judas goats who abetted him.

Living Water

Aramis was lost. D'Artagnan had no time to absorb it, as he looked at their situation. If D'Artagnan and Madame Bonacieux swam anywhere close to the bridge they'd be caught. And he could see vampires on the banks, vampires tracking them. Pointing them out.

"Madame," he said, wondering how long he could bear the chill of the water that seemed to leech life from his bones. "How well do you swim?"

She was doing something while treading water, something that—until he saw a garment floating down on the current—he could not identify. He then comprehended she was disrobing, and his eyes must have shown his dismay clearly enough to be seen by the light of the moon and at this distance.

"I swim well enough," she said through little puffs of breath, "when I don't wear three layers of petticoats, and one of them starched."

"We cannot make it to the banks here," he said. "There will be vampires."

"Of course," she said. "They dare not the water, which kills them. Running water. Living water they call it. They can cross it in boats or on bridges, but they cannot swim."

"Does it now?" D'Artagnan said, filing it away, should it be needed in the future. "I thought we could let the current aid us, and go down the stream a while, then get out where we may, up there, and there—"

"No," she said, giving a little shake of the head as she spoke. "Follow me."

"Where?" he asked, frowning. "Down the river—?"

"We'd never survive the water long enough to get sufficiently far away from the vampires. Besides, we'd be going out of the city, and toward the countryside, which is not safe. There are fewer people and more vampires. Follow me."

There was little for D'Artagnan to do—accustomed though he was to being the one to make plans and to decide things for himself—but to follow this woman as she set forth in furious strokes against the current. At least, he thought, the effort kept them warm, though it would undoubtedly tire them much too fast. He swam as swiftly as he could, irritated that he could not swim as well as she did.

His childhood in Gascony had provided the usual sorts of exercise that a boy sought—from running wild to swimming in the rivers—but not for the last three years. For the last three years, rumors of vampires abroad even in plain day, hiding in thickets or peering from the shadow of chasms, and of Judas goats who would kidnap one for a vamp's meal, had kept even D'Artagnan within sight of his father's house where there was nowhere to go swimming.

He resented being out of practice, and he was sure this imperious woman would think ill of him. In the impetuous way of adolescence, he forgot the danger they were in, or even the chance that she was leading him to an unsafe place. He must impress her.

Putting force into his strokes, he managed to distance himself from her, getting just slightly ahead, and felt ready to swim the rest of the length of the Seine, upstream, until he came to the origins of the mighty river when he felt her hand touch him, and saw her point toward . . .

A thicket of boats. There were, moored across the Seine, several boats. Some of them were permanently anchored or near enough, and in fact—for a fee—provided accommodation for such homely needs and occupations as clothes washing and for the water carriers to come and draw the water that they sold to the bourgeois in the city.

Suddenly it all made sense to him. Though these boats were guarded, surely they could show the guards they were not vampires! They could hide there until the morning sunlight made it possible for them to reach a safer destination.

He followed Madame Bonacieux willingly, but she never got to the boat. Instead, she veered toward a floating cluster of tree trunks. The people who cut down trees farther up the course of the Seine let them float to the city unfettered. They were marked and those who took them out of the river for milling or firewood then paid the originators of the logs a fee. At any time there were many of these trunks floating alongside the boats. Smaller boats sometimes took damage from the larger logs, and swimmers had to watch for them. Madame Bonacieux swam so that her head just peeked above the water between two of the trunks and then—presumably using her feet to propel herself—she pushed those logs and a few others ahead of her, as she moved, slowly, against the current.

It would be noticeable, D'Artagnan thought, logs floating against the current, but he imitated her. The river went around rocks, and there were eddies and whirls in the current that pulled the floating logs now this way and now that, but not for long. They couldn't go far this way.

She took a course toward the edge of the river. He, pushing six logs ahead and around him, following. He heard noises from the laundry boats and other boats anchored near them—screams and fighting. The vampires had assumed they'd boarded the boats. They must have gone over the bridge to the road—and along the road to the boats at incredible speed. There would be no safe place there.

The lady, however, swam to the riverbank, and, looking around cautiously, pulled herself up out of the water and onto the paved road, then turned to offer him a hand. He resisted an impulse to laugh at the small proffered hand. Young, he might be, and he knew well that he had not gained the weight of muscle and bone he would have in adulthood—he imagined he would be like his father had been, short but solid. But the lady was shorter than he and couldn't weigh nearly as much.

He spurned her extended hand, held on to a sort of parapet that presumably protected the city from the river's flood, and pulled himself up beside her.

"They're looking for us," she said. Her teeth chattered. No surprise, since all she was wearing was a soaked petticoat and an upper garment which, to D'Artagnan's hastily averted eyes, was not substantial enough to hide the rosy glow of her flesh beneath. He wrung his hair and then pulled the soggy mess away from his face, and nodded once. No use denying it. This had been a purposeful—

and masterful—ambush. They couldn't have sent that many of the strange vampires to cover the underside of Pont Neuf to capture just anyone. That would make no sense. Surely there was hunting aplenty in alleyways and corners of the deserted night city, and no use risking fighting at least one musketeer, and maybe two.

"So we should remain as hidden as we can," she said. "I know that they all share mind and memory, but these were sent with the intention to catch us. Surely it is not the mission of every other vampire in the city, only these."

"Yes," he said. "We must get away from the river and these vampires." He still heard sounds from the boats, as though the vampires were now ripping boards and tearing into any space where D'Artagnan and the lady might be hidden.

He extended his hand to her, and got the impression she hesitated before taking it. Together, slightly bent forward, they ran as fast as they could to the protection of a low wall, then ran hunched along it, so their shadows didn't show. But D'Artagnan heard the sound of steps closing in, surrounding them, and the same dry, rubbing sounds he'd heard on the bridge. The sound of long-dead, dried limbs moving. He couldn't think, he could only feel, the approaching mass of vampires. They were going to be taken. They were going to be captured. They were going to be . . . turned?

Aramis' voice echoed in his mind. *The lady is more important than any of us. Get her away.*

D'Artagnan pulled his sword out, but he could not possibly fight them all. He and Aramis had been unsuccessful. How could he, alone, win against this? He knew he couldn't. And yet he must get the lady away and free. He must save her at all costs.

I've never kissed a woman; I've never tamed a horse; I've never . . .

He leaned over to Madame Bonacieux, put his lips near her ear— her white and pink ear, framed in dark blond hair. "Lady," he said, "when I give you the word, run. I want you to run straight ahead, paying no attention to anything, till you reach the nearest street. Then run along the nearest street till you find a safe house. I presume you have places you know are safe?"

She gave him a dark look and whispered back, fiercely, "I am not a child! I have many duties and I—"

"Good. Then you know about duties. And my duty is to protect you. When I give the word, madame."

Suddenly her expression went from threatening to worried. "I don't want you to sacrifice yourself for me," she said.

He laughed a little at the idea that she could escape without his sacrifice, and said, "I don't want to sacrifice myself." But he could hear the vampires moving closer, ever closer.

And so could she, but before he could pull away and execute his plan, Madame Bonacieux seized his head, her hands at the back of it, and she pulled his face down to hers, and kissed him—a long, passionate kiss.

D'Artagnan was taken so wholly by surprise that he did very little at all as her tongue plunged between his lips and darted, daringly, into his mouth. For a moment—for an eternity—their mouths were joined. Though he knew she'd been in the same bracken river as he, he smelled roses, and seemed surrounded by the scent of rose petals. Her mouth tasted like distilled honey, like the sweetness of flowers on a summer meadow, like the first apple of the season. He moaned and, hearing himself moan, pulled back, startled, touching his lips with the tips of his fingers, as though to make sure those were indeed his lips and his fingers.

Then he shook himself. *I have kissed a woman*, not that it made him feel any better about what he had to do. Now to die with honor.

He whispered, "Stay here. When you hear me shout, run." D'Artagnan then tiptoed away from Madame Bonacieux, barely hearing her whisper something about "her rose and his spear" whatever that meant.

D'Artagnan crept with all the stealth he could muster through the dark streets. The vampires were coming from the river, that black swarm having crossed the bridge and moved on along the bank. They advanced blindly, and they certainly didn't know where the young man and Madame Bonacieux were. It reminded D'Artagnan of the way bats homed in on prey, seeming to feel for it out of the ether.

Thus the vampires were approaching, hesitating and rounding on them, slowly, slowly, but ever closer. Infallibly. Given enough time they'd find them. They'd surround them.

Merging with the shadows of the narrow streets, running from doorway to doorway, D'Artagnan went as far away as he could from where he judged the lady needed to go—toward the Palais Royale or some other safe house on this side of the Île de la Cité.

Far, far, as far from known streets as D'Artagnan could go. And then, when he judged his distance as adequate, he stopped, his back against a wall, his sword in his hand. Knowing it was a futile thing, but knowing he must shout and that his words must be plausible enough that the vampires were fooled and that they might as well be a cry for help, he screamed, "To me, musketeers! To me!"

In the dark shadows he could hear hundreds—thousands?—of footsteps shift and change direction toward him, and he more imagined than heard a single set of footsteps running away.

He held his sword and prepared to sell his life dearly.

Casting Lots

"Grimaud!" Athos said, as he saw his servant starting toward the stairs. "Let me do the honors." He was thinking that if someone had come, intent on killing or arresting him, perhaps he could give the others time to run. Certainly Grimaud could not buy them that time, not if faced with several of the cardinal's guards.

But as Athos tripped lightly down the stairs, he became aware he was followed. Porthos, not Grimaud, walked steps behind him.

"Porthos, my friend," Athos said. "I would wait at the top of the stairs. That way, if it should chance to be His Eminence's guards, you can escape with the others while I hold them back."

"Very funny," Porthos said. "But Grimaud is quite competent to lead a rout. I'm not so good at it."

Athos opened the door a crack, with his foot behind it, ready to close it and tell Porthos to run if it should be, as he expected, Richelieu's men. Instead, he found himself looking out . . .

For a moment, he couldn't make sense of what he saw, and when he did, laughter tried to make its way up his throat to his lips. It was Aramis, but he looked as though he'd been dipped, head first, in an unholy baptismal fountain. Unholy because the smell floating from him mingled the odors of everything the city discarded.

Athos' amusement stopped short as he noticed that, beneath the grime and the stained clothes, Aramis was bleeding. He couldn't see the stains of blood, but he could smell it, like honey beneath the foul stench. He stepped aside from his door, afraid of getting too near that smell or thinking too closely about it. But now he could see Aramis was too pale and that he trembled slightly. Easily attributable to being soaked to the skin, but loss of blood did the same. "My dear Aramis," he said, his voice—to his own ears—thick. "What—?"

"I jumped in the river," Aramis said, and his trembling increased. "After I managed to escape a multitude of old ones."

"Old . . . vampires?" Athos asked, pressing himself flat against the wall and motioning Aramis in past him. Aramis went in, and up the stairs, while Athos locked the door and followed him, willing his fangs to retract. He stayed behind enough that he didn't have to smell the all-enticing scent of blood, until they got to the top of the stairs, where Aramis turned and answered Athos' question. "Yes. Very old. I think older even than the ones we fought at des Fossoyeurs. They seemed . . . scarcely like animated creatures. More like . . . walking skeletons."

Athos shivered, imagining himself in that state, but aloud he said only, "Please, if you'd come to the kitchen? Everyone else is there."

"Not everyone else," Aramis said and sighed. "At least . . . D'Artagnan and Madame Bonacieux haven't come here, have they?"

Athos shook his head, as he took the lead down the back stairs to the kitchen. "No. Did you lose them?"

"I regret to say I may have done so," Aramis said. "At least, I told D'Artagnan and the lady to escape. I stayed behind to . . . to distract the attackers. I didn't know . . . That is, the vampires seemed to follow them, leaving me with so few adversaries that I escaped easily." He seemed to hesitate, just before they reached the kitchen. His steps stopped behind Athos, and as Athos turned to look at him, he saw Aramis swallow and shake his head. "I was in the river when I heard D'Artagnan cry, 'To me, musketeers.' But when I made it to the place from whence his voice came . . . there was no one there. Only—"

"Only?"

"His sword. Broken. Shreds off his doublet."

Athos wanted to ask if there were any churches nearby where the boy might have been taken, but he couldn't and didn't wish to tempt Aramis—who, from his scent, was bleeding freely—to go on a dangerous search.

Athos, himself would go as soon as he could. He doubted ancient ones were performing a blood mass, at least he'd never heard of their doing so. Their feeding seemed to be less orchestrated and more of a frenzy. So it would take time to summon younger vampires to the feeding. If there were a hope, Athos would find the boy.

He escorted Aramis to the kitchen, where the younger musketeer was met with distressed sounds from both Grimaud and Bazin. Grimaud wanted to bring forth the hip bath, but Aramis was as adamantly against it as Athos had been. Much to Grimaud's consternation, Aramis also stood by the sink's drainage hole and used water—at least this time from the well—to pour over himself and wash away the filth of the river, while he told in detail how they'd been ambushed on Pont Neuf and how the boy and Madame Bonacieux might be gone forever.

"So the boy has a special sense for vampires, it seems," Aramis said, and then, "Thank you, Grimaud," as Athos' servant offered a towel. Already the servants, who were as much comrades-at-arms as the musketeers, had managed to find one of Athos' suits that was a little smaller and tighter than the others for Aramis to wear.

While Aramis dressed, he said, "Or he is a very well-briefed Judas goat."

"A Judas goat?" Porthos asked. "But he killed vampires."

"Old vampires. Well, other than the guards of the cardinal, but for all we know Jussac and the rest had offended His touchy Eminence in some way and were due to die," Aramis said. He frowned. "What I can't stop thinking is that both his ability in the fights against the vampires, his courage in offering to enter the chapel, and his escaping with Madame—all of them are, after all, simple to explain if he is a Judas goat."

"But why would he warn you of the attack?" Athos asked, following Aramis' reasoning and wishing he didn't. Aramis' mind usually wended down the dark paths of the human soul and Athos' mind was dark enough without it.

Aramis gave a low mirthless laugh. His cuts, revealed while bathing, were all shallow defensive cuts on arms and hands. He bandaged his own left hand as he spoke. "Because he knew I wouldn't believe him, and this ensured I wouldn't suspect him. Afterwards—" He let go the cloth bandages and dropped onto a stool, covering his face with his hands. "—I let them capture her, Athos. She who was far more valuable than my wretched self."

Athos opened his mouth to say Aramis undervalued himself, but never finished, as there was a pounding on the front door. The same sort of urgent pounding he'd heard from Aramis.

Athos ran up the stairs and across the top floor and then down the stairs again. He was almost at the door when he noticed Grimaud behind him, and waved him away. Hoping that it was D'Artagnan and the priestess of nature at the door, he flung it open, though—prudently—keeping his hand on his rapier.

He was half right. Just outside his door, trembling, as soaked as Aramis but considerably less well attired, was Madame Bonacieux.

Her blond hair was so saturated with water as to appear greenish, and she had somehow lost all her clothes but her innermost—at least he hoped it was the innermost, else how she ended up in only it was a puzzle—petticoat and a translucent chemise.

Athos flung himself against the wall and said, "Madame, you do me great honor. The chevalier was just ahead of you. Please do come in."

She came in silently, her quick tongue for once stilled. As she walked by Athos, he smelled no blood but only a healthy human female drenched in river water. He couldn't help noticing, as he followed her up the stairs that he could see the creamy pink of her thighs through the soaked petticoat. Why this should bring up the same desire to feed as the smell of blood did, Athos did not know, but he knew that it disturbed him.

"It must seem quite strange to you, my coming here like this," she said, in a breath of voice, as she turned around. Her blush climbed from around her navel, visible through the soaked fabric

Athos looked away, "Madame, nothing that happens tonight seems strange to me."

She hesitated and tried to run her fingers through her draggled, matted hair, before giving up and sighing. "I know what I said, and the doubts I entertained on . . . on your behalf. But D'Herblay was so sure you were trustworthy that I . . . " She shrugged. "Well, the truth is, I find myself in the Île de la Cité, and I suspect my access to the Palais Royale will be blocked by vampires, therefore . . . "

"Therefore," Athos said, finding unexpected amusement in the midst of his worry for the young Gascon—surely her escape proved D'Artagnan was no adherent of the vampires—who might be, even now, the subject of a blood mass. "You thought you'd drop in on a secret and possibly dangerous vampire. Don't worry, madame, it all makes perfect sense to me."

"You mock me!" she said, managing to sound shocked.

Athos shook his head. "Not so much you as the madness that life has become." He bowed to the semi-clad, soaked woman, as he might have at court. "Madame, you do me great honor. Greater than you know, trusting me with your life and your soul. Greater than I would perhaps do myself. If you forgive me, D'Herblay, Porthos, their servants, my servant, and the young man we rescued are all in the kitchen."

She hesitated then. "I . . . I am not decent."

Athos, realizing the madness of asking her to bathe from a drawn water bucket in front of the sink, said. "Forgive me. It seemed less important than what might have happened to D'Artagnan. Unless he's likely to knock at the door in a few minutes?"

A sob tore through Madame Bonacieux' lips, leaving her looking surprised at the sound, as though not sure where it had come from. "No," she said. And then again, with a despairing tone, "No. He was . . . He drew the vampires away so that I could escape and there were so many of them. They swarmed past me, as if they didn't see me, I fear. I very much fear that he's . . . that he's been taken or killed or . . . or worse."

He nodded. "I fear so too. I was on the point of leaving in hopes of rescuing him from . . . worse . . . but . . . " He shook his head. "But I will make sure you are made comfortable first."

"No, no." She shook her head. "Forget me, go to him."

"I will, only give me a moment."

Down the stairs and into the kitchen, where he informed Grimaud that the hip bath would need to be set in his chambers and all made ready for a lady to bathe and, since they couldn't provide female garments, that Grimaud was to find something that might pass.

"You see, Aramis," he said. "Madame Bonacieux is safe. So it would make no sense at all for the boy to be a Judas goat."

"Unless he's somehow setting up our confidence," Aramis said.

"To get himself captured? Hardly," Athos said. But he didn't argue further. Aramis was being fed what looked like roasted chicken by Grimaud, who had opened one of Athos' best bottles of wine.

And welcome to it, Athos thought, as it was unlikely wine would ever again serve him. Porthos was sitting across from Aramis and discussing again the matter of the ancient ones, and how one could fight them.

Athos made sure no one was watching him and slipped—he hoped unnoticed—up the stairs.

Into Temptation

He bowed briefly to Madame Bonacieux and presented her with a blanket he had grabbed on the way. She wrapped herself in it, expressing her thanks.

"My servant will come presently," he said. "To lead you to where you may bathe. If you would . . ." He hesitated. "Don't tell my friends where I am gone."

Madame Bonacieux looked puzzled and he hastened to explain, "You see, Aramis believes that D'Artagnan might be a Judas goat."

"A—" The lady shook her head. "Of all the— The most hidebound, disgraceful—"

Athos managed a wry smile. He was all too aware of the disputes between Aramis and this priestess of an older religion. He suspected it had its roots in an attraction neither would acknowledge. "Just so," he said. "So if you would not tell the hidebound one where I'm going, he will not endanger himself. Moreover, your tale may convince him of our young friend's valor and innocence."

He was at the top of the stairs to the front door before Madame Bonacieux said, "But you, monsieur?"

"I?" he asked, looking around. "What worse can they do to me that they've not already done?"

He went down the stairs and was unbolting the door when he heard breathing behind him. He turned around, half expecting to see Aramis or Porthos or perhaps Grimaud. But, instead—pale and draggled, looking like someone drowned who had been dredged, unwilling, from the depths of the sea several days after death—was the young man they'd rescued from the blood mass.

"What are you doing here, Plant—Plat—"

"Planchet, monsieur."

"Planchet then," Athos said, annoyed at himself for having forgotten. He prided himself on his memory, his courtesy to the people under his protection, the people of whom he was liege lord de facto if not de jure. "What are you doing here?"

The young man bowed and made a spirited attempt to tug his forelock, which might have worked if his hair hadn't been severely caught back in a queue. "I will go with you, monsieur."

Athos shook his head. He wasn't sure whether the young man fully understood what he was, and he was not about to show him, not now, while he was still recovering from his own near escape. "No."

"Monsieur," the young man said, his face pale, his eyes shining, fever-bright and pinpoint-intense. "I must come. I must come with you."

"Planchet, you're a child. You could be my son. I am ordering you to stay."

The boy looked up. "I don't have parents. And your friend was taken while you were saving me. I owe him that much. I owe you that much. I must go with you, should you need help."

Should he need help! The idea struck Athos as so strange, that he barely managed to arrest a burble of laughter. He did catch it in time, and snapped his mouth closed with the effect of a groan.

That he should need this . . . child's help, alive or dead, human or vampire, begged credulity. A knot of quite a different kind formed in his throat, and he struggled to speak, managing it only in a voice that sounded pasty and thick. "Thank you, Planchet, I am honored. I—" He knew he could no more deny the young man's courageous offer than he could have sent D'Artagnan packing back to Gascony.

And see how it had worked for poor D'Artagnan.

"I thank you, Planchet, but *no*."

The boy's face filled with mulish determination. His chin jutted out, his eyes narrowed, and were this any other time, Athos would have remembered his own younger years and given in. But right then, with death being the penalty for a boy's impetuous folly; right then, when he had to go and rescue another young fool from his own folly, the last thing Athos needed was another death on his conscience. Another death . . . or worse.

He shivered slightly, imagining this determined youth as a vampire, then imagining D'Artagnan turned, and said, "Not now, Planchet. It is too dangerous out there and I'm not convinced ... that traps are not being laid down for my friends and myself." He shook his head. "What weapons do you know? How can you help defend me?"

For the first time, Planchet looked unsure, his expression mirroring the look of someone who takes a step in the blind dark and finds the ground not where he expected it. "I . . . " he said. "I used to throw rocks with . . . with a slingshot. When I was much younger, of course."

And now Athos did laugh, not in derision, but in shared amusement, remembering his own long-lost days of throwing rocks with a slingshot. He'd never been very good with it. He'd never managed to hit more than tree branches and, once, his mother's prized rosebush. "Your hand, Planchet," he said stretching his own and bracing so well for the appeal of warm, living flesh that he almost didn't flinch when it clasped his own cold fingers. "I will not take you today, young hero, but I will promise that I'll teach you to use a sword upon my return. Or better, perhaps, convince Monsieur Porthos to do so, as he used to teach fencing."

"But . . . " For a moment, Planchet was all wide-eyed surprise. "But, monsieur! I am but the son of a baker!"

"All that," Athos said with a wave of the hand, "must perforce be swept away—as are the past religious wars, the fights over which pathway to God was the right one, the bloodshed that sped far too many souls His way. If this war continues, we shall need every able-bodied human to keep the night at bay."

He stepped out the door and into the darkness. The night was no longer young. Stars were out, few and small, in the turbulent blue sky rayed with violet clouds. The moon seemed almost not real, in the middle of it, a shining blue beacon surrounded in a violet halo.

Now he was out . . . and alone. Where was he going? Athos blended into the darker shadows on the street, and kept his hand clasped on the hilt of his sword. As a vampire, and one trained in the use of his sword, he should be able to overcome anything that might threaten him, human or vampire.

But he was a newly-turned vampire, and he had not fed. What had Jussac called him? Halfling? The name fit. Neither human nor vampire, he felt vulnerable to both. Not afraid—or at least not the sort of fear that would induce cowardice; how could that be, when he would have welcomed death to release him from this, his tainted carnal prison?—but cautious, listening for every movement, every sign of life.

He heard none. Oh, if he fixed his attention he would hear mewling babes or their parents whispering behind the cross-marked window shutters on the windows at either side of the narrow street. But he bothered only with sounds on the street, and there were none to worry him.

He found his feet were taking him, as of their own accord, to that same church where he'd met his untimely destiny. And he found his feet were right. They should take him back there, as once tonight already they'd interrupted another ceremony in the place.

But he did not expect to find anyone there, human or vampire—and he did not. He stood outside the howling ruin, smelling the all-too-recent vampire deaths, and wondering if there were any others hiding in there, waiting for him. Waiting . . . for anyone.

He could only think that he'd not find Charlotte there, which brought his thoughts up short. Did he mean to find Charlotte, then?

When had his mind decided this, and why had it, and why did he feel as though it had betrayed him in reaching that conclusion without his conscious thought? Did he mean to see Charlotte because his body ached for her? Or was there a reason to see her that he could bring out in the full light of reason?

He clasped the hilt of the sword tight, till the decorations on it became imprinted upon his palm, and sighed. No. Just like his feet, his mind had made a logical plan. If he wanted to find D'Artagnan, he must find Charlotte, first.

The city was vast enough and even if you assumed the boy was in a church and about to be subjected to a blood mass—there were over three hundred churches in Paris, not counting cathedrals, chapels, or private chapels and shrines. He could not run through the streets, back and forth, until he found a particular one. And should it be across the city, he'd never get there in time.

But Charlotte was a vampire. She must, perforce, share that mental link all vampires shared. Even if she had not been the planner or the organizer of this plot, she would know which place, which church, which hiding place, the Gascon was held. And if she knew that, he could persuade her to tell him. He ran his hand back through his hair, not absolutely sure this was true, but willing it to be. He'd convince her to tell him where they'd taken the boy. He would find the youth. And finding him, either release him . . . or grant him mercy. Before he became what Athos was.

But this required Athos finding Charlotte, and quickly.

From her unruffled aspect the night before—aye, and from her appearance here a few hours ago, a phenomenon to which he understood there were limits of distance, she must live—No. Not live. She must have her lair nearby. Which meant he should be able to discover where.

He knew her tastes, his silver and ivory Charlotte's tastes. She'd reveled in being a countess and resented only that the castle at La Fère was not arranged according to the latest mode. She'd called it a wind-swept barracks and pouted when Athos had refused to remodel it into a more fashionable, airier habitation.

He closed his eyes. In this area there was only one house in which he presumed Charlotte would consent to live. It was a fine Italianate townhouse that had belonged to the de Montbelliards—a family of wealthy merchants who still held it when Athos had come to town, before they'd grown by degrees less wealthy, as their trade in luxury goods faltered and, finally they had left Paris, abandoning their fine stone and marble home to be taken by any enterprising vampire.

Athos guessed the moment Charlotte saw the house, she would have contrived to take it from whichever bloodsucker inhabited it. Not for his Charlotte the cold, dirt floor of some abandoned chapel or the filthy marble of some echoing cathedral.

No. He followed his memory of the location of the de Montbelliard house, down a narrow alley, across a broad street, then, in quickening steps, up stairs to its front door. And there he stopped.

The house shone from within with soft, wavering light. Either someone was using the finest candles, the kind of white wax that had once been used for divine services at the best churches and in the royal court, or else someone was using well-trimmed lamps. Light spilled forth from every window, and shone softly upon the pavement in front of his feet. The sound of a harp gently played came with it.

Charlotte wouldn't be the player. At least he never knew her to play an instrument. But she'd enjoyed music well enough.

His teeth ached, he was clamping them together so hard. Athos looked toward the double door, at the top of a broad marble stairway. Two large vampires, whom he recognized as the ones who'd tied him to an altar the night before, stood guard beside it. Athos shuddered and shook his head. He'd find no easy admittance there.

But there must be an entrance to the building. He walked around toward the alley that ran along the tall wall at the back of the house. Within lay gardens that he remembered as well kept and fragrant.

They were fragrant still. Though roses were out of season, he could smell them with his heightened senses. And he could still hear the harp from inside, joined now by dulcet laughter he knew all too well.

The laughter spurred him on. He climbed the wall, clumsily because it was a relatively new and well-kept wall, and there was hardly any places his feet and hands could grasp. He felt the skin on his hands tear and bleed on the rough stone as he climbed to the top of the wall and looked, blindly, toward the building.

His gaze was met with more light, spilling from an open window. The room he was facing at the same level as the top of the wall was a vast salon, luxuriously appointed. A carpet lay upon the floor and it looked to have the intricate designs of silk carpets from the orient. Athos' sight blurred.

In the center of the room, lying upon a blue and gold couch was . . . Charlotte. She reclined in the Roman fashion, and wore a diaphanous gown that allowed him to see the contours of her flesh beneath the fabric. Her feet were bare, long and sculpted, looking too fine not to have been created by an artist. Her breasts round, smooth, and swelling above the dress's deep neckline.

He could imagine the feel of her skin on his hands—cool, cool silk, but living and responsive as silk never could be. He could imagine lifting her diaphanous wrapping and—

He could remember her mind upon his, insistent, demanding he open mind and soul to her.

Like a sudden cold wave that submerges you on the sunlit ocean, like a freezing wind on a summer day, fear enveloped him, all-grasping. As much as he wanted her, he feared her more, with the unreasoning fear of the small and defenseless hunted by a powerful predator.

He climbed back down the wall and walked, dazed, along the street. He had to confront her. That much was sure. How else could he even hope to save his young friend? But how could he face her?

He thought of wine or spirits with longing and almost banished the thought from his mind before realizing most alcoholic beverages were clear liquids.

His body numb, his mind fixed on his need for drink, he stumbled along the alley on a well-known path.

A Dark and Dreary Journey

D'Artagnan woke up.

The lady! He thought, and half rose, pulling his body up. He could move no further. His hands were bound behind his back so tightly they demonstrated the unconcern of a captor who had gone beyond human frailty. The ropes binding his wrists were so taut they had almost dislocated his shoulders. Other thick ropes wound around his body. Something cold and hard—chains? fetters?—bound his ankles. He didn't have his boots, and for a moment was puzzled by this, as he'd kept them on even while swimming the river. But now they were gone.

Slowly, through his sluggish brain, like water trickling through a tight sieve, came the thought that he'd been divested of them so he could not escape. His doublet and shirt were torn. His breeches remained and still felt wet, the sort of residual clamminess one feels after clothes have dried on one's body a long time.

His head hurt, but he didn't feel injured. At least, there was no sharp pain anywhere, just a dull pain all over, as though he'd been bruised by a continuous and lengthy beating. He felt nauseated, though. His mouth tasted of river water, and his stomach seemed to sway within him.

He became aware that *he* was swaying, *all* of him, rocking to the rhythm of the floor beneath him, which was, in turn, being rocked, neither gently nor rhythmically, but constantly. He would sway, rock, sway, rock, and suddenly bump, in a way that held him airborne for a moment.

He swallowed against the bile rising in his throat and tried to open his eyes, only to find they were open but covered with a blindfold.

136

Whoever had captured him had tied him carefully, blindfolded him, and thrown him in a carriage. But why?

There had been vampires all around him when he'd been captured, but surely most vampires would simply have taken him to the nearest church and either turned him or shared him as a communal meal between them, drained to death. Who had taken him, and why?

He opened and closed his mouth, surprised to find it empty, shocked to find himself able to speak, as he said in a voice that emerged low and hoarse, "Let me go. In Jesus' name, let me go."

A boot hit his face, hard. The kick was so forceful it left him addled, for a moment, and it was so sudden that it took him a breath to understand that it had been a boot that had struck him, and not a hand, nor even the flat of a sword.

"Shhh," a voice said from somewhere above D'Artagnan. Above and to the left. He would be on the floor of a carriage. There would be . . . men? Vampires? On the seat or the seats. It would be worthwhile to know if there were one or two seats. And, if two, were both occupied? How many vampires were there? D'Artagnan couldn't even attempt to escape until he discovered these things. "Shush or we will gag you. And then if you cannot breathe so well, we'll be sorry, but you'll be dead."

D'Artagnan took a deep breath. He could well imagine if whoever had tied his hands together applied the same principle to gagging him, he would have trouble breathing or staying alive. He closed his eyes behind his blindfold, pretending to himself that he had some control over whether he could see or not, and tried to think.

He was on the floor of a carriage, utterly powerless, hurrying along what he presumed was a still-dark road. To where? The way the horses galloped, he couldn't be in the city anymore. No matter how large the city and how broad its streets—and some Parisian streets were indeed broad, though most were not—no carriage could move at this pace in the city without meeting with an obstacle. Yes, noblemen's carriages routinely ran down those on foot, but that in itself would slow the mad gallop down.

Even at night, even in besieged Paris, there were passersby. Even if those were often vampires. And besides, every broad road ended in a labyrinth of narrow alleys. Even in his short time in the city, D'Artagnan had seen fine carriages, elaborately ornamented with gold and painted with scenes of the ancient gods, doubtless relics from a more prosperous time, making their cautious way down the narrower streets. There was a reason, after all, that sedan chairs—carried by horses or men—were the most common form of transportation in Paris.

So they were outside the city and speeding . . . where? It felt like torture to D'Artagnan to be hurrying to a destination not his own, at someone else's command. But there was nothing he could do immediately, and he wasn't stupid enough to court another kick to the head. No. He must nurse his head and calm himself, so he would be ready to escape should an opportunity present itself. There were always opportunities, after all.

He'd resigned himself to this, and was disciplining himself to quiet, even breathing when the carriage lurched to a stop with the suddenness of a vehicle whose path is obstructed.

A sudden pounding against what sounded like a glass window, and the door opened. A current of cold air, tinged with the smell of pine trees, caressed D'Artagnan's face.

"What is it, then?" The male voice D'Artagnan had heard earlier spoke again, strangely with more peevishness than it had first displayed to the young Gascon. "Why have we stopped?"

"There are vampires, Monsieur Rochefort!" The voice had a cringing tone that implied its owner was bowing as completely as was humanly possible to bow, and would have fallen on his knees if he thought it might help. "Blocking the road."

The first man made a clicking sound and exhaled with a sound of great annoyance, "*Alors*, we do not have the time for this. Tell them to move by orders of the cardinal."

"I cannot, monsieur. They do not listen. They are all peasants and most likely have never even known the cardinal is their rightful lord. They're too far from Paris to feel the force of the master's mind. They are hungry, too. Starving. I think they want us and the horses."

The click of annoyance again. "And the two of you slugs know not how to deal with this? It would serve you well if I gave you to these wild vamps to feast on. It would be no more than your just deserts."

"But who would then tool the coach by day, my lord?" another man asked, in a voice that implied he knew very well the title wasn't real, but hoped that by conferring a noble honorific on the man—vampire?—he would, perhaps, receive the benefit of indulgence.

"It is your very great luck that I don't know where I can find replacements," Rochefort said. "Not here in the middle of nowhere. Very well, then, come, my minions. Come, my pets."

From either side of D'Artagnan there were rustling sounds. Of people? Creatures? He heard them rise, then feet—or perhaps talons—clicking past his head. The smell, slightly rancid, heavy, as if tainted with grave dirt, made him recognize what these were: ancient vampires. And they'd been sitting on either side of him—evidently so still their fetor was not stirred. But now their stench and the remembrance of what the creatures looked like—knowing he had been penned in so closely with them—made D'Artagnan feel nauseated again. He tried to discipline his mind and told himself that perhaps there would be a chance of escaping once Rochefort left the carriage.

But as he heard Rochefort's booted footsteps go past him, Rochefort said, "Mind the cub there. He's tied up tightly enough, even the two of you shouldn't be able to lose track of him. But stop him if he manages to get fanciful."

The carriage bounced as Rochefort disembarked, but D'Artagnan still heard breathing near him. He heard the vampires scuttle away, and pleaded, in a half whisper to the man—men?—left in the carriage, "Untie me and let me go. Then we can escape. We can be back to safety by daybreak."

Nothing but heavy breathing answered his plea.

From outside the carriage came the sounds of fighting, of swords clashing, of men—vampires—screaming. D'Artagnan resigned himself to waiting once more.

Whoever won that battle out there made little difference to him. He would be the trophy of the victors. Whether that meant more traveling in the dark, or a quick merciless death delivered by aged vampires, it was out of his hands.

He was no more than a pawn in a game he did not begin to understand.

Trading in Souls

Athos found the tavern, though it wasn't marked. No taverns were these days. It would amount to hanging out a sign promising any passing vamp plenty of victuals within. But he remembered the places where he and his friends used to drink till two days ago— places that looked just like the other houses from the outside, from their cross-marked doors to only the slightest glimmer of light escaping through cracks in the shutters.

He knocked on the door, and a voice from within said, "*Qui vive?*"

"A friend of the king," Athos answered, hoping the password hadn't changed. He waited, his heart hammering wildly in his chest, almost making him laugh because a dead heart should not beat so strongly.

But slowly the door opened. A small pale face, only slightly higher than Athos' waist, peeked up at him. The first time he'd seen it, he'd thought it was a child, but he knew it belonged to an old woman, the mother of the tavern owner.

"Madame Marie," he said.

She lowered her eyes and then looked up at him, taking in his hat, his face, the sword. Then she inclined her head again, "Monsieur Athos," she said, and stepped away, pulling the door open. Athos stepped in, ducking his head to get through the squat doorway. The tavern was kept dark—deliberately so, to prevent too much light escaping through the shutters—for which he was grateful, lest someone should notice his unusual pallor.

He felt his way cautiously in the gloom with his foot, to find the three worn steps that allowed him onto the broad, flagstone-paved tavern proper.

There were no tables. Granted, there had once been, but any tavern that could be proven to still operate now, would be brought up on charges of inducing men to be out of doors after dark, and thereby giving an advantage to the vampires. Under the king's law, taverns, like churches, were forbidden, even if for completely different reasons.

Groups of men stood huddled together, many of them wrapped in their cloaks, drinking grimly whatever there was to be had in this land in which vineyards were left untended and no grain was grown for bread nor brewing.

He wound his way among the groups, careful not to touch them, both to avoid bringing upon himself the craving for human blood and to avoid their feeling his icy nature. He could feel the heat of their bodies as he walked past. It was as though he were a cold void and they were warmth and life. He desperately craved blood—so desperately he could taste it in his mouth: the warmth of fresh baked bread, the joy of healing after a long illness.

He kept rigid control of his movements, rigid control of his thoughts. Life for him was death for others. And it meant losing his soul. It meant becoming . . . He did not know what it meant becoming. It was as if he were staring at a curtain that obscured a portion of the room. If he went beyond that curtain there would be something on the other side, but it would not be Athos. It would not be Raphael de la Fère either.

Moving his feet by dint of will alone, he made himself traverse the dimly lit, uneven floor with the same determination and blind urgency with which a traveler will face an unknown desert. Of one thing only he was sure. He could not face Charlotte sober. There were cravings he could not withstand.

In the past, alcohol had served as a barrier, a means to dull his senses and forget his guilt. Now he hoped it would serve to stop him losing what remained of his humanity.

Seeing him advancing, the host—standing behind a polished walnut table, rather than a bar—reached for a bottle, which Athos knew would contain red wine. Athos' drink of choice. Athos shook his head. "No. Armagnac," he said between teeth he'd clenched to forestall the instinct to attack the drinkers around him. He indicated how much he wanted with his fingers held apart, and tossed a Louis on the counter, where it sparkled briefly before being taken up by the disbelieving host. He looked up at Athos halfway between awe and fear and said, "Monsieur, that much . . ."

Athos shook his head. "Drink, not advice."

The man inclined his head—the bald spot atop it shining briefly in the light of the candles—and reached for the bottle from under the table, exposing his neck just long enough to display a large pulsing vein. Athos imagined tearing into it, imagined blood pouring into his mouth. He gripped the edge of the table hard and willed his mind to blankness. The host poured the liquid into a glass.

To Athos' surprise, unlike wine, which smelled as repulsive as water, the brandy smelled good. Almost too good. Like the blood coursing through the veins of the living, it gave off a sense of warmth and of the sun.

He reached for it with a trembling hand, clutching at the glass as though it were his hope of salvation and bringing it up to his lips, his hand shaking all the way. In the eyes of the host, Athos read a suspicion that the musketeer had already had a few too many.

The glass was at his lips, and Athos threw back the liquid, drinking it all, in a single swallow.

He set the glass down, quickly, and for just a moment thought nothing had happened—nothing would happen. Alcohol—even the finest Armagnac brandy—would now have no effect upon him.

And then the drink exploded within him. Or at least, that was the effect. As though he'd swallowed a seed of the sun, entire, and it had burst into flame and heat within him, singing along his veins, taking possession of his mind, overwhelming him with pleasure and horrible pain, the two together and intermixed like twins conceived jointly and born entwined.

He knew he screamed only because, through his tear-filled eyes, he could see everyone turn to stare at him.

Explanations tried to throng to his mind, but were evaporated by the bright light shining everywhere in his brain and by the pain coursing like fire through his veins.

Someone here, he thought, might know what this meant. Or perhaps not. How many vampires went drinking in common taverns? But they'd be curious. He must get out of this place fast.

Surprised he didn't trip on his own feet, feeling like his whole body was very far away from his burning mind, he almost ran out of the tavern and into the street outside, where the cold night air failed to sober him—perhaps because he wasn't drunk—but brought him to a consciousness of his problem.

He needed to get D'Artagnan's location—and predicament—out of Charlotte, and to manage, in some way, to tell it to his friends so that they might rescue the young man.

And he, himself, might be dying from ingesting alcohol, which would be yet a different way for a vampire to kill himself.

Alcohol buzzing through his body, clouding his mind, he walked as fast and determinedly as he could down the street, toward the house Charlotte had commandeered.

Getting drunk might not turn out to have been his best idea.

La Belle Dame

By the time he got to the house, his panic and the pain in his veins had mutated into a soft confusion that edged his vision in misty tendrils of pale yellow fog. He tried not to think this probably meant his brain was dying—or whatever it was vampire brains did instead of dying.

At the foot of the stairs, in front of his wife's palatial abode, he considered her guards. He'd had some vague idea—in so far as he'd thought about it at all—of returning to his perch on the garden wall and from there, with some jumping and a little care, to make it through the open window into Charlotte's sitting room.

But now staring up at the house, it occurred to him that her guards would attack him as quickly if he vaulted in through the high window as they would if he came in through the front door.

Or would they attack him at all? He did not know.

What Athos had learned of vampires, through the years of his life devoted to killing them, was that they were not fraternal or convivial or likely to hold friendship—or love—sacred.

Oh, they had rulers. In France, at this time, the cardinal was their ruler, and capturing him had been the greatest victory the vampires had won in this kingdom. But in another sense, they had no rulers and lived like wild animals, every one of them against all others. Even if they shared—or could share—their mind, it didn't make them love each other. And there was no way to guess how Charlotte truly felt about her errant husband. Her seduction attempts not withstanding, he had, after all, ten years ago done his best to kill her.

But if he were going to be attacked, then he might as well go through the front door. And if he were going to be received with open arms, whatever that might mean in these circumstances, he'd still rather go in through the front door.

He squared his shoulders and walked up the steps, or rather, he stumbled up them, at ever increasing speed. His legs felt liquid and as though they shouldn't be able to carry him; his mind was still suffused by what seemed to be mingled heat and light, pain and pleasure.

The vampire at the top of the stairs looked like he'd been a military man, veteran of a hundred campaigns before being turned. His hair was black, going gray at the temples, his eyes a bright, sparkling blue, his features crisscrossed by myriad scars.

He looked human and friendly, until you got close enough to catch, in his blue eyes, the hint of coldness, of detachment that marked him for a vampire.

But even that coldness was overlaid with a form of amusement as Athos managed to grasp one of the columns on the side of the doorway in time to stop himself from falling, and then had to spin around to look at the vampire guard in the eye. "I," he said. Realizing he had no idea what Charlotte called herself these days, he cleared his throat and said, in a voice as assured and full of his own importance as he could muster, "I am here to speak to Charlotte, Comtesse de la Fère." And then, realizing again how odd that might sound, added with a thunderous frown, "My wife!"

The vampire smiled, a smile that would have been friendly without the tips of his fangs protruding just beneath his upper lip. "Certainly," he said, "Milady is expecting you."

"Mil . . ." Athos said, again momentarily puzzled by the use of the word pronounced in English.

"Certainly," the guard said, and opened the heavy oak door, and stood aside, gesturing with his hand to welcome Athos within. "It is what *Milady* prefers to be called."

This idea put an uneasy twinge of discomfort in Athos' confused mind, a pang that grew into a finger of cold fear running down his spine, as he entered into a corridor that he vaguely remembered from his former visits to the de Montbelliards.

It didn't look that much different now. Unlike other places he'd seen that had been taken over by vampires, the house hadn't changed much. It was perhaps even cleaner and better furnished than when the de Montbelliards had lived in it.

A deep carpet covered the floor of the hallway—its jewel-like tones flashed in the light of the many candles burning in the wall sconces. Heavy, dark furniture loomed at every corner, reminding Athos of nothing so much as of his own furniture in his own home at La Fère. But the tapestries on the walls, and the paintings—floor to ceiling paintings, showing shadowy glades and half-naked maidens languishing under the whip of the merciless mid-day sun—were things he had never owned, nor could ever have owned, provincial lord that he was.

Everywhere, too, gold and silver glinted from pedestals that supported winged marble cherubs, twinkled in the threads of a tapestry that showed a waterfall, dazzled from the silver-plated form of a statue of a Greek maiden and her jar of water.

He walked past these splendors, dazed, looking only for his wife.

As it happened, he smelled her before he saw her, a smell of lilacs at full bloom that seemed to encompass him and pull him forward with near-physical tendrils through two archways, down a set of steps into a vast salon tiled in pink and white marble, past a virginal left unattended, a flimsy silk wrap draped across the carved stool next to it.

Charlotte's scent came from that silk wrap. Athos picked it up almost without noticing what he was doing, marveling at its translucence, at its intense peach-skin color, at the golden threads shining in it, which did not detract from its softness as it touched his face.

This wrap had enveloped Charlotte. It had touched her soft, scented skin, sliding around her. Her skin—he could feel as if he touched it now, silky soft, and as smooth as the wrap.

He stumbled half-blind through an arched doorway and into the room he'd first seen through the window from outside.

It had, in the de Montbelliards' day, been a vast receiving room stacked with tables, chaise lounges, and the sort of mannered, gilded furniture that had been fashionable when France still had great wealth and refinement of life. A time when no one would have believed that a grave, opened in the far Eastern reaches of Europe, would have such dire consequences for all of Europe, indeed, for all of the world.

Now the room contained only one chaise and no tables. On the couch Charlotte lay, gracefully resting. She wore a simple shift, white, covering from shoulder to ankle and leaving her arms bare. Made of silk so fine as to be translucent, it let her body glimmer through here and there: the rounded shapes of her breasts, crowned with pinkish-cream nipples, the narrow waist, the curve of her hip.

Athos knew there were other vampires—and perhaps other humans—in the room. He could sense them around him, half-see one of them playing a harp, and half-hear breath and music and movement. It didn't matter. For all his mind or body cared, he might have been floating out amid the stars, in the desolate loneliness of the eternal spheres with none but Charlotte. Charlotte, lying on her couch, white and gold against the blue upholstery.

"Raphael!" she said, as a command. Looking up, he saw her smiling at him, knowingly. She extended a hand; he fell to his knees and took it. It felt warmer than his, and much softer than any velvet. He dropped his face toward it and kissed along each finger, then along the back of it and to the wrist, where he'd swear he could feel her pounding pulse beneath the delicate skin. He kissed there too, worshipfully.

How many times in the last ten years had he longed to do this? How many dreams of mingled desire and dread had visited him, dreams in which his wife was not dead, in which he could touch her again, feel her, take her in his arms?

Every time his lips touched her skin it was as though he were a starving man taking a small morsel of bread. He savored it and yet it left him craving more and more.

He kissed up her rounded, soft and firm and living arm—living as no vampire's arm had a right to be. The smell of lilacs rose around him, intoxicating. Up to her shoulder, up and toward her neck, his hand straying to cup her breast, his whole body aching with desire.

"Stop," Charlotte said, her order unavoidable. He froze where he was. He couldn't have disobeyed her if he wished to. "Stand up, Raphael," she said, her voice soft but the command still as bare in it as the glint of a blade in the moonlight. "Stand and stay still."

He stood, his legs shaking, longing for her as he had once, in his human days, longed for a drink after a long spell without alcohol. His body wished to strain toward her, taut, desperate. But commanded not to move, he could reach toward her only with that slight, longing inclination with which a plant reaches for the life-giving rays of the sun.

She flowed to standing, just out of his reach, and walked around him, slowly, surveying his body. Her gaze seemed to him only dispassionate interest, like a horse buyer at a fair. Around and around him she went and for a moment, trembling, he feared she would address the others in the room; ask them what they thought of this new purchase, of his points and his muscles, his long legs, his powerful shoulders.

Instead, as she stopped in front of him, she said, softly, "Why did you come, Raphael? Why here?"

His tongue felt like an unyielding bit of cork in his mouth. He knew before, in the church, she—her illusion?—had been offended at his not having come simply to seek her. She would like it no better, would act injured if he told her he'd not come for her. And yet, the truth compelled itself to be spoken, because if he told her a sweet lie, chances were she'd see through it. She knew D'Artagnan had been kidnapped and therefore she knew why Athos was here.

"You know," he said at last, his voice slurred, forced out of his unyielding tongue, his stiff lips. "You know well why I'm here."

Her laughter rang out, like music falling softly on his buzzing ears. "Perhaps I do, Raphael. Which doesn't mean I don't wish to be told."

For a moment he wondered if she thought Athos had come to her out of desire. But no. Well did he know his *belle dame sans merci*. She was toying with him, inviting him to walk into her honeyed trap.

"I came for the boy," he said, his throat aching as though the words had been ripped through it, leaving it raw in their wake. "The Gascon. Tell me where he is."

A smile answered him, and Charlotte walked around him again, this time touching him here and there, now sliding a hand down his arm, then stopping to feel the curve of his buttock beneath his tight breeches. "Why should I?" she said and laughed. "Convince me I should."

148

She stepped back—one, then two steps giving the impression of a rehearsed dance. Three steps away, she put her hands behind her back, and stood surveying him, looking up at his face and down the length of his body to his feet, then back again. In that position, she looked very young, an impish girl daring him to do something.

He ached to touch her. He extended a hand toward her.

"No," she said, and the smile came and left again, traveling upon her lips but for a brief moment. Her tongue came out and the tip of it touched her lips. "Undress!" she said.

"Charlotte!"

Her laughter rang out, peel after peel of musical amusement, washing over the assembled crowd. "You wish for something of me, and you must pay forfeit. Undress!"

He stood incapable of moving. For the first time the others in the room became real. He could count them, even without turning his head to find all of them. There was the girl at the harp—just beyond Charlotte's left shoulder—her fingers still now, as though all her attention were riveted upon Athos and Charlotte. She looked very young, very blond, like a child just at the edge of adolescence. She was too far away for Athos to know whether she was human or not. Beside her was a young man, little more than her age. A nobleman, Athos would warrant, and was glad he was not so close that he could determine if the youth—who had an air of the de Montbelliards—was in fact their eldest son, either turned or held as a captive human.

Behind him, he could hear and sense at least four more people to his right, near the large window through which the night air blew its scent of flowers. On the other side there were at least that many people and probably several more, judging from the shuffling of feet, the sound of breaths being held—not fully but almost. The only breathing was so soft, that he'd need a vampire's enhanced senses to hear it.

He knew all gazes were on him, all eyes expectant. In his entire life, Athos had been naked only in front of his mother, his nurse, and Charlotte. Even Grimaud, who tended to him from early childhood, had never seen him completely unclad. Everything in him revolted at the idea of undressing here, in front of strangers. The horror at the thought was enough to almost sober him. Almost, but not quite.

He should turn and walk out. The Count de la Fère performed for no man. And no woman—or vampire—either. But his feet were rooted to the floor, and his open mouth could utter no protest save one inarticulate sound halfway between anger and pain.

Charlotte smiled at him. "If you would know where your Gascon is kept, you will do as I tell you. Now undress, I tire of this game."

Up went his hands, feeling like each was made of lead and weighed ten times more than their usual weight, to unlace the fastenings of his doublet. His fingers fought him as though each of them had become a small sentient being who, by balking the task, would make Athos recant. But he could not recant. He must know where D'Artagnan was, what they'd done with him, either to save the boy or to give him mercy. It was his fault that the boy was enmeshed in this. If Athos had not gone to Monsieur de Tréville's office. If D'Artagnan had not followed him and his friends to see what Athos' wound portended. If Athos had had the courage instead to put an end to his existence when he'd first known he was turned. If he'd done that, then D'Artagnan would not now be in what Athos was sure must be mortal peril.

He undid the lacing, pulled the doublet off, in a matter-of-fact manner, dropped it on the floor. In the silence now reigning in the room, it seemed to him that the fall of the velvet echoed as loudly as a bell in the night.

Next he'd have to remove his scabbard and sword. He hesitated at this thought. He would rather not be unarmed before a room full of vampires and Judas goats. But he didn't know how to be naked and still have his sword. And Charlotte had said he must be naked. Else, she'd not tell him where they'd taken the boy.

The metal buckle felt colder against his cold hands than it should have, and the leather too rough. His finger, clumsily, stabbed into the sharp metallic prong. A single drop of blood flowed and fell, and it seemed to Athos that the entire room held its breath. In the confusion, he pulled his belt off quickly and clumsily let his sword drop in its sheath. The clang of metal on wood sounded through the rooms, as he reached—quickly—for the hem of his shirt and pulled it up over his head. He felt his own hair falling back upon his broad shoulders like a soft whip.

Standing, bare-chested, feeling the gazes of everyone on him almost like a physical touch, he hesitated. The idea that these people whom he didn't know were evaluating his appearance and perhaps enjoying his nakedness, his vulnerability, made him want to cringe. Anger and revulsion mingled with an odd sort of rising excitement. He thought this eagerness was only because of Charlotte and despised himself for not being able to resist.

"Your breeches, Raphael," her voice was as crisp and loud as the sword falling on the floor.

He untied them quickly and dropped them, letting them fall over his boots. A titter answered this and, "Your boots, you fool."

He removed his boots, balancing and feeling as if he couldn't; dreading falling on his face. But he didn't. First one boot, then the other were forcibly wrenched and thrown from him as though they had offended him.

Words from Charlotte weren't needed, her look was enough to make him untie and drop his undergarment. While doing it, he noticed for the first time that there was a mirror behind Charlotte—a large old-fashioned mirror made of polished silver. No glass large enough to cover that expanse could be manufactured, of course. It reflected like a lake reflects, giving the image back cool and gray and distorted by strange ripples. In it Athos was long and lean and pale, his golden hair the only note of color. Reflections of his hair seemed to give him wings on either side, as though instead of only the name he also partook of the nature of the angel by whose name Athos had been baptized.

He stood a long while and wondered what Charlotte was going to do. She didn't move, nor did anyone else. He could still feel their relentless gazes on him and held still by an effort of will.

Charlotte sat down upon her couch, then lay gracefully again. She said nothing.

The breezes from the open windows caressed his body. He felt his body hair stand with their frigid touch.

Someone walked toward him, then all of them were approaching. Not hurriedly, but steadily, as though these were the steps of a dance. All of them. Closing in on him from all sides, save the side from which Charlotte observed, a half-smile on her face that reminded Athos of something he could not name.

First the harpist touched him, her hands cool and soft, caressing down the length of his back. Then other hands. He closed his eyes, his mind reeling. He didn't want to know. He didn't want to see. He didn't want to be present.

And yet the cool touch of vampires, the warm touch of humans tingled and gentled along his skin, touching him everywhere. And his body responded.

From the Terror of Night

D'Artagnan had to escape. He trembled with the urgency of it. He lay on the floor of the carriage, his nose pressed on the fine grit and dirt there, breathing hard. From outside came odd sounds—screams and slashes and the occasionally blood-curdling scream of dying vampires.

The horses, always restless, grew increasingly more so, pounding their hooves and tossing about, causing the carriage to rock and sway in place. But when it started moving forward—a horse clearly having taken it upon himself to run, one of the men in the carriage with D'Artagnan let out a muffled curse.

"I'll go, Jean," another said. D'Artagnan heard him leave the carriage and a few moments later the slow movement of the carriage stopped. But then there was another scream, and this one seemed to be not vampire but human and horse, mingled, and the carriage started moving forward, at first slowly, to the sound of trotting hooves, and then with increasing speed.

The two men above D'Artagnan exclaimed and were thrown against walls.

I must escape now, D'Artagnan though. *It is the only chance and the only choice.* He wondered if he'd survive the drop from the carriage that was now going at a fair clip, but as he saw no other escape, lest he were turned or, worse, used as the bait in a trap to take those more important than he. Dying seemed a third alternative and welcome, although D'Artagnan did not risk his life lightly.

This was the calculation of a moment. Before his captors could recover their balance in the swaying carriage, he squirmed until he was on his back and facing close to where he thought the door was—from a memory of hearing it open. He gathered his feet up, as the interconnected network of ropes nearly wrenched his arms out of their sockets. The carriage fortuitously swayed toward the door, so his body slid nearer it, and he let down his feet with all his might.

He felt them crash against wood and then he was airborne. In the echoing screams from above, he rolled down what felt like a steep slope covered in pine needles, leaves, and the occasional rock.

The rolling seemed endless and dizzying. He hadn't expected to be out in a single movement. He expected to have to open the door and then wriggle out to escape.

He rolled to a stop against what felt like a small shrub or a sapling, which suddenly gave way causing him to roll faster, farther. And then, again, suddenly he stopped.

His body bruised and scratched, he took a deep breath. Then another.

He was completely trussed up in—he assumed—the middle of a forest. He assumed, too, that pursuit would soon come, perhaps already nearer than he hoped. Whether the pursuers were his original captors or the vampires who'd tried to attack the humans and the horses, he neither knew nor cared. The difference was little: merely a matter of whether he would be killed or turned or used as a pawn.

There must be a way to set himself free. He heard a stream running nearby. Sharpening his ears, he heard the sway of great trees caught in the wind, above. He squirmed over the ground, creeping, till his head hit the trunk of a large tree. He'd free his eyes first. He rubbed the side of his face against the tree. Scratching his skin, till it fell raw, he persisted. The blindfold moved slowly, very slowly. He perceived a little light at the bottom of it, and rubbed harder. Sure he'd scraped vast swathes of his own skin and taken far too long, he finally managed to roll the blindfold upward.

He blinked at the relatively faint light of a moonlit night, still infinitely brighter than the darkness behind the blindfold had been.

As he'd expected, he was in a wood, with pine trees dense all around. He could not but shudder and be grateful that his head had not struck any of the massive trunks on his roll down the slope. However, the path of his rolling was all too visible in raw tears in the foliage and the accumulated mulch.

He must free himself. His eyes fell on several likely rocks nearby and he dragged himself to one. Slashing the ropes binding his wrists with the sharp edge of the rock cost him more patches of skin, but the ropes parted.

Restoring circulation to wrists and returning his shoulders to their proper position hurt more than the binding had, but he had no time to suffer through it, before his fingers—clumsy and numb—picked at his ankle bindings, finally using another sharp rock to slit them apart. And then, even as he stood—tottering, kicking away the remnants of ropes from his feet—he heard noise above. Voices and steps. *Pursuit!*

He dipped one foot in the rivulet which was very cold but also seemed to ease the abrasions and cuts. The depth was only up to his knee. And since the little river could be crossed by a determined jumper, it probably wouldn't protect him from the vampires, or at least from them sending the Judas goats after him.

On the other hand, if he crossed it and ran on the other side, the marks of his passage would be less evident. Arbitrarily, he decided to go up the current. But he hadn't gone more than a few steps than he heard the sounds of feet in boots and the curious rustling of dried leaves that heralded the progress of his pursuers.

Impossible to run fast enough. And he couldn't swim in this shallow water. Nor could he hide anywhere so effectively that the vampires' enhanced senses wouldn't find him.

He stood still, as his pursuers drew nearer and nearer; rustle and click and stomp of boots, scraping down the little slope, closer and closer to him.

Angel with the Sword

Athos closed his eyes and trembled as hands ran over him. He did not wish to acknowledge the responses of his traitorous body. So he stood, very still, his eyes closed, but the trembling he could not suppress.

"Open your eyes, Raphael," Charlotte said. "Now." He opened his eyes to watch in the polished silver mirror on the wall. People surrounded him. The indistinct nature of the reflections blurred ages, genders, and clothing. The only things he could clearly see were the hands, ranging from pale to golden, navigating the length of his body in well-practiced caresses. Hands intruded beneath his hair to caress the back of his neck, lingering with curious touch on the bite mark upon it. Other hands ran down the length of his back and luxuriated upon his rounded, muscular buttocks, yet others caressed his arms, his chest, his thighs. No one touched his burning erection.

He didn't wish them to, but his body did. His body longed for touch with desperate need. And the touch it longed for was Charlotte's. He looked at her with earnest, awful pleading. She stared back, her blue eyes full of amusement. A smile curled and uncurled the corner of her perfect mouth.

Someone knelt at Athos' feet. He did not look down. The mirror showed the tousled reflection of a dark brown head. The tongue touching his ankle made him jump, but Charlotte's quickly stifled, mocking laugh made him stop, hold himself impassive. Show nothing.

Only the trembling increased, as the tongue traveled up from his ankle to linger on the crease of his knee, then up again and around his thigh. He closed his eyes. He could not help it. His mind longed not to know and his body longed to imagine it was Charlotte who touched him thus, who laved, with careful and insistent licks up to the fold of his thigh and then slowly to the center of it, where—

The hand clap made him jump and open his eyes. The people who'd surrounded him scattered like scared birds, retreating to their previous perches. He stood alone once more, naked before Charlotte. Charlotte who had demanded to see him naked and defiled.

She stood up, languid and slow, like an immutable force that disdains to stop for any man, and certainly for something as insignificant as Athos. Approaching him with slow grace, she came so close he felt surrounded by her perfume. Her eyes, fixed on his, looked huge and blue. Eyes you could drown in. Up close, she lifted her face to his, and reaching up, pulled his lips down to meet her mouth.

He attempted to embrace her, but she took her hands from his head and pulled his arms down, forcibly. And then she kissed him. It was she who kissed and he who was kissed, not daring to move, not daring to take charge, not even daring to move closer to her. He longed for her body in his arms, for the feel of her soft, rounded curves against his burning erection. But he half expected that should he hold her so close she would vanish like a burst bubble and leave him nothing at all.

She kissed him carefully and thoroughly, their lips sealed to each other's, their tongues touching. Then her tongue pushed into his mouth to draw his tongue out. A sharp lance of pain and he cried out. She'd let her fangs extend and nipped at his tongue. As her curious, cat-like tongue lapped at his wound, he could feel her smile against his lips.

He tasted his own blood upon her tongue, and then she let go of his lips and kissed his chin. She trailed a pathway of kisses down his neck where she rested on the hollow of his throat so long that he thought she meant to bite him there and inflict a wound, the twin of the one at the back of his neck.

But she moved around again, kissing the hollow line between the two halves of his muscular chest, and the faint line of hair that grew down to his navel. She sank slowly to her knees as she did so and took her time, licking and nipping, as though she needed the flavor of his skin as much as he needed hers.

Athos tried to forget they were not alone. He could hear the breathing of the others, but it didn't matter. His world had contracted to Charlotte, on her knees, kissing now around his erect penis, refusing to touch it.

And then she paused, looking up at him, a smile on her lips, her blue eyes seeming to promise him delights only imaginable to those who are transported to paradise.

"Charlotte," he said, his voice hoarse. He reached out to touch her silken hair with his sword-calloused hand.

She smiled wider, her mouth open, the fangs showing beneath her top lip. And then she struck. Quick as an adder, her head pushed forward, and her fangs bit deep into the soft flesh of his inner thigh.

He screamed. His legs buckled and would have given out entirely, except suddenly there were hands supporting him in his position. No. Holding him in his position. Imprisoning him as perfectly as the ropes that had tied him to the altar on the night of his turning.

And then the excruciating pain of her bite turned to sweet joy. He didn't care what she did so long as he could go on feeling it.

He had no strength left, no determination with which to hold closed the door to his mind against which her mind pushed, insistently. What good was a soul if he couldn't have Charlotte?

As though a crack had opened in his mind, he felt Charlotte's presence. Not her physical presence—her petite body kneeling at his feet, but something else—a force, a strength.

It was like a thundercloud gathering all around him, if a thundercloud could be female and beautiful enough to take one's breath away. "Charlotte!" he said. Knowing her overarching, over-strong presence would devour him, he cried again, his voice clouded with fear, "Charlotte!"

Miraculously, as if in response, he heard the twin cries: "To us, of the king," and "To us, musketeers!"

He recoiled away from Charlotte, without thinking, but she was holding his thighs and there were other people holding him from behind.

Booted feet ran into the room. Musketeers. Disjointedly, like events in a dream, Athos heard the clink of swords, the shouts and exclamations of men. He smelled the miasma of a dying vampire. More boots stepped into the room. The hands holding him let go.

"To me, musketeers! To me, of the king!" echoed close by and behind it, beside it, obscured by it, Aramis' voice saying in a tone of disbelief, "Athos!"

Charlotte pulled back, withdrawing her fangs and smiled at him with blood-stained lips. She curtseyed. No one seemed to even see her. Unperceived by anyone but him, she slid among the musketeers and vampires engaged in combat all around. No one but Athos saw her slip out through a door at the back. The firm closing of the door was lost in the noise in the room, the deafening clang of swords meeting, and of the screams of dying vampires.

Athos stood alone in a room filled with musketeers. Some of the vampires lay dead on the floor, pouring out their smell that still registered in Athos' senses as enticing and appetizing and made him salivate despite himself. A musketeer whom Athos could not identify fought with a vampire in one corner of the room.

Athos was naked. He didn't know where his sword had fallen.

He felt someone thrusting fabric at him, finally seeing it was Porthos and the fabric was a sumptuous velvet cloak, not his own. He took it from Porthos' hands and wrapped it around himself, awkwardly.

People spoke, but not to him, though everyone cast him wide-eyed looks. Did they know what he was? How much had they seen?

He knew that what they'd seen wouldn't give him away as a vampire. But it would make them pity him. He clenched his jaw so hard his teeth hurt.

Snatches of conversation reached him. Someone reporting killing three vampires elsewhere in the house, "one a woman." Another reported rounding up the Judas goats. Athos despised himself before he could even form the coherent thought that he hoped the vampire killed wasn't Charlotte. And then he hoped it was. He would then be free.

And Aramis was extending him his breeches and other clothes in a bundle, at arms length. As Athos looked at him with uncomprehending eyes, Aramis said, "For the Lord's sake, my friend, take your clothes and dress yourself. There's a private parlor there, and I'll stand at the door." He narrowed his eyes. "If that matters."

Athos blinked. From what felt like a turgid, freezing river of thoughts, he picked a statement. He uttered through frozen lips, "It matters."

Aramis' look at him remained puzzled, as though he were trying to understand something, but he pushed the bundle at Athos once more, and said. "Go." With his hand he pushed Athos in the general direction of an open door to Athos' left. "Go, I'll stand guard."

From the weight of the bundled clothing, his boots and sword were somewhere in it. Athos allowed himself to be pushed into the small parlor—in fact a very small room, decorated all in pink and containing a chair and a desk. A bookcase full of bound books took up a wall, floor to ceiling. The window was open here, too, and the curtain furled in on the night wind.

Athos removed the cloak and shivered in the breeze coming from the window. He unrolled his clothes, finding his boots and his sword in the midst of them.

Putting them on was harder than he thought. It wasn't so much that he didn't remember what breeches were or how one put them on, it was more that he picked them up, then tried to put them on his body, but his hands and legs did not exactly obey his thought and the fabric reversed itself in his hands.

Aramis knocked on the door, a curt, impatient knock, "Athos?" Then opened the door almost immediately. Aramis' brows knit down over his eyes, and he shook his head. He opened his mouth as if to speak, then closed it.

Stepping into the room, he locked the door behind himself and said, "You will pardon me, my friend. There is no time for this. We must get out of here and fast. That . . . Your charming hostess left before we could catch up with her, and enough died that this place will be swarming with vampire avengers soon enough. Even now the armies of the night hurry toward us. We cannot engage in meditation or mourning."

Athos wanted to explain himself but his words caught, frozen within his sluggish thoughts. "Not . . . meditation or mourning."

Aramis let out his breath as though he'd been holding it too long and now his exasperation compelled it to exit with force. Wordless, he picked up Athos' clothes and dressed him. Athos was powerless to resist. Even as Aramis finished buckling on Athos' scabbard, shouts and the sound of swords were heard.

The door was thrown open with a sudden push that caused it to rattle hard against the bookcases. Porthos took up the entire opening. "Aramis, Athos, they've arrived. What is—"

"He's not himself, Porthos," Aramis said, and to a querying look from Porthos, "I don't know why, but we can't leave through the front door. He's in no fit state."

"Then—" Porthos said.

"I know the way through the back," Aramis said. "From . . . the old days."

Porthos entered the small room, looming. Behind him pressed the ragtag band that Athos had last seen in his own house: the young boy, Planchet, their servants, and—he blinked in surprise—Madame Bonacieux dressed in the attire of a musketeer and carrying a musketeer's sword. He forbore to ask whether the lady could use it. In his experience, she was a woman of surprising talents and he'd always thought their escorting her was more a matter of ensuring she was safe, than her only protection.

They all pressed into the small room, and Aramis pushed a lever by the fireplace. A panel beside it opened into a dark tunnel, into which they all pressed, with Aramis pushing Athos ahead of himself and Athos obeying, puzzled, wondering why he could not take his own initiative or even think through the puzzles facing him.

They came out into fresh air and relative light in the older part of the city by the river, and Aramis narrowed his eyes. "My lodging is this way."

He'd been in Aramis' lodgings many times. As they arrived, he noted with surprise that the large cross presiding over the small entrance room which Aramis pompously called his scriptorium still did not cause Athos any pang and it still did not appear to him as blinding light. But he'd let Charlotte . . . and he'd been in her mind. Or she in his. He had allowed her *in*.

How was it possible, then, that he was still whole? Could it be that his soul belonged to him still?

By Water and Blood

D'Artagnan lay down on the streambed, behind an outcropping of rocks. The freezing water leached all heat from his body and he felt himself becoming, by stages, numb and cold. He could go no farther without being seen, and in his state he was not up to fighting, certainly not up to fighting a multitude of pursuers. He lay down, underwater as much as possible, allowing his face to surface for shallow breaths.

If they were to send the Judas goats over the stream to do an exhaustive search, he would surely be discovered, for he was but a little ways past where he'd first dropped, and where—he saw—the remnants of his ropes were.

He heard them approaching, two of them talking and the rest making the peculiar clicking sounds of the aged vampires. When he put his face above water to breathe, he took in the smell of old vampires with the air. Down under the water again, he could hear them talking on the riverbank, but the sound was too distorted to understand what they were saying. The water warped the sound of their footsteps as well, so he couldn't be sure in which direction they were going.

He put his head above the water, just in time to hear the vampire say, "Well, he's not on this side."

"No, M'sieur Rochefort, and as I was sayin', if I was him, I would have crossed to the other side."

A silence in which he was sure Rochefort was looking across the bank, trying to discern signs of him on the other side. "You go, Jean," he said at last. "Cross over the water to find him on the other side."

"The water is shallow, sir, could you not—"

162

There was a silence and when Rochefort replied it was in the tone of a man who didn't like admitting anything that might be to his disadvantage, "You know it's not the depth," he spoke, dryly. "It is living water. Go over to the other side and see if there are signs of the infernal Gascon."

"Monsieur, I'd be glad to, but . . ."

Rochefort clicked his tongue. "Yes, yes, your leg. What possessed you to jump out of the carriage in full career?"

"But monsieur—"

"Not that the other idiot was any better or came to a better end." In a voice full of disgust, "Humans. I'd trade them all for a passel of monkeys, if one could feed as well from monkeys as from humans." A pause. "That branch there, yes, bring it over."

There were sounds of rustling and clicking and then a branch landed, so close to D'Artagnan's head that it barely avoided hitting him. And in the next moment he had to move as the branch shook, moved, then creaked alarmingly and, with a loud crack, gave way.

D'Artagnan whipped sideways to avoid the end near his head, but didn't avoid a grazing blow to his nose. He was gently feeling this offended body part with his fingers when he heard, "Let go, let go. No, you can't save him. This scheme won't do."

A keening, somewhat like when a vampire was pierced through the heart echoed, loud and brief. D'Artagnan, daring to peek ever so slightly above the water and the rocks, saw one of the ancient ones in the current.

He was . . . dissolving, like spun sugar upon water, his legs disappearing from under him, as he fell forward, and then his face and arms dissolved, causing the scream to stop. Scraps of ancient fabric and a yellowish foam drifted past D'Artagnan.

On the bank, two men or rather a man and a vampire—the well-dressed, dark-haired, powerfully built one was likely Rochefort; the other—a simply dressed, slight man leaning on a crutch—looked on with wide eyes and a shocked expression.

Rochefort's face changed to a look of distaste. He brushed what must be imaginary drops of water from his clothes, and made a face. "That will not do," he said. "That was the sturdiest branch. We will go farther down the river to where there is a bridge."

D'Artagnan waited, not sure the words were true or had merely been pronounced for his benefit. But man and vampire walked on and, little by little, the band of ragged, bony wraiths of ancient vampires moved down the river.

When their voices had vanished from his hearing, he considered. It could be they'd made sure he heard their conversation and that it was just a ruse.

On the other hand . . .

On the other hand, he could not stay in the water much longer. Even now, his body was so numb from the cold, he felt as though he might be dead.

He moved a little. At first he crawled, on hands and knees, away from the voices, feeling the silt and sand on the streambed and little darting touches he believed were fish. He crawled past a bend in the rivulet, shaded by tall trees. And then he stood and ran. He ran headlong down the stream.

His legs hurt, his lacerated feet stung, and he was quite sure he was on the verge of collapsing from hunger and tiredness and cold, but he ignored all the many pains and complaints of his flesh to run. To run till he could run no more, and then he left the river bed and crept on aching feet down a rocky scarp back on the same side where he'd left, because the one thing of which he was sure was that the vampires and their minion meant to search for him on the opposite side. He crept up and up and up slowly, expecting to find the road the carriage had traveled, but road and river must diverge, because he found himself, instead, on a narrow beaten dirt path. To take it might make a convenient route for those coming after him to follow. But not to take it would leave behind a trail of broken leaves and trampled grass that his pursuers could easily follow.

Listening for talk or footsteps, he walked as fast as he could along the path.

Casting Lots

Aramis' lodgings were not as large as Athos'. Just three rooms, all of them well furnished in a way belying Aramis' vocation.

The grandiosely named scriptorium to which they were admitted had a vast desk, several elaborately carved wooden chairs and, behind the desk, hanging from the wall, a dubious reminder of the occupant's call to the priesthood—a painted Madonna smiling down in blessing upon those assembled. But since that Madonna was a comely and ripe young woman with golden hair, large blue eyes, luscious lips, and a bared breast she offered to the fat and happy baby on her knee, it took more than the halos painted around both heads to convince the onlooker of the worshipful intent of the image. The two crucifixes, one on each side wall, were elaborately wrought, their golden embellishments shining by the light of the single candle burning at the foot of the Madonna.

Athos had seen the other rooms. They would have surprised any casual visitor with their spare monk-like sobriety—perhaps not surprising in Bazin's case, but almost shocking in Aramis'. He wondered how many of the visitors would believe the exquisitely groomed, exceedingly well-bred musketeer—for all his claims of a vocation to the priesthood, interrupted only by the arrival of vampires—slept on a bed that was little more than a blanket over a hard board. Or that his room contained only that, and a vast and oppressively plain wooden cross upon the wall. Or that the space on the wooden floor in front of the cross had been polished by the long wear of two knees, those two knees belonging to Aramis? He would almost swear none would believe that beneath the musketeer's exquisite tunics, carefully ornamented doublets—belied by the smile that played, fugitive, on the musketeer's face—hid a hair shirt, turned inward and tightened to produce near-unbearable discomfort.

Athos himself had not believed it when he'd first seen it while assisting Aramis, wounded after a fight with vampires. And only his enhanced senses, which now allowed him to smell the blood raised by the punishing garment, convinced him Aramis was still wearing it. It was not the smell that suggested he was wounded, just a hint of living blood at the surface of the skin.

You wouldn't know it from the way Aramis pushed Athos into a chair, invited Madame Bonacieux and Porthos to sit. Nor from the smile on his face as he whispered something to Bazin, who vanished into the tiny kitchen behind the bedrooms. The other servants and Planchet went with him, leaving the three men and the priestess of nature alone in the scriptorium.

Athos held his hands on his knees, feeling their solidity with something akin to surprise.

"Athos," Porthos said. "What can you mean by—"

But Aramis held up a hand. He stepped very close to Athos. So close that the smell of the blood beneath the laceration of his hair shirt was torment. "Athos," he said, "tell me only one thing. Do the crosses on the wall bother you?"

Athos looked up, first at one crucifix and then at the other. He shook his head, because his throat felt too dry to speak. He thought distantly that Charlotte had drunk her fill and that he must be nearly drained again. Not that his strength had ever been that which a common vampire should have. And here he stopped, pondering *common vampire* and would have laughed could he have remembered how.

Aramis' gaze was still upon him. Athos thought he'd marked how Athos stared at each of the crosses in turn. Aramis let out a long, drawn out breath, almost like a sigh. "I was afraid . . ." he said. "I feared . . ."

Athos nodded. "I drank," he said, his voice coming out harsh and raspy. And to the look of alarm in Aramis' eyes. "Armagnac. Not . . ." He shrugged. "I drank because I feared meeting her without doing so. And then . . . " He opened his hands as if to explain that the madness of the night had not been his fault, and those whose fault it had been he would have been unable to explain if pressed.

Aramis did not press. Instead, he got up and went through the back door into the depths of his lodgings. And if I'm really lucky Athos thought, savagely, he will return with a stake and end forever my miserable existence.

But Aramis came back with a bowl of something foul smelling resting on a cracked saucer. He handed bowl and saucer to Athos and said, "Drink. It is warm but not hot, and I believe you need warmth right now. Not that I understand precisely how this operates in vamp— in someone like you, but I think you are in shock, and I suspect why. But I need you to speak, and you cannot speak till you've recovered. Drink. Bazin has made more."

Not sure whether he should be grateful for Aramis' attention or mortified at having to drink more of the foul-tasting liquid, Athos forced himself to drink.

The horrible taste woke him, and the feeling of liquid flowing into him helped. He drank a cup, and then another. Porthos and Madame sat in silence. Porthos looked embarrassed and Madame mulish. Athos wondered what each of them had seen and how they felt about what they'd seen.

He himself was not sure how he felt about what he'd seen, much less what he'd done. Another bowl of broth was pushed on him. He drank obediently, wondering if the broth would serve as expiation for his sins, and then reminding himself that vampires were already outside forgiveness . . . but remembering Aramis had said perhaps not.

And then, halfway through his fifth cup, he drew his breath and it turned into a sob. Aramis fetched the chair that stood behind his desk, and moved it in front of Athos. He folded his hands upon his lap and leaned forward. "You drank to have the courage to see her, but Athos, why must you see her at all?"

"I thought," Athos said. "That she would tell me where D'Artagnan was."

"And did she?"

Athos shook his head. "She told me that I must pay forfeit."

Aramis clucked his tongue on the roof of his mouth, the sound echoing too loudly in Athos' ears. "Fool. If the boy hadn't told us you'd gone out and if we hadn't followed you close enough, we'd never have known where you'd gone or what had happened. As it was, we stumbled upon you coming out of the tavern, and from there we followed. It was a matter of minutes to gather enough musketeers to rescue you."

"Minutes," Athos echoed. "How many?"

"Fifteen," Madame Bonacieux said dryly. "Did you think you'd survive her glamour longer?"

"Glamour?" Athos turned his puzzled gaze to the lady.

She made a sound that indicated derision and opened her mouth, but before she could speak, Aramis did. "You were under her glamour, Athos. You've felt this before and withstood it, from the vampires we duel."

Athos sighed. He could see he would have to explain, lest Aramis wonder what had possessed him, more or less literally. "It is not the same," he said, softly. "None of those other vampires were my wife."

"Your wife?" Aramis said, at the same time Porthos said, triumphantly, "I told you."

"Please be still, Porthos. You told me Athos had married a vampire, which is neither sanctioned nor plausible."

"Plausible or not," Athos said. "It is nonetheless true."

"You married a vampire?" Aramis said, at the same time Porthos said, "I meant he is married to a vampire. His wife was changed."

Athos made a gesture with his hand, meant to convey denial. "No. My wife was a vampire when she married me. She says so at any rate." He frowned. "And I believe she is telling the truth. She . . . I didn't know she was a vampire. She looked like . . . she pretended to be the sister of our priest. Three months into our marriage, we went for a ride and she . . . she's a splendid rider . . . she rode ahead of me, until she ran into the branch of a tree, which rendered her unconscious. I rushed to aid her and when I cut her dress, to help her breathe, I saw the branded mark of the fleur-de-lis upon her shoulder. Faded, mind you, and covered in cosmetic, so I'd never perceived it by candlelight. But in the light of the morning sun it was unmistakable."

"A hidden Judas goat!" Porthos said.

"Very acute, dear Porthos," Athos said, regretting his voice came out hollow and bitter. "Indeed, a hidden Judas goat. In that moment, filled with revulsion at what I loved so well, I performed what the law would have executed upon her for hiding what she was. Because she was a Judas goat and she had not informed me of this, and was, therefore, a branded criminal—possibly planning against the unturned, certainly breaking the king's law—I hanged her from a nearby tree."

He saw the flinch in Madame Bonacieux' features, and Porthos said, "But—"

"But there might have been a mistake?" Athos said. "At the moment I did not even consider it. I felt . . . betrayed." He looked at Aramis. "I believe I don't need to confess to the sin of pride. The vampires had been besieging my domains for a decade, slowly cutting down those on whose labor our prosperity depended. And now, I thought, a Judas goat had insinuated herself into my house." He looked up, but met no condemnation in Aramis' dark eyes. "The doubts came later, in the days, in the weeks that followed. The doubts sent me running from my house, unable to bear the memories of our days together in my beloved home. I told people I felt called to fight the vampires, but it was no such thing. I needed to fight the vampires, to kill . . . to kill my own damned pride most of all."

"These doubts are foolish," Aramis said. "Were there a mistake or a doubt, she would have told you before you discovered it. She would have let you judge of the justness of it. That she hid it and lied to you . . ."

Athos inclined his head. He did not want to think either of his rashness in killing—as he thought—the woman he loved, or of the doubts and guilt that had pursued him for years over her—she who had turned out, after all, to be a vampire. "She told me she'd been a vampire all along. When I was turned. She was the one who turned me." His hand went up to his neck to touch the first bite mark she'd given him, which hurt still like a fresh firebrand.

"But you said you were riding," Porthos said. "In the sunshine I mean."

"Yes," Athos said, then understood what he had said and how odd it seemed. "But . . ." He shook his head. "She was in the sunlight, and yet she tells me she was a vampire then."

"Are you sure she *is* a vampire?" Porthos asked. "What I mean is—"

"She turned me."

"She had him under glamour tonight," Madame Bonacieux said, her voice crisp. "But the question is, was she a vampire then?"

Athos turned to her. His vision blurred. He saw her shape but not the details and not her expression. He spoke to her shape, "I hung her from a branch. She didn't struggle, because she was unconscious. But I waited . . ." He shook his head. Though he couldn't see whether she showed disbelief, he spoke as if she did. "I beg you to believe I'm remembering correctly. The scene has haunted my nightmares for years. She could not have survived it unless. . . ."

"Yes," Aramis said, sounding cool and collected and calling Athos' gaze to his imperturbable countenance. "There is no doubt at all she is a vampire. And there is no doubt, I presume, she can withstand the sunlight. It is unheard of, and it must be explained, but it is not in doubt. Athos . . . Did she ever tell you where they took D'Artagnan?"

Athos shook his head. "No, she never—"

He stopped, because before he could say there was never time or opportunity, he recognized he knew—knew with certainty as though she'd told him—D'Artagnan was alive and where they were taking him, had an inkling of why they'd captured the young Gascon and perhaps even a hint of why his wife could walk in the sunlight of the living when even Athos, not a full vampire by a vampire's own account, could not.

"She didn't tell me," he said, softly. "But I know."

Remnants

D'Artagnan didn't know how long he struggled, his feet weary and sore and bleeding. He walked in the dark night with no way of measuring time or judging how close dawn might be. It seemed like an eternity of walking, measured on his torn feet, on his aching legs.

At first he thought only of going away, of getting away from the road and those searching for him. It was some time before his mind noted the disarray of the desolate fields, and that there were no signs of life anywhere. No farmer tilled these fields. No livestock huddled in the early spring morning chill, not even an old woman collected wood.

Which brought him to other less happy thoughts. What had happened to those peasants? There had been vampires on the road. Local vampires. Rough peasants, who didn't recognize the rule of the cardinal.

He imagined peasants, crowded into their hovels through daylight and hunting at night, draining any man and livestock within reach. *They want us and the horses,* echoed in his mind with an ominous tone and he shivered. Every shadow and every bush seemed to him a menace and he walked warily.

Most warily of all, he approached a largish house set in the middle of a cottage garden gone to rambling wildness. Though it was early spring, and the winter had killed most of the plant growth except for the pine trees, it was easy to see where the beans had grown to encompass most of the yard, in what was now a mass of dried leaves.

The house seemed to be long-abandoned and, looking closer, D'Artagnan felt it must be. The chicken coop in the back was quite deserted, the door open. There were no pigs in the sty. From the house

171

itself there came no smell of cooking or of fire and no sound of living. Which didn't mean—D'Artagnan thought, even as he eyed the pink tendrils of sunrise starting to color the ink-blue sky in the east—that the house was deserted. Vampires didn't cook or, that he knew, didn't keep fires burning. They gathered in the dark and ambushed humans, and needed neither market gardens nor chickens and pigs.

Yet he had to brave the quiet interior of the cottage. He had to look for water and, if possible, for any stores of food the home might still hold. For a while, he had been aware of his hunger and thirst; now his throat felt parched and his tongue as though it were glued to the roof of his mouth.

He entered the house cautiously. Spider webs gave way as his face or fingers brushed against them. Rather than being annoying, these encounters were reassuring. No matter if vampires had no need of pigs or chickens, or other food, they would need to move now and then and they would, perforce, break the webs with their movement.

Feeling a little bolder, he walked in, the webs like ghostly fingers on his face. The bottom floor consisted of a kitchen and a large room that had probably been parlor, hall, and gathering place. Judging by the state of the fireplace, the last ashes wet and dried again and then wet again. No fires had been kindled in a year, maybe more.

Up the uncertain staircase, parts of the steps eaten out by mold and mildew. Up all the way to a half upper floor where a partition divided two rough chambers, both of them with rotting straw mattresses. He felt wholly reassured when he saw there were no clothes anywhere and no sign of human bones. He released his breath in a great sigh of relief. He would picture the family here as having gotten away from of the vampires in the countryside. And perhaps it was so, or perhaps they'd been turned. Or perhaps they'd been caught in their flight. But in D'Artagnan's imagination he would have them escape and be living somewhere away from danger and vampires, in some well-secured village in the countryside where the bloodsuckers had not managed to penetrate.

He descended the staircase again, carefully. The treads gave out under his feet twice, and he stepped away just in time. But the floor at the bottom was steady.

D'Artagnan needed food. He went back to the shuttered kitchen. The sky was now frankly pink and fingers of light crawled in through the open windows, seeming solid as they fell on spirals of dust raised by his passage. It was a simple kitchen, and not far different from his mother's own kitchen in Gascony. Noblewoman she might have been, but the lady of a domain so small it could have fit in the Cimetière des Innocents in Paris, and barely wealthy enough to compete with the better-off farmers. The most fortunate farmers in Gascony were no better than the poorest farmers elsewhere in the country. At least until the fields stopped growing rocks, which heaven knew the good Lord owed Gascons for the help they'd lent France in all its wars, and for saving France from itself over and over again.

He remembered his father, after a session of sword practice, telling him that the vampires would be around until God sent the Gascons to defeat them.

As it dawned on D'Artagnan that he had been smiling at the reminiscences of home, the smile vanished from his face. He looked around the kitchen again. There was a cupboard built atop a storage container. That would be flour for the daily baking, he thought. He didn't want to guess how spoiled the flour would be. Judging by the mattresses upstairs, it would be rotted. But opening the bin disclosed there was no flour, save for a dusting of something at the bottom that might well be sawdust. Of course, the grain supply had failed long ago in villages that had not kept the vampires out. Sowing and harvesting required many men and long hours of work together. Hard to do after your neighbors became vampires.

He felt suddenly very tired, or rather he felt as if the tiredness he'd been keeping at bay had dropped on him like a heavy blanket. He almost swayed under the weight of it, but he felt hunger warring for his attention and forced himself to totter to the other corner, where a wooden trunk stood. He didn't have any great expectations. In most households, such trunks contained a quantity of salt preserving some pork. The salt, by now, had gotten damp and the pork would be spoiled.

But when he opened the box, he was greeted with the smell of apples. There were perhaps a dozen, wrinkled and shrunken, dried within their skins, but their heady fragrance giving witness to their unspoiled nature. Next to them, wrapped in a slightly dusty linen towel, which hid another, cleaner linen towel, was an unopened wheel of cheese.

D'Artagnan found an overturned table in a corner of the kitchen where, fortunately, the roof overhead seemed to be sound. No rain had rotted the wooden table. He set it on its legs and wiped frantically at the dusty top with his sleeve. He found a stool nearby which, though it shook when D'Artagnan set upon it, neither cracked nor gave the impression it would give out under him.

A quick search of the shelves in the corner brought to light a set of ceramic cups, from which he chose the one that looked least encrusted with dust. To eat the cheese he needed water. And he meant to eat the cheese. He limped out the back door, holding his cup.

The hoped-for well was to the left of the kitchen door, its mouth bordered by stones that had miraculously not fallen. It was capped too, with a still-intact oak cover. Even more surprising, the rope on the pulley above—though black with age—proved sturdy to his pull. Once the cover was removed and D'Artagnan pulled the rope up, the bucket that had been suspended halfway between the top of the well and the water proved reasonably clean and sound, the wood dry and only a little dusty.

Like a man possessed, D'Artagnan worked the pulley getting the bucket down, then up again, the weight of water pulling at his arm muscles and making him feel every sore place and every injury. Up and up and up until he held a bucket of cool, clear water. He'd have drunk it, he thought, even if it had come up green and slimy and bearing a croaking frog.

He used the first bucket to wash himself and his cup, then filled the cup from it, and tottered back into the kitchen.

By the time he'd eaten two apples and managed to find the stump of a knife with which to cut a few slices of cheese, the sun was full up, warm on his back as he ate. Birds sang outside and the air brought a heady scent which he thought were roses but must have been some other flower. It was too early for roses.

The vampires wouldn't come searching him in full daylight, he thought. He could get a good long distance from them.

But he wondered how far he was from Paris? How long had the carriage rumbled along the road, before he had woken. How long

174

would it take him to get to Paris and to a place where he could claim the protection of the musketeers, the protection of his friends?

On his way to Paris he'd ridden his horse and stopped only at hostelries surrounded by healthy fields, heralding an area not blighted by too many vampires. Could he find one of those on foot and tired? Could he find them before night and vampires overtook him?

There would be no denying he was tired. Tired enough to drop where he stood, he thought. How would he fight against vampires— either the ones from which he escaped or wild ones who had once been peasants and who might now overtake him?

Blinking in the light of day, the languor resulting from a full stomach overtook him. His feet hurt, sore and cut from his escape. His legs ached with fatigue. His shoulders and neck remained painful from being bound in an unnatural position. He had to rest.

Much as he longed to go up the stairs and look for a still-whole blanket he could stretch on the dusty floor, he dared not. If he lay down horizontally, he'd almost surely sleep too long.

But here, on this awkward kitchen stool, leaning on a rickety kitchen table, he'd rest his eyes only a few minutes. And then he'd make a bundle of some of the cheese and apples and walk in search of anyone who could tell him where he was and where the nearest safe village was.

He was asleep before his head touched his folded arms.

Duties and Delusions

"What do you mean she didn't tell you but you know?" Porthos asked.

Athos knew Porthos would have used more forceful words were it not for the presence of the lady. He struggled for the right words to explain. "You see, when she came to me in my bedroom before—"

A gasp from Aramis and Athos amended, "Though that was just an illusion, you understand, but I thought it was . . ." He paused and took a deep breath. "No. What you said, before, Aramis, about the ways one can . . . one can lose one's soul. You alluded to it without . . . without elaborating." Without, in fact, naming it. "One of those ways is the pleasure of . . . of carnal congress."

Athos looked up. His cheeks would be flaming if they could. As it was, he felt a little heat on them; he must have got enough liquid into his body—even if not blood—for it to react. But Aramis was not blushing, just surprised, his eyes open very wide. Athos met his gaze and nodded once. "I don't think you understood the nature of this temptation. You see, it is not carnal congress as such but that vampires use . . . the moment of . . . of surrender, being immersed in pleasure and . . . and all the emotions that surround it, to touch your mind, to . . . to commune in mind as well as in body."

Aramis nodded in turn. "I've suspected something like that. Did she—?"

"I believe so, though not . . . not fully. She had just . . ." He made an inarticulate sound of frustration at the inadequacy of words to cover events so primal and so devoid of words. "Imagine your mind as a walled garden, with a gate through which one must step to enter the garden. I'd allowed her to slip her hand in and lift the

176

latch on the gate, but the gate was only opened a bit." He frowned. "It was enough. Maybe too much. I could feel . . . I could feel her presence, her . . . essence. I think it happens gradually, over time. You surrender to another vampire over and over and, in the throes of repeated pleasure, each time they enter further into your mind, they conquer it, they merge their minds with it, till eventually you are one with them and with all other vampires, and everything they see you see, everything they do, you know. Even when you're physically apart." He paused, trying to force feelings into words. "I don't know if it would take that long with her. I know only that as her mind touched mine my . . . she was . . ." A deep breath and he again tried to bring order to thoughts that insisted on running in all directions at once like unbroken horses. "I believe she's very old. Very, very old. I had the feeling of the passage of time, unmeasured, endless. Time . . . Time before Rome and Greece. Time before we have names for the civilizations or the languages."

"She's not one of the ancient ones!" Aramis said. "She cannot be. We have determined all those old ones, beneath their grave dirt and filth, are two thousand or so years old, no more. Nor does she look like that."

"Unless she's using her powers of illusion," the lady said.

Athos shuddered and felt his throat constrict at the thought of having taken one of the ancient vamps to his bed, of having wedded one under the appearance of—

"Impossible," Aramis said. "The old ones simply can't. They don't have . . . their minds are devoured by the collective mind till they are no more than walking corpses controlled by the collective mind, so that one of them, or even the collective mind in them could no more produce an illusion than—"

"It was not," Athos said, "the collective mind. It was her own. By which I mean, it was a . . . an individual mind I touched and one that . . . she had the . . . it felt like her mind, from what I know of her." He closed his eyes, avoiding looking at Aramis, afraid of what his friend's expression might show. He knew the feel of her well enough, the beauty and the allure overlaying something else. Something as cold and cruel as the edge of a blade. "But that's not the important part," he said with an effort.

"I'd say the existence of a creature who is one of the old ones, but who looks like she does and who can walk in the light and the sun is important!" Porthos said impatiently.

Athos opened his eyes and directed what he hoped was a quelling glare at Porthos. "Yes, my friend, but that is not the point. The point of this conversation, and what I meant to convey to you, is that they're taking the boy, the Gascon, back to Gascony as fast as they can possibly travel. There was . . ." He rushed to speak further as he saw them staring uncomprehendingly at him. "There was the suggestion of haste, the feeling that they were using relays of vampires and Judas goats driving the carriage day and night and that it was of the utmost, frantic urgency to get D'Artagnan back to his ancestral domain."

Porthos ran his hand over his forehead and eyes and said, "But in the Lord's name, why?"

Aramis asked, "Well, that absolves us of responsibility, does it not? What business is it of ours what happens in Gascony? At a guess, it is the result of some feud or event in his land, surrounding his domain. Nothing to do with us."

Protest rose in Athos, but he didn't know why nor how to express it. He had no time for it, anyway. The lady rose, looking, if possible, more curvaceous in her borrowed musketeer's attire than in her feminine clothes—which Athos would guess were somewhere in the depths of the river. She took three paces to the heavily curtained window, then back again, her brow furrowed, her eyes narrow. "Father D'Herblay," she said, turning to Aramis, and in the safe secrecy of this room, using his proper title.

Aramis and a dozen others, judged strong enough by the leadership of the church that swore allegiance to the pope and not the cardinal, had been given the opportunity to take orders in a secret ceremony before the seminary was dissolved. Then they'd been sent into the world, in the expectation none of them would survive very long but that, while they lived, they might be able to stem the tide of evil. They could bless salt and water, they could baptize, they could give sacraments.

With their brief light, they could not stop the vampires, but they could delay them and pray for a greater power to stop them. Aramis had once told him that of the initial dozen only two remained.

They must keep their ordination secret, lest vampires target them particularly. To that end, they had been granted dispensation from the vows of chastity, so that they might not be conspicuous in a society determined to enjoy itself as much as possible while the world burned around it. Aramis had been careful to earn quite the worldly reputation at court. But he was a priest, nonetheless, and the serious look he gave Madame Bonacieux acknowledged the full gravity and danger of his calling.

She, in turn, clenched her fists, and let words pour from her lips like stones tumbling in a landslide. "What a vile, base denial," she said. "Is that not how your holy founder denied his divine master? *I don't know him?*"

Aramis frowned in annoyance, his lips thinning, "Madame!" he said. "There is no call to mention Saint Peter, no need to refer to the Savior. I do not know this Gascon boy. None of us do. He has been a cipher, an interloper, from the moment he followed us from Monsieur de Tréville's office until now. I've seen no signs that he's not a spy for the vampires, a more advanced form of Judas goat." He stood, clearly bothered by having to look up at her while she glared down at him. Standing, he overtopped her by a head and could scowl down at her and look superior and disdainful. "Look at what happened while the boy and I were escorting you to the palace. Have we ever before met with such a reverse? How did the vampires know to wait for us under that bridge?"

Madame made a sound in her throat, that was part laughter and part disdain. "Oh that is rich, D'Herblay! Rich indeed. Are you suggesting *he* chose the route?"

"Not chose it but—"

"He did not even know it, D'Herblay, don't play the fool." She shook her head. "You don't know the boy, you say, but I do. He is a brave and gallant man—not a boy except in age. He was foolish enough to follow your instructions in getting me off the bridge, but equally brave and gallant in convincing me to run away while sacrificing himself." She looked up at him in appeal. "How can you say he's not our responsibility and we have nothing to do in this situation."

"Very easily, madame," he said, looking down at her with—Athos thought—his coldest and most aristocratic bearing. He often used the same demeanor to prevent Porthos questioning him about something. His attempts to do the same to Athos had always failed. It was, Athos knew, not what Aramis did when he was sure of himself and certain of his position. It was what he did when he did not wish his decisions probed or thoughts plumbed. "Clearly if they're taking him back to Gascony, the reason for his capture concerns whatever happened in Gascony before he came to Paris. If it involved us, then they would have killed him or turned him on the spot. If they are taking him south, it is a matter having to do only with him."

She set her hands on her hips, looking younger and also more down to earth, her court-manner stripped away by anger. "Rubbish. Whether he was sought for himself or his association with us matters not. He was captured because he wouldn't let them capture me. He's gallant and pure of heart and—"

"And you hope he would materially help you with those rituals to which, you told me earlier, your husband was unable to lend assistance?"

Her hand flashed through the air, white and purposeful. The impact of her hand against his cheek was so stunning it seemed like a clap of thunder. Only the mark of her fingers, red against Aramis' skin, gave witness to her fury.

She stared at him, mouth agape, as though surprised at her own action. She curtseyed, incongruously, in her borrowed breeches. "I beg your pardon, monsieur, that was intemperate of me."

He raised his hand to his offended cheek. "I thought intemperate was characteristic of your religion, it being all about nature and doing what you wish while dressed in the cloak of faith."

She clenched her fists. Her small white teeth bit at her lower lip. "Well, at the very least," she said, "we are not pious fops who go about doing what we wish and claiming we do it only to disguise our vocation from the vampires."

He opened his mouth but before he could speak Porthos was between them, a hand raised in front of each combatant. "Let us not re-enact, in Aramis' scriptorium, the wars of religion," he said. "It is not which of our faiths is better, nor what we believe. We long ago established, did we not, that whatever works against the vampires is of God and needs no other justification and no other excuse?" He looked from one to the other. "I thought we were allies in the war against the greater evil."

Both parties muttered something that might be assent—the lady blushing pink, Aramis paling white—but Porthos shook his head. "The matter is not which of you is right about any of this, but only if we should go after the boy and rescue him. And, if we choose to intervene, then what course we should take. This has nothing," the usually inarticulate giant added, "to do with whether we are responsible for his predicament or not. Good God above, sir and madame, we do not go into battle against the vampires because we are responsible for their being here, or for their depredations against our fellow men. How could we be? If we rescue the boy it will not be because we owe it to him, having gotten him in trouble, but because he's a fellow human whose life is at risk. Did we owe it to the boy Planchet to save him? No. Yet we rushed in imperiling our lives." His eyes slid over Aramis and to where Athos still sat in his chair. "What say you, Athos?"

"I—" He took a deep breath. "I think we should rescue him. I felt the urgency of his position. Enough to want to find him and prevent his . . . suffering my fate. But it is now almost morning." Seeing Porthos glance toward the curtained window, he added, "I can feel the approaching daylight, the . . . pressure of it. I can do nothing until night. Even if I manage to stay awake, not all the will in the world will save me from burning in the sunshine. Whatever my . . . whatever Milady does to avoid it, it is a secret not known to me. Nor do I have the fortitude of vampires, or even—right now—of men. I must rest."

"Well, then," Porthos said. He shook his head and looked at Aramis, appealingly. "Aramis, it is clear that Athos wishes us to rescue the boy that he thinks we . . ."

Aramis glared at Porthos, "And I think it is foolishness and a great deal of stupidity which I would not expect even from you, my friend. Would you have us traipse all over the countryside leaving the performance of our true duties unattended? The chances of our being able to survive the journey are slim enough, even if it's just the two of us. But by our departure, we leave our duty at the palace unfulfilled. Already Athos, being wounded and out of the rotation, has left one opening in the musketeers. Add to that my rotation in the special guardianship of the queen being left untenanted. And pray, consider Madame Bonacieux will have to make her way to and from the palace by herself."

"No. Madame Bonacieux will not," she said firmly. "Because Madame Bonacieux does not need the escort of all of you gallant chevaliers." She favored them with a withering glare. "Nor your moral guidance to do what must be done. Madame Bonacieux knows her own ethics require her to rescue those in need and help the helpless. She will be making her way to Gascony as soon as she can inform her colleagues amid the guardians that her place by the queen must be filled, and she can procure transportation." She curtseyed again and turned her back on them.

"Madame!" Aramis said, and Porthos, "You can not mean it."

She turned before opening the door. "Oh, I assure you I very well can. I shall see you when I return, messieurs. Or not at all."

Opening the door only a crack, she slid out. Her exit admitted the faintest of rosy sunlight into the room—enough to make Athos feel uncomfortable, but not enough to hurt him.

She slammed the door behind her. Aramis said, heatedly, "Of all the exasperating, annoying females."

Athos could only think that in this situation, as in most others, his new condition made him less than human. Unable to follow Madame Bonacieux to the street and get a horse immediately, or trace the young Gascon to his homeland, to rescue him from whatever foul ensnaring plot awaited him there.

Let Us Not Fall

D'Artagnan woke up. The kitchen was suffused with pale light and, for a breath, he thought he must have slept no more than minutes. But standing, his legs cramped, dispelling this notion. He could see out the kitchen window the sun setting in a glory of gold and red in the west. The sun.

He reeled, partly from his cramping muscles and partly from surprise, and held onto the table. He must be on his way. He must. Or would it be safer to hide here, to sleep, to wait the morning's return and with it the safety of daylight that would keep his pursuers at bay?

It was a difficult decision. His pursuers might track him here—though he'd been careful to obscure his path and leave no traces—or they might not. It was less likely he would stumble on local vampires if he stayed hidden in the farmhouse. Clearly the house had been empty for months, possibly for years. It would not be searched by vampires now.

He stood straight again and stretched. He would get another bucket of water, and clean himself, then find a blanket and lay down on the floor, after eating another apple or two and a bit of cheese. This would allow him to be well and truly rested by morning.

But he'd taken no more than two steps into the darkened area before the doorway, when a hand shot out and closed on his arm.

D'Artagnan screamed, his free hand lashing out, his whole body attempting to twist away from the grasp of his captor. But another hand closed on his arm with crushing force, holding him immobile.

Peering into the gloom, he saw Rochefort, wearing a full cloak, his dark face peering from the folds of its hood. He saw now what he hadn't distinguished in the gloom of night: the gentleman had only one eye, the other was covered by an eye patch. And with that, together with the name, he remembered vague references heard among the musketeers in the antechamber to Monsieur de Tréville's chambers. Was it only two days ago? This must be Rochefort, the right-hand vampire to the cardinal, who was said to be the power behind the power behind the throne.

D'Artagnan had heard he was a dangerous creature, and those given a choice would rather tangle with the cardinal himself than with Rochefort.

D'Artagnan tried to twist out of Rochefort's grasp. To bite the hands holding him. In vain. He fixed his bare feet on the dusty floor and tried to pull his arms away, but it was to no avail. Whatever Rochefort was, he had a grip of iron. Besides, a pack of ancient vampires was emerging from the dark, clicking and rustling, their odor enough to gag D'Artagnan and to stop all thought. His captors held him firm, pulled his arms behind him and tied him with what seemed an excess of rope.

He noted, as though in a dazed dream, that the ancient vampires were also cloaked and cowled. They grabbed him with many hands, carrying him with little effort and throwing him into the carriage. This time they threw him on one of the seats. Rochefort sat beside him. D'Artagnan's brief glimpse of the carriage revealed no more than a pitch-black lacquered frame and door, with the coat of arms of the cardinal emblazoned on the door. A mangled-looking Judas goat sat on the driver's seat.

An opposite door opened and the ancient ones gathered inside the carriage, one sitting on the other side of D'Artagnan, the others filling the seat opposite, with the rest piling onto the floor, in what appeared to D'Artagnan to be unnatural positions.

"I see I underestimated you," Rochefort said. "I shouldn't have. You are a dangerous man, my little Gascon. I should have suspected it. After all, I knew your father."

D'Artagnan's body, tightly bound, went rigid. "Did you? Then you know you should not speak to me of him. Not further."

A booming laugh answered him. "Ah. Yes. The hot D'Artagnan blood. Your father was just as intemperate. A damn fine dueler though. They should never have turned him against his will. I could have told them it would not work. If they had asked me . . ."

D'Artagnan chose not to take Rochefort's bait. He would be thrice damned if he discussed his murdered father with this thing, or let the creature catch even a hint of D'Artagnan's heartbreaking grief. It was clear Rochefort was hinting at knowing who had turned D'Artagnan's father. D'Artagnan ignored the vampire and stared straight ahead. If Rochefort wished to tell him who had turned D'Artagnan's father, he would do so. If he didn't wish to tell him, D'Artagnan would not demean himself with asking.

They rode for a moment in silence. After a while Rochefort said, "It was very sudden, wasn't it? Unexpected. I understand you were not home."

D'Artagnan turned his head to glare at him.

Rochefort let out a curt laugh. "I knew your father when we served together in the musketeers, boy," he said, and, his voice going distant and soft and far away, "At the dawn of the world, when we were young."

D'Artagnan could not hide his surprise, which in turn brought another laugh from Rochefort, more genuine this time. "You think that all of us are born vampires or even choose our side willingly? Look at your friend, the Comte de la Fère."

D'Artagnan had surmised that Athos was a count. Hearing the title did not surprise him enough to wring expression or words from him. There was only the sound of horses at full gallop. Rochefort looked at the heavily curtained window, swaying and rocking in the speeding carriage. The curtains didn't spring open because they were pinned at the sides, and also pinned together in the center. D'Artagnan wondered if he could distract Rochefort long enough to somehow tumble against the windows and pull the curtains open.

"Your father should have told you," Rochefort said. "He should have told you about your line and your house and what was so important about it." He raised an eyebrow at D'Artagnan, "I suppose he didn't."

If he wanted D'Artagnan to tell him what there was to tell, he would be disappointed. Not reacting also seemed to keep the vampire talking.

"What I don't understand," Rochefort said, "is why they felt they had to die."

This brought an answer from D'Artagnan, "Perhaps," he said, "they had no taste for damnation?"

Rochefort shrugged. "If you believe in all that," he said. "I suppose it matters."

"I suppose you don't?"

Another shrug. "Even if I believed, there are ways to avoid damnation. Blood willingly given from a victim does not harm the state of your soul, provided you do not drain them. I expect your father had enough retainers, friends and acquaintances willing to feed him and the lady your mother."

D'Artagnan felt sick.

"I imagine if you were turned you wouldn't feel the same, my boy," he said. "It's easy to be a vampire. Very easy. The pains of mortality are gone, you need not sleep as much, and wounds heal quickly." He touched the patch over his eye, reflexively. "Feeding . . . feeding is a glorious mix of food and passion . . . and you are feared by mere mortals. You're harder to kill and you can live forever."

D'Artagnan looked at the wraiths that filled the carriage. Rochefort called this living? He turned his head and with great accuracy spit in Rochefort's face.

He expected the man to backhand him, or at least to swat him and send him flying across the carriage. Instead Rochefort laughed. With a lacy handkerchief, pulled from his pocket, he wiped at his face and looked at D'Artagnan intently with his one good eye. "You are foolish beyond measure, my boy. You have immortality offered to you on a plate and you refuse it with contempt."

"Perhaps," D'Artagnan said, speaking through clenched teeth. "But if I remember correctly, the last people who accepted the offer to become like onto the gods, knowing good from evil . . . well, it did not end well for them."

A surprised look, and then Rochefort laughed again. "Indeed. The legends of mankind never cease to astonish me."

"Where are you taking me?"

"To your father's house, my boy. For your inheritance."

And though D'Artagnan did not know what Rochefort meant, one thing he knew for sure: soon either he or Rochefort would lie dead. One or the other. The two of them could not live in God's green world at the same time.

Into the Dark

Athos woke up with his heart pounding so madly his chest hurt. He did not remember dreaming. He did not even know if vampires could dream or if the state they plunged into during daylight was like death or simply sleep. He knew, though, by some instinct, that night had fallen upon the city.

Sitting on his bed—the curtains of which were open, though the curtains on the window were tightly shut—confirmed his suspicions. Outside, the noises were not those of the waking city, but the sounds of Paris at night. Few voices, the sparse and distant sound of horses and carriage wheels. Somewhere nearby a wolf howled desolately.

He'd have thought it was a dog in other times, but most dogs, like men, had fallen prey to vampires.

Getting up, he hurried to the window and pulled the curtains aside enough to see, through the lead-paned windows, the dark, velvety stillness of night. He flicked the curtains open, then opened the window itself, letting in the cool night air. It smelled of smoke, of the cooking odors always present in the city, of horse manure, of flowers, but most of all it smelled of cooling breezes and late afternoon.

From the smell he tried to guess the day, which he thought must have been warm, in the way some days in spring were warm, like a thin promise of the coming summer stretched taut above an underlying coldness that was much larger and stronger. And which at nightfall had overcome the warmth altogether.

He took a breath, two, realizing this was much like a blind person telling the features of someone they could not see by reading the face with extended fingertips.

Instead of concentrating on thoughts of the daylight world that would never again be his, he wondered why he'd awakened with his heart speeding and a sense of purpose—of urgency pushing him to act.

Jumbled images of the night before ran through his mind. Charlotte, lying on a couch, more desirable and rosier than when he knew her before. He thought of her touch on his skin, and the pain in his thigh surged. Her head inclined, her tongue lapping at his blood.

But no, that wasn't it. That couldn't be it. There was a different feel to the excitement, the mingled fear and desire now coursing through his veins was not the same exhilaration he'd had on wakening.

And then it came to him, entire, like Athena from Zeus's head. He'd woken convinced he must go to Gascony and rescue D'Artagnan. Of course he must. The way would be arduous, though perhaps less so for Athos than for mortal humans. He would face some unique perils in traveling only by night, but he felt responsible for the boy. Whether the vampires had meant to capture him all along or not, he'd surely been pulled out of his safe bed to fight vampires in the street through seeing Aramis and Porthos fighting them almost in front of his lodging. From there his capture was inescapable. If the boy had not chosen to join in their fight, on their side—if Athos had ended his own life instead of going to Monsieur de Tréville's office that morning—it would all have been avoided. Therefore Athos must go to Gascony. He must find the D'Artagnan domain and rescue the boy before the vampires did whatever they planned to do.

His pulse quickened. He then perceived it was even more than that, feeling the pricks of half-formed thoughts he didn't want to admit to. He felt certain, from their mind contact—if that's what you could call the experience of her mind and soul overwhelming his—that this was her plan, that taking D'Artagnan to Gascony was in her interests and meant something to her. He also felt sure she would be there. Danger and desire rose in him. His fingertips brushed the wound on his thigh, which burned with pain and heat such that he felt it should glow through the hem of his shirt.

He looked out at the star-sprinkled night and took a deep breath of the city smells on the cool night air. He would go tonight.

He started to walk to his door, ready to call "Hallo, Grimaud," when he comprehended his servant could not have been sleeping all day and would therefore be tired. He couldn't in good conscience take Grimaud either, though the man had accompanied him on all the travels. Grimaud's sleep habits and his needs were now so different from those of Athos that traveling in company would, perforce, be unbearable.

A pang of regret made his breath catch and then he shook his head, accepting the inevitable. He would have to find where Grimaud kept Athos' clothes. Not just his shirt, but his spare doublet and hose and breeches. He would need, he thought, two pairs of riding breeches and two, no, three doublets. And some hazy number of shirts and undergarments. The idea of how many exactly he might need—he estimated with three days—or in his case nights—of riding to Gascony and back, this left three, perhaps four days in which to solve the problem and either set the boy free from the vampires or die trying. So that made it close to a fortnight. He knew he changed his shirt and undergarments every day and he knew this luxury was not common. He also knew he could not pack that many clothes and expect to carry them without hindrance, in his saddle sack.

He had no more than opened the clothes press when Grimaud entered the room exclaiming, "Monsieur le Comte!"

Athos often thought this was Grimaud's favorite phrase and marveled how Grimaud could make it mean so many different things. Right then, his tone was—obviously—one of exasperated reproach.

Grimaud was fully dressed in a russet suit, complete to his boots. Athos said, "Have you not retired yet? Have you dined?"

"Monsieur le Comte," Grimaud said again, his voice full of injury. "I would not . . ." He shrugged. "I am here to serve you, which I can't very well do if I must accompany you all night long and then stay awake during the day. I stay awake just long enough in early morning to make sure that the merchandising is done and anything procured you might need, and then I'll retire to be awake at night."

Athos felt his eyes fill with tears, his vision blur. There was much he wished to say—such as *then they will think we are both vampires*, or perhaps *you don't need to*—but what he said was, "I thank you. As it happens, though, I must go out of town on a . . . I must travel to Gascony, so all that will be needed is for you pack my saddle sack and then you may have leave for close to a fortnight."

He could feel Grimaud's body stiffening and his shoulders

squaring before he focused his gaze on him. "If I've given offense . . ."
Grimaud said, his voice stiff and proud.

"You've given no offense, but I can't ask you to travel with me
by night through the countryside and sleep by day. You would be
thought a vampire, and they will know that I am one."

Grimaud was a small man. Certainly small when compared to
Athos. He said, and perhaps it was true, that in his youth he'd been
taller. In late middle age, however vigorous, his gray hair had joined
a slight curvature of the spine and a general sagging to presage the
coming indignity of old age. He did, however, manage to give Athos
the impression of towering. "My lord," he said, "when your illustrious
father asked me to look after you, he did not say I was to cease my
care, should you be turned into a vampire against your will. I do
not wish to desert you. I had foreseen you might want to travel to
Gascony, of course, and I have packed the saddle sack. Unless you
wish to dismiss me from your service . . ."

"No," Athos said. "Of course not. I might think you foolhardy for
wishing to serve a vampire—"

"I have no wish to serve a vampire, sir. I wish to serve you."

Athos bowed his head, feeling suddenly curiously humbled. There
was nothing he could tell Grimaud to convey the mix of pride and
fear, the sense of not being worthy of this loyalty, which would not
completely undo both of them. So he said, instead, "We shall leave
almost immediately. Retrieve my horse—and obtain one for yourself,
since the matter is of some urgency and your mule will travel far
too slowly to overtake D'Artagnan's kidnappers. I must also give
Monsieur de Tréville some excuse for leaving town. I realize mine is a
secret that can't be kept forever and that sooner or later, in some way,
Monsieur de Tréville will discover it and perhaps feel obliged to—"

"You shall tell the captain you are taking the waters. To help heal
your wound—the wound he thinks you are recovering from."

This brought Athos' head up, his brow furrowing in confusion.
"The waters? In Gascony? Grimaud, the captain is a Gascon himself;
he will know there are no famous waters in Gascony which are good
for the healing of wounds."

"No," Grimaud said, and pursed his lips. "*You* are forgetting the
captain is a *Gascon*, m'sieur. He might know there are no particular

waters, but if you tell them that some have been found, in the vicinity of Pau or Tarbes or some such place, whose efficacy in healing wounds rivals all the others in France, he will believe you. No. More than that, he will not question it."

"Of course not," Athos said, and now he could feel his lip twitching in earnest, amused by both his servant and the prideful folly of Gascons in general, and of his captain in particular. It was a folly all the more amusing since it was one of the very few nonsensical beliefs the man—who was to Athos like the representative of God himself— was allowed. "He will think it is only fair that God, having thought it fit to fill Gascony with rocks and precipices and to make her the center of wars, should now have compensated her by making one of her cities the source of all healing. By God, you have it, Grimaud. We shall go to take the waters." He frowned slightly. "I must pen messages to Porthos and Aramis, so they will know where we've gone. I can get servants of the captain to deliver them to their residences."

"Certainly, Monsieur le Comte," and now the words were paternal and indulgent. "But you must have three cups of broth before we go, and you must—"he surveyed Athos with a critical eye, as Athos stood in his shirt and bare feet, in the hallway. "You must wear breeches and boots. I know it is not my place to say, but you must not go out bare bottomed and barefooted."

"Oh, then," Athos said, on the crest of a surge of relief that his trusted servant could still joke with him. "Oh, then, I shall not, for I know that in all matters of dressing and demeanor you are the authority."

Grimaud tried to look stern, but it would not hold. "And a good thing too, for how you would manage your clothes on a trip this length I do not know, but I know for a fact you'd arrive not fit to be seen."

Not fit to be seen. Surely that, but who would he been seen by? Vampires and . . . other vampires and Charlotte.

For the ten years he'd thought her dead, he'd not been able to get her out of his head. What chance had he now that she was alive and masterful and, seemingly, commanding his every breath?

Together Again

Monsieur de Tréville's offices teemed with life and light. Athos had not expected otherwise. Not only had the sun just gone down and, therefore, most of the musketeers were still within their duty, but this was the time in the evening when Monsieur de Tréville would be handing out the assignments for the night.

For all his repeated injunctions that the musketeers were not to patrol in those areas of the city that had been allotted, by treaty, to the vampires, or that they weren't—under any circumstances—to provoke the guards of the cardinal or to become embroiled in duels, the real instructions he gave were quite different. De Tréville said what he had to say to obey the treaty between the king and cardinal, so the musketeers received their instructions in his prohibitions. The captain would say, "And you, D'Alphonse, are absolutely not to patrol the area from the Barefoot Carmelites to the rue des Anges. You are not to take Josse with you. Do not to stay alert for any appeals for help and do not to interfere with the guards of His Eminence in the performance of their duties." But he would mean they were supposed to do exactly what he'd told them not to do. It was a game everyone knew and everyone played.

So the musketeers in their best garb—such as it was these days—would crowd the residence, after their dinners and routs, and wait till the captain called them to, particularly and with intent, hand out his prohibitions.

They thronged the receiving room, dueling for space on the stairs, calling boisterous jokes across the room. At Athos' entrance all talk stilled. The two men who'd been mock-dueling up and down the stairs stopped. Heads turned toward him.

192

"*They know,*" Athos thought, then chided himself. It wouldn't take their knowing, and it would be unlikely they could guess he had been turned. None of them called him out, or even gave him more than the bare room necessary to walk between two rows of them. They were so close he could feel their body heat.

To be honest, they'd always given him only the space necessary to walk between them and no more. The space was a mark of respect. As for the silence . . . the silence was no more than was natural when he'd broken protocol so dramatically on his last visit by collapsing on the floor of the captain's office and having to be carried out. Having drunk broth—too much broth, curse Grimaud—all too recently, he felt his cheeks flush and walked quicker toward the stairs. His foot was on the first step of the broad marble staircase leading to the captain's office. He was headed toward Gervase at the top, ready to ask him to announce his presence to the Captain, when someone called from the mass of musketeers in the hall, "Athos, how is the wound?" All of them turned to look at him.

He spun around, forcing a smile on his face. The consciousness of all their bodies so close to his, the feeling of their heat, his desire to feed, were unbearable. He had to resist gritting his teeth and making his face wooden. Instead, he smiled pleasantly and spoke in what he hoped was a natural voice, "Very well, D'Ingelger. I am healing. It still pains me, of course, but . . ."

"The fighting last night can't have done you any good."

He allowed his smile to widen, carefully disciplining his facial muscles to display no more than the ordinary. "Indeed, D'Embocage, but that is what must one do when friends call."

And then remembered there were those in the crowd of musketeers who had seen him at the de Montbelliard house last night. Someone—many—here had seen him completely naked—completely naked with Charlotte's fangs and lips fastened onto his thigh.

They wouldn't know he was a vampire, but what they thought he was doing there in that state, he didn't know. His stomach lurched within him, the broth, which always felt heavy on it, seeking to explode through his lips. He wouldn't allow it. By sheer force of will he kept his smile and betrayed his nervousness only by removing his gloves carefully and methodically. Even then you'd need to know him as only Grimaud did to know this was his favored method of giving his hands and thoughts something to do when worried. Likely they will think I am embarrassed, he thought. Which was true but also not, because he was, in fact *mortified.*

He forced himself to say, conscious of the constraint in his voice, "And I am sure they will return the favor another night." His voice echoed too high and shaky, but he thought that was exactly how it would sound if he were still mortal and had been found in such a state, even if he had no history with the lady. Even if she weren't his wife. "I . . . I thank any of you who were in the raid that freed me from compulsion at the old de Montbelliard place."

No one admitted to it, but several heads dipped, and Athos turned quickly away, feeling as if he were suffocating in his own embarrassment and rebelling against his own need to monitor his every word, almost his every thought.

Up the stairs—the play-duelists moved aside to let him pass—all the way up to the landing where Gervase, Monsieur de Tréville's thin and worn-looking manservant, bowed to him. "Monsieur!"

Like Grimaud, Gervase had the knack of being able to use one word and make it mean many, many things. What it meant, right now, was that he was pleased to see Athos and trusted Athos must be recovering nicely from his injury. And did he wish to see Monsieur de Tréville?

"If at all possible, Gervase, I would like very much to see the captain, as I must inform him in a matter of much importance."

"Certainly, monsieur," Gervase said, and, opening the door, announced Athos, then stepped back to let him pass.

Monsieur de Tréville wasn't alone. He rarely was. It was his habit to interrupt an audience when a petitioner with a great claim appeared, and to conduct several talks at the same time.

He stood, in full court dress—even if his royal-blue velvet doublet had started to look a little faded around the edges, the ornamental embroidery pulled in places—talking to a group of musketeers to whom he must have given their negative assignments for the night. He waved them aside and extended both hands to Athos, smiling. "Ah, my valiant Athos. I knew that you'd not long be able to stay away from your duty. You've come to report to me, have you not?"

Athos inclined his head. At all times it pained him to lie to his captain and now more than ever, since his very existence, his presence here was a lie. "Pardon me, Captain, but no, not yet. You see, the wound is paining me, and I thought—"

"Not a discharge!" the captain said, looking up at him, as though wondering if this was the same Athos he knew.

"No, sir. Of course not. When you did me the honor of accepting me into the regiment, I swore to you that I would serve as long as France needed me, as long as we were besieged by vampires. I would not withdraw my word now."

Monsieur de Tréville's features sagged with relief, but he said, "Well, then what is it you seek of me? I know you are on leave until you are recovered . . ."

"Since my wound is paining me more than it should, and because some miraculously beneficial waters have lately been found in Gascony, I've been persuaded that partaking of these waters would speed my recovery."

Monsieur de Tréville stepped away from Athos, his gaze still fixed on the musketeer. Athos tried not to even consider what the captain might be discerning that so alarmed him. "But," Monsieur de Tréville said frowning, "surely to ride two or three days to Gascony could not possibly be good for a wound?"

Athos swallowed, "I believe the benefits will outweigh any ill effects of such travel," he said.

The captain scrutinized Athos as though hoping to distinguish some ominous sign. Athos wished he knew what it was so he could avoid it.

Of all the behaviors that vampirism had forced on him, he despised this prevarication most of all. He would endure ten times the craving for blood, fifteen times the fact that he had to drink what tasted like stagnant water, just to be able to talk to his captain—and, indeed, to everyone he admired or trusted without disguise.

"Well," the captain said at last. "I suppose Porthos and Aramis will be going with you?"

"In fact, sir, they—" he said, ready to explain he didn't think it fair to demand that they should travel to Gascony, when it was his wound and his problem.

However, just at that moment, Gervase opened the door and called out, "Messieurs Porthos and Aramis," and stepped aside, allowing Athos' friends to enter.

Unfortunately Porthos liked lying even less than Athos. Even more unfortunately, Porthos was also less skilled at dissembling. He stepped in, saw Athos, and said, "You, here?" Then stopped at a glare from Aramis.

"I meant," Porthos said, with the feel of having changed sentences mid-speech, "we went to your lodgings and you and Grimaud were absent."

"Yes," Athos said, tersely. "As you see, I was here, to—"

"I presume," Monsieur de Tréville said, before Athos could think of words double-edged enough by which he could warn his friends of the story he'd just told the captain. "You two have come to volunteer to accompany Monsieur Athos to Gascony."

"Indeed, sir," Aramis said. But there was no disguising the look of shock that came over Porthos' face, as he looked at Athos.

"I have come," Athos said, trying to head off any possible uncomfortable revelations, "to request permission to take the waters at the newly discovered hot springs in Gascony."

"Of course," Aramis said smoothly, "in Tarbes." Which would have been perfect, had not Porthos at the same time said, "In Pau."

The captain looked from one to the other; inquiringly at Athos and even more so at Aramis and Porthos.

Were they about to get one of Monsieur de Tréville's famous set-downs? He was quite capable of raking even the most respected and best of his musketeers over live coals when they displeased him. And now, from his narrowed eyes and his glare, it appeared he was about to do so. His cutting references and terrible put-downs would then be transmitted to the crowd downstairs by one of the observers in the office. After what some other musketeers had seen the night before, it seemed to Athos it would be easier and far less painful if the earth should open and swallow him whole. Even if the yellow and white tile floor of Monsieur de Tréville's office could in no way be construed as *earth*.

Monsieur de Tréville was quiet a long time, and when he spoke at last, it was to say "Messieurs," spoken with eerie, terrible calm.

Athos tried to look impassive. Bad enough when a scolding started with *you men,* but if it started with *messieurs,* it was guaranteed to be most vitriolic and memorable. The captain's acidic barbs would repeated all over town for weeks.

But, instead, he said, mildly, "Messieurs, if you would leave me with Athos, Porthos, and Aramis, we have matters of interest only to us and His Majesty to discuss."

Athos recognized Monsieur de Tréville was talking to the others in the office and that he had just spoken the only words that would give them privacy. In the old days, he'd heard, it was impossible for Monsieur de Tréville to have a private tête-à-tête with any of his musketeers without other musketeers listening outside the door. Whatever had been discussed was then spread far and wide. But these days, hemmed in between the treaty and the need to protect the helpless and fight the vampires, Monsieur de Tréville often required privacy to keep from falling into traps set by the cardinal.

The men filed out quietly. Monsieur de Tréville followed them as far as the door, which he closed. He then turned to Athos and said, "Speak. Why must the three of you go to Gascony, and why did you decide this independently from each other?" He waved his hand at Aramis, "Not you, Aramis. I know your glib tongue, and I know you'd give me a perfectly reasonable explanation that would even be the truth after a fashion. But I prefer the real story, as I have a sense that you gentlemen are in over your heads."

He retreated behind his desk and sat down, which he only did when he expected a lengthy discussion.

If only you knew how far over my head, Athos thought. Aloud he said, "The truth is, it concerns the Gascon whom you met the other day." And, in reply to Monsieur de Tréville's blank look, he said, "D'Artagnan, the young man just arrived from Gascony."

"Oh, him," Monsieur de Tréville said. "I thought he might well be a Judas goat."

"Yes, I did too, sir," Aramis said, "and part of the cardinal's plans to entrap us."

"I see," Monsieur de Tréville said. "Do go on."

Athos went on. He told an edited version of their dealings with D'Artagnan which left out the reason the Gascon had followed them and pretended he had come upon them as they started the duel with the guards. From there he told the story until the boy was kidnapped.

"Kidnapped," Monsieur de Tréville said, smoothing his beard in a pensive gesture. "Or ran away having discovered that he was getting too enmeshed in a deception he could not carry on?"

"I feel sure it was a kidnapping, monsieur," Athos said, "as does Madame Bonacieux." He explained his reasoning much as he had to Aramis.

Monsieur de Tréville looked at him, long and hard. "What if," he said, "it is the cardinal's intention to have you go to Gascony on this fool's errand, while he enacts some plan here in Paris which your presence would have destroyed?"

"You'll still have the other musketeers, sir," Athos said, soberly.

"And I no longer think the young man is a Judas goat," Aramis said at last. "Madame Bonacieux might be many things, intemperate being one of them." As he spoke he lifted his face and Athos thought he could still distinguish a faint reddened mark where her hand had struck him. "But she is no fool. And she has . . ." He opened his hands, palm out, as if to signify inability to explain. "Something else, which her faith and its practice gives her. She . . . senses people. Some she trusts and some she doesn't, but I've never known her to be wrong. Remember last year, when she said Nazaire . . . ?"

"Ah, yes." De Tréville pursed his lips in distaste, recalling the one instance of betrayal in the corps. It still rankled even though a year had passed.

"Well," Aramis said, "Madame de Bonacieux trusts D'Artagnan so much she said she was going to Gascony to rescue him herself."

"*Sangre Dieu*," Monsieur de Tréville said, sitting straighter. "Did she go?"

"I don't know, sir, though she informed all our colleagues—Rabbi Isaac and Pastor Monfort and the others—that she will be gone for some time as . . . as have I."

"I see," Monsieur de Tréville said. He looked at them a long time, and then, finally, spoke again. "Of course, even if the boy is not a Judas goat, that does not exempt him from being used as bait in one of the cardinal's games."

"It does not exempt any of us," Athos said, quietly, thinking of himself and all the events of the last few days.

Monsieur de Tréville sighed. "I shall grant you gentlemen a fortnight leave of absence." He took a leaf from his desk, dipped his quill and wrote rapidly, blotted, then folded the page. He then put pen to another page. "You will be going to Pau—unless Tarbes is more convenient," he permitted himself a smile at their expense, "to take the waters for your chest wound, Athos. Your comrades will escort you." He extended the first folded page, which Athos took. "This gives you the ability to tell anyone you are on orders to go as soon as possible and to stay as long as you need to, and that Athos' recovery is of great importance to me. This one," he offered the second folded paper to Athos, "this states you are on urgent business for His Majesty, the King. I know in the countryside the king's name doesn't hold much sway. Still, it might serve you good stead."

"Thank you, sir, I don't know how to—"

"Do not bother," Monsieur de Tréville interrupted Athos' gratitude. "However—" he got up, and offered his hand to each of them in turn "—you will wish to be aware that I believe there is great trouble brewing. I've had intimations there is something afoot. I do not know what, but I've learned to know when Richelieu is attempting something. Also … also he seems to be afraid of someone or something …"

Perils of the Roads

They'd not gone very far, when they found the road blocked by a large log. Aramis rode up close to determine if they could force their horses to jump it, and came back to where Athos and Porthos waited—their servants and the boy Planchet, who refused to be left in Paris, at a distance—and said, "There are other logs beyond this." His face was contorted with worry. "If we'd tried to jump this one, the horses would have been lamed on the other side," he said.

"Then we move the logs," Porthos said, and started to dismount.

Athos shook his head. "Do not, my friend," he said. He walked his horse nearer his friends, so they could speak at little more than a whisper. "If many logs were felled together," he said, "and laid across the road, that must mean it is a trap. If we dismount, chances are we will be set upon." He looked up at the sky to determine the position of the moon. "One hour or two till dawn," he said. "Aramis, where is the last place you saw that might be safe for us to take shelter?"

"An hour back," Aramis said, wearily. "But if we are to make it to Agen, we must use this road. It is the only road passable enough for horses. There are, I believe, some goat-paths, beaten dirt only, which can be used to progress south, but we'd risk our horses being lamed or worse."

Athos sighed. "Barring," he said, "the ability of my lady wife to withstand daylight, then the people who felled these logs will be asleep come morning."

Porthos frowned, "Why do you think they are vampires?" he asked.

"Because, Porthos, if the nearest safe place is an hour back, and this trap was set in the dark of night, that must mean those who man the trap are not afraid of anyone. If they are not afraid of anyone,

200

it must mean they are vampires. Who else in this desolate a place would be so confident?"

Aramis nodded. "So, we go back to the nearest village that had lights and seemed to have people about at sunset, and we find a place to bed down. And then?"

"I said nothing about finding a place to bed down," Athos said, smiling. The cunning Aramis could, at times, seem as slow as Porthos, who at least had the excuse of being uncomfortable in company. "We will go back to the nearest village and see if they have something resembling a carriage."

Aramis' eyebrows flew up.

"Or, failing that, an oxcart. It will slow us but not stop us through the day. We shall pay some rustics to move these logs," he waved a hand in dismissal. "Then we will progress as far as we can during the day, till we come to what looks to be a safe place to sleep. If we pause in late afternoon, no one will notice much if we depart again at nighttime."

"But how will an oxcart fit your purpose?" Aramis asked.

"It will," Athos said, "if it has an empty barrel on it, or perhaps a load of straw." From anyone else, Aramis' reaction would have bothered him, but he knew the sudden laughter bursting out of his friend was not intended to humiliate him. "Stop laughing, Aramis. A pretty thing it is, indeed, for me to travel this way. Grimaud will be most displeased at such an affront to my dignity."

Aramis' face went grave. "None of us wishes to displease Grimaud," he said. "We'll play it according to your plan, but if we are going to comport with rustics, you must wear this." From the depths of his sleeve he retrieved a plain—and old—silver cross on a chain. Looking at Athos, he added, "You said that the cross does not bother you."

"No, it doesn't. Only I have a great fear I might bother it," Athos said, and to Aramis' look of total incomprehension. "I am a vampire. Won't it be sacrilege to wear the cross? Won't it, by itself, damn me to lose my soul?"

A tight smile flew across Aramis' lips. "Not if you are not disturbed by it. You can't deem yourself unholy yet. Bide your time my friend. You might yet find a way to damnation." And then, seriously, "Don't reject yourself before you are rejected."

He handed the cross to Athos, who held it in his hand a moment before slipping the chain around his neck. He felt he was somehow committing a dire offense, passing for a mortal when he was not. But he knew enough not to repine. *Don't reject before you are rejected.* After all, for ten years he'd condemned himself for a murderer, when it seemed Charlotte had been a vampire all along. Perhaps he should forbear hasty conclusions.

"I think," he said, "that we'll have trouble leaving here." He added, "One of us should go ahead of the servants and the others behind, since I feel they'll attack us from behind."

"I was about to recommend that myself," Porthos said, and maneuvered his horse around the mounted servants, pausing to convey instructions to Mousqueton. Athos saw the servants draw stakes from their cloaks. The musketeers drew their swords.

As they started to canter down the road back to the last safe village, figures came out of the darkness behind them. They were armed with pikes. If they could get close enough, the assailants could trip the horses. Athos shouted a warning, and they spurred the horses to a gallop, half expecting to find their progress blocked. But they did not. The vampires had not expected retreat as a means of escape.

They were halfway back to the still-human settlement when Athos thought that if he lived a thousand years—and as a vampire, he might—he'd never forget those figures. Shambling creatures, who'd once been peasants and were now lost somewhere between human and animal, their clothes filthy and in tatters and their eyes filled with nothing but hunger.

Home Exile

It was the smells of home that made everything worse, D'Artagnan thought, as he sat in this same carriage in which he'd been imprisoned for two days. He could smell the pine trees, the flowers just starting in the fields. When the curtains of the carriage were open, at night, he could occasionally glimpse the round, rocky outcrop of a bastide—one of the fortified towns of Gascony. Sometimes when he slept—he would never have believed he could have slept while tied up in a carriage, but he did, such was his fatigue from three days of continuous travel—he dreamed he was home, and that his mother was shaking him awake from an awful dream. *There had never been any vampires*, she said. *He was to wake this minute.*

He did wake, still confined in a carriage, with His Eminence's right-hand—or perhaps left-hand—vampire, and several wraiths that had been vampires for longer than D'Artagnan could imagine.

On and on the horses devoured the road. Day and night, the carriage wheels trundled beneath. When they stopped, even to allow him to relieve himself or to procure him food, he was never untied, and Rochefort was always at hand.

It wasn't until they got to the Comminges—the carriage straining up steep slopes, then rolling perilously close to the edge of narrow mountain roads—that D'Artagnan truly knew they were taking him home. Rochefort had claimed they taking him to father's house for an "inheritance." It appeared the vampire had told the truth, but what he had meant by an inheritance D'Artagnan, as the only son of an impecunious house in impoverished Gascony, had no idea.

If D'Artagnan had a choice, he would rather die a thousand painful deaths than see the land of his birth, much less his home again. He would not be able to see the sun-warmed walls of his homestead without thinking of his mother, without hearing her voice.

And yet, more and more, his thoughts drifted to that part of Gascony that was his home. If he closed his eyes, he could hear the mountain cascades and smell the wildflowers in the fields. If he tried hard, he could hear Gascon men call at each other in the language of the region, the language spoken at home by noble families and by villagers, peasants, and merchants all their lives.

They stopped at a village with a roadside hostelry. The locals, D'Artagnan had quickly discovered, could not refuse custom to a large carriage even if it were filled with vampires and the horrible old vampire-wraiths.

The carriage rocked as Rochefort got out. He came back with a flask. D'Artagnan had become used to this. With his hands bound behind his back, he was not able to eat, unless Rochefort held the food. Rochefort had learned early that D'Artagnan's teeth made a formidable weapon which could and would snap at fingers that close. He now would purchase some sort of gruel or soup in a flask and feed D'Artagnan that way. D'Artagnan had tried spitting out the food or refusing to swallow it, but that simply resulted in going hungry.

It was soup this time. Chicken broth with vegetables and ground grains, and even in this most bland of dishes, D'Artagnan could taste the garlic and rosemary of Gascon seasoning.

As soon as he was done, Rochefort descended from the carriage. D'Artagnan heard him speaking outside and was surprised—from what words he could catch—that he was speaking in Gascon. He edged closer to the door of the carriage, moving into the seat Rochefort had occupied. The wraith sitting by him made no effort to move, so D'Artagnan crept all the way to the edge, where he could look through the open door.

Outside the moon was full, the sky was a deep, dark blue, and a light breeze played on the branches of pine trees and grasses. From what he could see—a fork in a road, with an hostelry planted solidly in between, its name just visible on a faded sign, proclaiming it in Gascon: The Musketeer's Head. He swallowed, knowing where he was. Bagnères-de-Luchon, a few hours horseback journey from home. It sat in a narrow basin, little more than a mile across, where the River One flowed into the Pique.

He closed his eyes, trying to shut out memories of coming with his friends to bathe in the rivers, in what now seemed like the golden afternoons of his childhood. Oh, they knew there were vampires, that they were dangerous, and even that they were everywhere or near enough. They didn't know vampires would ever come close enough to their safe, happy lives to make any difference. And then Luchon had become half-occupied by vampires, a miniature version of Paris. The vampires seemed to be smart enough to allow about half the population to remain human in order to keep the land tilled and the wool spun, to keep a semblance of regularity over the deep, dark chasm of life with vampires. D'Artagnan's parents had forbidden his visiting there and then at other villages, until he was confined within his native bastide, its deep walls and bell tolling to keep vampires at bay.

Behind his closed eyes, he saw a handful of small boys, slick and tan, playing in the basin, darting in and out of the water. Those sun-splashed, happy boys seemed to belong to another world, perhaps another species.

He woke up to "Jean, come," spoken loudly by Rochefort.

"Milord?"

"Come."

Rochefort resumed his seat in the carriage. The man, Jean, entered the carriage with a halting step, dragging his injured leg—a result of the runaway horse incident at the beginning of the trip. He paled at the sight—or perhaps the smell—of the wraiths.

Rochefort reached out, his hands grabbing Jean around the shoulders and pulling him down. His fangs tore into the man's neck without warning, prompting a scream. But then Jean quieted. A sudden moan escaped him, as though having his blood sucked were a sensual experience. His body went lax, his eyes rolled into his head.

D'Artagnan stared, unable to look away, but wanting to do so more than anything. Rochefort pushed the man from him and got up, wiping his bloodstained mouth. Outside, D'Artagnan heard him speaking to the hosteler and to another man. From the words, it seemed obvious that they'd acquired a new Judas goat to tool the coach.

He still could not tear his eyes away as the wraiths took over sucking Jean's blood, wherever they could attach. Jean looked like a rag doll, boneless, spineless, a pale and poor imitation of a human.

He knew death had come to the man; he could smell the former contents of Jean's bowels. And, as the wraiths tossed the broken human from the other door of the carriage and down a steep embankment, D'Artagnan sat, unable to move, until a lurch from his stomach made him lean over and empty the recently-drunk soup onto the floorboards and—mostly—outside the carriage.

He'd just finished when Rochefort reentered the carriage. He did not ask D'Artagnan why he'd been sick, or the wraiths where Jean or his body had gone. Instead, he took his seat in the carriage, muttering something about damned nuisances.

At his sign the carriage moved, rolling through the still night. D'Artagnan turned his face toward the side with the window, hiding as much as he could against the wooden wall of the carriage, and sobbing. He hadn't cried like this since he was a very small child, tears rolling down his face unchecked.

But he could no more stop it than he could stop breathing, and so he cried—for those young boys long ago who didn't know what vampires were or what they could do. For Jean. For himself. For the whole of humanity now consigned to unending damnation.

De la Fere

The blood tasted sweet, hot in his mouth. It ran in a steady rivulet down his throat. He didn't know whose blood, only that her neck was long and slim and the little bit of her ear he could see was a delicate conch-like pink-whiteness that gave the impression of transparency.

Her hair—he was sure it was a woman—fell, dark and heavy over the arms he'd wrapped around her shoulders. She smelled of the sun and summer and long careless days. Her skin was soft, soft against his fingers, his bare arms, his chest.

He'd just ripped into the pulsing vein on her neck, quieting her brief scream of pain. Blood poured into his mouth. It warmed him and filled him with joy, as a cup of hot chocolate had done on a bitter winter day when he was very small. But there was more to it than that, he thought, as he suckled desperately at the open vein. It was the pleasure and innocent union of the infant with his mother, but also the heated adult consummation of fleshy desire. The blood had a spicy edge, a feeling of the forbidden.

He could feel his spirit intertwine with that of his victim, could feel both her pleasure and her fear in her struggles, which grew feebler and feebler, until a great sigh escaped her and her body went limp in his arms, He turned her to look at her face and—

Athos woke up. His heart beat a mad drum in his chest and he was hot, burning. Was it the sun? Had he been caught in the sun and . . .

Opening his eyes showed him only night, a blazing full moon above, and around him the relative stillness of the dark woods, punctuated by the noises of crickets and birds, by the sound of some creature crawling in the undergrowth and something else making a moaning sound in a tree. The pine branches swayed in the wind above, filling the air with scent.

He lay on the ground, half atop his cloak and half covered by it, panting with the exertion and shock of his dream. He threw the covering away from him, trying to feel the cool spring night air on his body. He undid his doublet, but it did not help. He could still taste her blood on his tongue, hot and spicy, spicy and hot, warming his cold body and returning it to a semblance of the life that had been taken from it.

He untied the laces that held his shirt closed at the throat. His mouth felt dry and hot, craving the remembered taste of blood. He felt his hands tug at the fastening to his breeches, and caused himself to stop, forcibly, from touching an erection that throbbed with unsatisfied longing.

He remembered her struggles against him, her half-hearted attempts to escape, her moans of pleasure.

The brisk air didn't cool his skin at his chest or throat. He had swallowed three cups of broth for his supper, warmed over the campfire, but he felt as if he hadn't eaten in years. He needed food. But the thought of broth made his stomach twist.

He wanted blood. Her blood on his tongue, her body in his arms, her surrender, her craving, his craving. He needed living blood, from a living vein.

Then he smelled it, heard it. The scent of living flesh nearby, the sound of breaths drawn, the pounding of living hearts.

Here, lying next to him, seven necks offered that fountain of sweet life that he'd dreamed of, that satisfaction to the thirst he felt growing, unslaked, within him.

If he drank just a little. If he controlled himself. If he . . .

He remembered the taste of the blood and its precious flow, calming his many aches and pains, his despair. Calming everything, as her body, pliant and warm in his arms, made him feel as if he were alive again. The power to take her life made him feel as if he were better than he'd been when alive.

He listened to the pounding of heartbeats. He imagined his teeth tearing into flesh, creating an open tear from which blood flowed, hot, spicy.

His own moan startled him, and his erection hurt so it felt like an individual thing, independent of him, craving satisfaction as much as he did, feeding his need.

If he fed just a little.

But something within warned him it wasn't so. If he waited, if he let himself start—tearing skin and flesh with his fangs, lapping at the flowing blood—he would not be able to stop. Not until the body he was holding—warm, soft, living—lay dead in his arms, while his victim's blood—he cared not whose—coursed in his veins. He would lap and suck and—

He was on his hands and knees, crawling fast through the undergrowth, away from the camp. Morning would come in an hour or so. They had bedded down in the early hours of the still-dark morning, with the understanding he'd return to his barrel on the back of the oxcart for the day journey before daylight.

Stung by pine needles, skin lacerated by rocks, he scrambled away from the camp, from his sleeping comrades, from their sleeping servants, sure that if he remained he would tear open the nearest throat, he would drink living blood, he would . . .

His body craved blood and physical release entwined, and both together could not be satiated. Not here. Not now.

"Monsieur!" Grimaud, in a whisper, his voice hoarse. "Monsieur, what is wrong, are you ill?"

He heard the steps behind him. Doddering fool. Athos would rip into his throat, he'd rend—

No! "No," he said aloud. "No. Come no further. Stay." He dragged himself to standing by clawing himself upright on a young pine sapling, feeling it tremble with his push.

"Monsieur le—"

"No, you fool," Athos tried to shout. His voice came out more growl than human voice, and he was afraid that Grimaud would not arrest. His heart was pounding so loudly, he would not hear the man's footstep behind him. He let go of the tree.

He ran, tottering, blindly, snapping branches and kicking rocks, slipping and scrambling back up again: running into trees, then edging around them.

He tripped over something and, falling, felt a warm body under his extended arms. It was warm and furry and squirmed under his grasp. He felt for the vein at the neck, without thinking. He could not have stopped himself if he had tried. His teeth sank into the vein.

Warm, living blood poured into his mouth. He was in his dream again and it was her blood, warm, heady with her scent of summer and sun.

He nursed and suckled and suddenly, remembering the feel of her in his arms, of her voluptuous body, his body erupted in pleasure as the blood trickled to a stop.

He opened his eyes, suddenly cold and sober; aware that his undergarment felt wet and clammy. The thing he'd grasped, the thing whose life he'd sucked in great, gulping pulls, was a wolf pup too young to have run at his noisy approach. It lay in what had been a safe nest beneath the roots of a great tree. The mother wolf must be hunting.

Athos wiped his mouth with back of his hand and marveled at the red streaks left. He took deep breaths. He willed his fangs to retract.

"Monsieur," Grimaud's voice said nearby.

"I'm well, Grimaud. I'm . . . well." His mouth tasted metallic. Looking at the corpse of the pup, he was afraid he'd vomit what he'd just ingested and thereby make the pup's death more atrocious. He dragged himself up, forcing himself to look away. "I am well."

Looking up he saw Grimaud eyeing him dubiously and was gratified to see the stake, clasped tight in Grimaud's hand. He wiped his mouth with the back of his hand again, and said, "It was a dream, I think."

As Grimaud took a step toward him, he said, "No. I can find my own cloak."

But when he returned to the camp and lay down, awake, staring up at the darker shadows of the pine tree branches again the lightening sky, he knew that whatever creatures might go in stealth through the dark woods were not half as terrifying as the beast in the darkness within.

Betraying Memory

"We will untie your hands," Rochefort said, as they tossed D'Artagnan back into the room in which he'd slept from his earliest memories until three weeks—could it truly be only three weeks?—ago. "So you may care for yourself. But make no attempts at escaping. There will be two guards outside the door and two more outside every window."

D'Artagnan verified. How could he not? He crept to the door and looked through the sliver of space underneath at the feet pacing back and forth. Two feet in heavy boots. Rochefort had said men, but D'Artagnan presumed he meant vampires. Or perhaps not. There was no way to tell, and, exhausted from the mad travel, D'Artagnan couldn't stand against either. No, he had to find another way out.

On the other side, at the base of the tree that almost touched his window, he could tell the two men moving confidently in the darkness of the night, had to be vampires. Which made the idea of opening the window, shimmying down the tree and attempting to escape a foolish one. Not that he intended to do it, D'Artagnan thought, as he rolled his shoulders, trying to make his arms stop hurting like the blazes.

He sat on his bed, on the feather eiderdown his mother had stitched, made of her old dresses. Pink satin and blue silk and embroidered linen flowed one into the other, like little cushions filled with down. It was old. D'Artagnan had slept under it every winter of his young life. He traced his finger along the stitchery, feeling his eyes swim in tears.

His room took up the western corner of the second floor, and its window—in daytime—admitted enough light to make the scrubbed, polished oak floor glow like gold.

How to get out of his room? Thoughts of hurling the clothes press through the door and then leaping over it, a sword in each hand, stabbing at each of the guards outside at the same time swept briefly through his tired, disordered mind.

A rueful smile played across his lips and he touched his fingers to his lips, as if to assure himself of the expression. Such feats of derring-do were, of course, beyond him. However, if a certain three musketeers were at hand: Porthos could hurl the clothes press and, swords flashing, Athos, Aramis, and he would leap out the window ...

D'Artagnan didn't even have a sword.

He rubbed at his chin, which was starting to feel scratchy with stubble—though he didn't have enough growth yet for a proper beard. If only they'd given him a blade to shave with. He looked toward the basin with a wild hope of a blade's presence and of picking the lock with it, slitting one of the guard's throats, and then perhaps appropriating one of their swords ...

But there was no blade by the basin. Why should he expect there to be? After all, the vampires might be evil, but they were not stupid.

He drew up his feet to sit on the eiderdown, hugging his knees to his chest. His feet were filthy, crusted with blood and dirt from his escape attempt and being barefoot the whole rushing trip.

There was no way to escape. He would have to sit and wait until Rochefort or his vampires disposed of him in whatever way they saw fit.

Jumping to his feet in the fury of this thought, he aimed a fierce punch at the wall and hurt his hand on one of the many metal fleurs-de-lis that ornamented the wall. He recalled a dim memory of a time when the walls of his room had been waxed wood paneling, without any decoration. What had led his father to ask the village ironsmith to make these fleurs-de-lis and to set them all over the walls?

He stepped back puzzled, rubbing at his chin again. Seen from one side it seemed to make no sense, and from another, it was all a mad dream. He didn't know how old he was, but the memory of the walls being bare and warm waxed wood paneling came back to him, until his father had commanded these ornaments installed—an odd fancy in a room that was used as a nursery for a small boy—D'Artagnan could not have been more than four years old.

Thinking back on it, he was sure he had thought his father had done it because D'Artagnan had in some way displeased him. He ran his fingers along the cool metal of the flowers, feeling their rough edges. Why would his father consider putting them in D'Artagnan's room to be a punishment? The emblem was associated with the royal house, to which D'Artagnan did not belong. He supposed that he should not feel insulted, though, to be treated like a prince, though the symbol was now used as a brand for undeclared Judas goats. But D'Artagnan did not think his father was accusing him of being a Judas goat, or of treachery. Or at least—he sniffled, his eyes being unaccountably close to overflowing with tears—his father had always seemed to him a sensible man, and he wouldn't have expected a very small boy to understand such an insult.

Dredged from a deeper memory, at last D'Artagnan recalled his father had been furious because D'Artagnan had gotten out of his room, to which he'd been sent as a punishment to *"cool your abominably hot temper, young sir."*

He could just hear his father saying it . . . probably not a single memory but a composite of the many times he'd been sent to his room for just that sin when he was young. He rubbed the bridge of his nose, the thought of getting out of his room foremost in his mind. But how had he done it? Probably, he thought dismissively, by simply opening the window and slithering down the tree, something he'd done as recently as a month ago, simply because he did not wish to worry his mother when he went out to drink at a tavern late at night.

But no. Scraps of memory crept back to him. There had been a hole, a tunnel. He frowned. From his room? Impossible. He was on the second floor. He didn't doubt that the house might have a secret passage here and there; it was certainly old enough. Doubtless, it had been built on the ruins of previous houses, so indeed, secret passages might have been left incidentally, if not in truth.

He slowly recollected rough stone walls, and a labyrinth of passages, some of them crumbling plaster with traces of paintings upon them. He frowned at the unlit hearth in a corner of his bedroom. Did he go into the tunnel through a hole that opened in the wooden paneling by the fireplace? He was sure of it . . . well, at least as sure as he was of anything he remembered from childhood.

Squatting by the fireplace he tapped the wood panels around it. The dull thud of wood where it backed against the ancient stone walls was a disappointment. But in an area just to the left of the fireplace, a significant area sounded hollow under his knocking knuckles.

D'Artagnan sat back on his haunches, on the oak floorboards, and stared with a frown at the panel. There was a hole there, so it might be true there had once been some sort of passage. Maybe. Perhaps it merely was a boarded-up door to the next room which might be one of the linen store rooms. Though it seemed to him he rarely heard anything from that room, and from his memory there was a remembered space between the two. He frowned again. Which would be there, if there were a passage.

Kneeling, he examined the panel again, and noted a fissure running all around it, but there were no similar gaps around other panels. The crack was hardly discernible and resembled, he told himself, a badly fitted panel. Or, of course, a very well-fitted door.

A deep sigh escaped him. What if there were a secret door? He would never find the way to open it. He scratched at the fissure with his fingernails, but didn't dare try to knock through the panel. Not with two guards stationed outside the door. He did not intend to end up as tightly bound as he'd been on the trip here. That left . . .

Thinking hard, he dredged up a vague memory of having opened the door by stabbing at a knot in the wall. Yes, he'd pushed it and the door by the fireplace had slid open. And being a young boy he had . . .

It was madness. But all the same, he remembered hearing the sound and looking—over his shoulder and to his left—as the door opened.

He positioned himself on his knees, approximating the height he had been at age—what age?—four, yes, four.

If you were the father of a small boy who had just found the way to get out of his room . . . a way—because D'Artagnan could not believe his father would be so careless as to put his small son in a room with a secret passage leading somewhere—that you might have forgotten or never known about, you could change the boy's room, but he would remember the secret door. D'Artagnan smiled ruefully remembering his younger self—of course he would return to that room to use the passage again. Or you could just hide the wooden knot with a fleur-de-lis, in a sea of other similar fleurs-de-lis. If he was right, that was why his father had undertaken such an otherwise senseless expense.

He pushed at various flowers on the wall. He pulled them. He crawled on his knees the length of the wall, fiddling with each flower, pulling the petals, the crown, pushing the knots. Nothing happened. Of course, a careful father, might also have disabled the operation of the door. But then . . .

Tears prickled in his eyes again. He was so tired. And the only thing he was sure of was that Rochefort and his minions would return to make him . . . He couldn't think what they'd want to make him do, except that he was sure it would leave him wishing for as simple an end as poor Jean's.

In frustration, he punched a flower or two again, then out of despair, started trying to twist the iron ornaments. Two of them twisted, insecure in their attachment to the wall, but nothing happened as they turned. He heard a sharp keening of frustration escape his lips, and bit his lips together forcibly. Such a sound might call his captors. He grabbed hold of the twisted fleur-de-lis, pushed and pulled at it furiously, then leaned on it, fully resting his forehead against another.

Behind him, he heard the sound of a small door creaking open.

Down, Down, Down

The door was small and narrow, barely large enough to admit D'Artagnan. He looked through it. After a narrow passage, there was what looked like a broad hole and . . . something, D'Artagnan didn't know what. If he crawled into this hole, there was a chance he would end up stuck further on.

On the other hand, it was possible that it led all the way through to . . .

Where? Confused images, memories of emerging from the tunnel on the hillside, outside the walls of the bastide. If that were true . . .

He frowned. Right. One thing was certain. Even if the passage led only to the kitchens or just outside the house walls, it led outside this room. He entered the passage backwards squeezing in, both because his shoulders were his broadest part and because he wanted his head nearest the entrance to the tunnel, should he need to reverse.

Crawling backwards on his hands and knees was frightening, all the more so when he pulled himself completely into the tunnel. A small handle allowed him to slide the hidden door closed from the inside. After he pulled the panel halfway, it clicked the rest of the way shut by itself.

D'Artagnan felt trapped, but controlled his quiet panic as he kept creeping backwards until he came to the slightly broader end of the tunnel where, looking behind and beneath his body, he could see a tunnel continuing and leading vertically down. It wasn't till he was hanging by his elbows, his shoulders straining with pain and bruised muscles screaming, that his feet found the rungs embedded in the wall. He climbed down, rung by rung, eventually coming to a pitch-dark passage. Feeling his way with his fingers, he followed a smooth, plastered wall for what seemed an endless length of time. He was unable to tell if he was going farther from the room or returning to it, but a blind sense of direction told him he was getting away from his room by degrees and, finally, from the house itself.

In memory, the journey was completely different, but he'd followed the tunnel in daylight then. He guessed there must be holes or other conduits overhead for the attenuated light of day. In the darkness, there were none.

He could feel his way more than he could see it. Feeling cooler air and, suddenly, no longer constricted by the walls and ceiling of the tunnel, D'Artagnan slowly, cautiously, stood. Keeping one hand on a cold, damp, rough stone wall, he took a few steps. From the sound, his footsteps were treading the floor of a cave; from the feeling of the air, even from the immenseness of the dark around him, twirling and enveloping him like a living thing—he knew he was in a vast space. It didn't feel like a corridor but like a salon or a cathedral.

As he came to the end of the wall he'd been following, a passage opened to his left and another to his right. Turning to the left, he felt the floor go down a step and took it. Two.

Something touched him, enveloped him. It felt, at first, like an enveloping chill. And then it reached in, grabbing and twisting his emotions, making his heart pound, his pulse race, his feet hesitate—he could not descend the next step.

He stopped, his foot midair. Advancing or even leaning in that direction increased his perturbation. Pulling back, the fear subsided. He considered pushing against the terror, simply because he'd been raised with the idea fear was a bad thing and should be conquered. But he remembered the horror he felt at Jean's death, and the sheer recoil of disgust. There were perils not worth defying. He turned the other way, following the other wall.

The fear subsided. His heart returned to its ordinary rhythm. Step by step, he followed the corridor until he felt fresh air on his face. It came, he determined, from directly in front. Extending his hands, he felt his way forward until they encountered an irregular rock surface. He could feel colder air blow and the smell of the night and the outdoors. He discerned from his touch that the stone—a boulder of some sort he guessed—was roughly round in shape.

He pushed at it, tentatively, then again. No movement. He pushed again, putting his aching shoulder to the burden and pressing with all the weight of his body behind him.

The rock swayed, and a little space opened. Not enough to walk through, but enough to squeeze out on his back. The scant moonlight coming in through the opening showed D'Artagnan what might be an ancient Roman fresco on the wall he'd been following.

He slid into the opening on his back and, pushing hard, managed to shove himself out, inch by inch. He ignored the sound of ripping cloth, the painful scraping of the exposed areas of his flesh.

Emerging on the other side, aching and more bruised than before, D'Artagnan took stock of the situation. He stood on the inside the meandering walls of the bastide, near the second watchtower. He took a deep breath in relief. Even if there were vampires loose in the town, it would be more dangerous outside its walls at night than in. He could see a man atop the watchtower; from his look and the fact he kept a little fire near him, he thought it was a mortal and not a vampire. Which did not mean D'Artagnan would be so foolhardy as to hail him.

He needed someone he could trust. Monsieur D'Astarac, he thought. His father's accountant and boyhood friend, whose son, Pierre, was D'Artagnan's own boyhood friend. He would go to the D'Astarac house and ask asylum and—he looked down at his battered feet—for new clothes, or at least boots. He would lay all before them and ask them what to do.

He couldn't go back to Paris, he thought, when his own town was facing this much strife. But what he could do remained to be seen.

His body in pain, and sore of foot, staying within the shadows close to the walls, hiding at the sound of any passerby, he walked the remembered streets to his friend's house.

His feet took strides as much upon memory as upon real cobblestones. If he ignored his stinking and tattered clothes and his throbbing body, he might be a boy again, and his only fear that his mother would discover he was out alone.

Sanctuary

"**G**ood heavens, boy, what happened to you?" Monsieur D'Astarac said in a shocked tone. Only an old a family friend would refer to the lord of the domain as "boy," but D'Artagnan had been in and out of his house for years, first as his son Pierre's young playmate and later, as both grew, to go on rides or hunting with Pierre. Besides, the D'Astaracs were minor nobility—if D'Artagnan remembered properly—and Monsieur D'Astarac would have been a lord himself, save for having been born a third son.

D'Artagnan felt a blush warm his cheeks, but spoke resolutely, "I beg your pardon, monsieur, but I was ... that is, I was kidnapped and have escaped capture."

"Well." Monsieur D'Astarac stepped back from the door, opening it fully onto a hall that was, like Monsieur de Tréville's, paved in tile, in this case yellow and black, and allowing D'Artagnan to step into a home lit by many candles and furnished in a way that was more comfortable and richly appointed than D'Artagnan's own. D'Artagnan had never thought of it before, since the fact his family was accorded more respect had blinded him to the relative wealth of his friend's family. But now faced with the tiled floor, mellow polished wood surfaces, and a feeling that this was far more hospitable a haven than any he'd entered in a long time, he allowed himself to be blanketed by a feeling of security as Monsieur D'Astarac closed the door behind him and called, in his assured voice, "Cecile, Cecile!"

His lady wife arrived from within and looked shocked at the sight of D'Artagnan while her husband spoke rapidly. "The boy was kidnapped and clearly maltreated. You must get the servants to fill the old tub with warm water for him. Prepare the bed in the green bedroom. Oh, and tell the cooks to prepare food for him, for he can't have eaten well in some time—have you, my boy?"

Overwhelmed, D'Artagnan shook his head, and allowed himself to be led through various rooms. By the time they got to the green room, a large hip bath was already waiting, full, in front of the roaring fireplace, and everything laid out for his comfort. He bathed, flinching at the touch of soap on his skin, every inch of which seemed to be abraded, cut, or bruised. But after he had bathed, he slipped into the dressing gown they'd provided, an affair of silk and lace unlike anything he'd ever owned, but which felt soft and comfortable against his skin.

He'd asked for a clean suit of clothes and boots, and though Monsieur D'Astarac had teased him about not needing such for a while yet, the fact was that morning would be coming soon—even if in this opulent house, with the curtains closed to keep in the comfortable warmth of the fire, he could ignore that for a while.

So, rather than argue, they'd given him a clean suit of clothes borrowed from Pierre, who was similar in size to D'Artagnan, and he felt like himself again, even if Pierre's shirt and breeches, doublet and hose—without being bright or gaudy—were all of much better quality and much newer than any that D'Artagnan owned. The boots, too, were almost new. One thing they didn't provide for him was a sword, and after his time in Paris, he felt almost naked without it.

However, when he lived at home, he had not worn a sword unless going out, so he could imagine that Monsieur D'Astarac would not think of it—not to mention that a sword, scabbard, and belt were costly items not lightly loaned. Upon reflection, especially since, after the last few days, he couldn't imagine going about unarmed, he took the straight razor from the side of the tub, folded it up, and put it into his right sleeve. He was grateful he'd been allowed to shave, as they might not have thought about it, since both Monsieur D'Astarac and his wife seemed to think D'Artagnan was all of ten years old.

He had barely wrapped himself in the dressing gown, when there was a knock at the door. At his word, several servants came in. Ten male servants—far more than he'd ever known the D'Astaracs kept—entered and exited the room, taking out the bathtub and towels and removing any indication that he'd bathed.

In no time at all, as though this were one of those dreams in which things came about just by wishing, two chairs and a table had been set in the room. On the linen-covered table lay a silver platter with a small roast chicken, accompanied by roast potatoes, and a meager bowl of withered apples, which reminded D'Artagnan of the apples he'd eaten in the ruined cottage. There was also cheese, of course, a bottle of wine, and a goblet.

Monsieur D'Astarac, himself, came in after the food, took one of the seats at the table, and motioned D'Artagnan to take the other. "Eat, my boy, eat. You must be famished. I've eaten already, and as you can see we couldn't find much to serve you at this hour, so I will not join you. But if you will allow me to sit with you, perhaps you can tell me your adventures as you eat.

"I heard, of course, that you had gone to Paris, after . . . well . . . It was a sad business, my boy." He made a face. "Your father and mother . . . gone like that. Not that one cannot help but salute them for their decision and their fortitude of mind. They did not wish to be vampires; no matter how much it was forced on them, they would not do it." He inclined his head. "We heard you'd gone to Paris . . . to stay. But now you're back, and in such a state . . ."

With a sense of relief, of almost joy, D'Artagnan poured out the story of his adventures. Monsieur D'Astarac interrupted only now and then with questions that encouraged more detail, understanding D'Artagnan's horror in seeing Jean killed. "There, there, my boy," he said reassuringly. "While I'm sure it's terrible to see a man killed like that, you must admit he was a Judas goat and it could be said . . ."

"No one deserved that," D'Artagnan said, heatedly.

A slow gaze examined him, but then Monsieur D'Astarac looked very sad and shook his head. "No, perhaps not." He tapped his fingers on the top of the table and said, in a tone designed to distract D'Artagnan from the thought, "What did you say, earlier, about escaping from your room through a secret passage?"

D'Artagnan poured out the whole story to him, complete with his father's decision to encrust the room in fleurs-de-lis.

"Ah," Monsieur D'Astarac said, "that would have been the year before your honored father offered me the post as his accountant and I was put in the way of several other lucrative business deals, which made it much easier for me to move here. Though we'd known each other as boys, of course, long ago. So you see, I'd never heard of your escapade." He smiled. "I imagine you were a handful as a four-year-old. You still were at six, when you became friends with Pierre."

At this, D'Artagnan wondered why he hadn't seen Pierre and opened his mouth to ask, but Monsieur D'Astarac grinned. "He's away from home, of course. Believe me, if he were home, he would be here this minute, to see you. Like brothers you were, and I often said he had more in common with you than with the parents who brought him into the world."

Monsieur D'Astarac stood and went to the window. He seemed to consult the curtains at length—at least he looked at them for considerable time—and then spoke in a ponderous voice, "You'll be desiring your bed, I'm sure. I should leave you to sleep."

D'Artagnan rubbed the middle of his forehead, suddenly realizing that he hadn't slept beyond fitful dozing in the carriage in a very, very long time. He said, "Yes, I should be seeking my bed, sir. Thank you for all your kindness."

But once he'd lain in bed, he could not sleep. He could do nothing but stare at the distant ceiling, wondering what to do next. Was his house occupied by vampires? And if it were, how did he rid the house and the village of them?

Monsieur D'Astarac had told him next to nothing about the situation. D'Artagnan had noticed the bells no longer rang over the city. Had all of it been taken over by vampires in his short absence? Or had it become a mini-Paris, with two divisions, night and day, vampires and humans?

It couldn't have been taken over by vampires, could it? Not completely, otherwise the D'Astaracs would have left or been turned. He twisted the other way upon his bed, feeling the deep feather bed adjust under him and the razor press against his wrist.

He'd forgotten to remove it from his sleeve. In the morning, he must ask for a sword.

He turned again. Lucky the D'Astaracs had been awake and dressed. At two hours before dawn, this was not always a given, nor even, in fact, expected. Of course, maybe he'd just returned from one

of his business trips. How fortunate that all their servants had been
up too. He thought of the well-dressed, liveried servants, who'd come
in with bath and table and dinner. They couldn't have all dressed so
quickly and in the dark, just minutes before. While he had never
been a servant, he had lived with servants all his life, and he knew
that not even the best servant in the world could look that way after
being suddenly awakened. How odd they'd had the whole house
awake . . .

He shifted in bed again. How could it be that in such a large
house, there had been so little food? The one scrawny chicken and
bits of aged cheese and a few old apples. He remembered how in
years past, the house would be redolent of roasting meat and spices,
of burnt sugar and cooked fruits.

The region must be starving indeed, if this family had to do with
so little. Not that the rest of the house, from their clothes to the
multitude of candles gave the impression of scarcity.

He banished the matter from his mind as something he could
not think about now. He was sure there must be an explanation,
but none he would discover now, half asleep as he was. Instead, he
thought of Monsieur D'Astarac's fascination with the location of
the tunnel, exactly what it felt like in it when he'd taken a step and
felt as though he were submerging himself in evil. He'd even asked
very carefully where the rock was that hid the exit from the tunnel.

Which surely went to prove that men retained always, within
themselves, a bit of the child. Monsieur D'Astarac had, in just such
a way, listened to Pierre's and D'Artagnan's adventures when they
were very young.

With this came a pang of longing for Pierre and the wish that
his friend were home. As understanding as Pierre's father might
be, D'Artagnan felt sure that—though Pierre had always been
more faint at heart than D'Artagnan—he would have entered into
D'Artagnan's sentiments more exactly and been able to understand
what disturbed D'Artagnan and how he needed to know what was
happening in the bastide.

Restless, wishing he weren't so tired, wishing he could know more
about the town today, D'Artagnan got up from the bed, kicking
aside the eiderdown. He went to the window and pulled the curtains

wide. There were two pairs of them, both tightly shut. A surplus of curtains that D'Artagnan didn't remember from before—when, admittedly, he'd had little reason to open and close curtains—but which seemed to him, now, as excessive.

On the other side of the impressive buttresses of fabric, there was a cool, clear morning, with the sky just brightening in shades of coral pink and pale yellow. There were noises from the wakening town, though it seemed to D'Artagnan that it was quieter than it had been, once upon a time.

Even the D'Astarac's house was quiet. Very quiet. There was no more than the sound of hushed footsteps up and down the stairs, and those infrequent for a house with so many inhabitants, between family and servants.

He frowned. A house this quiet at early morning? The scant food, though other signs of wealth remained. So many servants, more than he ever remembered the D'Astaracs having. And the whole house awake before daylight. He fingered the material of the curtains and frowned.

He was being suspicious of nothing, he was sure, but . . .

Another thought intruded, uninvited. How did Monsieur D'Astarac know about the death of D'Artagnan's parents? It had all taken place just hours before dawn, while the servants in the house lay sleeping, while even the housekeeper was not up. When the housekeeper had awakened, D'Artagnan had dug shallow graves for their ashes, put crosses over them and told the housekeeper his parents had been killed by a vampire—which was the truth.

Short of someone digging up the graves and finding no bodies, and even then . . . How and why would Monsieur D'Astarac know they'd been unwillingly turned and not . . . ?

He shook his head. No. It was impossible. But he remembered thinking that as cautious as his father was, only a trusted friend could possibly have got close enough, without suspicion, to turn him. He felt a cold finger of foreboding run down the back of his neck.

If only Pierre were here. He could talk to Pierre and Pierre would make D'Artagnan laugh at such absurd suspicions.

Yet he could not sleep. He would explore the rest of the house. He would see—he was sure—windows open in the hallways and in the rooms, and the D'Astaracs sitting in the parlor in the sunlight.

All these suspicions and horrible thoughts would vanish like snow in summer.

He went to the door and tried the handle, but it would not turn, and forcibly pushing it did nothing. The hair now stood fully on end at the back of his neck.

What had he done? He'd escaped one captivity only to find another. He redressed completely. Feverishly, he removed the linen from the bed and tied sheets end to end. He was three stories up, and he knew that the sheets would not reach the ground. Looking out the window, he saw one of the D'Astarac servants lurked underneath, casually leaning against the wall of the house.

A Judas goat, D'Artagnan thought, and knew he could never go that way. But looking down he saw an ornamental frieze that ran around the house. The ledge was wide enough—just barely—for his feet. The sheets would reach—just barely—that far. If he walked along that ledge, he could reach the lower roof next door and climb onto it. Once there, he could study another way down.

He closed the shaving blade and slipped it into his sleeve again. Then he tied the end of the sheets to the leg of the bed, pulled the rest over to hang out the window. It fell barely short of the ledge.

He prayed the guard would not look up. And he was off.

From on High

Walking along the ledge was harder than D'Artagnan had expected, requiring holding on to window ledges and ornamental molding. Every window he passed—and he noted there were seven—showed curtains or shutters, tightly closed against the light of day.

At least his prayers held, though it seemed to him it took endless time to cross the front of the building. The guard did not look up. And by the time D'Artagnan reached the lower roof, he was sure the man was a guard, meant to keep him in the house, and that the D'Astaracs were vampires. The silence in the house and the closed curtains had confirmed it. He wondered only about his friend Pierre.

Gaining the neighboring roof, he climbed to the other side of its sloping length, careful to position his feet so that no stray roof tiles would fall below. At length he made it from rooftop to rooftop, quietly, till he was near where a stone cistern touched the edge of an eave. From the stone cistern he jumped to an abandoned trough on a house at the edge of town. And, from there, to the ground, where he fell almost on top of a very young boy.

D'Artagnan jumped back. He started apologizing profusely, hoping this child wasn't a Judas goat who would denounce him, hoping that—

He stopped sharp, as the face of the boy came into full focus and he recognized the rounded face, the blue-gray eyes, the slightly parted lips of Madame Bonacieux, however well disguised in a suit of dark wool cloth, having bound her breasts so that no hint of her soft loveliness showed through the male apparel.

"Madame!" he whispered.

And he had her in his arms, warm and pliant and smelling of roses, her lips finding his with almost desperate hunger, her body glued to his.

"Madame!" he said again, in quite a different tone, as she allowed him to pull back enough to look at her. Not that it wasn't flattering to be kissed this way. They'd parted with a kiss and it was fitting they should reunite with one. His body felt lighter than it had since she'd last kissed him, his heart soared and he bent his head to her and kissed her again, deep and long. He still felt hesitant and not sure exactly what to do once their lips were joined, but she led him, gently, her tongue on his.

He parted again, suddenly wondering what those inhabitants of the town who were awake would feel if they saw their lord kissing a boy outside a house on the outskirts of town. On a long drawn breath, his fingers pulling back straggles of her honey-blond hair that had gotten loose from beneath her hat and framed her face as though in a nimbus of light, "You? Here?"

"I scried," she said, and took a deep breath. "On a pond, early morning. It showed this place and how to get here, and it showed your falling from above. I thought, to be sure, it had to be wrong, but . . ." She drew in breath again, like a woman drowning, and she pulled him to her again and kissed him hard, before releasing him and smiling tremulously up at him. "I cannot tell you how and why I came," she said. "We . . . I do not wish to talk here. The rumor in the countryside hereabouts is that half of your town is vampires and Judas goats, and no one knows which half, save that the leader of the vampires is one Monsieur D'Astarацs and the leader of the humans his runaway son, Pierre."

"Pierre," D'Artagnan said, and half laughed. "Pierre, my friend, who was always more like me than like his parents, as his father says."

Madame Bonacieux gave him an odd look, as though wondering what he meant by that, and D'Artagnan shook his head. "It is a long story and painful. But where can we go, that we can talk? If we could speak to Pierre . . ."

"Likely you could have, two days ago, but now the vampires have taken over your house, and the humans have taken refuge some-where, no one is sure where."

"Oh."

Her small hand dug into his arm, holding close. "If you will listen," she said. "We must find a safe place or a place we could be . . ." She frowned again. "You wouldn't know where an ancient temp— No, wait, you almost certainly would not. How about . . . do you know of any standing stones hereabouts?"

"Standing . . ." he said, and frowned. "Do you mean like the King's Men?"

"If those are standing stones, ancient ones, I most assuredly do."

"Outside the town. A mile or so. The legend is that a king and his men were turned to stone there, and stayed thus, forever. Other legends say that if the stones are ever moved, that will be the end of the world."

She frowned at him a little then gave him her hand. "Take me there."

They judged it better not to go through the town gates. You never knew which side the guard might be on. But D'Artagnan, a son of the region, knew the place where a couple of stones had fallen and been put back up, which could be removed to allow a young man and woman to squeeze through at the back wall of the town without exciting notice.

D'Artagnan remembered his father saying that a town could never be secured against the vampires by stones. You had to be vigilant every moment. Too bad he had relaxed his own vigilance.

While they walked to the standing stones, under the growing light of day—D'Artagnan grateful for Pierre's boots and even more grateful that Pierre was still alive and that he'd not been mistaken in him—D'Artagnan told her the story of his adventures.

She, in turn, told him about Athos' misadventure and about what he'd found out. "Now, I'm not sure why the vampire allowed him to see that," Madame Bonacieux said. "For you can be sure she did, considering what vampires are and what they do."

It worried D'Artagnan too, as did the idea that there was some significant thing or event of great importance, to which he was so integral that the highest ranking vampires in France had dragged him all the way back to Gascony.

"I think," he said, thinking of D'Astarac's interest in his story, "the vampires wanted to know where that secret tunnel under my house was."

She frowned up at him, her pretty nose wrinkling. "Do you know how vast the cave the tunnel leads to is, or where the branch that you felt was evil goes?"

D'Artagnan shook his head. "It was pitch dark. Deep, dark, blind. Now, the memories I have of it . . . " he shook his head again. "It might mean nothing." And to her quizzical gaze. "I was very young and might have confused it with other places and times. I remember a vast cavern and the sound of a river somewhere, and also several paths, branching off from it."

The look she gave him was worried. "And the feeling of evil."

"I don't remember that from when I was young," he said. "Perhaps I never went near that place." He thought about it. "If I'm not confusing it with somewhere else, there were paintings too."

"Paintings?"

"Or at least drawings," he said. "With lots of painted blood. I remember the blood."

He wished she did not look so worried. Given what blood had come to mean for humanity, the idea there were paintings of blood in a cave made him feel distinctly uneasy, and her expression did not help. "What can it be, though?" he asked, forcing a smile onto his face. "It's not as though the monsters aren't walking our streets already. How much scarier can anything underground be?"

She took a deep breath. "I'm thinking of all the vampires they've released from underground tombs."

D'Artagnan shivered. During his whole life, his happy childhood, had there had been a sleeper army of vampire wraiths underneath his house waiting? Had he never been secure at all?

"Sometimes," Madame Bonacieux said, "these vampires and the secret of their existence are passed in families from generation to generation. Sometimes it is because an ancestor of a family, long ago, was a Judas goat and kept such a place as a shrine, performing certain rituals believing they kept the vampires alive. The knowledge passed from generation to generation until it was a religion. Most of the blood gods, I think," she said, "who have tainted human religion from the beginning were of that nature."

D'Artagnan started to say that he did not believe any of his ancestors could have been Judas goats, then had to admit he did not even truly know people he'd been acquainted with all his life.

The idea of his ancestors worshiping those creatures, though, made him squirm with discomfort. "What," he asked, "would be the reason for them wanting these armies of old ones?"

She shrugged. "No one knows, but they seem intent on freeing all of those that they can from their captivity, and letting them out to wander the world of the living. They must serve some purpose. Are those the stones?"

They'd crested a hillock, and had come into full view of the stones on the slope just below. There were thirteen large stones, one of them as tall as two tall men standing one atop the other, and then twelve more surrounding them, which were just a little taller than Porthos and twice as broad around. They were local granite, roughly hewn, their surfaces covered in lichens and mosses. Although they were clearly man-made, they blended naturally with the grassy slopes surrounding them.

The lady ran to the stones and then walked around, touching now this stone, now that, with the look of someone who is greeting old friends. "Strange," she said. "That it is not on a mountain top, or at least a hilltop, you know these circles often are."

Before he could point out that they were in a small hollow atop a larger mountain, she frowned at him and smiled. "Doesn't mean much, though, as they are a protective lock. These are, sometimes, when they are placed as protection. They are put where they are most needed."

She walked around the circle, touching here and there again. D'Artagnan leaned against a standing rock, warm from the sun. The stone felt almost human there, behind him, as though it were supportive and calm, a friend or a relative. The lady certainly treated them as such, bowing to the one in the center, smiling at and touching the others.

She returned to him. "It will do. I don't know what it is set to guard. The shielding here is too strong to feel whatever it is protecting us from." She looked around and smiled a little. "But it is very alive and very good, and it is the ideal place for what I have to do." She looked at him with defiance in her eyes, though he wasn't sure what or whom she was defying. "Monsieur D'Artagnan," she said, "we are threatened and besieged all around. I have some scant power that comes to me from my worship of the goddess, and from being her faithful servant. I will need all that power to extricate us from this situation and perhaps—" she hesitated "—to help prevent the dark ones from unleashing the horror of more vampire wraiths upon the world."

He took a deep breath. "Whatever you need of me, my lady."

The defiance remained, but now her eyebrow lifted, and a brief, secretive smile trembled upon her lips. "As may be. But let me explain, first, as I know some have problems aiding with the rituals of another religion."

He remembered Aramis' words and couldn't help smiling back at her. He sobered, though, as she said, "My power is of a particular kind. The goddess to whose worship I am devoted is a fertility goddess. Do you understand my meaning?"

He shook his head and she sighed. "My goddess derives her power from . . . . Her favored mode of worship is the . . . union of male and female, the . . . act," she blushed deeply, "that can lead to the conception of a child. Are you willing to participate in this, to call her favor upon me so I can fight the evil of vampires?"

He could scarcely believe it, and when he believed it at last, he could scarcely take it in. These things did not happen to him or—he thought—to any male outside fevered dreams and fantasies. Perhaps he *was* dreaming. Perhaps he was still tied up in the carriage, surrounded by vampires, unable to escape except in dreams.

A deep breath, and he felt his fingers upon the rock, the rock rough beneath them, and he thought, *I am not dreaming*.

He nodded once at her. "But you are married, madame," he said.

She smiled. "Ah, but I am married according to the rites of my religion, and when my husband cannot provide the necessary . . . ah, services, he has given me license to do what must be done. My estate in the mundane world requires the protection of marriage, but my estate in the sacred world requires that I be free."

"I said I would do anything needed, lady, to help in the fight, and I meant it." He inclined his head, almost afraid to see her expression;

embarrassed and trembling and afraid she would say it was all an elaborate ruse.

Instead, even though her laughter rang in a merry peal, there was no derision in it. She led him by the hand and stood him by the biggest stone. In local lore, it represented the king. "Wait here, while I draw the circle that will keep us safe while we perform the ritual."

He leaned back against the stone and watched, as she took from a pouch at her waist a small cup, a flask, a cloth bag, four candles, and a very small pottery container. From the boot of her male outfit she pulled a wicked-looking knife wrapped in leather and in silk. She unwrapped it, reverently.

It was hard to know exactly what she was doing, but the ritual and all the gestures involved looked as complex as what he had watched at mass for so many years. She poured water from flask to cup, then shook something white from the bag into the cup. She murmured some words under her breath, for all the world like the priest at mass. Walking around the outer circle of stones, she sprinkled water from the cup onto each stone, muttering something again. Then she came back, and taking the first candle she used the contents of the ceramic container to light its wick. Walking straight to the stone facing north, she intoned, "Power of the North, oh noble guardian, bestir yourself from your cold, wintry depths! Come stand by and protect us as we perform these, our necessary rituals." Lighting another candle from the wick of the first, she set it down at the stone facing south, and then paced to those facing east and west, placing candles. She then brought out her knife.

She walked up to D'Artagnan. Her eyes were wild and, for a moment, D'Artagnan—remembering stories from classical times and the madness of the bacchantes—feared she would plunge the knife into his heart. Instead, she leaned forward and kissed his lips, momentarily. "I am now going to cut the circle out of the world," she said.

"I beg your pardon?" he said, not quite believing what he'd heard.

She laughed again, a laugh that combined nervousness and amusement. "I am going to cut the circle we stand in out of the world, in a metaphysical sense. It doesn't matter," she said, seeing the lack of comprehension in his eyes. "It is all very complex and would take forever to explain, but for our ritual to succeed we need to avoid interruption, so I will now remove us in spirit from the common world of humanity and onto another plane. We'll still be here physically, but our spirits will not. It is very important that you understand," she said, intently, "this circle is sacred and drawn in my own energy. Once the ritual is completed you must wait until I've broken the circle with my knife before you step out. Do you understand?"

"Will it . . . kill me, if I do it wrong?" he asked. His life had been so strange these last few days that it was not beyond belief that a line drawn upon the ground by a knife could cause his death.

She shook her head. "No. Not physically. But it will render us both vulnerable. It will make the circle itself weaker, less able to keep the harmful forces at bay, perhaps even the ancient vampires . . ." She sighed. "Do you know the story of Romulus and Remus, together, building the sacred wall within which Rome would one day stand?"

He nodded. "And then Romulus killed Remus," he said, "so he would be king alone."

"That's one of the stories, but there's an older one, which is told among those who believe as I do. The wall was a sacred circle, as is the one in which we stand now. My people say that Remus saw a bird flying by and, to catch it in his net, forgot about the ritual and stepped over the wall, breaking the circle before Romulus could break it properly. The pain of it drove Romulus insane, and he killed his twin with the sacred knife. He grieved afterwards, but he knew he had not been himself while caught in the throes of the broken circle."

D'Artagnan warily eyed the sharp knife in her hand.

"They were young men," she said. "Raised rough and living rough, and violent by nature. I'm not threatening you with death. I'm simply saying that breaking the circle, unbidden, could have very bad consequences for both of us."

He nodded solemnly, and she walked around the circle, drawing on the earth with the tip of her sharp, sharp knife. Then she stuck the knife in the ground in front of the king stone and proclaimed, "I have cut us out of the plane of men. We now stand between planes and everything we do is sacred."

And then she advanced toward him.

The Power of the World

She kissed him again, brave and bold. Her nimble fingers undid the ribbons that tied his doublet together. She removed it carefully, gently, as if D'Artagnan were either too old or too young to do this for himself. Indeed, right then, his arms felt like running water and his legs little better. The razor fell from his sleeve as she took the doublet; turning, she set the closed implement beside the garment on the grass, amid the stones.

He feared she'd think he was a fool for not acting, not helping, not doing anything, yet even more afraid of acting or doing something and being thought an even worse fool. Only one part of his anatomy was quite sure of itself—his erection grew, and as she pressed her body against him, he thought she could feel it. In fact, he was sure she could feel it, and it changed the smile she gave him. It was more knowing, broader, secretive

She plunged her hands beneath his shirt and helped him remove it, then stepped back and removed—in swift and efficient movements—her own doublet and shirt, which she set near his. She danced close up to him again, her hands stroking down to the small of his back as she embraced him.

Her hands were not as soft as he expected. There was some callus there, the result of working with her hands he supposed, though he had no idea what type of manual labor her craft might involve. Nor did he want to stop to find out, as she caressed him from shoulders to waist, then back again.

Her firm breasts pressed against his bare chest, filling him with sensations remarkably akin to those from a raging fever. He went hot and cold, shivering uncontrollably.

His hands lifted, slowly, without real strength. Once they touched her skin and felt the rounded, swelling silk-softness of her bosom, he felt rejuvenated, and couldn't have helped himself any more than he could have stopped his own heart with sheer will.

His mouth followed his hands, and then his hands were struggling with the ties to her breeches, pulling them down. She stopped him long enough to remove her boots, without which she would have become tangled in breeches and hose and boots.

As soon as she was nude, he undressed himself, a feat not so easily performed, since one of his hands was still busy on her shoulder, and rounding the curve of it to her arm, muscular and yet softer than any arm he'd ever felt.

Every portion of her fascinated him, and he wanted to feel it all, enjoy all of her. He freed himself of boots, breeches, hose, and pulled her roughly against him. She had incongruously long legs for such a short woman, though her wide hips and broad breasts lent her silhouette more balance than he'd thought.

He kissed her lips, her eyes, the hollow of her throat, trailing down to follow the curve of her shoulder . . .

Their first coupling was brief and clumsy, tumbling upon the grassy ground, falling upon her and entering her almost all in one movement. The feeling of warmth and sweet confinement was too much, something he had only dreamed of before, and he spent in her almost immediately.

She waited, caressing all the while, and then she rolled him onto his back and sat astride him. His erection returned almost immediately. This time she guided him within and she controlled the movement, forcing a slow rhythm on his impatience, tormenting him with touches and kisses, as she led him up a seemingly endless slope of pleasure to a long-delayed and satisfying summit.

Waves of pleasure washed over him, each higher than the last. Heat or joy or perhaps music—all his senses being scrambled and mingled and impossible to tell apart—swirled about them, as the pleasure opened like an abyss and swallowed him, and he fell, headlong, into a joyous semblance of death or godhead.

They made love again and again, heedless of the time, lost in a world of their own and smiled upon by a benevolent divinity, in which neither hunger nor hurt intruded.

When it was over, he lay on the grass on his back, surprised to see that it was early evening and the sunset sky a dark, dark red, like spilled blood.

Madame Bonacieux got up and bowed to him, a small, precise bow. "I thank you, monsieur, for your help in worship." A small smile played on her lips, but he couldn't tell if it was pleasure, or amusement, or politeness, or a combination of all of those.

"Capture him!" The words, shouted by Rochefort dissipated the veil of satisfied pleasure and D'Artagnan bolted upright. Looking over his shoulder he saw a mass of the ancient vampires hurtling toward him.

It didn't work, he thought, *they are free!* And, reaching for the razor blade from beside his doublet, he charged out of the circle, ready to defend his lady.

A twinge, like the feeling that makes one's hair raise in the middle of a thunderstorm, told him he'd broken the circle and he heard Madame Bonacieux scream, "*Stop!*" But too late.

He turned around, ready to reenter, just in time to see her doubled in pain, but it was too late; he was swiftly overtaken by the writhing mass of vampire wraiths. He slashed about him with his blade, but even as he thought his sword would have been ineffective against this multitude, his blade hit a bone and snapped in two.

He thought of Jean, being drained of life; his pause cost him any advantage he might have had. He was thrown onto the grass, held down by the wraith vampires.

His last vision as he was dragged backward was of the hoard of ancient vampires—a swarm of darkness—toppling one standing stone, and then another.

It is the end of the world.

That Fool Man

Athos relished riding for once, on this very strange trip. Throughout the last few days they'd been traveling during the day to avoid snares laid by vampires on the roadways they must use. In a previous village, where they had stopped to water their horses, they had been fortunate to find an abandoned racing gig that must have been some young man's pride and joy before the vampires came. It was musty and disused and needed repair, but upon inspection, it became clear the top of the seat would come off, and if Athos lay inside it, with the seat covered by a scrap of tapestry, no light could penetrate.

Hiring four horses to pull the gig had been more difficult, as their own horses were not broken to harness. The horses they'd found were rather short in the back, but despite this they made excellent time.

Athos did not complain of the accommodations since, while in the seat, he slept deeply, with the somnolence that affected vampires in daylight.

But at the end of the day today—being so close to D'Artagnan's domain and having heard stories of a vampire carriage heading toward it—the musketeers had decided to press on, ignoring their fatigue. They'd left the gig and the horses that pulled it with a farmer.

After allowing their own mounts to rest a few hours, they were now bent on pursuit.

This had left Athos to ride again with his comrades, but without worry of sleeping near them.

Whether staying in hostelries, or camping in the forest or by the roadside, he had always taken care to sleep away from his friends. He'd noticed, though, every time he woke, Grimaud woke too, as though he'd trained himself to wake when Athos stirred. Knowing

Grimaud always had the sharpened stake at hand was an odd sort of comfort.

Since the awful night and the wolf pup, he'd taken great care to have broth by him as he slept. The horror of tasting it was usually enough to sober him from the dreams that were becoming, unfortunately, all too frequent.

But tonight, Athos would not think of stakes or of his horrible dreams. He was riding free under the stars, on Samson, his night black horse, hand-reared by him from a colt. He'd calmed and accepted that Athos presented no danger to him, so they had resumed their former good understanding, in which Samson moved as if controlled by Athos' own thoughts.

Given their perfect coordination and the fact that Samson had been galloping without rider all day and was therefore far less tired than the other horses, they kept outdistancing his companions and riding well ahead. Finally Athos remembered there might be dangers that needed all of them together. He reined in his mount enough for the others to catch up with him.

After riding Samson madly and freely through mountain roads, nearer to the edge of the precipice than Athos would trust any other mount, they'd found themselves in relatively open country, the road winding between trees on one side and a grassy plain on the other. Reining in Samson, Athos noticed there was an ancient circle of stones on one side and, in the distance, a lone bastide. He also recognized his friends were getting just far enough behind that it might be dangerous should he encounter trouble first—or if trouble overtook them from behind.

The thought of trouble took his hand to his sword, as a tatterdemalion figure burst out of the stone circle, yelling, "That foolish man, foolish, idiot! You must do something!"

The creature looked all the more frightening because it wore a man's clothes, but it had the long, flowing blond hair of a woman. It seemed too that it had dressed hastily, for it had breeches but no hose, and its doublet was pulled on askew and sideways.

Athos thought it was some sort of tramp, or worse; he imagined it was a lure thrown by the local Judas goats who perhaps found creatures of this type enticing.

But as the creature came closer, it said, in a voice full of female tears, "Monsieur Athos."

He did not let go of his sword nor push it back in after pulling it out of its scabbard a palm or so, but he did frown and look closer at her. Under the tousled hair which formed an obscuring curtain in front of her face, and the clothes which he recognized for Grimaud's own second-best doublet and hose, he now saw Madame Bonacieux' tear-stained face, her wild eyes.

She still wore her rose around her neck, he noted. Had she not, he'd have thought she was turned. But as it was, he said only, "Madame," in a tone of shock, as she came very close and lay her hand on Samson's mane and looked up at Athos with eyes that were so tear-filled and intent as to seem almost blind. "Monsieur Athos," she said, "you must help that foolish man."

"What man, madame?" he said, recognizing depths to her speech that he couldn't quite understand and that the word *foolish* conveyed an odd sort of affection, perhaps love. "Of whom do you speak?"

"Monsieur D'Artagnan!" she said, and started pouring out a wild tale of D'Artagnan dropping off a building, and other stories, stranger and darker. Something about a sleeping battalion of ancient ones poised to take over the world, about someone who had almost lured D'Artagnan without a fight, about passages and secret rooms, and a primeval painted cave.

She was in the middle of it, when the rest of them rode up. As with Athos, it took them a moment to recognize the lady. But when they did and she told her story again, Aramis seemed to grasp it better than the rest of them. "A sacrifice," he said. "They mean him for a sacrifice, but ... *Ventre saint-Gris!* What can be so special about him that they would go all the way to Paris to capture him and bring him back here? Surely there are other virgins in—"

He was interrupted by a snort of derision from Madame Bonacieux who, blushing deeply, immediately covered her mouth with her hand. "I beg your pardon, but he is no longer, that is to say ... "

"No," Aramis said drily, "no, I imagine he isn't. But even if he were, surely there would be other virgins in Gascony, and nothing would justify their going so far just to capture him and drag him here."

She shook her head. "I don't think that is it," she said. "I think they needed to know where the entrance to the tunnel was located."

"Surely, madame, they could have looked," Porthos said absently, looking with half-closed eyes at the walled town as though evaluating it for weaknesses. "Not that large a place, and I would think if one of the entrances was the hole by the wall, it would have been easy to find."

She shook her head and waved her hand. "These mountains hereabouts," she said, "are as full of holes as cheese. It wasn't that it was difficult to find a hole, or even a hole that led to a cavern. It wasn't even finding a cavern underneath D'Artagnan's house, even if it is known that it should be there. It is more that I think once in the cave beneath the house, which might be—let us remember—centuries old, they would need someone to help them find the particular cave they're looking for." She pulled her hair back with both hands and said, "I believe I have proof of this, after a fashion, that is . . . He did sense an evil down there, and I think that's where the vampires want to go."

"But why D'Artagnan?" Athos said, thinking of the young Gascon. He remembered an open countenance, perhaps a little too prone to showing all his thoughts upon his features. He then remembered what Aramis had said about D'Artagnan sensing the old vampires massing on Pont Neuf when Madame Bonacieux, certainly more trained to the task, didn't. "Oh," he said, "you mean he is a sensitive for vampires?"

She shook her head, then shrugged. "More than that," she said. "I would think that . . ." She bit her lower lip. "I think there is a reason the house was built on top that cave," she said.

"You mean . . ." Aramis let a laugh tear through his lips though his expression gave every appearance of fighting it. "I was right all along, while being wrong. That he's a Judas goat—a hereditary Judas goat, raised to protect vampires."

"Yes. No. I mean, I don't believe he knows anything about it, or even that he cared about it at all. I am sure he is what he seems to be—an open and amiable young man, a vampire orphan who, detesting the breed, determined, by all that's holy, to fight them. Also, what I heard in the town is that his father was one of the most determined fighters against the blight of vampirism spreading through the countryside." She shook her head. "I don't mean he was raised to be a Judas goat, nor that his father was, for that matter. Simply that at some time, probably thousands of years ago, one of his ancestors was chosen for the duty of guarding the army of the undead."

Athos frowned, and grimaced. "Not his fault then."

"No," she said. "His only ability is being able to tell where large groups of vampires are. You see, he would be linked to them by rites performed by his ancestors in this place where he was born."

"Madame," Aramis said. "Are you telling me they're using him to locate the army of vampires?"

She nodded, twisting her hands together in distress. "As it is, we've wasted far too much time already. We must rescue him!"

Aramis gave the impression of reining in his horse, though the animal had been stopped for a while and showed no signs of impatience other than the occasional stamping of a hoof on the packed dirt of the path. "I believe not, madame. It is unlikely we would be able to save him, and if we follow him into a cavern deep underground, we'd be trapped there with the army of the damned. It seems a lost cause, madame, and that we came this far for nothing."

She made fists of her hands and, for a moment, seemed disposed to pummel the neck of Athos' mount. But before Athos could do more than put out his hand to grasp her wrists and stop such a foolhardy movement, she controlled herself.

She opened her hands first and turned them toward the musketeers in a gesture of helplessness, then she clasped them on the thighs of her breeches, in great handfuls of fabric. "No, monsieur, you don't understand."

"I understand," Aramis said, his lips gone thin and aristocratic again, and his head tilting up a little, as if to emphasize his superiority over his circumstances, "that you have a lively concern for the young gentleman's circumstances, but—"

"No!" she said. "You do not understand. Stupid man!" She shook her head. "These stones were put here to prevent the sleepers wakening. There is a strong quieting spell on them that would keep the vampires asleep beneath them, should anything happen, only that . . ."

"Only that?" Athos said, noticing, for the first time, that about half the stones—including the one in the center—were toppled.

"Only that the stones were overturned and desecrated," she said, frowning a little and turning to Athos, looking at him only, as though he were her sole dependence and her last hope. "The key stones were toppled by the vampires, and now the stones no longer protect." She gave a loud sob, though her eyes remained dry. "And these stones . . . I don't know if it is about the army of vampires or . . . or whatever they protect, but D'Artagnan told me if they were ever violated it would be the end of the world."

"Madame," Aramis said, somewhere out of Athos' range of vision, somewhere at the periphery of the group, somewhere out of sight. "Surely you know every circle of stones has that legend attached to it."

But Athos didn't pay any attention to him and neither did Madame Bonacieux, because they both were thinking of D'Artagnan down there with a menace so greatly primitive that men of a civilization long lost had created this circle of massive stones to protect the world from it, seeking to keep it inviolate through the centuries.

Athos could feel something dark and dangerously seductive nearby. It felt like his pull to Charlotte and her desires, the glamour they'd said he'd been caught under. Only this was stronger and somehow more frightening, like being caught in a river current pulling him inexorably toward it, yet fainter than a whisper he'd strain to listen to. "I think this legend is true," he said gravely. His voice was heavy with meaning, and Aramis gave him a look of enquiry. Athos sighed in reply. "I can't explain it, Aramis, not coherently. I feel the pull of something dark and dangerous . . . it's like the pull of a river approaching a rapids. I have felt this pull since I was turned. I felt it for the vampire who turned me. But now I feel it—and much stronger—for whatever lays—probably no longer asleep—beneath those stones."

Aramis studied Athos' face in silence for a long moment, while the woman stood by, her face pale with anxiety. "If you will not help me," she said at last, "I will, once more, have to go by myself and do what I can to rescue him."

Porthos shook his head. "We will come," he said. "Of course we will come."

Aramis could only slowly nod in agreement.

Mutiny and Turmoil

"You will wait for me here," Athos said to Grimaud, reading mutiny in his servant's eyes.

"If that is your wish, Monsieur le Comte," the man said, his voice deceptively meek.

Athos sighed. "Grimaud, it is not that I don't prize you or wouldn't wish your company, but this is likely to prove . . . " He paused. He'd almost said, *Likely to prove my death*, which he felt was true, even if the concept of his death had altered somewhat now he was a vampire. And yet, if he said it, he knew as he knew himself that Grimaud would only insist all the more on going along. Athos, who had lost his father when he was only ten, had no idea what promises Grimaud had made to the old count, whom he'd served so faithfully for decades. But whatever it was, he was sure it involved keeping Athos from all danger that could be averted until—possibly, his father having spent most of his life in such an endeavor—a successor to the lands and title were assured. Perhaps even after, since Athos' father had been inordinately fond of his young son.

Athos took a deep breath. "It is likely to prove the end of the world if we fail. And if we fail, you are to return to La Fère," he said. "Make it ready to withstand the onslaught to come and help my successor as best you can." His successor being the rather dull cousin who now governed the land on Athos' behalf, but all possible help would be needed, including divine intervention.

Grimaud pushed his lower jaw forward in an expression of obstinacy that made it far more credible than ever that he had served as a fighting man. "Monsieur le Com—" he started.

Before he could do more than open his mouth, Porthos spoke. "No, Grimaud, your master is right and you must do as bid." It was so rare for the shy musketeer to speak with such a commanding voice that Grimaud stopped his speech and looked at him, astonished. "For you are, by far, the most experienced fighting man of all our servants and Planchet has no experience at all. It is our duty, sworn, to fight for others, but it is not yours, my friends." His kind gaze encompassed the group. "Bazin would probably do better to pray for all our souls and the world itself, and Mousqueton . . . " He smiled affectionately at his own servant. "It is my wish, Grimaud, that if I should die, you tell Monsieur de Tréville that Mousqueton becomes, at my death, my adopted son and my successor to the tunic of the musketeers and my spot left in the rotation. I do believe Monsieur le Comte was right when he told you to look after his domain. I've met that cousin of his. What do you think Monsieur le Comte's father would say if he were left without resort to your wisdom, and the domain fell to vampires? No. You must return to La Fère to guide the new lord and train the boy, Planchet, to wait on the lord's son, so that together both will know that vampires must be fought."

"Will you do that, Grimaud, my friend, my second father?" Athos said, extending his hand to his servant.

For a moment the man neither spoke nor moved, and Athos thought his gesture would be rebuffed. In the others, too, there were signs of mutinous rebellion boiling just beneath the surface. It peeked out of Mousqueton's furrowed brow, because Mousqueton— and Athos had no idea what his history was, though from something Porthos had said once, he thought the young man had been left a vampire orphan very young—might be honored beyond speech at the idea of becoming his master's adopted son, but he also loved Porthos with all his heart, and gloried in Porthos' exploits. Perhaps he was afraid he was not quite good enough to become a musketeer. He looked at Porthos, his eyes wide, and a hint of protest started to form at his frowning mouth.

Then there was Bazin who, in the last moment, had crossed himself twice and set his hands in prayer five times, but whose right hand nonetheless kept caressing the stock of his stake in its scabbard. And Planchet—well, Planchet was good and furious and, Athos would guess, putting all his will into stopping himself from telling them he would see them in hell before he stayed behind while they went to risk their lives. This from a boy whose greatest martial accomplishment was the pitching of stones at birds.

All of it seemed to hang on Grimaud's lowered head, his hands gripping the horse's reins. If he raised his face and it showed Athos a rebellious expression . . . if he uttered as much as a sound of protest—

But when Grimaud's head came up, his hand did too. He clasped Athos arm just below the elbow, his grip strong enough to be painful. "Be careful, m'sieur," he said, his voice clouded with tears. "You are too good, too fine to throw yourself away without need." The sincerity of his voice shook Athos to the core.

How could the man say this, this man who had seen Athos that disgraceful night in the woods when he had allowed the inner beast to rule?

"The world needs you, Monsieur le Comte, and many like you. Your mother said you were sent by the warrior archangels to battle evil, and, sir, I've seen nothing to make me disbelieve it.

Grimaud's eyes, ordinarily so calm and sensible, seemed to burn with an inner fire. "Go with my blessing," he said, and hesitated. "My son."

Athos felt tears prickling his eyes, at this acknowledgment of their relationship which both men knew to be true, but which neither would have otherwise admitted, hiding instead behind the facade of their roles and class differences.

"Thank you," he said clasping Grimaud's arm in turn, in a greeting of war-brothers, then letting it go. "You will wait here," he said, looking at the other servants and finding that, though Planchet was looking at Grimaud with admiration and Bazin with shock, they no longer seemed to wish to dispute the order to wait. "If we do not return or you have reason to fear we will not, you are to go and fulfill your destinies and continue our fight for us."

He wheeled his horse around and looked at the others. "Now we must go to the town, and Madame must show us the way to these catacombs beneath the wall. Be prepared, for I think the town guard is a vampire."

"He is," Madame said. "Or at least he might be, since the leadership of the town ricochets every day between Pierre D'Astarac, the leader of the mortals, and his father, the leader of the vampires. As well to be prepared, for as soon as we enter the town, at the very least the Judas goats there will try to stop us, and perhaps worse. They tried to kill me! I spent the day in magical battle with them, and I am exhausted."

Athos inclined his head. "As well, then, madame, you tell us where the entrance to the cave is, and then you wait here, with my friends."

She shook her head. "No, monsieur," she said, her voice almost sweet in its absolute unshakability. Turning to the servants, she said, "One of you, lend me a horse. I will try to return it, if you need to retreat. Has anyone a spare sword?"

"Madame!" Aramis said, sounding shocked. "Will you try to fight when your profession is—"

She rounded on him like a furious cat, her pretty little face distorted by a snarl. "The same as yours, Father D'Herblay, and you fight because in these sad days we can't be contented to simply pray for people's souls. If we do not also defend their bodies, it will all be for naught."

"But for you to pretend to be a warri—" It was perhaps clear only to Athos that behind Aramis' censorious attitude hid a very real concern for Madame Constance Bonacieux. Of different religions they might be, but in the last several years of hard fighting, holy men and women of all religions had learned to trust each other and even to admire each other, and those two were no exception.

Athos had always suspected beneath their endless quibbling on theology, the nature of the divine, and her highly inappropriate behavior for a female, there lay an emotion that if not romantic love, was a platonic love. He could tell from the frantic expression in Aramis' eyes that he aimed to save the lady if he could.

But she was in no mood to see it or to credit his kindness. Even if she had been, Athos thought, the truth was a that woman like her, who did battle without fear in the spiritual realms and in such an unorthodox way, would not now stay still and meek awaiting her rescue. Instead, she rounded on Aramis, fury in her eyes and voice, "*Pretend* to be a warrior?" she said. "Oh, such presumption, when you know all of us, all who are chosen to guard Her Majesty are as well able to defend her physically as spiritually! How can you say that? You must know I trained with arms and in unarmed combat too, before I was accorded the honor. I was—" She raised her small face up, so that in the light of the moon she looked undeniably proud and strong. Were she a little taller and male that pose would be the thing monuments were made of, to be extolled to future generations as examples of the steely qualities of their ancestors. "The only daughter of a musketeer, and by him trained in all the arts of combat as though I were a boy. I beg you to believe I can fight as well as any man, and better than most."

Aramis opened his mouth, but said nothing, and Athos seized the opportunity to say, quietly, "Planchet, let her have your horse. If need be, you're light enough to ride double with Grimaud till you can acquire another. As for a sword—" He reached into his own luggage. He always brought extra swords, because experience had taught him swords still got broken or lost. "This, madame," he said, extending her a sword in its own scabbard, "is my second best sword. Wield it in honor and do not stain it with surrender. It has not been accustomed to that."

She reached for the sword and for just a moment, their fingers touched—hers warm and vital and alive, his cold and hard and dead. A vision of his body pressed against hers, his fangs piercing the smooth pale skin of her neck, made him recoil. The beast, he thought, was dangerously close to the surface, brought there by the tension in his muscles and nerves, by the inexorable, continuous pull of the . . . thing beneath the earth.

Madame Bonacieux did not seem to see it or sense it. She adjusted her attire, buckled the scabbard on, and looked up, "Even though we have different ideas of honor," she said, "I will use it to protect the weak and defend the defenseless, and I'll never surrender it while living."

He inclined his head. "I can ask no more."

Then they were mounted, galloping fast toward the gate.

It seemed strange to Athos—for they'd stopped at the approach to the town long enough so that someone was bound to have seen them, and, certainly, if something so important were going on, surely the vampires would have no wish of seeing it disturbed—but there was no massed battalion of vampires at the gate. A single sentry stepped toward them, shouting, "Halt in the name of the—"

His fangs, his pallor, his whole demeanor left no doubt of what he was, nor did the stench that poured forth from his severed neck, as Madame Bonacieux swung her sword in a broad arc. They galloped through the gate, coursing through what must once have been a comely and vibrant main street, with sundry establishments on either side, as well as handsome and stately houses now gone to seed. Shutters were closed and fastened on some houses, yet others had the sills thrown up and opened wide. The sound of clashing swords could be faintly heard from somewhere to the north of the town.

Athos thought this explained why the gate had been left nearly unguarded. There was fighting in the town proper, and by the sound of it, a massive force was engaged.

"This way," Madame said. When they came within sight of men and horses engaged in open battle, she leapt from her horse with a grace that gave the truth to her assertion of having been raised as a musketeer's page. "This way, my friends, and let your horses go. They'll return to the servants, won't they?"

Athos nodded. Musketeer horses were trained to return to the last stop on the journey. He leapt from Samson. None of the others protested. Instead, they dismounted, slapped the horses on their flanks, and briefly watched them go. They all knew when entering a fight of the kind ahead of them that horses were just early casualties, and might take you down with them.

She pointed at a massive stone ahead of them, and the deep dark hole beside it. "There," she said, "from Monsieur D'Artagnan's description, that is the entrance to the underground caves."

The hole was defended by rank upon rank of vampires, most of them the mindless vampire wraiths. Attacking them was a motley group of men, some looking like noblemen or well-to-do bourgeois, and some ragged, desperate-looking peasants who had probably, in happier times, been farmers and tenants. The weapons being used against the vampires included—in addition to swords, pikes, scythes, and shovels—some stranger implements that Athos couldn't even identify, despite a youth spent on a rural demesne.

As he drew his sword, he hesitated. Not all foes were the easily identifiable vampire wraiths and, as ignorant strangers joining this fray—in which foes and friends alike had known each other all their lives—they might inadvertently put those they wished to aid at risk.

Knowing it was foolhardy, but the only sure way to recognize their own side, he shouted, "To me, musketeers! To me, of the king!"

Captive

The cave was dark, and D'Artagnan did not like being dragged into it. Vampires held him on all sides. His hands were tied again, and his feet hobbled by rope, barely allowing him to walk.

They pulled him into the passage he'd earlier avoided. Several of the vampire wraiths surrounding him carried torches. As they tugged him deeper into the cave, traveling over a stone bridge spanning an underground river, he noticed that the cavern narrowed into a tunnel, and the tunnel walls were painted. At first he caught sight of trees and animals, and of the hands of men—many hands, drawn with ochre, colored in bright red. Hand upon hand upon hand.

The sense of horror, the sense of being immersed in evil, suffocating and inescapable, overcame D'Artagnan. He wanted to run, to scream, anything but continue to go farther into this tunnel and toward the evil he felt.

But he could not resist it. There were hands all around him, and all his struggles did no more than further tighten the hold they had on him.

The vampires didn't speak, not even Rochefort or the couple of other vampires who still looked like the living. The ancient vampires didn't even make their clicking sounds.

Animals were portrayed on the walls, caught in the flickering light of the passing torches, animals D'Artagnan knew were not native to this region. There were what looked like the elephants he'd seen in illustrations of books about other lands, as well as lions, and great horned beasts.

As dread filled him, D'Artagnan sweated with the effort not to scream. It was as if he were a cup and fear was a liquid poured into him, a full measure and overflowing his vessel. He felt feverish and trembled, his heart racing. He couldn't run away, but still tried to hold himself back from the place where they were dragging him. He couldn't do much more than lean back, nothing, certainly, that would stop their inexorable movement.

Deeper, deeper, deeper. The ground opened like a mine shaft in front of them. Vampires jumped down first, then handed him down like a bound package.

Here the paintings on the torch-lit walls were different—vulvas and erect penises, lewdly painted with extreme realism upon the walls.

D'Artagnan was fairly sure he'd never got this far as a small child. Even as he averted his eyes from the obscenely detailed drawings, he knew he would have remembered this.

He tried to wriggle out of the holding hands, but he didn't stand a prayer. His attempts drew no more than a laconic, "Hold him," from Rochefort.

D'Artagnan felt as though the evil in which he'd been submerged was now far above his head. It was as though he were at the bottom of an ocean of evil, only no ocean had ever been like this. Not unless the ocean had a hole at its end, a pit colder and more evil than all the rest surrounding it, pulling everything into its abyss.

The vampires gazing upon him were very intent now. Even the pebble-like eyes of the vampire wraiths seemed to shine like polished glass, and their tongues—black and withered—lolled out of their mouths between their fangs.

The corridor was filled with cobwebs, as though no one had come this way in centuries, perhaps in millennia.

Strangely, the drawings in this area looked more accomplished than the ones in the more accessible caves. The others had been exact and realistic, but these looked like paintings he'd seen in the homes of great noblemen, or the walls of undesecrated churches. They looked like living, breathing people, as if they could walk out of the wall.

Their clothing was odd, though, resembling that of the statues of Greece and Rome, the fabric looking almost translucent.

As D'Artagnan watched, the vampires started setting torches down on the floor in prepared holes in front of painted scenes.

The first torch was set in front of a woman, beautiful and blond, wearing a tunic so diaphanous she might have been dressed in cobwebs. There were flowers in her hair, and were it not for her open mouth, D'Artagnan would have taken her for the representation of a goddess or a saint. But her open mouth fully displayed her bloodstained fangs.

The vampires moved faster, placing torches quickly, first revealing a crowned king, then a man resembling him, both of them hauntingly familiar in a way that D'Artagnan couldn't quite pinpoint. Then the woman and the crowned man mating were displayed—in every possible position—and finally the woman alone with hands open, and from her hands flowing a multitude of vampires.

D'Artagnan couldn't stop the keening of fear bubbling up from his throat, though he didn't know why, he hated showing that weakness. Fear had filled him and overflowed, and he felt as if every hair on his body were standing on end, and all his skin had turned to gooseflesh. The feeling around him was as strong as the stench of the old vampires.

As each torch fell into place, D'Artagnan saw that Rochefort and the other recent vampires had retreated, and he was now only in the hands of the old ones. His heart surged with hope, but on the other hand he was sure Rochefort would never have left him alone if there was any hope of his escaping.

Down and down the vampires dragged him, ignoring his feeble struggles. But D'Artagnan's brain worked through all his fear, and he marked that all these vampires wore swords and he would wager all of them knew how to fight. He swallowed hard and tried to calculate. Could he grab a sword with his bound hands, or perhaps bring them near the flame of a torch?

He marked where the torches were behind him. First, to bring his wrists near the flame, then to grab a sword. He couldn't explain it, but he thought the more recent vampires had left because the sense of evil discomfited them as much as it terrified him.

They passed a giant painting of the crowned man. No, not a man, but a vampire, sucking his double's blood. Then on the next panel the crowned vampire rose with the sun—D'Artagnan was sure of it—behind him, commanding what looked like armies of vampires, covering the entire panel.

D'Artagnan marked just where a torch was, behind and to the right of him, and swiftly leaned back. The pain flared, excruciatingly, in his bound hands as they touched the flames, and then around his wrists as the rope caught.

The vampire wraiths tried to hold him, but he twisted out of their grasp, breaking his charred bonds and grabbing the torch on the way. As the flames touched the older vampires, they flared up and burned like kindling.

D'Artagnan jumped back from the heat of their conflagration, falling to his knees on the stone floor of the cave, dazed, his feet still bound.

Circling his torch around him, he kept the still intact wraiths that came near him at bay.

By Sword and Blood

The ranks of the living opened to admit them, to give them passage to the very front, where a foolhardy group of humans spearheaded the penetration into the terrible ranks of the vampire wraiths.

Up and up they swept, cutting a swath through the vampires, continually replenished by others boiling out of the dark hole itself. Athos vaguely remembered something about a secret passage from the house itself, and doubtless vampires were going down into the caves that way, to keep this entrance guarded. He guessed that the house itself would be teeming with vampires and any attempts to penetrate there would be even more ill-fated.

Athos cut and parried, stabbed and swung, in the movements he'd practiced every night for years. He tried not to smell the blood of the vampires, like the finest Armagnac brandy, poured onto the cobblestones. Up and up and up, his mouth watering and the horrible and pressing call of something from within those caves shouting at him to *come, come*, until he found himself, at the very tip of the vanguard, back to back with a young, dark-haired man, who reminded him of D'Artagnan.

"Monsieur," he shouted to the young man, "is D'Artagnan down there in that cave?"

There was a moment of hesitation and—either because the young man wasn't sure whether to trust Athos, or because he was killing a vampire with a broad stroke of his sword—the young man's back moved against Athos'. Then came the answer, "He is, and we're trying to rescue him before they turn him!"

Athos bit his tongue before he could say that he feared what they intended to do to him was far worse than turning. Athos was unsure

255

just what that might be, but it could cost more than a single life. It could, he thought, cost them the entire world. The sucking dry of all humanity, the conquest of the world by vampires, once and for all, world without end. The prospect both horrified him and made his pulse quicken in a way that terrified him. He could feel the beast stir and fight within him, trying to escape.

"I am Pierre D'Astarac," the young man said. "I am Monsieur D'Artagnan's best friend. It falls to me to rescue him!" He didn't ask who Athos was, but the implied question was clear.

"I am—" Athos started, then knew his assumed name wouldn't do here and now, not when this might be his last battle. Let disgrace and crime flee because he would die worthily. "I am Raphael, the Comte de la Fère," he said. "I serve in the king's musketeers, and I too am Monsieur D'Artagnan's friend, as are the others with me." Even as he spoke, they were approaching the entrance to the cave, surrounded by the corpses of vampires, stepping on them, feeling the ancient bones crack beneath their feet, smelling their death-smell all around.

Pierre gave the others a sweeping look. They'd moved up front, displacing Pierre's own comrades. "It is an honor," he said, "to fight beside such valiant men."

"We've heard of you," Athos said. "And it is an honor to fight by your side."

"You understand the caves within are filled with vampires," Pierre said. "It is likely we will not escape this."

"They have toppled the standing stones," Athos said, somehow feeling as though that act reflected the danger in which they stood.

"It is the end of the world, then." Pierre said. "Let us prepare to make it end as well as we can."

Something in his bright exclamation, and the way in which he embraced the idea of his coming death—not with welcome, but without fear—made Athos laugh. "I see you *are* Monsieur D'Artagnan's best friend!"

"Like two brothers," Pierre said, "from infancy."

Athos was about to say that Pierre would have made a great musketeer, when he felt Pierre startle, his back tensing on the other side of Athos. Pierre's voice sounded hollow as he said, "Here comes my unnatural father, monsieur, whom it is my duty to fight. Continue within, take your friends—rescue D'Artagnan!"

"Foolish boy," an aged voice sounding like Pierre's grown old and dry called out. "You'll go no farther than this, Pierre. You have run your course."

A clash of swords and Athos dared look over his shoulder, to see the boy fighting a large, muscular vampire. Could Athos still pray, he'd have said a prayer for Pierre D'Astarac.

Fighting Inward

Porthos took Pierre's place, and pressed harder than Pierre had toward the mouth of the cave, his sword slicing vampires, while he called out rude and amusing taunts. This was one of the few times in which Porthos found his tongue, perhaps because while he was engaged in killing he need not fear offending.

"Ah, Monsieur Bloodsucker, *bien*, let me see those pretty fangs before I slice your head off your shoulders. And you, monsieur, don't be shy. My sword shall pierce your heart."

They fought with their swords, defended with cloaks rolled around their arms and used as shields, pressing deeper into the ranks. Soon, the small group from Paris had become separated from the group of locals. As was perhaps understandable, a good number stayed behind, guarding Pierre.

Vampires surrounded them. It was a horrible strategy, Athos thought, but it didn't matter. All that mattered was to get to the boy on whom the fate of the world seemed to hinge.

Madame Bonacieux defended the rear, her sword as deadly as any of theirs, and the sudden scent of roses spoke of her spreading her blessed petals around. Still, he was not surprised when a scream echoed from her—given her unprotected position. "I am wounded," her voice said, wavering only a little. "I shall defend, but I cannot advance."

He had no idea what she meant by defending, but assumed she meant to use her arcane arts. A strong smell of roses and a flash of light indicated he'd been right.

Porthos slipped back, still taunting, to guard their unprotected flank, and Aramis pressed his back to Athos. He fought furiously on in silence; his pace, more frantic than that of Athos, took them

258

into the ragged hole in the earth, past the stone opening—irregular and jagged, like an open mouth with bare teeth. Athos felt a shiver run up his spine, and smote the ancient vampire facing him all the harder.

What were they doing, he wondered, fighting their way into this dreadful place, only to be trapped within with vampires all around? But inside him a voice called, strong and loud, *Come, my son, come.*

The pull was not that of his father's presence—his upright, elderly father who had always stood by what was morally right, sometimes a little inflexibly—nor was the voice that of the old count's. Instead, it was something more primal—darker, colder, more seductive—calling with an irresistible allure.

The beast within Athos reared its head and screamed, *I come, I come!*

Athos' sword flashed and cut, smiting, in the almost perfect darkness of the cavern. The vampires screamed, and the smell of brandy rose all around. Athos' mouth was parched, and dry, and he thirsted, thirsted with horrible longing for that liquid that he knew, with absolute certainty, was corruption and horror.

His arms hurt. The warmth of Aramis' back against him was torture. The beast thirsted and wanted to turn around, pull Aramis into its vise-like grip, and feast on his living blood.

The voice in him screamed: *Come deeper. Come faster.*

Porthos had somehow got detached from the two of them, and was now surrounded by vampires. His voice could be heard merrily calling, "You two go ahead. I'm good enough to defend myself. Come on, monsieur. Ah, you will, will you?"

Athos felt his heart turn within him. Porthos—even Porthos—could not possibly defend himself from the group of vampires that besieged him on every side. Yet he heard the continuous death screams of vampires, and smelled the rising scent of vampire blood, and Porthos' merry jests continued fast and loud. Athos knew, knew as he had always known, that the end might come thus for any of them, and that this might be the time when none of them would walk out alive.

Not walk out, not walk out, the dark voice, full of authority, called. *Come my son, and the world will be ours.*

He felt a kiss, a rubbing against him of a dark wind. They had, somehow, without his realizing it, fought their way into a corridor, fighting down steps and into another cavern, and the voice in his head was deafening, demanding, unavoidable.

Come, it called, and Athos came, fighting more strongly, more desperately. It seemed that the vampire wraiths ahead of him gave way, falling easily—as easily as the wheat he'd once scythed, helping his father's tenants with the harvest after so many of them had been unwillingly turned.

Come, the voice called, and Athos came.

"I am surrounded," Aramis called out. "You go on, my friend, go on."

Athos, who hadn't noticed that Aramis had fallen behind, could not have stopped himself going if he tried to.

The wraiths moved out of his way, and he ran, stumbling, into the corridor ahead.

Vile, Abject

D'Artagnan had grabbed a sword from amid the ashes of the burned wraiths and cut his feet loose, jumping up and killing the remaining wraiths.

He trotted back along a corridor that paradoxically seemed much, much longer when he was running back on his own, torch in one hand, sword in the other.

The pictures on the wall—displayed by the torchlight—made him shiver, and he tried not to look. He soon realized the way seemed longer because he'd taken another, more direct path, than before. It made a strange sense to him that, of course, there were multiple paths. Torches burned on these walls as well, illuminating more paintings. The same woman was depicted again, and again the same man with a crown.

There were also scenes of harvest and seeding, scenes of what looked to D'Artagnan's confused mind like a multitude of slaves working for the royal pair. More scenes of feeding. Always and onward there were scenes of vampires feeding on humans, of blood dripping, of golden cups filled with blood.

He tripped on skeletons, and on the dusty, spun-sugar remains of ancient vampires. He wondered if he'd lost his way and was going the same way, round and round.

His head felt as if it were exploding, his mind seized with the same dull confusion that he'd experienced when he was very young and had a fever. Everything ran together, till he was no longer sure that he was in this labyrinth under the earth. Perhaps he was a small child, in his bed, suffering from bad dreams and hallucinations.

But even in his worst nightmares, he could never have imagined the sheer evil surrounding him. He wanted to run toward the surface, wanted to escape, but it was like being at the bottom of the sea and not knowing in what direction the surface lay.

In his native mountains, in winter, he'd heard of people buried by snow, who—with no clue as to direction—could not find their way out and who, in confusion, dug deeper and deeper rather than toward the surface, dying in their attempt to get out.

He heard noises, too, from the other tunnels. Suddenly, with startling clarity, he heard the sound of someone approaching—running fast, and with an odd gait, as if partly on all fours, the hands now and then helping the feet.

D'Artagnan's mind gave him the image of the Minotaur, part man and all beast, charging toward him. The thought came to him: Perhaps the mythic Minotaur had really been a vampire, never part bull at all? Were all the monsters and horrors of human history built on the ugly reality of vampires?

He pressed himself to the wall, sword in one hand, torch in the other, and prepared to sell his life dearly.

But when the person appeared into the full light of torches, looking toward the wall and pausing for a moment before resuming running in the strange position—almost as if he had forgotten how to walk properly—D'Artagnan was shocked that he wore the hat of the musketeers. He was bare from the waist up, displaying a muscular torso; his hair was golden and familiar.

When he turned toward D'Artagnan, a shock of recognition startled the Gascon. *Athos.*

He stopped himself from calling out as he saw Athos' face more clearly. His features were pale and drawn, as if carved in white marble. Were it not for the convulsive movement of his throat, as though he were swallowing, over and over, trying to clear an obstruction, D'Artagnan would have thought his face was paralyzed. But his throat moved, as did his body, scrambling inhumanly along the passage.

The most frightening thing of all were his eyes—Athos' wide, jade-green eyes. They seemed bigger than ever, opened to an extreme, glittering like ice in the light of the torches.

His eyes burned with a fever like nothing D'Artagnan had ever seen or experienced before.

The shock, the feeling this was—somehow—not Athos, kept D'Artagnan still, pressed against the wall. That Athos didn't notice him, but ran past him and down the dark corridor, filled D'Artagnan with more fear than he'd felt at any time in this gloomy, evil place.

It was, he thought, as his throat closed, worse than seeing a horrible monster charging toward him. It was worse than any demon or imaginary Minotaur. This was the ordinary mingled with the abhorrent, as if he'd opened the door to his kitchen as a child, and found his parents cooking and eating the neighbors.

A shudder shook his entire body, as he stared at Athos, running down the dark hallway and dropping, effortlessly, into the open shaft in the ground.

D'Artagnan recalled the staring eyes, the rigid, fixed features, and it reminded him of the painting of the vampire king and his near-twin. Their familiar but not immediately identifiable features reappeared in D'Artagnan's memory. Both looked . . . like Athos. They could be members of the same family.

With utter horror, he realized that he would have to follow Athos. He didn't want to, but he was sure there was more at stake here than his own desires.

Memories of the scenes on the wall assailed him. The man resembling the king opening a chamber, lighting yet more torches around what looked like the sleeping king; the mortal being drained of blood and then the vampire king rising.

Swallowing hard against the bile rising in his throat, blinking to keep sweat from his eyes, D'Artagnan followed the receding sounds of Athos' passage. Not this time, he thought. Not this time, no, not the fields and the willing slaves overseen by vampires who pretended to be gods and goddesses.

Not if D'Artagnan could do anything to prevent it.

Blind

*C*ome!

And Athos went, tripping over his own feet, blind and lost and full of nothing—nothing—but the driving need to obey that voice.

His feet moved of their own accord, caves and galleries and endless corridors moving past him. He could no more stop and look at things, no more defend himself, no more fight the compulsion than he could stop breathing.

His sword fell from a numb hand, and he removed the cross from his neck by pulling so hard on the chain that it broke, then dropped it to the ground. He stepped on it as he ran. It ceased to matter.

His clothes were tight, suffocating him, and his vision came in narrow, focused snatches amid what seemed to be fog.

Through it all the call, irresistible: *Come, my son, come.*

His fingers fumbled at his doublet, untying it, pulling it off. He tore his shirt off, completely unable to understand how to pull it over his head.

Still, the first picture on the wall, with a torch burning in front of it, made him stop. He blinked at it, in shock, as Charlotte's lovely face smiled at him. He swallowed hard against what seemed to be a constriction in his throat. Charlotte. He wanted Charlotte. Needed Charlotte. The bite marks she'd given him, at neck and thigh, pulsed like living fire—the pain was pleasure, too, the pleasure pain—and his whole body was a bridge stretched, long and thin, over an abyss of need.

He swallowed hard again. His mouth felt so dry, but he didn't want blood. He wanted . . . he didn't know what he wanted. Charlotte.

Come, the voice said, again. It was a male voice, but it had the same effect as Charlotte's and it drove him with the same need. He must get to it, he must.

Glimpsing a wall painting again, he saw what looked like his face, but was not his face, and there was a man lying still, like a crusader dead atop his tomb, like the stone effigies in the church of Athos' childhood.

Come, Raphael.

It was his father calling, though it wasn't his father. Athos jumped down a shaft and ran down another corridor, feeling as if he'd done this before, as though his entire life had aimed him at this moment and dropped him here to . . . what? He didn't know.

On the wall there was a picture of himself being bitten, drained, by a crowned version of himself. He remembered the pleasure of Charlotte's teeth on his neck, and he longed for it with a painful desire.

Come, I will give you what you need. Everything you need. I will satiate all your longings.

In the Peril of Death

D'Artagnan followed Athos as he ran past all the torches, past all the places that had been marked, into the dark corridors beyond.

He followed Athos in the dark, as Athos shuffled, now more animal-like than ever, scratching at the walls, touching them as though he had to find his way by coming in contact with certain points.

Coming up behind, D'Artagnan saw that the points Athos had touched were where frescoes of the vampiric queen and the king were. A frisson of fear ran down his neck.

It was as though Athos were in a trance and being called.

He remembered legends his grandmother had told him, when he was very young. How the people of old used to pick a king for a year, a king they killed to improve the crops, and to preserve their one, true, immortal king.

Of course! The vampire king's double, sacrificed to . . .

To what?

D'Artagnan thought of the standing stones. *The king and his companions.* They'd guarded something deep and evil. If they were ever overturned, it would be the end of the world.

Madame telling him his ancestors had been devoted to the army of vampires that slept beneath his house. The picture didn't fit. It was like looking at a stained glass window in the dark and not being able to tell which pane was the wing of the angel, and which the tail of a demon. D'Artagnan blinked.

No. It had never been an army. It was the king of vampires, the king who would reunite with the queen. Together, they'd enslave humans and make them all into armies of vampires.

266

Sweat dripped down his naked back. He wished they hadn't captured him when he was completely naked. He wished they had let him dress.

And yet—there was something right, something proper about facing ancient evil naked, with nothing but a sword.

He knew, all of a sudden *knew* with absolute certainty that what was painted on the walls was the truth and not some fantasy or some foreseeing. Here—or rather outside, where the fields now lay fallow, the forests overgrown—in the fields and mountains of Gascony, and all over the rest of the world, unless he guessed wrong, a king and queen of vampires had once ruled over a captive and helpless humanity.

Harvests had been grown, and livestock tended to nourish humans. But those humans had been no more than livestock themselves for vampires who were worshiped like gods and goddesses.

And then—though the walls didn't tell of it, he knew it was so—something had happened. The humans had rebelled. They'd fought back. Step by step they'd fought back, until the king and queen—perhaps more than one king and queen—were immured in caves, sleeping, awaiting the call. Recalling all the legends of sleeping kings and sleeping warriors made D'Artagnan shiver.

His heart pounded. Vampires, sleeping under the earth, waiting for reawakening. He was sure, suddenly deadly sure, that there had been spells or some force which his ancestors could not break, and therefore they had built their house over the cave of the sleeping vampire.

His ancestors were not worshipers, but prison guards, keeping the vile things confined, keeping watch, a secret duty passed from father to son through the centuries, through the generations, till somehow the idea of where the passage was had been lost, but not its purpose or its reason for existing.

D'Artagnan imagined how frightened his father must have been when he found his small son wandering the secret corridors. Yet he hadn't dared close them off for good, because the watch must be kept.

He heard Athos stop ahead, and stopped in turn, raising his torch just a little, not wishing to call attention to himself. Athos, in his trance, didn't seem to notice light or movement.

He'd come to a large boulder, like the one that had blocked his exit at the end of the passage, beneath the town wall.

There were symbols there, graven in the rock itself. Crosses, stars, a rose. Sacred symbols, D'Artagnan thought, probably carved by the religious guardians who tried to keep this place inviolate.

Athos ran his hands over the rock, as if not sure what he was doing, and then, to D'Artagnan's horror and surprise, he put his hands up and started scraping at the rock, seeking to move it.

It was firmly wedged, and as Athos fought with it, his fingers left long bloody streaks on the gray surface of the boulder. Little whimpers emerged from the musketeer's frantically working throat. He must have torn more than one nail off by the roots. But he continued trying to pry his fingers into the space between the rock and the wall, trying to pull.

And, unbelievably, the massive rock started to move.

It should have forever resisted the efforts of a single mortal or even of a single vampire. But it didn't. It moved slowly, inexorably, accompanied by Athos' sobbing groans.

The King

There, there, now, that will do, the voice in his mind said as Athos—bleeding, in pain—moved the stone just enough to enter the chamber.

The royal chamber, his mind supplied, and he nodded his head in understanding, as he squeezed past the granite, feeling the broadcloth of his breeches tear and catch, till all he had left on his body were the tatters of his clothes. It did not matter.

His fingers hurt—lacerated and mangled, most of his nails torn. His legs hurt from his nonstop run down the endless corridors. That too didn't matter.

What mattered was that he'd finally found the chamber to which he'd been called. Entering it, he felt as though he'd emerged from unbearable pressure into sudden relief. It was like being kept underwater, without air, and now here, at last, he could breathe.

The chamber itself was large and almost sumptuous, the sort of room one would expect in a palace or a temple.

It was all natural, Athos thought—a vast underground chamber, with a vaulted ceiling above, on which someone had painted a blue sky and a huge, glowing sun.

In the middle of it, on a stone that might be bed or altar, lay a man. No, not a man, a vampire. He looked like Athos himself, but larger, taller. He lay on the stone bed, his face impassive, his hands crossed on his chest. By his side lay a sword.

Athos' first attempt at touching him did not work. Any attempt at approach was met with rebuff, as though there were an invisible dome over him, an inverted vast bowl of glass, forbidding all approach.

You must break the wards.

Wards. Guards. He walked around the floor, which was made of soft sand, following the edge of the barrier in a perfect circle.

His eyes, now used to the dark, distinguished on the ground a cross, a rose, a star, and other older symbols, including what seemed to be the numeral eight turned on its side. They were made in stone and in metal, carved and molded.

He pulled at them, and it was like lifting endless weights. They dragged his arms down, but he pulled, and continued pulling, fighting, struggling.

The rose came loose first, and he tossed it over his shoulder, then the other symbols, one by one. He could now approach the king, and his heart was filled with peace and contentment, singing with joy.

Good, good. You've done well.

Something in Athos fought like a man kept prisoner in a chamber of stone, but it was no match to that voice gentling him, calling to him, *You've done well, my son. Now come closer. Closer. Closer.*

He obeyed, trembling but rejoicing, longing for . . . longing for the feeling he'd had when Charlotte drank his life. Though this creature was a man, he felt the same toward him as he'd felt toward Charlotte, the same need, the same longing.

Something small and ignored at the back of his mind told him this was wrong, this was terrible, this was an illusion. Glamour, all glamour . . . His lips formed the word and pronounced it, trying to ward off whatever it was that was holding him captive. "*Glamour.*"

Closer. One of his hands was reaching out, touching the cold, cold arm of the king.

The king opened eyes like burning embers, eyes that called and bound like flames in the darkness. Eyes made of ice and fire and primeval need.

He moved fast. Athos couldn't have moved if he'd tried to.

In a single, seamless movement, the king sat up. His hands, like bands of iron, tightened on Athos' shoulders.

His fangs pierced the vein in Athos' neck like daggers. His lips, cold, cold, cold, fastened on Athos' skin, and sucked.

Bliss and pain entwined blotted out all thought.

Only Human

D'Artagnan dragged himself to the hole left between rock and wall of the cave, forcing his body to step closer to what rational sense told him to run from.

There was, as he'd expected, a sleeper, a king of old, just as the legends spoke of, sleeping till he should be needed. Only, he now realized, the legends never told just why he was needed.

He watched, frozen in place, as Athos approached the king. The musketeer moved like a sleepwalker, touching the king's arm, then exposing his neck.

Everything that made him a musketeer rose in D'Artagnan, all that had brought him to this place in time. The boy who had a damnably hot temper, the young man who could never be disciplined into behaving, the man who'd gone to Paris to kill vampires. All of them rose in him, overpowering the feeling of the fear that was blanketing his reason, making all thought dull and slow.

His fury moved him. He didn't know how or why. He didn't pause to think that Athos was, after all, a vampire. He didn't pause to think that the creature who slept here must be powerful, very powerful, and have resources beyond physical strength with which to crush such as D'Artagnan.

No. All he could think was of the paintings on the wall. The king, drinking the blood of the half-mortal resembling him, and then rising with the sun, impervious to its rays. He and his consort becoming unimaginably powerful and controlling the whole world.

D'Artagnan took his sword and charged the vampire king, knowing it was likely to be the last thing he did. Almost without knowing he did it, he shouted, "To me, musketeers, to me, of the king!"

Waking

The pleasure and pain together blotted out Athos' mind, made him forget everything. But his own true mind and thought—like a man locked in a stone chamber—pounded on the walls and doors screaming. He was aware of himself as a location, a thing, inaccessible to the body losing strength in the grasp of the vampire king; unresistant to the grip of the fangs on his neck, to his life evaporating.

And the voice in his mind whispered: *What other purpose can you have, little one? What greater purpose but to allow your king to live forever and rule forever?*

Not my king, Athos' voice surged. Inside. He tried to form the words, but his lips were like something carved in stone and inaccessible. *Not my king.* The prisoner locked in his own body tried to rise, a scream forming inside him, *To me, musketeers, to me, of the king!*

As if by miracle, he heard the shout echoed, nearby and close, and in a Gascon accent.

Athos' eyes flew open, answering a call that had been his reason for waking and sleeping now for over a decade, his reason for moving, his reason for fighting.

His eyes focusing, he saw the boy charge the vampire king, sword in hand. He felt the king move, as though it were his own body that moved, the massive arm drew back and struck at D'Artagnan's head as the boy awkwardly tried to charge and behead the king without hurting Athos.

The king's fist, more massive than any human fist, stronger than any vampire strength, caught the boy on the side of the head and sent him flying.

For a moment, for a bare second, his fangs pulled out of Athos' neck, ripping flesh and veins as they did, and the king's grip became fractionally less strong on Athos' shoulders.

And Athos' mind was free. His lips, finally able to move, shouted the words, "To me, musketeers. To me, of the king!"

I am your king, the voice in his mind said, trying to sound as compelling as it had before, but with something akin to hesitation behind it.

"Not my king," Athos said, as he twisted, and reached for the sword beside the king, the sword that had been left by him as he slept through the untold millennia. "Not *my* king."

The vampire discerned what Athos was doing, and grabbed both the sword and Athos' shoulder. Athos wrenched his shoulder, feeling as if he'd dislocated every bone, and, screaming against the pain, tightly held on to the sword. The king lifted it and Athos with it, as he refused to let go—and used the sword as a handle, pulling it back and flinging the sword and Athos away from him in one swift movement.

Athos flew through the air and landed, every bone and muscle jarring, against the hard stone wall of the cave, hitting his head very hard. He could feel the blood running from the torn vein at his neck, and his shoulder hurt as if it were on fire.

Every breath drawn into his body hurt his chest hurt, too, as though the knock had injured his lungs or his heart, or perhaps cracked his ribs. He felt his eyes close. It had been a good try, while it lasted.

Footsteps, heavy, as if bearing a great weight, approached, and then there was the sound of the king of vampires kneeling beside him. A gentle touch on Athos' shoulders told him the sovereign of the dark was about to resume feeding.

"To me . . . musketeers," Athos said, in little more than a whisper. "To me . . . of the king."

As though the words were invisible strings pulling at his battered body, he surged to his knees, twisting free of the grip on his shoulders, ignoring the pain. With the sword of the vampire king clasped hard in his hands, he took a swing at the creature who tried to grab him again.

The swing was no harder than what a child or an old man might manage. The sword was almost too heavy for Athos' ravaged body. It started with hope, but lost all strength when it hit the vampire, and then slid harmlessly down the vampire's chest, leaving a shallow cut in its wake. It brought Athos down with its weight.

The king looked shocked, raising his hand to his chest, as though he couldn't believe the cut on his skin or the blood on his fingers.

"To me, musketeers," Athos said, his voice slightly stronger. "To me, of the king." He dragged himself up, and tried another riposte at the king. This bounced harmlessly off his arm, making another shallow cut and causing more blood to flow.

The blood smelled strong, intoxicating, and Athos inhaled deeply. While the king looked puzzled, Athos mustered another attack, this time managing a cut across the king's scalp and face, crying again, "To me, musketeers! To me, of the king!"

He didn't expect anyone to answer him. The boy, he saw, had fallen against the wall as limp as a flour sack, and remained motionless. He looked dead, and might well be.

But the gallant Gascon had acquitted himself better than Athos. He had not let darkness control him. He had fought as a free man. Hell would lose its fires and the sun would go out before Athos allowed the boy to have died in vain. "To me, musketeers! To me, of the king!"

He had no strength. Everything hurt. The sword was almost as tall as he was, and it weighed too much for his arms at his full strength, much less now.

But come hell or the devil, Athos was going to kill the king or die trying. "To me, musketeers. To me, of the king!"

The king's fist shot out again and punched at Athos. He caught him in the head. It was like being hit by a hammer. Athos' skull rattled. His vision blurred. He heard a low whimper, and recognized it was himself.

"To me, musketeers," he said, gritting his teeth against the pain. "To me, of the king!"

No one would answer. He was the only one here. The only one who could keep France free. The only one who could keep the world free. The only one who could avenge the young Gascon who had saved him from a fate worse than death.

Up went the sword, Athos' arms hurting. Up and up and up, as if by an incredible feat of strength, by the power of a miracle, by the power of prayer. Up and up and up, slowly, slowly.

And the vampire king smiled, reaching with his giant hand for the sword, intending to wrest it away from Athos. Intending.

Athos swung. "To me, musketeers!" It seemed to him that the weight of the sword itself pulled it and himself along with it, until his feet left the ground and he jumped a little, landing on the other side, the sword completing the arc to bury itself in the sand and the force pulling Athos with it to sprawl him on the ground.

He looked up through blurry eyes at the king. There was a very small cut in the king's neck. He would now finish what he started. He would now drain Athos. Athos could not move, even if he tried.

But I AM your king, the voice in his mind said, in shocked surprise.

And then slowly, very slowly, as though it were beyond space and time and the law of mortals and the world, the king fell. He fell sideways, like a large tree falls. As he hit, his head rolled from his neck, ending near Athos' own head, looking at him with reproachful eyes.

The scent of the most intoxicating of all liquors enveloped Athos, full of temptation and promise. Athos gagged and turned on his side, to vomit without choking.

He didn't have much in his stomach. Just a few drops, and then endless dry heaving, which left him even more exhausted.

He imagined he'd been nearly drained again, and then, with the battle . . . But he'd won. If he died now, it would all be worth it.

A Life for a Life

D'Artagnan woke up surrounded by the most foul odor he'd ever smelled. It seemed to him as though he'd traveled a long distance away from his body, but he came to suddenly, with a shock. He ached; the soreness of bruising, the pain of having hit the wall.

Memory trickled back more slowly. He'd tried to attack the vampire king, and managed nothing but to get himself thrown with force against a wall. By now Athos would be dead and the king—

The sheer terror of the thought caused his eyes to fly open. He sat up, as the room seemed to spin around him. He swallowed hard against nausea clutching at his stomach.

The way his eyes failed to focus and his suddenly disturbed sense of balance made him feel as if he'd drunk too much, but even so it was enough to see there were two bodies in the room. Two.

He blinked. Athos lay nearby, on his side. Judging from the liquid by his mouth, he'd been violently ill. By his side lay the vampire king's head, his body a little further off, surrounded by black blood trickling into the sand.

Athos' upper body was a mass of cuts and bruises; the place where the vampire had bit him was a deep trench oozing very little blood— which meant Athos would be nearly drained.

What *did* happen when one drained a vampire?

D'Artagnan didn't know. He imagined, considering the animal instincts that seemed to animate the creatures, that it made them all beast, all thirst, and caring for nothing but satiating themselves. Only perhaps that was true of all other vampires. All vampires that weren't Athos.

D'Artagnan tried to raise himself to his feet. He must get out of here. He must get help. The feeling of evil that had twisted and wrenched all his thoughts was gone. His mind was clear.

But standing only made the room spin, and he fell back to the ground, heavily. Walking, let alone running, was impossible.

By supreme effort he managed to get onto his hands and knees and transverse the two sword lengths that separated him from Athos. He must find a way to save the musketeer, vampire or not . . . he must.

He touched Athos gingerly on the shoulder and saw the musketeer's eyelids flutter. For a moment his heart clutched, tight within his chest, afraid of what would look at him from Athos' eyes.

But Athos blinked once, then twice; it was undeniably his eyes and his gaze that looked back. "D'Artagnan," he said, or rather formed with his lips, with no sound. Then he made an attempt to clear his throat. "D'Artagnan. Go. You are free. Give me mercy before you go. I can't . . . I'll not get out of here. I can't. *Go, quickly* . . . Tell the others how I died."

D'Artagnan felt a lump form in his throat. He could feel the tightly controlled hunger, the despair behind Athos' words. And he understood what Athos was saying. The vampire musketeer was drained and he had fought while drained. Even the way he'd kept himself, by dint of broth, would not heal him now, not in time to get him out of here. And yet, D'Artagnan tried. "I'll crawl out," he said. "I'll get help. If our friends . . ."

Athos shook his head. "No," he said. His voice was little more than a raspy whisper. "No. If I wait . . . any longer . . . I'll attack whoever . . . I'm barely keeping the beast under control. I couldn't . . . if I wait . . . it will win."

D'Artagnan looked into the jade-green eyes and saw the beast trying to take over, trying to erupt. As if from very far away, a memory came to him, of Rochefort saying that if blood were freely given, feeding would not destroy the vampire's soul.

He swallowed hard, then chuckled and saw the surprise in Athos' eyes and shook his head. *I went to Paris to kill vampires,* he thought. *And now, I'll feed one.*

The Beast and the Angel

"Y ou cannot mean it," Athos rasped, as the boy made his offer and explained what he had learned from Rochefort.

But D'Artagnan meant it, just as he'd meant the offer to fight by their side in that alley, just a little over a week ago. Brave and gallant and foolish beyond measure, the Gascon bent his head, and pulled his disheveled black hair out of the way. "I'd prefer you don't take more than you need. I would prefer you don't drain me," he said, his voice tight and trying to be strong, but with an edge of trembling behind it.

"But . . . Can we trust Rochefort?" Athos said, even as his fangs descended, even as his whole body hurt with the desire to feed. "How can we? What if—"

"He wasn't lying," D'Artagnan said. "I'd wager on it. I'd . . ." He laughed. "I *am* wagering my life and your soul. He wasn't lying, Monsieur Athos. He was genuinely puzzled as to why my parents had not done this." He lay down beside Athos, offering him his neck.

Athos' finger seemed to move of its own accord, tracing the blue vein under the young man's olive skin. So soft, so warm, so alive. He'd resigned himself to death. He'd accepted it as the price to save mankind, and now—

"Please," D'Artagnan said, softly. "If you don't take what I offer, we will, neither of us, leave here. When I hit my head against the wall . . . I cannot walk. I cannot traverse those long corridors of stone on my hands and knees or reach those places one must pull himself by the force of his arms . . ."

Athos understood. But it seemed to him no more than a difficult reasoning, a way to justify what he really wanted. What he really wanted was to tear into the living vein under his finger. His lips followed his finger and touched, just touched, the warm pulsing vein beneath the soft skin.

He pulled back, by a superhuman effort. "You don't know what you're offering. What if I can't stop? What if—"

"It is a risk I will take," D'Artagnan said. "And less dangerous than trying to crawl out. Please, let us dare it, and perhaps save both of us."

Athos could no more have stopped himself from taking the proffered blood than he could have stopped himself breathing.

He let his head move, as though pulled by a force stronger than himself. He let his lips touch the young man's neck. His fangs were out already.

He tried to make the piercing of the skin as soft as possible, but his craving had its own power. His fangs bit deep into the youth's neck.

D'Artagnan trembled and a long exhalation escaped him; his body tensed and a low, deep moan escaped him, just as the blood poured out and onto Athos' tongue.

Hot blood, living blood. Nothing like the experience of draining the wolf pup. This was like feeding and like drinking. The finest liquor, the best food.

And his mind linked to D'Artagnan's, feeling the pleasure that coursed through the young man's body, the same pleasure that had consumed Athos at being drained, and feeling at the same time the pleasure of draining, the pleasure of feeding.

Oh, Charlotte, he thought. *No wonder you fell.*

He heard D'Artagnan's heart beat slower, straining. D'Artagnan's warm hand clasped his cold one, hard.

And Athos told himself, *No more.* He would not kill the boy.

The beast raged, wanted more, but Athos pushed it down, controlled it. He pulled back from the living vein, painfully willing his fangs to retract.

Opening his eyes, he saw D'Artagnan look back at him. Alive. The boy was alive. Athos would keep him alive. He didn't need another death on his conscience.

The beast was pushed away, locked tight within him. It was there. He could not deny it. He could feel it clawing at him, demanding more blood, demanding the pleasure of sucking a life, of consuming it entire.

But even as he looked at D'Artagnan, and saw the blush climb to the Gascon's cheeks, he felt the blood he'd swallowed speeding to every broken corner of his body, healing him, erasing his fatigue.

"Are you—" He asked D'Artagnan. "Did I take too much?"

D'Artagnan shook his head slowly. "No. Did you take enough?"

Athos rose to his feet. "I believe so," he said. Somehow, in the grip of his frenzy, he'd gotten rid of doublet and shirt and lost his sword, but his cloak, twisted and dirty, was still clasped around his neck. He now unclasped it and wrapped D'Artagnan in it.

His tiredness, his pain was but a memory. He lifted D'Artagnan easily, with one arm, and with the other lifted the vampire king's sword. And walked out to meet any perils that might come.

This Son of Mine

It seemed to Athos he walked for miles. Not that it was tiring, but more that he didn't know what would meet them at the other end, or even if it would be day or night.

Most of the torches in front of the pictures had guttered to embers, but even dimly lit, Athos averted his eyes from Charlotte's painted countenance. He could feel her shock, her grief, her rage, even at this distance. He did not know where she was, but he could feel her pain at the death of her true consort.

I was never her husband.

D'Artagnan was very quiet, though alive, his heartbeat and his warmth reassuring against Athos' chest.

He passed a place where it looked like someone had burned a lot of old vampires. Bones stuck out of a black, burnt mass at odd angles. "I found that they catch fire," D'Artagnan said, guessing his thoughts, or perhaps they were still linked through the mechanism of feeding.

"Yes," Athos said, looking at the remains. He climbed up and out of two shafts, pushing D'Artagnan upward with an ease he wouldn't have believed possible, and then pulling himself up, by force of his arms. His shoulders still hurt. They felt bruised, but nothing like the pain he had felt before.

But worry pounded his mind and wormed into his brain. Would his other friends even be alive? Would they emerge from this cave into a town entirely controlled by vampires?

Along another corridor, and, suddenly, a voice boomed and echoed, "Athos? D'Artagnan?"

Athos leaned against the wall, holding D'Artagnan, weak with

281

relief, recognizing Porthos' voice. He replied, as heartily as he could, "To me, musketeers! To me, of the king!"

As Aramis and Porthos appeared around a bend in the tunnel, Porthos limping, Aramis cradling his arm, Athos saw Aramis' eyes alight on D'Artagnan bundled in the cloak. His eyebrows rose. The only words Athos could find were those of scripture, "This son of mine was dead, and is alive. He was lost and now is found."

And he knew he was speaking as much of himself as of D'Artagnan.

To Paris

"It was badly done, Athos," Aramis said. He'd tested Athos' retention of a soul by means of blessed salt and cross, and now Athos—properly dressed, in a spare room in the D'Astarac home—now free of vampires—wore a crucifix once more. "You didn't know if it was true. The boy might have found himself facing a true vampire."

How to explain to Aramis, the desire, the need, the inability to refuse, the fear that if he denied the beast, the beast would take over. He didn't try. Instead he said, solemnly. "We'd both have died, otherwise. You'd never have found us in time."

Aramis drummed his fingers on the window sill of the shuttered window. Pierre had killed his father in fair duel, cleansed most of the town—the stragglers were being hounded out of the bastide, even now.

The standing stones had been righted, though they now guarded nothing more dangerous than a tomb and some paintings. The hard part had been explaining to Pierre that Athos might be a vampire, but he fought vampires. D'Artagnan's testimony had been near useless.

"He's a Judas goat now!" Pierre had shouted at Athos, looking revolted. "*Your* Judas goat! That's how Judas goats are made. D'Artagnan won't be able to resist you."

It had taken the salt and the crucifix to convince Pierre, and he was still jumpy around Athos, still acting as though he expected the musketeer to attack him. And why should he not? Athos would not trust his beast, so why should anyone else?

"From what I can understand," Aramis said. "You killed the vampire king at the only time he could be killed. After he woke and before he finished feeding on the ritual sacrifice."

283

"I was the intended sacrifice," Athos said, slowly, frowning. "I think Charlotte meant for me to follow the boy. Kidnapping the boy, bringing him here was a trap for me, all along, even if they needed to know where the king was."

A knock on the door and Grimaud's voice, "Monsieur le Comte, the . . . Madame Bonacieux . . ."

"I'll tell him myself," the priestess of nature said. She burst into the room, none the slower for the bandaged wound all knew to be on her leg, although hidden under the very proper petticoats she'd returned to. She, like Pierre, treated Athos somewhere between a hero and a monster. But she'd been nursing the boy for these two days and a night and a half. Athos turned, suddenly frightened. He didn't feel that the boy had taken a turn for the worse, but—

"It is not about him," she said, her voice curt. "It is about a scrying. While we were here," she said, her voice catching. "Her Majesty the Queen was left with insufficient guards and . . ." Madame Bonacieux shook her head. "She has disappeared from the palace. No one knows where she is. We must go!"

"Yes," Aramis said. "As soon as possible, we must go to Paris with all speed. We must find the queen and rescue her."

Athos looked bewildered. "But it shouldn't matter," he said, feeling as though his victory were snatched away from him. "We killed the vampire king. We . . ."

Aramis shrugged. "And yet the vampire queen still lives, and there are still vampires in the world. If they capture the throne of France we'll still be lost. And there's no reason to allow it. We have killed a vampire king, the most ancient of all vampires. We should be able to rescue Her Majesty with not much trouble. You must see it falls to us, Athos."

Athos felt the words pass through his lips before he knew. "To me, musketeers," he said, his voice soft, and sad, accepting of his destiny. Vampire or not, he served a cause greater than himself. "To me, of the king."

⚜ The End ⚜